This is a work of fiction. Characters, places and incidents are products of the author's imagination or are used fictitiously. They are not to be construed as real. Any resemblance to actual events, locales, organizations, or persons, living or dead, is entirely coincidental.

Jasmine's

Eye

Chapter 1
The Dream

I come from a town in Alabama that is smaller than some, but bigger than most. Except for the modern-day cars that would pass along the streets, one would think this neighborhood could have come straight off of a 1940's post card. We live in a genteel old southern house that you would expect to see a little old lady living in, but we loved it. Our two-story house was built in the 1930's with four bedrooms, three bathrooms, a formal living and dining room, and an old country kitchen. Mama told my grandmother that my daddy got this house for little of nothing in a foreclosure sale. She said they were going to fix the place up, and make it the envy of the block, but instead it became the eye sore of the block. The inside of our house was nice, but the outside needed some repair. We didn't care. Our house was still the biggest in the neighborhood. I live here with my mama, Michelle Patterson, and twin brothers Jonathan and Jordan. My two eight year old brothers' look just alike except one is slightly smaller in size than the other. They are the same height, but both of them are a foot shorter than me.

Jonathan and Jordan wanted braids in their hair, but mama said, "With your caramel colored skin, and those dimples, you two would look like two little girls."

So instead, she had the barber to cut their hair into a short afro. My brothers hadn't gotten into any real trouble yet, but they are always getting into something.

My grandmother said, "Those boys must have come from God to test the limits of our patience and mercy," and I think she was right.

I don't think I look anything like my bothers, or mama. I think I might have resembled my grandma maybe sixty years ago. I am ten and a half years old with sandy brown hair, and hazel green eyes. My skin is brighter than my brothers, and I have this ugly birth mark on the back of my right leg that looks like an eye. My brother Jordan calls it my evil eye, but my grandma told me that I was privileged to have it, and some day I will come to know the meaning of the mark. My mama was a good-looking black woman with average coffee colored skin. She's a slender framed woman in her forties, and she is a very hard worker. Outside of church, I never saw her wearing anything except for her suits. Mama worked her way through school, and got a job at a financial office. Lately, we don't get to see very much of her because she has two jobs now. She still works at the office in the daytime, but now she works as a sitter for Miss Betsy Jenkins in the evenings. It makes me kind of sad that we don't get to see her as much as we did before, but mama said, "If we want to keep eating and sleeping here, I have to go to work."

I know she tries to spend as much time with us on the weekends to make up for the time she can't spend with us during the week, but I still miss her.

My grandma would pick us up from school, and take us to her house until mom got off work. We never called my grandmother *grandma,* or *gram* or anything that a normal child would call their grandma. My grandmother's name is Bertha Thomas, but the only name my grandma wanted to be called is Big Mama. Now, you would think that no elderly black lady would want to be referred to as *Big*, especially when she is slightly overweight, but my grandma loved it. I think it made her feel a little more special than the other grandmas. Also in the South, you never answered your grandma, or any older person as anything, but yes ma'am or no ma'am. Anything else was downright disrespectful. I loved going to Big Mama's house after school. She would have snacks waiting for us, and she would teach us card games that my mama did not want us to learn. Later on in the evening, we would have to do our homework. Sometimes Jordan wouldn't have all of his homework finished by the time my mama got there. When mama finally came to pick us up, I could hear mama and Big Mama going at it in the kitchen.

Mama would say, "Why don't make him start on his homework earlier? You know it takes him more time than the other kids."

"All kids need time to just be kids. You can't have school all day, and night too, Michelle. Give that child a break, and give me a break." Big Mama said firmly.

My mama just looked at her like she had just eaten something bad. Then she turned her head slightly looking out of the corner of her eyes when she said, "Jordan, you better not have another bad grade in math again."

Her expression changed, and I knew she was too tired to argue, so she told us to get our things, and go to the van. Jordan has never been a very good student. Once, mama thought he was going to repeat the second grade. She talked the principal into letting him go to summer school. Jordan hated going to school in the summer when we were out having fun, but he got passed the second grade. My brother Jonathan was one of those annoying people who always knew the answer before anyone else did. Even though he was really smart, he would always do dumb things, and get into trouble with Jordan. I often wondered how somebody could be so smart and so stupid at the same time.

Today, mama came to pick us up earlier than usual. She didn't go to work at Mrs. Jenkins's house today. Mama said she asked her friend Sharon from church to sit with Mrs. Jenkins today. I could tell mama had been crying. Her eyes were swollen. She was pretending everything was all right in front of me and my brothers, but we knew something was wrong. Big Mama told mama to come into the kitchen, and taste her new mint tea. I have never been the kind of person that would miss the opportunity to listen in on a conversation that I wasn't supposed to hear. So, while my brothers sat in front of the TV trying to imitate sounds like the alien from Mars on a cartoon show, I crept towards the corner of the kitchen door. Big Mama had two glasses of tea in her hands as she walked back to the table, and sat down.

She motioned to mama to sit, and said, "Have a glass of tea with me."

Mama slowly walked to the table and dropped into the chair. With her eyes still looking down when she brought the glass of tea closer to her. Big Mama didn't say anything for a moment and then suddenly she looked very sad herself. "Baby, tell me what happened in court today?"

Mama didn't say anything at first. She picked up the glass of mint tea, and took a big sip. She hesitated for a moment and said, "He brought that little twenty-year-old hood rat, which I found in my house, to court. Can you believe he had the nerve to be so blunt about his affair? He said I was too old and too slow for him now. He needed something new."

Big Mama sat there shaking her head looking down at her tea. Then she looked up. "What did the judge say about all of this?"

Mama looked back down at her glass. "She said that he should apologize to me, and the kids for bringing that nasty woman into our house. That he would have to pay child support, and I would have custody of the kids. That he will have visitation rights every other weekend, and we have to work out an agreement for the holidays."

Now, I know that the judge didn't call my dad's girlfriend Tammy, a nasty woman, but I knew my mama was mad. When mama finally looked up she said, "He gave me the house and said, 'I know you won't have it *long.*'"

Big Mama's mouth flew open in surprise when she heard this. "Why would he say that?" She asked.

I could see that mama was about to cry. She tried to hold back the tears as she said, "Because he told me before he left that he could survive without me, but I couldn't survive without him."

With that said mama couldn't hold back the tears anymore. She got up from the table and walked to the counter. She tore off a piece of paper towel from the holder to blot her tears.

Big Mama shook her head then stood up and walked over to mama. She put her arm around her, and turned her shoulders to face her. With a slight smile, and a concerned look on her face she said, "Well baby, that man is a fool. He left you over two months ago, and hasn't come to see his children once. You are still going to work, still paying the bills, and you look good. Thinner than I would like, but good. The children will adapt to this change faster than you will expect, but you should believe what God said to us. We can do all things if only we believe in him. So, you just go on. Who is he to tell you what you can't do? If you are going to listen to any one, you should listen to God first."

Finally, mama started to show a little smile. "Well, I don't know what I would do if you weren't here."

Big Mama raised her head slightly, and said, "Live! You would live. Just like the rest of the women in this country who are dealing with divorce."

The sadness in mama's face returned as she looked outside the kitchen window saying, "How could a man that once said to me, that he loved me since high school, and that he would die for me could possibly treat me so badly?"

With no more emotion on mama's face, the tears started to pour down her cheeks again. It seemed as if she was emotionally drained.

Big Mama sighed with her hand still on mama's shoulders and said, "Sometime, time is the only thing that will tell you what is truly in a man's heart."

I was leaning so close to the door threshold that my pony tail was spotted by Big Mama from the side of the door.

Big Mama yelled, "Jasmine! Is that you?"

I had to think fast. "No Big Mama."

"Come here girl." She said with her hands on her hips and a stern look on her face. I could tell she wanted to smile, but she didn't like the idea of me snooping.

"How long have you been outside of that door?"

"Not very long, I just wanted a glass of water." That was the first thing I could think of to say, but Big Mama knew I was not telling the truth.

"Umm Hmm. Don't go telling your brothers what you've heard here, okay?"

"Yes ma'am," I said trying to look as innocent as I could.

Mama dried her face with her hands, and turned from the window saying, "We'd better go."

The ride home was a quiet one. My brothers had fallen asleep in the back of our old minivan. I wanted so much to ask my mama what happened, but I knew better than to push the issue. Looking out of the van's window at the buildings and street lights, I could see the people of the light. Now, these were not like normal people. These people were surrounded by a strange eerie light. I have never been afraid of them because they've always given me a kind of peace, but the dark ones were scary. They never smiled at me. They only looked at me then walked away. My brothers thought I was crazy when I told them this.

I told Jonathan I saw a person on Big Mama's front yard, and he said, "What person?"

"The lady by the steps."

He looked at me, and said, "You're crazy." Then he turned and walked straight through her. My mouth fell open, but the lady just smiled and disappeared.

I ran through the house into the kitchen, and pulled Big Mama's hand out of the dish water saying, "Big Mama! Big Mama! There was a lady on the front porch!"

She just looked at me, smiled. "Child that lady has always been there. She watches over the house for me. Don't know what I would do without her here."

"But Big Mama, Jonathan said he couldn't see her," I said as I was still breathing very hard.

She just laughed and told me, "Child most of the world can't see these beings. Why most don't even see them until it is too late."

I was so confused by this. I asked, "What are they?"

Laughing even harder she said, "Child they are angels sent by God himself to watch over those that follow him." I was shocked. I couldn't believe I could see real angles.

"Big Mama, how come you see them, and I can see them, but no one else can?"

She just smiled, and said to me with a big grin on her face, "Because baby, we are Seers."

"Seers?"

"Yes baby, you are like many women in our family that can see them. They are our protectors, and one day they will help guide us to the light."

Then I thought about something I had seen in front of Alley's house. "Big Mama, what are the scary dark ones?"

She stopped smiling, and looked very sternly for a moment, and said, "They are the fallen angels that follow after Lucifer. You know him as the Devil. I have never seen him, and I don't want to. He is truly pure evil, and soon those that follow him will have the same fate. They can't hurt you unless you listen to them, so stay away from that house. Also, don't tell your mama that I told you about this. She hates it when I talk about this stuff. She hoped that this would pass your generation, but I told her it is God's will. So, don't say anything about this, --okay?" Big Mama knew I was dying to say something to someone, but I knew she was right. Besides, no one in their right mind would believe me anyway, so I told Big Mama, okay.

When we finally got home, my two brothers were still a sleep in the van. Mama called Jonathan and Jordan, but they didn't move. Mama got out of the van, and opened up the back door. Then she climbed in the back, and shook Jonathan and Jordan. Jonathan finally woke up. He staggered out of the van, and walked to the front porch. Mama gave me the keys, and told me to let Jonathan into the house. Mama was still trying to wake Jordan while I let Jonathan into the house.

I was about to go inside myself when she said, "Jasmine, come here, and help me with Jordan."

I tried to shake Jordan, but he just looked at me, and said, "Leave me alone!"

Then I remembered that I left my water gun on the front porch steps. I got out of the van, and ran to the steps. When I picked up the water gun and it still had water in it. I ran back to the van. As soon as mama sat Jordan up, I squirted Jordan in the face with the water gun.

Both mama and Jordan yelled at the same time, "Jasmine!"

"Well, you wanted him up, and now he is up!" I said as I backed up.

The shock from the water splashing into Jordan's face woke him up quickly, and made him mad too.

As he tried to wipe the water off his face with his hands, he yelled at me, "I am going to get you back, you know this!"

I stuck my tongue out at him, laughed. Then I walked into the house. He tried to jump out of the van to grab me, but mama pulled him back.

Mama shook her head in frustration saying, "Jordan I don't have time for this. Just go into the house, and go to bed."

I ran up the stairs to my room still elated by what I just did to Jordan. I was so happy because I had finally got him back for all the times he tormented me. I put on my pajamas, turned on my favorite froggy night light, and got into bed. It didn't take me very long to fall asleep. I had a dream that Alley and Plump, my two best friends, and I were playing *Double Dutch* outside in the front yard when suddenly my dream was interrupted by a vision of a lady running in the woods. She was a white lady with long brown hair, and beautiful blue eyes. Her right hand was turned inward toward her wrist. I don't think she could use that hand very well, and her mouth seemed to droop a little on one side. She was wearing what seemed like an old night gown that was covered in dirt, and blood. Her nose was bleeding, and her left eye had a huge bruise on it. I knew she had been beaten really badly. She ran deep into the forest terrified that someone was following her. She jumped down behind three large boulders trying to hide from whoever was chasing her. She sat down behind the boulders trying to be as quiet as she could.

Then I heard a man's voice with a deep southern accent yelling, "You can't hide from me! I know these woods like the back of my hand! Tried to call the police on me, will you? I won't leave these woods without you, and you won't leave here alive!"

She could hear her heartbeat pounding in her ears as she tried to quiet her breathing. A stick cracked. She knew he was getting closer. She searched frantically for a weapon of some kind on the ground, and spotted a small broken branch. With the curled hand, she tried to scoot the branch toward her. The footsteps grew closer and closer, but it was too late. She heard the loud cock of the hammer of the riffle as she felt the barrel pressed against the back of her head.

"Leave it there, or I will shoot the rest of that worthless piece of shit hand of yours off," said the man in a low sinister southern accent.

I could see the woman trembling as she slowly raised her hands in the air. "Please," she begged the man, "who is going to take care of our child if I die?"

The man gave an evil laugh, and said, "Someone better than your worthless ass."

Without another word he pulled the trigger. The sound of a gun shot rang out over the forest. The woman's body sailed face forward towards the ground.

"No! No!" I woke up screaming terrified from this nightmare.

Mama came running in my room yelling, "Jasmine, wake up! What is wrong with you? Stop yelling before you wake up the whole neighborhood."

I could hardly catch my breath. When I finally did, I said, "He shot her in the head! The man chased her in the woods, and shot her in the head."

Mama just looked at me for a moment, and said, "I am going to have to tell mom that she can't let y'all watch those scary shows on TV anymore. Every other night y'all wake up screaming about something you've seen on TV. Come on Jasmine. It was just a dream, and it's time to get up anyway."

"Mama, I didn't see this on TV, and it didn't feel like a dream. It felt like I was there." I was still breathing hard when I said this, but I could tell she didn't believe me.

Mama looked up at me saying, "Jasmine how could you have been there when you're still in bed?" Mama got up to walk to the door. "Now get up," she said. Then she left the room.

When I finally got out of bed, I couldn't stop thinking that this wasn't a dream. The lady's face seemed so real to me. This so-called dream felt like more of a memory of some kind. Then I thought well mama must have been right after all, I'm still in bed. After I finally got out of bed, I went into the bathroom, took a shower, and got dressed. Almost everyday mama would comb my hair into two ponytails. I wanted her to style my hair like one of those pictures in the magazine I saw on her bed, but she said that those hairstyles were too mature for me. When mama finished my hair, I went downstairs into the kitchen, and sat with my brothers at the kitchen table. Mama came downstairs in her robe and put a plate of egg, bacon, and toast on the table.

"Y'all eat. I've got to go and finish getting dressed," she said.

After she left the kitchen, my bothers, and I started to pile our plates with egg, bacon, and toast. Jordan stopped eating, got up, and went to the pantry. I saw him take something out, but I couldn't tell what it was. Next, he went to the refrigerator to get some juice, and took two small cups from the cabinet. He filled the cups half way, and put the juice back in the refrigerator. Then he came back to the table with two cups that had what seemed like vegetable juice in them. He sat one of them on the table in front of me, and took a sip from the other.

Then he said, "It's good. Take a sip."

Now, I knew that anytime my brother set anything down in front of me with a smile, I knew this meant he must be up to no good.

I picked up the cup, sniffed it, and held it toward the light. "What is this?"

"Oh, it's only vegetable juice," Jordan said with that same smile, "Just try it."

I sniffed it again and without another word, I put it on the table. Then I started to eat again. Now both Jonathan and Jordan looked at me curiously.

"What's wrong? Just taste it," Jordan demanded.

Now, I know the smell of hot sauce. In the South, it is as common as ketchup. I looked up at him, and said, "I don't want any. You drink it."

Jordan stopped smiling, and looked as if his feeling were hurt.

"It's just veggie juice. What? You don't trust me?"

I looked at the cup, and then I looked back at him. I hesitated for a moment then said, "No."

Jordan looked back at me with a disgusted look, and rolled his eyes. Jonathan reached across the table, and grabbed the cup.

Jonathan said, "Well, if you won't drink it, I will. I am thirsty." He turned the cup up, and took a big gulp of it. Next, he slammed the cup back on the table, and put his hands around his throat. His eyes were bulging. His face turned a deep shade of purple. I turned back to Jordan, and he just sat there with his mouth open.

"Jonathan, are you all right?" I finally asked. He got up, and ran to the sink. He turned the faucet on high, and put his head under the running water.

Then Jonathan let out a yell, "Mom!"

I turned back to look at Jordan who had already left the table. He grabbed his back pack, and ran outside.

Mama ran down the steps, and said, "What is wrong with y'all?"

I just sat there with my mouth opened, and pointed towards the cup. Mom ran to the table. She picked up the cup, sniffed it, and yelled, "Jordan!" She put the cup back on the table, and walked over towards the sink. Mama pulled Jonathan's head from under the faucet. "Are you all right?" The color in his face had come back to normal as he struggled to answer yes. Mama took the towel off the kitchen counter and dried his face. Then she said, "Come on you two. Let's get in the van."

When we pulled up in front of *Red Cliff Elementary School*, mama said, "Jordan I'm going to have a talk with Big Mama today to make sure you have some extra chores to do."

Jordan grabbed his backpack, slide across the seat after Jonathan saying in a monotone voice, "Yes ma'am."

I got out of the front seat, and waved goodbye to mama. Mama turned the motor back on and waved back to us.

"You three have a good day, and stay out of trouble," she said as she drove away.

It was now the second week in May and every kid in school had summer vacation fever. Most of our final exams were over. The only thing that was interesting this day was the dodge ball game we played in P.E. In my school and neighborhood just about every kid had a nickname. My nickname is Jay-Jay. On my team was one of my two best friends nicknamed Plump. Her real name was Bernadette Burns. Plump was a chunky little black girl with a short afro. She had a cute round face and big hips too. Plump always felt that her size was an advantage against boys. Alley was my other best friend on my team. Her real name was Alexandria Hope. She was a little white girl with long brown hair, and big beautiful blue eyes. When she smiled one of her baby teeth was missing. This just added to her charm. I always thought she was pretty even though her clothes were old, and she was sometimes dirty. Today, we had our gym clothes on, and this was the first time I could see the big bruise that took up most of her forearm. It seemed to me that she was either getting more bruises, or that now I could see them more because of the change to lighter clothing. Derrick Johnson, also nicknamed Teach, was on our team. He also was a good friend of mine, and my brothers. He was a light skinned black boy with dimples like my brothers. Finally, our last player was Buckey. Buckey's real name was Jack Simmons, but he was named this because of his buck teeth. He had pale white skin with blue eyes and his blond hair looked almost white. He was shorter than Teach, but he was great at playing dodge ball.

On the other team, were two of the class bullies, Todd and Timothy Peters also nicknamed Toad and Stool. But, no one said this to their faces. Outside of P.E., the hallways gave them another opportunity to torment students together. They were bigger than anyone in our class, and both had brown hair, and freckles on their pale faces. Happy was a little white boy whose real name was Roger Davis. Happy had blond hair, and brown eyes. Compared to Toad and Stool, Happy looked like the short man on their team. Of course, Happy got his name because he is the happiest go lucky kid in school. Katherine, also known as Katie, was a quiet little black girl with pony tails all over her head. Her skin was the color of dark ebony, and she was missing a tooth too. Lucky was the last player on their team. Lucky's real name is Steven Smith. He was a tall skinny white boy with curly brown hair. Steven was called Lucky because his life was saved twice from getting hit by a car. Our teacher heard the story, and said, "This boy sure is lucky," and that's how he got his name.

Coach Jody Carter was the referee for both teams. Everyone liked Coach Jody. He had grayish brown hair, and blue eyes. He was shorter than the average man, but he was athletic.

There were four balls on the center line of the court. Each team was lined up on opposite sides of the line. When Coach Jody blew the whistle, we took off towards the balls. Toad was the first to get a ball. Plump and Katie's heads almost collided before Plump got the next ball. Teach tried to get a ball, but Happy beat him to it. Alley ran for the last ball, but Lucky dove, and slid grabbing the ball from the floor. Plump hit him with the ball before he could get off the floor.

She turned to him with her hands on her hips saying, "Nana, nana, boo, boo! Sucker!"

When Toad saw that Lucky was the first teammate to go to the bench, he got mad. He swung the ball as hard as he could and hit Teach in the stomach.

Coach Jody blew the whistle. "No excessive roughness! Play Ball!"

As Teach went to the bench I turned, and asked if he was all right. He nodded his head saying yes.

Toad saw us, and said, "Jay-Jay and Teach sitting in a tree--."

"Shut up Todd!"

"Make Me!"

Coach Jody blew the whistle again shouting, "Stop talking and play ball!"

Then he blew the whistle again. I picked up a ball, and threw it at Toad, but I missed. He and his terrible brother both picked up a ball, and hit me. One ball hit my side, and the other knocked me off my feet. I could hear them laughing as I walked to the bench. Once I sat down, I stuck my tongue out at both of them. Plump threw the ball, and hit Stool in the head with a loud wham sound. Alley picked up a ball sailing it across the gym floor hitting Happy on the leg. Toad swung a ball at Plump. The ball hit her on the butt causing a loud booming sound that echo throughout the gym like a gong of a large bell.

Everybody said, "Woo!"

Plump just turned around, and gave Toad an evil look. Buckey sailed a ball at Katie, and missed. Toad swung a ball at Alley. She ducked out of the way, and he missed. There were so many balls flying. So much ducking and dodging we could hardly keep up. Then we heard a loud crash from the ball. Katie was out. Next, Buckey was hit by a fast ball Toad threw, and he was out. The game came down to Toad and Alley, or shall I say between good and evil. The kids were riveted to their seats. Who would win this *David and Goliath* game? Both Alley and Toad picked a ball up off the gym floor. Toad was swaying back and forth, bouncing the ball with a big smile on his face. Alley wasn't intimated by his bravado. She stood her ground. Toad swung the ball sailing it towards Alley's head. She ducked, and swung the ball back just as fast hitting Toad in the chest. The blow sent him sailing to the hard floor. Our team jumped to their feet. They were cheering, and laughing when Toad got up. He was so angry his face turned a crimson red. To be beaten by a girl was too much for the bully of *Red Cliff Elementary School* to handle. He picked up a ball, threw it as hard as he could and hit Alley in the head. The blow caught her off guard, and sent her crashing to the floor. Her head hit the floor with a loud smack. Coach Jody blew the whistle with both of his hands up in the air in a fit of anger, and shock as he ran to Alley's side.

We all turned towards Toad as coach yelled, "That was an excessive use of force, and bad sportsmanship! You could have really hurt her. Tomorrow you will run ten laps around this gym, and write two pages on what it means to be a good sport."

Toad folded his arms across his chest, and stormed out of the gym.

"Come on everybody. The bell is about to ring. Go to the locker room, and change for your next class."

After saying this, Coach Jody turned, and walked away. As I reached down to grab Alley by her forearm to help her up, suddenly I could see a vision of her father in their kitchen yelling at her. I could see this as if I was there. He was walking back, and forth yelling, "You better clean this shit up now."

He grabbed her arm, and punched her. He hit her as if he was hitting a grown man. Then he flung her toward the sink. "Clean this shit up now! I'll be back, and it better be clean!"

As he walked out of the room, the tears just poured down Alley's cheeks. Her eyes were swollen and red as she rubbed the bruise that took up most of her forearm. Without another sound, she turned toward the sink, and began to wash the dishes. Suddenly, my mind was back in the gym. I was standing there holding Alley's arm, and a tear came down my cheek. Alley looked curiously at me.

"I'm okay. What's wrong with you? Are you all right?"

I let her arm go, and stepped back. "I'm okay. Sorry?"

"Yeah," Alley paused. "Let's go," she said.

I didn't tell her what I'd seen when I grabbed her arm, but I finally knew how she got all those bruises. Now was not the time to tell her what I'd seen, so I decided to wait until after school.

The last class I had was Mrs. Jackson's history class. Mrs. Jackson was nothing less than long winded. Her class always seemed to make time standstill. When the bell rang, I couldn't wait to run out of class, but we all had to line up at the door. We all walked out of the door in a single file line down the hallway to the front double glass doors of the school where we waited to be picked up.

I walked over to Alley, and said, "Come over to Big Mama's house with me. You know she won't mind."

"Yeah, but my daddy will mind. I can't Jay-Jay."

"Alley, I'm worried about you. I know he hurts you." She turned her face from me, and didn't say anything. "Alley, can I do anything to help you?"

She didn't look back at me. She just held her head down, and said, "No one can help me."

I've never seen her look so melancholy, and defeated before. I knew how afraid she was of her father, so I didn't push the issue. She looked up, and saw her father's car coming toward the school.

"I've got to go."

My eyes followed her as she walked away with her eyes still toward the ground and her face was drained of any emotion. She got into the car, and shut the door. With a little smile, she waved toward me from the car. Then she was gone. I looked back, and saw my two brothers getting into Big Mama's old car. I walked towards Big Mama's car still wondering about what happened to Alley. I got into the car thinking to myself, I'm just a kid, what I can do? With that last thought Big Mama drove away.

Chapter 2
To Big Mama's house we go

As Big Mama drove away, I saw the angel again, but this time she had tears in her eyes. Then something strange happened. I saw her mouth move, and I heard a voice in my head saying, "Help her."

I just sat there with my mouth opened thinking, *they can talk*. I have never heard an angel say anything before.

Big Mama looked in her rearview mirror at me, and said, "Who can talk?"

Now, I know I didn't say anything out loud, but Big Mama knew what I was thinking. "Angels! Angels can talk?"

"Why yes baby. Didn't you know that?"

"I've never heard them talk before," I said to Big Mama still looking baffled by this new revelation.

"Oh yes baby," Big Mama laughed, "they talk to anyone who wants to hear them. Sometime when you really need one just call him or her, and one will come to you."

Now, I thought to myself, how can I call an angel? They aren't in the phone book. "Big Mama, how can you call an angel?" I asked.

"Well baby, you just pray, and if you know their name you can call it. But first you must ask God to forgive you, and then they will come."

Jonathan and Jordan just sat there looking at each other shaking their heads, and then they looked back at Big Mama.

Suddenly Jordan said, "Big Mama, you're not going to call any angels when we get to your house, are you?"

"No child," she laughed again, "besides they only come when you really need them."

Jordan looked relieved by her statement.

"Good. For a minute I thought you were going cra--."

Big Mama looked back in her rearview mirror very sternly. "Watch your mouth, Jordan. Your mama talked to me about what you did this morning, and I have something special for us to do today."

When we finally got to Big Mama's house, Jonathan turned to Jordan and, said, "I'll race yah to the door."

Jonathan got out of the car running. Jordan scooted across the seat, and took off behind him. It was a close race, but Jonathan won. They both slammed into Big Mama's front door.

"Boys stop before you break down my front door."

Big Mama's house was a small old yellow shotgun house. People called these houses this because they had no curves. In other words, you could shoot a shotgun, and the bullet would go from the front of the house to the back without hitting a thing. The house had a small front porch with a metal couch on it. When you walked inside of the front door, you would be in the main part of the house. This is where we stayed most of the time. The den had an old floral couch, and loveseat with a solid green colored easy chair. The coffee table in front of the couch was a carved dark wooden table with matching end tables. The TV was on a rolling metal cart, and there were some old pictures around the room. Big Mama had a big plant by the window that took up most of the wall. In the kitchen was an old metal table, and chairs. The kitchen was small, and it had linoleum flooring with pale yellow walls. A window stood over the sink that looked onto the side of the neighbor's house. The café curtains had an ugly fruit design on them. Down the hall was a guestroom on the right, a bathroom on the left and Big Mama's room was in the back. On the side of her room was a small laundry room that went out to the back porch. The porch is where we would normally play our card games. The back porch was screened in, and there was a small metal table with four metal chairs. The one thing I loved about this porch was the old wooden swing that hung from the roof.

Big Mama told Jonathan and me to go into the backyard while Jordan did his homework. Jonathan and I played with a hula hoop, and climbed Big Mama's old magnolia tree while Jordan sat sulking, and doing his homework. About an hour later, Big Mama brought out a big cloth bag of what looked like beans, and leaned them against the metal chair. Then she went back into the house, and brought out two large bowls.

She placed them on the table in front of Jordan, and said, "Let me show you how to shell peas."

She picked up a bean from the bag, split it at the top, and ran her thumb down the center releasing the pea down into the bowl.

"Now, the peas go into this bowl, and the shells go into this one," she said.

"Oh no." Jordan sighed. "Do I have to do that whole bag today?"

"No child," Big Mama laughed. "But you will be helping me out for a while."

Jordan and I stopped playing with the hula hoop, and walked toward the porch. We were curiously wondering what Big Mama and Jordan was doing. As I approached the metal table, Big Mama had a hand full of beans. I had never seen these kinds of beans before.

"Big Mama, what are these beans called?"

"Field peas," she said with a little smile. "Black folks would eat them all the time when I was growing up, but now days with all the fast-food restaurants people just don't take the time to enjoy them anymore. Come, and sit down with us. You two can help. Tell me, how was school today."

No one answered. As we sat down, and started shelling peas, Big Mama said, "Jordan how was school today?"

He just shrugged his shoulders, and said, "It was okay."

Big Mama turned to Jonathan, and asked the same question. Jonathan said that he made an A+ on his math exam. Now, I knew Big Mama wanted to hear more about Jonathan's test than this, but my brothers have never been big on conversation. Big Mama just said, "Great Jonathan."

Then she asked me. I spared no detail. I told her about the dodge ball game I played at school. I told her how Plump was hit in the butt with the ball that made a loud sound. Big Mama just laughed. Then I told her how Alley won the game when she was hit in the head by a ball Toad threw at her. Big Mama asked if she was all right. I said yeah, but she was mad.

Big Mama sighed and said, "I knew something was really bad about those two when I first met them at your school. If they don't change their direction in life, I'm afraid they'll be lost."

"Well Big Mama, that's not all." Then I hesitated and looked at my brothers. I didn't want to sound crazy in front of them so I just said, "T--Toad had to do laps around the gym, and write a paper on being a good sport. That boy is so mean. When I asked Teach if he was okay, Toad said, 'Jay-Jay and Teach, sitting in a tree…' Can you believe that? We are just good friends. Big Mama, why can't girls be friends with boys without someone saying we are going together?"

Big Mama just leaned back in the chair and said, "Of course you can be friends with boys. You can be friends with anybody. Don't listen to that mean kid. He's just jealous that he doesn't have any friends as good as yours. You know this reminds me of a story I was told when I was about your age. It's not one of my stories, but I think you will like it just the same. The story is a tale out of Africa. There was a boy named Yera, and a girl named Syrah. Oh child, they were the best of friends. They would go swimming together and play tricks on each other. No one was able to separate the two of them. As they grew older, people didn't like it when boys and girls spent so much time playing together. Now back then, girls and boys didn't go to the park, or on a date like today. At a certain age, a girl would have an arranged marriage by their families. That meant the father would choose the daughter's husband. Well, Syrah had reached the age of marriage, and her father chose a man for whom she just did not like. His wealth made him an arrogant man. He didn't care about her. He just talked about himself all the time. But she had no choice. She was promised to him, and that was that. Syrah's husband to be didn't like the fact that Syrah spent so much time with Yera. He grew jealous of their relationship, and used his powerful influences to force the leaders of the tribe to send Yera off to war. Syrah was heartbroken. Do you know what she did?"

We all were staring at Big Mama shaking our heads. Big Mama laughed, and said, "She left her house in the middle of the night to find him. She found out where the battle was, and she went to join him. She disguised herself as a warrior, and went off to fight. People on both sides where swinging swords around, and shooting arrows. An arrow almost hit her in the head, but she jumped back before it did. She saw Yera fighting a mighty warrior from another tribe. This warrior was about a foot taller than Yera, and had a huge spear. Yera fought the warrior gallantly, but the warrior was too strong for him. The warrior stuck the spear right in Yera's heart. Syrah saw him fall to the ground. For a moment she was devastated. Then she looked around, and saw a sword on the ground left by a fallen warrior. She grabbed the sword, and ran toward the mighty warrior. She stabbed him in the back before he could turn around. The mighty warrior fell to the ground like an old log in the forest. The battle was so fierce that no one noticed her dragging Yera toward the forest. She kneeled beside Yera as he lay dying on the ground.

With tears in his eyes, he said, 'I will always be your friend,' then he was gone.

Syrah sat there wailing over his dead body. Then she began to pray to her ancestors. She begged them to bring him back alive. She asked the ancestors to let his spirit live beside this land as a reminder of their friendship that will never die. Then she spoke the words of a native spell, and cloud of pure white smoke covered them. When the smoke settled, Yera was gone, and a small fruit tree stood in his place. Syrah realized the spell did not bring him back as he was before, so she wrapped her arms around the tree, and prayed to her ancestor to never leave his side again. The same white smoke surrounded her, and when it faded away, her feet grew into the ground like roots. Her body became a vine, and wrapped itself around the tree. The tree, and vines remained there as a testimony to their undying friendship."

"Wow Big Mama," Jordan said still elated by the tale. "Was that a true story?"

"No child! Ha, ha. It is just a story, but it does teach us to stay true to our real friends."

Curiously I said to Big Mama, "Big Mama, why do they pray to their ancestors?"

"Well, some people believe in worshiping their ancestors like gods, or something. As if they had some kind magical power. Ha, ha. But you and I know that some of our relatives can't help us here in this life, so what can they do for us when they're gone." She laughed again. "No, no baby, we know where our help comes from."

We shelled peas until the sun went down. Big Mama always had a way of making something even as small as shelling peas seem fun. We filled that enormous bowl of hers with peas. Then we went into the house. Big Mama started to make dinner while Jonathan and I did our homework at the table. Jordan was still sulking because he didn't get to play outside with us. He just sat on the couch watching TV, and kicking a ball around with his foot. Neither Jonathan, nor I had a lot of homework to do. We only had one more exam to take on Friday. After Tuesday, school would be out for the summer. Jonathan finished his homework before I did, and went into the den to play checkers with Jordan. I finished my study sheet, and went into the kitchen to talk to Big Mama.

Big Mama had washed and packed most of the field peas in freezer bags. Then she stored them in freezer except for a few she left in a bowl for dinner. She put the remaining peas into a pot she had boiling on the stove. Then she put a piece of ham hock, and spices into the pot that made the whole kitchen smell good. Along with the peas, she prepared baked lemon peppered chicken, collard greens, and corn bread. Big Mama has always been a very good cook. I was getting so hungry just thinking about the food. I suddenly realized why I had come into the kitchen in the first place. I wanted to talk to Big Mama about something that had bothered me all day.

"Big Mama, I want to ask you something."

Without looking at me she said, "Go ahead baby."

"Well, today I saw a big bruise on Alley's arm, and when I tried to help her up, I saw something."

"What did you see?" Big Mama stopped stirring the pot to face me.

"I saw her father yelling at her. Then he grabbed her by the arm, and punched her really hard. He threw her towards the sink. Then he told her she better clean this kitchen up now, and he would be back."

I know better than to tell Big Mama exactly what he said. She hates profanity. Just thinking about this again made me want to cry.

"Big Mama, do you think that this was real?"

Big Mama just looked at me with her mouth slightly open, and turned back to the pot.

"Yes baby. I think it was real."

"Big Mama there is something else. The angel asked me to help her."

Big Mama turned to face me.

"You are too young to deal with something like this. I will go to your school, and have a talk with principal Whitaker tomorrow."

I was horrified. What have I done? I didn't want to get Alley into more trouble.

"Big Mama, please don't tell principal Whitaker about this. Her dad will get really mad at her. I don't want her to get into anymore trouble."

I was about to cry when Big Mama said, "Don't you worry about it. I won't let her dad hurt her. The angel said you have to help her, so we will. Besides, if I don't say anything, he will hurt her again. You don't want that do you?"

I shook my head, and held my face down. With one chubby finger Big Mama lifted my chin saying, "Don't worry, I won't tell anybody else." She gave me a little smile, and said, "Go to the table. It's time to eat."

After we finished dinner, I helped Big Mama put the dishes into the dishwasher. Big Mama finished cleaning the kitchen, and grabbed a bunch of bills off the counter. She put the bills on the table, and sat down to read them. I went over to play a game of cards with my brothers. We were playing a game on the floor when we heard a knock on the door.

Big Mama got up to answer the door. "Who is it?"

"It's me." Mama was here to pick us up. My brothers and I ran to greet her at the door.

"Well Mom, was Jordan good today?" Mama asked with a slight grin on her face.

Big Mama turned to face Jordan, and said, "Oh yes. He has been an angel, and he promises not to play anymore tricks on his sister. Isn't that right Jordan?"

Jordan just shrugged, and said in a very monotone voice, "Yes ma'am."

Mama walked towards the kitchen table to put her purse down when she spotted an eviction notice on the table. Mama read the letter very quickly to herself, and turned to face us.

"Mom, please come here for a moment. Kids y'all go back to playing your game while I talk to Big Mama for a moment."

Mama sat down in front of the bills. Big Mama walked to the kitchen table looking a little concerned, and a little outraged.

"Michelle, this is none of your business."

"I'm sorry Mom. I wasn't trying to be nosey. It was on the table when I put my purse down."

"It's okay darling," Big Mama sighed as she sat down on the other side of the table. "After your father died, it has been hard making the ends meet. Everything keeps going up. I have to take money away from one bill to put on another. And, we won't even talk about the medicines I have to buy."

"But Mama, why didn't you ask me or Pete for help?"

"Child, your brother can barely take care of himself. Besides, you have enough to deal with. No, this is my problem, and I have to deal with it in my own way. I've lived here for over thirty years now. I've had so many good memories in this house. It will be sad to leave it, but I know it is time to go."

"Mom, where will you go?"

"I've been thinking about moving into a retirement home. It's fully furnished. Small though, but you can go to the cafeteria if you don't feel like cooking.

Mama looked shocked. "A nursing home? "

"No baby, it's a retirement community. People can take care of their basic needs."

"No Mama. You will have to stay with us."

"I'm not charity."

"I know you're not. That is not what I'm saying. You are precious to us, and I can't bear to see my mother go to some nursing home."

"I told you. It's not a nursing home. Besides, I can't stay here."

"Come stay with me. Your home will be my home."

Big Mama sighed as she said, "I just can't stay for free. That would be charity."

"Mom, you still have bills to pay even if you move in with me, so let's make this deal. You can continue to take care of the kids, and help me around the house as payment to me. How does that sound?"

"Michelle, I can't let you pay all the bills."

"Why not, I'm doing it now anyway, and if I had to hire a babysitter it would cost me even more money. Please, say you will stay with us."

"Well, I have to pay something. I just can't stay there free."

"Okay, if it will make you feel better you can help me with the groceries. So, will you stay with us?"

Big Mama thought for a moment, and said, "Okay."

Mama was elated. I could see a smile on her face clear across the room.

"Are you sure? I don't want to be a burden to anyone."

Mama's smile faded a little. She reached across the table to grab Big Mama's hand.

"Mama, I'm tired of people treating older women like used cars. When we get older, people want to just trade us in. This never happens to men. Where is the Hugh Heffner version for women? As we grow older, we are smarter, more confident, and more beautiful than we were in our youth, but society treats aging women as discarded waste. I mean it mom. You are precious to me. I need you, and that is the truth, but I want you to stay with me too. I've always wanted you to come, and live with us. If it wasn't for James, I would have asked you a long time ago. You could never be a burden to me. We are two adults, and like I said before, my house is your house."

Then I saw a tear rolled down Big Mama's cheek. Both mama and Big Mama stood up, and hugged.

Mama turned, and said, "Guys guess what? Big Mama is coming to live with us this Saturday."

We jumped up, and cheered. Big Mama stood up. "What? Why so soon?"

Mama looked back at Big Mama, and said, "Because the notice said you would have to pay, or be out by the end of the month. James is coming to get the kids this weekend, so I will have all day to help you move."

Big Mama's face looked very sad. I could tell she didn't want to leave.

Then mama said, "I know you hate leaving this place, but you told me once if you don't make a change for the better, then nothing will change."

Big Mama looked back at mama, and smiled. "Have you always listened to me?"

"Yes, I've always listened to you even when I didn't do what you said. Like maybe I should've thought a little longer before I got married to James." Big Mama just laughed. "Get the kids to help you pack tomorrow, and I will be here by ten on Saturday. Is that okay?"

Big Mama shook her head in agreement saying, "Yes."

"Good," mama said as she pointed to the door. "Kids get your stuff it's time to go."

The next morning mama was downstairs before anyone else. While we got dressed, mama prepared cereal and raisin cinnamon toast for breakfast. When we came downstairs, she said we had to hurry up today. She had to be at work early for a meeting. Jonathan sat down at the table still half asleep. I sat down, and started to eat. I was so hungry. Jordan was giggling, and pointing when he sat beside Jonathan. Jonathan was so tired that his head was nodding back, and forth. Mama got up to get some juice and fruit from the refrigerator. Before the next spoon full of cereal could get into my mouth, Jonathan's head fall back with his mouth open. He was sound asleep. I sat there with the spoon half way to my mouth, and with my mouth opened. Jordan was giggling so hard I thought he was going to fall out of his chair. He didn't make a sound though. Jordan got up with a sneaky look on his face. He peered down into Jonathan's eyes to make sure he was asleep. He got close to his ear, and then burp! Jordan burped was so loud and long Jonathan almost fell backward over his chair. Both Jordan and I laughed. Mama was startled too.

She turned around suddenly saying, "Jordan, say excuse me!" Jordan was laughing so hard it took him almost twenty seconds to speak.

"Excuse me. Ha, ha, ha." Jonathan just gave Jordan an evil look, and started eating again.

"Jonathan," mama asked. "Are you okay, honey? Did you get any sleep last night?"

Before Jonathan could speak Jordan said, "Nope. The nerd stayed up until one o'clock studying for his science test. What a joke."

"You're a nerd!" Jonathan shot back.

"Hey, stop it now," Mama said ending the confrontation. "Jonathan, do you want me to ask your teacher to let you take the test on Monday so you can stay with Big Mama, and get some sleep?"

Jonathan shook his head saying, "No, that's okay."

Now, unlike Jonathan, Jordan hadn't studied at all. While mama was in the mood for letting someone stay with Big Mama, Jordan thought he would give it a try.

"Mama I'm tired too. Can I take my test on Monday?"

Mama looked at him sternly, and said very loud, "No!"

Jordan was taken aback. "I just asked. You don't have to snap."

"Look at the time. Come on guys. Everybody, eat your breakfast. I have to get to work early."

Getting to school early for me was never a good thing. Even though this was the last Friday of the year, I was ready to go when I got there. Mrs. Smith English class was the first class I had. The students had to write a paper on our summer vacation, and I was the first to read mine. If it wasn't bad enough that I had to stand in front of a class full of bored ten year olds who were making faces and talking, I had Toad in my class. I would rather eat dog poop than speak in front of this class.

As I started the read my report titled, *My Summer Vacation*, when Toad yelled, "Louder!"

So, I spoke so loudly that everyone jumped in their seats. I told them I was going to summer camp where we would swim, hike, and do other fun stuff. I told the class how we would barbeque on the Forth of July, and celebrate my brothers' birthday.

Toad yelled, "How stupid is that to celebrate their birthday on Independence Day! You're Stupid!"

"You're stupid. My brothers were born on the Fourth of July."

"That will be enough Todd," said Mrs. Smith. "Anymore out burst from you, and I will take a letter grade off your report. Continue Jasmine."

I finished my report with our summer vacation to the Gulf. This was a trip we took every year, but I didn't tell them that.

When I finished, Mrs. Smith said, "Class, give Jasmine a hand for that fine report."

The class gave a dismal applause as I sat back down. One by one each student gave his or her report. Finally, the bell rang, and I was out of the class before anyone else.

After lunch, the day seemed to go by very slowly. I had one more exam in Mrs. Jackson's history class. This was the last class of the day, and the one I hated most. I've always hated war stories. People talk of war as if it were a game. As if killing thousands of people at once is just a big number. I guess they would have to be on a battle field to change their opinions. This was madness to me, but here I was answering questions about World War II. When the bell rang, it was a relief to be out of this class. We lined up at the door to go home. As we walked down the halls, I could hear kids cheering because this was the last full week of school. When I looked around, I didn't see Alley, but I saw Big Mama's car in the parking lot.

Plump walked up to me, and said, "Are you going to *Lee Community Center's* summer camp this year?"

"Yeah."

"I am too. Where is Alley? I wanted to ask her, but I haven't seen her all day."

I knew where Alley was when I saw Big Mama's car, but I didn't say anything.

"She probably has gone home already," I replied.

She knew something was up by the unconvincing way I looked.

"Jay-Jay what's up?"

"Nothing," I lied.

"Oh, that's my mom. I got to go. See yah later."

When she left, I saw my brothers and Teach talking outside by the steps. I walked over to them, and asked, "Where is Big Mama?"

Now, I knew what she was doing, but I didn't want my brothers to know I knew.

Jordan said, "Big Mama is inside talking to the principal."

"What did you do Jordan?" I said still pretending not to know.

"Nothing. Maybe she's in there because you did something."

"Yeah, right."

Jonathan looked as if he was about to pass out. Teach walked over to Jonathan, and asked, "Jonathan, are you all right?" Jonathan barely lifted his sleepy eyes to see Teach.

"I'm okay."

I could tell he was upset about something. "Jonathan, how did you do on the test?"

"Okay, I guess, but I fell asleep on the last five questions." I laughed a little, but I could tell he didn't think it was funny.

I put my arm on his shoulder and said, "Hey, cheer up. You're still the smartest guy in this school. You might not get the grade that you wanted, but you'll pass the course. Don't worry about it."

"Yeah Jonathan," laughed Teach, "you couldn't possible do any worse than Jordan here."

Jordan glared at Teach as we all laughed. Then I turned, and saw Big Mama coming out of the front doors of the school. She waved at us from the doors to follow her to the car. Both my brothers and I said goodbye to Teach as we walked to the car.

Once we were in the car I said, "Big Mama, how did it go?"

Without her usual jolly smile, she looked back in the rearview mirror, and said, "We'll talk about it later when we get into the house."

Jordan turned to me with a surprised look. "I thought you didn't know why Big Mama was here," he said.

"I didn't."

"Then why did you ask her how it went?"

"That enough Jordan," Big Mama stopped him before he could ask another question. "She didn't know exactly what I was here for. A . . . And, what is wrong with Jonathan?"

Jordan and I turned to look at Jonathon. His head was held back, and his mouth was opened. He was sound asleep again.

I turned to Big Mama, and said, "He stayed up late last night to study for a test."

Big Mama cranked up the car and backed out saying, "Jonathan can sleep in my bed while y'all go outside."

As we drove away, I saw the angel on the steps waving goodbye to me.

When we got to Big Mama's house, Jordan got out of the car, and ran to the backyard to play.

Then Big Mama got out of the car, she turned back to me, and said, "Go on to the backyard, and play with your brother. I'll talk to you later."

I ran to the backyard, and put my backpack on the patio table along side of Jordan's. Jordan and I raced up the old magnolia tree to see who could reach the top first. Once we got to the top of the tree, we could see the whole neighborhood including the ice cream truck that was coming down the street. As fast as we went up the tree, we came down just as fast. We ran inside and asked Big Mama for some money. Then we ran outside, and just caught the ice cream truck at the corner of the block. We sat on the front steps eating our popsicles, and telling our worst stories about Toad and Stool. Then we went back to the backyard to play a game of *Red Light/Green Light*. Big Mama came out on the back porch to take our backpacks into the house. She came back outside with two bowls, and some fresh green beans.

In the middle of the game I said, "Jordan, I want to talk to Big Mama."

"What? Now?"

I knew he was irritated with me, but I just had to find out what happened at school today. Jordan turned from me, and ran back to climb the magnolia tree. Once I was on the porch, I climbed into the big swing, and begin to rock.

"Big Mama, what happened at school today?" I was praying that she wouldn't send me away.

She looked at me for a moment, then said, "Well sweetie, I came to your school about twenty minutes before school let out for the day to see your principal. I told the principal about the big bruise on Alley's arm, and that she should investigate it. I waited in the office while the principal asked Alley's teacher to bring her and her father to the office. He came in wearing an old t-shirt and jeans with his dirty spiked blond hair. He looked like he had been working in the yard, or something. Even though I didn't see any dark angels around him, I could tell this man was under their influences. He got really nasty with the principal when she asked him about it. He said she fell down the basement steps, but he didn't feel that she needed to go to the hospital. I knew he was lying, and I think the principal thought so too, but we can't prove it. Anyway, they will send a social worker to his house to check out his story."

Big Mama seemed saddened by this story. "Big Mama, do you think he will hurt her again?"

"No. Honey, he would be a fool to put his hands on that child again now."

"Could you see what he did to her?"

"Oh, I could see that, and a lot more that he has done."

"Big Mama, are there many more Seers like us?'

Finally Big Mama started to smile again. "Yeah, there are a lot of Seers like us all over the world. Mostly women though."

"Why?"

"Well, in some places around the world women are considered weak, or less than men. Just because we aren't the same as men doesn't mean we are less than men. Our strength comes from different places to unify this world. Besides, God uses the meek, and humble to do his work. 'Blessed are the meek' for their inheritance is great," she grinned.

"Does that mean that women are better than men, Big Mama?"

Big Mama began to laugh out loud. "No, no. God has given men a special purpose to be good stewards of the Earth, and its people. Only the devil has come to kill, and destroy. We are supposed to follow the Almighty's way, and protect his land, and his people."

"Why the land, Big Mama?"

"In order to have life here, we have to have the Earth. Baby, the Earth can survive without us, but we can't survive without it."

Then I thought to myself, *did Big Mama answer my question?* Before I could speak, she said, "Nobody is better than anyone else. It doesn't matter if they are rich or poor, black or white, nor man or woman. Man thinks in such small terms. Only God is supreme. If you think of yourself as better than anyone else, then you must also think of yourself as a God."

"Do you know of any other Seers?"

Big Mama thought for a moment.

"Well, I'm not sure, but I believe that she must have been. During the evil times of slavery in this country, Harriet Tubman made over nineteen trips from the North to South to free slaves. To steal a slave was a crime. She could have been killed at any time, but this didn't stop her. She freed slaves from 1849 to 1857. I don't know, but she had to be a Seer to come this many times without getting caught."

"Who got caught?" Jonathan said as he entered the back porch still half asleep.

"Big Mama stood up, and said, "Well, everybody it's getting dark. Let's go into the house. Jordan!" She called out to him.

Jordan was dangling on a low limb when he flipped off to his feet, and walked into the house.

Chapter 3
Pee-Pee

When we came though the back door into Big Mama's house, there were no more pictures on the walls, or mementos on the coffee tables. Big Mama was already packed, and ready to go. Coming down the hallway into Big Mama's house was like walking through a maze. There were boxes lined up on both sides of the hall. Big Mama made her way back to the kitchen to cook dinner. She didn't pack the games, so we would have something to keep our minds from being idle. Big Mama always says that an idle mind is a Devil's workshop. Anyway, we pulled out the game that you spin the dial, and whatever color it lands on you have to put your foot or hand on. Jonathan and I pulled out the mat, and Jordan had the dial. Jordan gave the dial a spin, and said, "left hand blue."

Jonathan's and my arm crossed as we put our hands on the blue circle.

"Right foot red," he called out as we tried to balance ourselves. Jordan spun the dial again.

"Left foot green."

I tried to pick up my left foot to touch the green dot, but it was too far away. I slid down, and hit the floor. I made such a loud thump landing on the floor that Big Mama stuck her head out of the threshold of the kitchen.

"Is everybody okay in here?" She asked.

"Yes ma'am," we said in unison.

"Be careful," Big Mama said. Jonathan was laughing so hard he sat down too.

"It's my turn," yelled Jordan. I took the dial from Jordan while Jonathan and Jordan stood on the other side of the mat. I spun it.

"Left hand purple," I said.

Jonathan reached across Jordan to get to the closest purple circle. This made it harder for Jordan to get to a purple circle. Jordan had to reach across the mat to the third row. I spun the dial again.

"Right foot blue."

Jonathan swung his foot passed Jordan to a circle on the first row in front of him. Jordan struggled to reach a blue circle because his hand was so far away. When he finally managed to put his foot down on a circle in the second row, we heard a boo-up!

I yelled, "Ha, ha, ha! Jordan passed gas!"

"Shut up!" He shouted.

Jordan's head was still down with his arm, legs stretched out, and his butt was still in the air. Jonathan was laughing so hard I thought he was going to fall over.

"Shut up Jay-Jay! At least when I pass gas, I don't put holes in my underwear."

I was insulted. I wasn't going to take that. "I do not Jordan! With your stinky self," I shouted furiously.

All this time Jonathan never stopped laughing. He laughed so hard that he fell over, hitting Jordan's leg. This sent both of them crashing into four boxes that fell to the floor. Big Mama rushed out of the kitchen with a spoon in her hand.

"What on Earth are y'all doin in here?"

Jonathan and Jordan just sat there pointing at each other. I was still standing there in shock with my mouth open.

"Are y'all okay?" Big Mama asked. We just nodded our heads in unison. "Boys, pick these boxes up, and nothing better be broken."

"Yes ma'am," we answered her in unison.

"Play something else!" Then she left the room.

We started playing cards, but Jonathan got bored with this, and quit. So, Jordan and I played *Solitaire* together while Jonathan watched TV.

"Dinner's ready. Y'all get to the table," Big Mama shouted.

Even though Big Mama is moving tomorrow she still made a meal that was fit for a king. We ate green beans, candy yams, fried corn, and thick juicy fried pork chops. These pork chops were so tendered you could cut them with a fork. I loved Big Mama's cooking, but I knew when she came to live with us, I would have to cut back. I didn't want to be a Big Mama myself at the tender age of ten. After we ate, everybody cleaned off the table. Big Mama cleaned the kitchen, and my brothers and I were so full we just lay around on any furniture that was left. We watched TV until mama knocked on the door.

When mama came into the house, we could tell how shocked she was to see how much Big Mama had packed. After mama greeted us, she said, "Wow mom, did the kids help you pack all of this today?"

"No, no. I packed all of this while they were at school. I knew they would be tired from those tests they had to take, so I did it myself."

Mama looked at Big Mama with a slight grin. "Yeah right. You just didn't want them to break anything."

"Well, that too." Big Mama laughed.

Mama looked around, and turned towards us. "Kids, it's time to go. Mom, I will have two movers here tomorrow with me, okay?" Big Mama shook her head in agreement. "Let's go," she said as we waved goodbye to Big Mama.

In the van, Jonathan was wide awake. Jordan wanted to go to sleep, but Jonathan kept playing with him. I was getting so sleepy that my eyes started to burn. Every street light we passed began to look like blurry stars. The more street lights we passed, the faster I faded away until I finally was asleep.

It wasn't long before I had a dream about Big Mama's homemade apple pies. I could smell those baked apples and cinnamon as if I was there. Big Mama cut a slice of delicious pie, and put it on a plate for me. The pie was still warm. I could see the steam coming from it as I grabbed my fork. I was about to cut into the pie when my dream was interrupted by a vision of Alley's father standing on a street corner downtown.

From the flashing lights, and loud music I could tell he must have been standing on the outside corner of a nightclub. I looked up, and saw a sign that read: *Dance Machine*, in neon lights. I knew this place. This is where the big kids hung out on weekends. I've always wanted to go there when I got older, but what was Alley's father doing here? He was too old for this club. My mind was like a motion picture camera as I watched the action going on around me. As I moved in closer, I could hear everything. When I got close enough to Alley's father, I saw two boys surrounding him. I heard the first boy say, "Hey Billy, I brought you another customer."

Alley's dad looked suspiciously at the both of them. "Who in the Hell is this? Did you bring the cops with you boy?"

"No, no Billy." The first boy said trying to calm Billy down. "He's too young to be the police."

Alley's dad still looked at him suspiciously. "Prove it. Let me see your ID."

The second boy pulled out his ID from his back pocket, and handed it to him. Alley's father snatched it from him, and read his name and address out loud. "Just so you know. I know your name, and where you live, so don't try and screw me." Then he gave the ID back to the second boy.

The first boy said, "Hey man, he's legit."

Alley's father's short blonde spiked hair and blue eyes made him look menacing in the dark. "So, gentlemen, what will it be?" Billy asked.

"Give me a dime bag of meth," the first boy said. He gave Alley's father a fifty-dollar bill, and Alley's father gave him a small bag of crystal methamphetamine.

"What will you have?" Alley's father asked the second boy.

"Give me a--."

"Hey, I ain't got all day. Stop screwin around before the cops come by here."

"Okay, okay," the second boy said, "give me what you gave him." Then second boy gave him a fifty-dollar bill for the bag too.

"Nice doing business with yah. Oh, by the way, I know the cops too, so don't fuck with me."

As he walked away, I heard "*Jasmine, Jasmine! Get up!*" I woke up to the sound of mama calling me. "Come on," she said. "Let's go into the house." I walked out of the van wondering to myself if Alley's father really sold drugs? I've have always known there was something really bad about this man, but I couldn't believe this.

When I got to my room, I changed into my pajamas, and jumped onto the bed. Then I heard mama arguing with someone on the phone. I got off the bed, and walked downstairs to see what was going on. I sat on the bottom steps listening to mama's conversation. I heard her say, "James, you haven't seen your kids in two months." She paused, and then said, "It is not my fault. Maybe it's your ghetto girlfriend's fault. James, don't do this to your kids!"

The more they talked, the madder mama got.

"So, you're not coming to see your kids?" Mama paused. "Fine!"

She hung up the phone. I could hear the chair move in the kitchen as mama sat down. I moved slowly from the steps, and walked around the corner to the kitchen door. I could see her elbows on the table, and her face in her hands. She was crying.

"Mama, are you okay," I asked.

"Yeah baby, I'm okay. What are you doing up?"

"I was going to the bathroom when I heard you on the phone. Was that daddy?"

"Yes, it was."

"Is he coming to get us tomorrow?"

"No."

"Why not?"

Mama looked at me as if she wanted to say something else, but she decided not to. "Your dad said he and Tammy are going out of town this weekend."

"It's okay mama. We can help you and Big Mama move this weekend."

"That's sweet of you honey." Mama dried her face with her hands quickly and said, "I got to take the trash out."

She walked over towards the trash can, and pulled the bag out tying the ends of the bag together. Before she picked the trash up, I said, "I miss him too."

"I know sweetie. I do too. Now, it's time for you to go back to bed." Mama picked up the bag, and I followed her to the door. Once she opened the door, we noticed that it had begun to rain. Mama sighed. "Now I really miss him."

Mama covered her head with her sweater, and walked down the steps to the trash can sitting on the curve. After putting the trash in the can, she turned to find a dog sitting in front of her. The dog was dirty, and wet. It was a big yellow dog that looked like it hadn't eaten in some time. Even in the rain the dog had a cute happy face, and it was waging its tail. Mama stood there for a moment just looking at the dog. Then she said, "Hey boy, are you lost?"

She patted the dog on the head, and motioned for the dog to follow her. Without any fear, the dog followed mama into the house. Both mama and the dog came into the house soaking wet. They walked towards the kitchen. The dog sat down in the middle of the kitchen floor. Mama walked back to the laundry room to get some dirty towels.

"Here Jasmine, dry him with these. He's dirty anyway, so I don't think he will mind. Now, let me see. Do you think he might want some leftover chicken?"

Mama opened the refrigerator, and pulled out a plate of chicken. She grabbed two plastic bowls from the dish drainer, tore the chicken off the bone putting it into one of the bowls.

"Jasmine that's enough drying. Here, put some water in this bowl, and put it on the floor."

Both mama and I put the bowls on the floor at the same time. The dog wolfed the food down so fast I don't even think he chewed it. Then he drank half the water in the bowl. Mama went back to the laundry room to fold up some more dirty towels for the dog. She made a makeshift mat for the dog, and put it near the hot water tank.

"Mama, are you going to keep this dog?" I asked curiously. I was still amazed she let this dog into the house.

"No, he's not our dog, but I can't let him out on a wet night like tonight. I'll let him out in the morning."

The dog left the kitchen, and lay down on the makeshift mat.

"You see Jasmine," mama said with a smile, "He has made himself at home."

This was the first time I've seen mama smile in months. It's truly amazing what an old smelly wet dog can do to change a person's mood.

"Come on. Let's go to bed," she said.

Before mama left the kitchen, I looked back at the dog. He had put his head down, and closed his eyes. I have never seen this dog before, but I could sense he felt at home.

The next morning, we all had to get up early to eat breakfast. The second we finished, we all got into the van to go to Big Mama's house. Mama said she was going to ask Uncle Pete to help us, but we all knew how he was. Uncle Pete had a drinking problem, and we all knew it. Mama said he has to want to stop, or nothing will work. I know she was right. No one could stop Uncle Pete from getting a drink if he wanted one. He would always find a way.

When we turned the corner in front of Big Mama's house, there were two men standing by a moving truck, and Big Mama was sitting on the metal couch on the front porch. When we got out of the van, Big Mama said, "Hey, the truck just got here before you did, so we waited until you got here before we started. You see, these two good looking young strong men are ready, and at your service. Ha, ha."

The two men just blushed, and grinned.

"Come on guys, before my mom embarrasses y'all anymore." Mama said.

When we walked into the house, Big Mama had separated everything she wanted stored from everything she wanted to take with her. She told me, and my brothers to get the boxes in the hall, and put them into the van. We worked hard moving everything out of the house until it was almost lunch time. Everything in the small house was gone. The house seemed like it had been vacant for years. Looking at it this way made me a little sad.

The truck was filled to its capacity, and so was the van. Mama got the storage information forms from the men, and then they left. Big Mama sat up front with mama in the van. My brothers and I had to squeeze together on one side in the back seats. Mama didn't want to leave Big Mama in the house by herself, so she said she would ask Sharon to come back with her to get her car. Mama drove to a drive-thru restaurant for lunch, and brought it home for us to eat. Mama unloaded the food from Big Mama's refrigerator first before we sat down to eat.

When mama finally sat down with us, she said, "Mom, I don't think we will have to buy any groceries for at least month. Wow, that was a lot of food. Why do you buy so much when you lived by yourself?"

Big Mama had a big piece of the sandwich in her mouth when she said, "Well, I have never gotten used to cooking for one. Besides, once the kids started coming over, I needed to. Also, your brother comes to see me sometimes, and he's always hungry."

"Well, maybe we can keep our big meals for Sunday, okay?"

When mama said this to Big Mama, I knew she would be slightly disappointed. "Well, okay," she replied.

I quickly finished my food because I wanted to see how Alley was doing.

"Mama, can I go outside?" I said hoping she wouldn't ask me where I was going. I didn't want to tell her where I was going because I know she would say no.

"Okay, but don't go far, and come back before dark."

I ran outside the door, and walked around the corner. My neighborhood was a multi culture community. Mrs. Madison's house was across the street next door to Plump's house. Mrs. Madison was an elderly feeble widowed white lady with long gray hair she kept in a bun. All the kids loved to go to her house because she would give us candy, and apples. Sometime she would even make sandwiches for us in the summer. Across the street, and one house down from Plump's house is where the Sanchez family lived. They are a Hispanic family with a son name Carlos. Carlos was the same age as my brothers. He would come to our house to play with my brothers from time to time. Down the street there was a store owned by a Muslin man named Haysem Muhammad. We would stop there after summer camp to buy sodas, and candy. Finally, there was Alley's house.

Alley's house was on the same side of the street as Carlos's house. She lived in a small white house that had a huge metal gate surrounding it. I've never been inside of the gate because I was too scared. Dark angels come here. I saw Alley in the window, so I waved to her to come outside. Alley came outside wearing jeans, and the same dirty t-shirt she had on yesterday. She met me at the fence.

"Hey Alley, do you want to come to my house, and jump rope with me?" I asked this because there was no way I was going to stay at her house.

"Okay," she replied.

A lady came out on the porch. The lady had very pale white skin with dark circles under her dark brown eyes. Her hair was shoulder length, but it didn't look like she had brushed it in days. I could tell she must have slept there in her clothing.

"Alexandria, where are you going?" The lady asked.

"I'll be back."

"Well, you better make sure you're back before your father gets home."

"Okay!" Alley yelled back at her. Alley came out of the gate, and walked back down the street with me.

"Who is that lady?" I asked.

"She is my father's girl friend."

"What is wrong with her? She looks sick."

Alley looked back to see if she was still standing on the porch, but she was gone. "She is sick. She keeps bringing my dad this cold medicine, but I think she needs to take it."

I knew I didn't like this woman, and I had just met her, so I asked Alley, "Do you like her?"

"No."

"Alley, where is your dad?"

"He said he had to go meet this police man."

I thought to myself that her dad and the police just didn't go together. I knew it was more to this story, but I didn't pursue it. "Alley, what happened at school yesterday?"

She looked at me, and hesitated for a moment then spoke. "My dad was angry. He thought that I had been talking to someone."

"He didn't do anything to you, did he?"

"No. He said I better keep my mouth shut about what goes on in this house. Then he said a social worker will come to the house on Monday."

"Are you scared?"

"A little, I guess."

"Hey," I said with a little smile, "I know what will cheer you up. Let's go get Plump, and play *Double Dutch*."

"Okay," Alley said with a slight smile.

We turned the corner and walked across the street to Plumps house. We waved to Mrs. Madison who was sitting in her rocker on her front porch.

"Girls come back, and see me before you leave. I have something for you," said Mrs. Madison.

"Yes ma'am," Alley and I said in unison. We walked to the front door, and I knocked. Mrs. Burns came to the door.

"Hey Mrs. Burns. Can Plump come over to my house?" I asked.

"Yes, hold on a minute. Bernadette! Your friends are outside." Mrs. Burns turned, and left the front door. We could hear Plump running to the door.

"Hey, guys. What's up?"

"Do you want to play *Double Dutch* with us?" I asked.

"Yeah! I want to turn first."

"Okay," I said, "but we have to stop at Mrs. Madison's first."

"Mrs. Madison! Does she have candy?" Plump asked excitedly.

"I think so," I replied.

"Good, I don't know what I would do without Mrs. Madison."

Alley leaned towards my ear, and said, "Lose weight." I giggled.

Mrs. Madison gave each of us a candy bar. "What are you girls up to today?" She asked.

"We are going to play jump rope at Jay-Jay's house," Plump replied.

Mrs. Madison stood back smiling with the grin on her face. Then she said, "When I was your age, jumping rope was my favorite thing to do. Why I could do all kinds of tricks while I turned the rope. Yep, that was fun stuff back then."

Mrs. Madison was so nice to us, and I see how she likes to jump rope. I thought it would be a good idea to ask her if she wanted to jump rope with us.

"Mrs. Madison, would you like to play jump rope with us," I asked curiously to see what she would say.

"Well child," she giggled, "I don't see how I can since I can hardly get my leg over the rope." She laughed again. "Nope, you kids go on, and I'll have fun watching over here."

We thanked Mrs. Madison for the candy bars, and waved goodbye. When we got to my house, mama and my brothers had unloaded everything out of the van. Soon Mrs. Sharon drove up, and mama and Mrs. Sharon left to go get Big Mama's car. All of us walked up to the porch. When we got there, the big yellow dog was sitting on the porch.

Plump turned to the dog, and asked, what's this?"

The dog sat there happily wagging it tail. He looked like he was smiling.

"He came by here yesterday," I said.

"Will he bite?" She asked suspiciously looking at the dog, and then at me.

Shrugging my shoulders I said, "He hasn't bitten anybody so far. Hey, I'm going to get the ropes."

I looked back to see Alley and Plump petting the dog. I ran back to my room, and found the ropes as fast as I could. When I came back, the dog was sitting on its hind legs, and Plumps hand was in the air. When she put her hand down, his front legs came down.

I looked at Plump, and said, "What are you doing?"

"Nothing, I just put my hand up like this, and he sat up. Look, I'll show you."

Plump, put her hand up in the air, and the dog followed it. When she put her hand down, he sat back down. "See!" She said.

There was something really strange about this dog. I could understand what he was feeling. I knew he wanted to play with us.

I turned back to everybody, and said, "Come on guys, let's jump rope."

Plump and Alley grabbed both ends of the two ropes, and begin to turn them. We had a song we sang anytime we played *Double Dutch*. Whatever the lyrics call for in the song, the jumper would have to do the movement. If the song says touch the ground, you would touch the ground. If the song said turn around, you would turn around.

By the time Plump and Alley started counting, they would turn the ropes even faster. I was jumping so fast that I could hardly catch my breath. The dog was running back and forth from Alley to Plump. The rope caught my foot, and I went down. The dog ran over, and licked my face. Both Plump and Alley said, "Yuck!" I got off the ground and dusted myself off.

Alley said, "My turn."

I took the ropes from Alley, and started to turn them with Plump. We started singing the song again. The dog never stopped running from Plump to me. I knew this dog wanted to jump. Alley didn't last as long as I did. She got to three, and said stop. I gave the ropes back to Alley and said, "Wait a minute. I think this dog wants to jump."

Both Alley and Plump looked at each other, and turned back to me. "What?" They said in unison.

"Dogs don't jump Jay-Jay," Alley shouted to me.

I put my hand up, and said, "Wait a minute."

I walked over to the middle of the ropes, and whistled for dog to come over to me. I leaned over toward the dog who just sat there swaging his tail. Then I said, "Plump, Alley, y'all drop the other rope, and just turn this one." They dropped one of the ropes, and Plump threw it out of the way. "Now," I said as I stood up straight, "--on the count of three turn the rope slowly; one, two, three."

When the rope came over, the dog and I jumped at the same time. Plump and Alley's mouths stood open in amazement. They kept turning the ropes. My brothers came to the door. When they saw the dog and me jumping, they walked down into the front yard where we were jumping.

Jordan said, "Look at that dog jumping. Did you teach him that?"

It was hard to talk, and jump too. I said, "No! H . . . He just . . . wanted . . . to . . . jump."

Jonathan came down the steps shouting, "I want to jump!"

Before I could say no, he had jumped in beside us. Then Jordan jumped in on the other side of me. All three of us, and the dog were jumping rope. Mrs. Madison got out of her rocking chair to watch. Big Mama came outside on the porch, and just watched with her hands on her hip. Mama and Mrs. Sharon drove up about the same time. They got out of the cars. Mama was carrying a big bag of dog food.

"What on earth have they taught that dog to do?" Mama said with a very surprised expression.

The moment the dog saw mama, he stopped jumping, and ran to greet her. I stopped jumping when the dog left. The rope stopped at my foot. Jonathan and Jordan both jumped thinking I was going to turn again.

I stepped over the ropes to greet mama. When Plump and Alley started turning the rope again, both Jordan and Jonathan fell.

"Hey!" They shouted together as they got off the ground, and dusted themselves off.

We all walked over to meet mama and Mrs. Sharon. Mama looked back at Mrs. Sharon then she looked at us. "Who taught that dog to jump rope?" She asked.

"I didn't teach him. He just wanted to jump," I replied.

"Well Michelle, you have one unusual dog," said Mrs. Sharon shaking her head. "Here are your keys, Michelle. I have to go."

"Okay, I'll call you later." Mrs. Sharon got back in her car, and drove way.

"Take this dog food in the kitchen, and feed the dog for me Jordan."

Jordan grabbed the bag, and said, "Come on Pee-Pee."

"Why do you call that dog Pee-Pee?" I asked.

"Well, when I did this." Jordan put the bag of dog food down and put his hand to his ear, and stuck his tongue out at the dog. The dog showed his teeth, put his tail between his legs and walked away. There was a little trail of urine as the dog came over, and sat behind me.

"You see. That why I call him Pee-Pee."

Everyone laughed.

"Stop making that dog pee Jordan, and take that dog food into the house," mama shouted.

"Come on Pee-Pee," Jordan commanded. The dog followed him into the house. Mama went inside the house, and we played until it was dark. Plump went home, but Alley stayed with us for dinner. I asked her if her dad would mind that she stayed so late and she said he wouldn't know because he wouldn't be back until tomorrow. After dinner mama took Alley home.

Chapter 4
Uncle Pete

      Church service at A.M.E. United Baptist Church was always an event for my family. We all dressed up in our Sunday's best for service. I put on a pretty white dress with embroidery around the hem. The dress came with a pink satin ribbon that tied in a bow at the back. Every Sunday my brothers were dressed just alike. I don't know why mama did this. It was hard enough telling them apart without them dressing alike. Today they had on navy suits with bow ties. They looked like *Twiddle Dumb*, and *Twiddle Dumber*. The mother of the church was Mrs. Pugh. She was almost ninety years old, and she loved to pinch my brother's cheeks. She would tell them how cute they were, and they would always get embarrassed. The problem was that Mrs. Pugh had no teeth in the front of her mouth. She would spit every time she called my brother's names. They hated this. They would try to avoid Mrs. Pugh, but she would find them anyway. Big Mama had on a green suit with a green feathered hat. Big Mama had a hat for just about every suit she wore. She had almost the same number of wigs as she had hats. I often would sneak into her room at her old house, and try her hats on. Now, mama really looked very nice. She had on a silk pink dress the really complimented her curvy figure. Her hair was pulled up with soft curls falling gently around her face. It was nice to see mama dressed up even if it was only on Sundays.

      The church's interior was almost completely white except for the altar, and the crimson and pine benches we sat on. I sat by Big Mama. My brothers sat between mama and me. Our church had one of the best choirs ever. This choir has won ten competitions over the past two years. They have sung at the State Capital's Christmas Ball for the governor of Alabama. The people at my church were never quiet when the choir would sing. They would clap their hands, and pat their feet. Sometimes people in the crowd would shout out an '*amen*,' or two before the song was over. Even after the choir stopped singing the people still were shouting *amen*, or *praise the Lord*.

Reverend Jackson Howard III held his hands up to quiet the audience, and said, "Church let's give the choir a big round of applauses for that great rendition of '*How I got over*.'"

The audience clapped, and shouted amen again as the organist continued to play. Reverend Howard put his hands out again to quiet the audience.

He began his sermon by saying, "What's in Hell do you want?" My brothers and I gasped when we heard this. He said it again. "What's in Hell do you want?"

I just sat there thinking to myself, *did he just curse*? I looked over at Big Mama who was just smiling, and clapping her hands. She never looked back at me.

Then I looked back at the reverend who explained saying.

"It seems to me like everybody is trying so hard to get there as fast as they can, so I want to know. What is it in Hell that you want?" He asked.

I looked back down the bench where my brothers sat, and they were both giggling. A man sat behind us with an old straggly beard. His brown striped suit was older than he was. It seemed to me that the man was falling asleep. Every time the minister preached louder, the man behind us would jump. Then he would say something that sounded like a muffled *amen*. The man did this so many times that my brother Jordan jumped too. By the time the reverend finished his sermon, my brothers and I turned to look at the man to see if he would give us his last amen, but he didn't.

After church service, the reverend would stand in the foyer to greet the members, and shake their hands as they left the church sanctuary. In our church there was a lady named Mrs. Leola, the church gossip queen. She was older than my mother, and she wore all black like the "*Wicked Witch of the North*." Mrs. Leola was a person for whom I have never heard her say a nice thing about anyone unless she was being sarcastic. When we walked down the aisle to greet the reverend, mama greeted the minister first. My brothers and I were in the middle. Big Mama was on the end. Mama shook Reverend Howard's hand, and told him what a good sermon he preached. I could see Mrs. Leola coming toward us. Mama, my brothers, and I walked toward the doors. Big Mama stayed back to talk to the minister.

Before mama could turn around, Mrs. Leola was there.

"Well, hello Michelle," she said with an evil grin.

"Hello," mama replied.

"Well, I just wanted to know how you and the little ones were holding up. I heard about the nasty divorce you've gone through. That kind of thing could just devastate a person."

"We're fine Leola," mama said flatly.

Then Mrs. Leola leaned over, and said in a low voice, "Well, from what I heard, he brought his girlfriend over to your house. Now, I know that had to be devastating."

I could see the rage in mama's face. I knew the only reason mama didn't say, or do what she wanted to do was because she was in the church.

"Leola, I don't care to discuss my personal business with you now, or anytime in the future. Especially in front of my children, so for only now I will ask you nicely. Please leave."

"Well Michelle, I was only trying to help you, you know. I guess some people can't be helped, or hang onto a man."

Then Mrs. Leola turned, and walked away. Big Mama walked over to us looking very concerned.

"What's wrong?" She asked looking at all of us. Mama was still staring at Mrs. Leola gossiping with some other ladies standing by the office door. We could tell that the ladies were laughing, and talking about us. Mama's face was so angry that it seemed at first that she wanted to fight. Then she lowered her eyes as she fought back the tears.

She looked back at Big Mama, and said, "Nothing, come on y'all. Let's go."

When we got home, everyone changed out of their dress clothes into something more comfortable. Mama, my brothers, and I put on shorts, and t-shirts. Big Mama wore an old pink house dress with flowers on it. Mama and Big Mama started cooking dinner while my brothers and I set the table. Big Mama turned the stereo on, and put in an old *"Mahalia Jackson"* CD. Big Mama loved all gospel music, but *"Mahalia Jackson"* was her favorite. Mama and Big Mama were talking, and laughing in the kitchen when we heard a knock at the front door.

"Answer the door Jasmine," mama said.

When I opened the door, it was Alley. My brothers finished setting the table, and waved to Alley as they passed us walking outside.

"Hey, let's get something to drink before we go upstairs."

Alley grinned, and said, "Okay, but do you have a Soda?"

I shrugged my shoulders, and said, "Let's go into the kitchen, and see."

Alley and I walked towards the kitchen together. Alley stopped at the kitchen threshold while I plundered through the refrigerator.

"Hi Mrs. Patterson. Hi Mrs. Thomas. Whatever y'all are cooking smells good!" Alley said.

"Would you like to stay for dinner today?" Mama asked.

Now, there were two people who never had to be invited to dinner, and that was Alley and Uncle Pete. Anytime they showed up mama would feed them.

"Yes ma'am," Alley replied with a toothless smile.

"Here, I've found a soda. Come on."

As Alley and I started to walk out of the kitchen, Big Mama said, "Stop." She walked over to Alley wiping her hands off with a towel. "Child, didn't you have this on yesterday?"

"Yes ma'am," Alley said with a bit of embarrassment.

"Why didn't you change your clothes," Big Mama asked softly.

"This was the cleanest thing I had left."

"Did you bathe today?" Big Mama asked her out of curiosity.

"No ma'am."

Big Mama shook her head in shock saying, "Never have I seen a child in this poor condition. Baby, go upstairs, and take a bath. Jasmine let Alley barrow some of your clothes, and I will wash hers."

"Yes ma'am," we said as Alley and I walked out of the kitchen. We went upstairs to my room where I found a t-shirt, and shorts for Alley to wear. Alley turned to me with a strange look.

"I have no underwear," she said.

I thought for a moment and then I pulled out a new pair of underwear I haven't worn. I gave Alley the underwear saying, "I don't want them back."

Alley laughed. "Okay," she agreed.

Alley liked our newly remodel bathroom. The bathroom had double sinks, new stone tile floors, and a corner whirlpool tub. Mama decided to fix this bathroom after she remodeled her own. I turned the facet on.

"Would you like bubbles?" I asked.

"Yeah! Your bathroom looks like a picture in a magazine. I might never come out of here."

"Oh yes you will. Especially when my brothers have to use it, and then you may never want to come back in here again." Alley just laughed. "Just leave your clothes outside of the door. When you get dressed, let's play cards, okay."

I left the bathroom, and Alley put her clothes outside the door. When I picked up Alley's jeans, I saw a vision of Alley's father. I was frozen in some kind of bad day dream. I couldn't move. Alley's father was drunk when she came through the front door. The room was dark except for the TV light. Sitting there on the couch, her father's face and hair looked white as his pale eyes shined in the darkness. He was wearing a "*Falcon's*" t-shirt with a pair of blue jean shorts. He had a beer in his hand that he balanced on his knee.

"Where have you been?" He asked. The sound of his voice startled her in the darkness.

Then she spoke, "Jay-Jay invited me to dinner, and Mrs. Patterson drove me home."

"Really now," he said with a smirk. "You spend more time with those niggers than you do here in your own house. Why don't you invite that pretty little black friend of yours over here sometimes? I think I could cook up something special for her."

Alley turned to go to her room when he said, "Where are you going? Come over here and talk to me for a little bit."

Alley was terrified. She knew how he was when he was drunk. She wanted to run, but it was too late.

"Sit down. I ain't goin to bite yah." He grabbed her arm, and pulled her to the couch. "You know you're starting to look just like your mother. Come here."

He pulled her back forcing her to lean against his chest. He put his hand under her shirt.

"Looks like you're starting to get boobies. Let's see what else you've got." He slid his hands from her chest into her jeans. A tear rolled down her cheek as Alley sat there trembling.

"I have to go to the bathroom," she cried out.

He took his hand out of her jeans, and let her go. "Okay, okay," he said, "but hurry back."

Alley ran to the bathroom, and locked the door. She sat behind the door with her hands wrapped around her knees, and cried. Suddenly, I could see the jeans in my hand again. I stared at the bathroom door for a moment then I picked up the rest of Alley's dirty clothing, and ran downstairs. I rushed through the kitchen to put Alley's clothes on top of the washer in the laundry room. Then I left out just as fast as I had come into the room. I could hear Big Mama calling my name, but I didn't stop. I ran into my room, and shut the door. I sat on my bed with my hands wrapped around my knees. I put my face in my knees, and cried. I could sense the terror, and humiliation she felt. I couldn't believe that her own father would treat her like this. I stayed there crying with my face in my knees. Alley walked into my room dressed in my clothes, and her hair was still wet. She walked around my bed, and sat beside me.

"Jay-Jay, what's wrong?" She asked.

How could I tell her what I saw without making her feel worse? "Alley, I want to tell you something, so don't think that I am crazy. I can see things."

"What?"

"I'm serious. Alley, I can see things, and I have seen things about you." Alley turned her face from me.

"What have you seen?"

"I saw your father touch you in the bad way."

Alley's eyes lowered.

"Alley, I am not trying to embarrass you. Please don't be mad at me, okay."

"What else have you seen?" She asked.

"I saw your father hit you."

"How could you have seen this?" She glared at me in shock.

"Alley, I don't know how, but I can. Big Mama says that I'm a Seer. Alley, I'm not crazy. Tell me, did your dad do this?"

"Yes." Alley said reluctantly.

"Does he do it a lot?" I asked cautiously.

"He does hit me sometimes, but only when he's drunk will he try to touch me. He thinks that I am mom, or something."

"Alley, has he done anything else?"

She shook her head, and said no.

"I hide from him when he's like this. Please don't tell anyone about this. You know how people talk about me at school already. If someone finds out about this, I could never live this down."

I knew how she was harassed at school about the way she looked, so I agreed. Then I thought for a minute, and said, "Alley, you can hide here."

"What?"

"I'll let you in anytime day, or night."

Alley looked at me with a bit of concern. "Are you sure? What will your mother say?"

"Alley you're here all the time anyway. She won't care. Besides, the angel said I had to help you."

"What angel?"

I knew by now Alley must really think that I was crazy. "Don't worry about the angel. You can hide here." Then I leaped across the bed, and hugged her. "I'll help you." I let her go, and sat beside her.

She looked at me with a slight smile, and said, "Jay-Jay, you are so lucky to live here with your mother and Big Mama. I wished I had my mama. I don't have anyone that loves me."

I grabbed her shoulder, and said softly, "Yes you do. We just don't live with you."

Then we heard the door bell ring. We ran downstairs and it was Uncle Pete.

Uncle Pete came in the door behind Jonathan and Jordan.

"What's up?" Uncle Pete shouted. "And who might this young lady be?"

"Uncle Pete this is Alley," I replied.

"Well, hey Miss Alley. You sure got a funny name. Were you named after a street corner, or something?"

"No, no Uncle Pete, Alley is her nickname. Her real name is Alexandria."

"Well, tell me something," he laughed.

Everyone knows that Uncle Pete has always been a sharp dresser. He always had his shoes polished, and his afro neat. Uncle Pete was the coolest man I have ever known.

Uncle Pete walked toward the kitchen, and shouted, "What's up?"

Mama and Big Mama replied with a dismal, "Hey, Pete."

"What's cooking? I am as hungry as a mother f--. Oops!" Both Big Mama and mama turned to look at Uncle Pete very sternly.

"Dinner will be ready in a minute," said Big Mama.

"Good, good," replied Uncle Pete. "Hey let's liven this place up."

Uncle Pete turned off the gospel music, and turned the radio to some R & B music.

"Come on and show me what you got," he said as he called me, Alley, and my brothers over to him.

We formed two lines. My brothers where on one side, and Alley and I were on the other. Uncle Pete was dancing down the middle.

We were dancing from side to side saying, "Go Uncle, go Pete, go Uncle, go Pete . . ."

I have never seen the dance Uncle Pete was doing before. When he got to the end of the line, he did a split, and jump back up again. Everyone screamed, "Woo!"

Then I came down the line with my hand in the air dancing, Jordan yelled, "Wave you hand in the air. Wave them like you just don't care."

Jonathan came down the center break dancing. We started laughing so hard that nobody could say anything. Alley came down the aisle dancing very conservatively.

We all said, "Go Alley, go Alley . . ."

Suddenly Big Mama came out of the kitchen dancing down the center shaking her hips from side to side.

We shouted, "Go Big Mama! Go Big Mama . . ."

Finally, Jordan came down the aisle break dancing like Jonathan, but this time he wanted to do the split like Uncle Pete. He jumped down, and when he landed, we heard a big rip.

"Oh no!" Jordan shouted.

We all stopped dancing. The room fell silent. Then everyone broke out in hysterical laughter as Jordan ran upstairs covering his backside with his hands. He ran as fast as he could upstairs. Mama came to the kitchen threshold.

"Dinner is ready. Where is Jordan?"

"He ripped his shorts, and ran upstairs," Jonathan said.

Mama started giggling. "Well, go get him. Tell him to change his shorts, and come to dinner," she replied.

Once Jonathan and Jordan came to the table, Big Mama asked Uncle Pete to say grace. We all put our heads down.

Uncle Pete said, "Dear heavenly Father, we thank you for this food. Now, under the roof, and over the tongue look out stomach because here it comes."

Everybody broke out in laughter except Big Mama. Big Mama gave Uncle Pete a very stern look. "Pete, watch your mouth. That's the Lord you're praying to."

Uncle Pete lowered his eyes, and gave Big Mama a pitiful look. "Yes ma'am," he said.

Then he turned to me grinning, and winking. Dinner on Sunday was a big event. We ate pot roast with carrots and potatoes, green beans, broccoli and rice casserole, and homemade rolls. For dessert Big Mama made a peach cobbler, and we had vanilla ice cream to go with it. This was one of the best meals we've had this year. Most of the food was devoured except for half of the roast, and half of the peach cobbler. We all got up, and cleaned the table off while mama and Big Mama cleaned the kitchen. Uncle Pete sat on the couch telling us stories of the war, and he added a few jokes to liven the stories up.

Then he stood up, and said, "I'm thirsty! I'm going to get something to drink."

Big Mama and mama gave him a sarcastic look and said in unison, "Bye Pete."

Alley, my brothers, and I walked Uncle Pete to the front door to say goodbye. After Uncle Pete left, my brothers left me and Alley at the front door. Alley and I walked outside onto the porch.

"I have to go too," Alley said.

I didn't want her to go back to her house after what I have seen, but I knew she had to go.

"Alley, do you need a ride home?"

"No, it's still light outside. I can walk. I'll be okay."

I walked over to her, and touched her arm. "Are you sure you'll be okay?" I asked.

"I'll be back if I'm not okay."

I watched her go up the street, and turn the corner. I wondered for a moment if she really would be all right. Then I turned around, and saw Pee-Pee on the porch. We walked back into the house together.

*****

School ended Tuesday at noon with a big party. I think these last two days of the school year were probably the best days of the whole year. After school, Big Mama took us to a restaurant, and bought us some ice cream cones. We ate the ice cream, and played on the restaurant play ground. Then Big Mama drove us home. My brothers and I were playing in the front yard when Carlos came over to invite us to his birthday party on Saturday at two o'clock. I ran towards the backyard to tell Big Mama about the party. When I opened the gate, Big Mama was wearing a wide brim straw hat with garden gloves on her hands. She was sweating too. It was a hot day. Pee-Pee was sitting under a tree panting very loudly.

"Big Mama, are you okay," I asked.

"Yes baby. This is just a little sweat. I have been digging up the grass, and loosening the dirt to plant my garden. No garden will grow in the shade. So, I am digging it here in the sunshine. All plants need sunshine."

Big Mama hummed as she pulled up weeds, and turned the earth. She had cleared a four-by-four feet section of grass in about an hour, and a half. Then she stopped, and looked at me. "Baby, did you need something?"

Standing there in amazement at the amount of land she had cleared, I had forgotten why I came back here.

"Big Mama, Carlos has invited us to his birthday party on Saturday. Can we go?"

"Well, I don't see why not." Big Mama said as she wiped the sweat from her brow. "I'll tell your mother tonight, okay. Later on, we can get a present for Carlo. I wouldn't want y'all to go empty handed to a party."

With a big smile and excitement, I said, "Great. I'll go tell Jordan and Jonathan."

By the time I came back around the house to the front yard, everyone had left. They knew better than to leave without telling someone where they were going, so they left a note on the porch under a rock. The note read:

> *"Big Mama, gone to the store with Carlos.*
> *Jordan."*

Suddenly, I became very lonely. I knew that Plump would be at her grandmother's house in the daytime. I wouldn't see her again until summer camp started. I hadn't seen Alley since Sunday. It's not easy being the only girl in the family. I walked around to the backyard, and gave the letter to Big Mama. She stopped raking, and took the letter.

"Those boys should have come, and told me this before they left. If they aren't back in ten minutes, we are going to go, and get them. They aren't going to like it if I have to go get them either. I swear those two boys give patience a whole new meaning."

Big Mama put the letter in her pocket, and started turning the earth again. I went into the house, and got a bowl of water for Pee-Pee. I sat under the tree rubbing Pee-Pee's back while he lapped up most of the water.

Big Mama stood up saying, "Woo! I believe it's getting too hot even for me out here. That's enough digging for today. Come on. Let's go into the house."

I got up, and followed Big Mama to the back door. Before we got half way up the steps, Big Mama said, "Stop!" Pee-Pee was right behind me. Big Mama put her hands on her hips, and said, "If that dog is going to stay in this house, he has to take a bath."

"A bath? But, this isn't our dog."

Big Mama looked at me as if I said something really crazy. "Well, he might as well be your dog. Y'all feed him, and he sleeps here. Why your brother even named him."

"I know, but mama said he might belong to someone else."

"Oh, forget about that. Your mama isn't going to give this dog back if someone did say he was theirs, so if he stays here, he's going to have a bath."

Big Mama went into the house, and got out our old plastic swimming pool. She put it on the patio, and filled it half way with water from the hose. Then she boiled some water in a teapot on the stove, and put the boiled water in the pool to warm the water. I put my hand in the water, and it was just right.

"Don't put him in the pool just yet. Let me get his leash and collar," said Big Mama.

"A leash and collar? Where did you get a leash, and collar Big Mama?"

"Your mama picked it up from the store when she bought the dog food. She left it in her car. She just brought it in the house this morning before she went to work."

Big Mama and I turned to see Jordan, Jonathan, and Carlos coming into the backyard carrying sodas.

"Just in time boys," Big Mama said with a grin. "Put those sodas down on the table over there, and y'all help Jasmine wash this dog."

We didn't have any dog shampoo, so Big Mama gave us some dish detergent.

"With this dish detergent, he should be squeaky clean," Jordan said.

We washed the dog twice with the dish detergent. I made sure that the boys didn't get the soap in the dog's nose, or eyes. We rinsed the dog with the hose, and took him out of the pool. As soon as he got out, he shook from his head to his paws. He got all of us wet.

"Catch him!" Big Mama yelled.

Before we could grab him, Pee-Pee took off. He ran around the yard in a circle. I could sense that he thought that if he ran fast enough, he could get the water off. I knew if we didn't stop him, he would roll around in the dirt.

On Pee-Pee's last lap around the yard, I stood in front of him, and said, "Stop running Pee-Pee!"

The dog stopped in front of me. He sat there wagging his tail panting. Big Mama gave me the collar, and leash. I put the collar and leash on the dog, and lead him into the house. Once we were inside, I took the leash, and collar off. He lay on the towels, and went to sleep. About an hour later, Pee-Pee was dry. His coat changed from a dirty dingy yellow to a beautiful shiny golden color. He looked like a show dog. When mama got home, she couldn't believe this was the same dog.

"As clean and pretty as he is, we can't let him sleep on those dirty towels. When I get off work tonight, I will buy him a new bed," said mama.

Pee-Pee curled up into a fluffy yellow ball, and went to sleep.

Chapter 5
Big Mike

This morning we all ate cereal. Big Mama told mama she had to go to her social and savings club meeting, so she wouldn't be able to sit with us tonight.

Mama knew she didn't have time to find anyone else, so she said, "Guys, I guess this means that you are coming with me. Y'all have to be ready when I get home tonight. I don't have time to wait for anyone, okay."

My brothers and I said, "Yes ma'am."

"Mama, can I bring my *Jacks*?" I asked

"Yes, but you will have to keep up with them. I won't be able to help you look for them when I am working."

"Okay." I got up from the table, and put my bowl and spoon in the dishwasher. Then I noticed in the laundry room that Pee-Pee had a new bed. The bed had a dark forest green trim with fluffy cream cotton colored center. I could tell Pee-Pee loved the new bed. When I looked at him, he wagged his tail, and seemed to smile at me.

Mama called me from the table saying, "Jasmine, let the dog out."

I didn't call Pee-Pee, but somehow, he knew to follow me. I walked out of the kitchen to the front door with Pee-Pee at my heels. I opened the door, and Alley was standing there.

"Good morning, Alley," I said. "What are you doing here so early?"

Before Alley could answer Big Mama shouted, "Alley would you like some cereal?"

Big Mama was leaning so far down from the kitchen table to see who was at the door that I thought she might fall.

"Yes ma'am," she replied.

Big Mama got up from the table to make Alley a bowl of cereal. Alley and I sat down at the table when Big Mama put the bowl of cereal in front of her.

"I'm going outside to work in the garden. If anybody needs me, that's where I'll be, and boys don't go anywhere without speaking to me first," Big Mama said sternly.

Both Jonathan and Jordan said together in a very monotone voice, "Yes ma'am."

Mama stood up, and grabbed her purse and bag. "I have to go too. Bye guys."

We all said goodbye to mama as she left for work. Jordan and Jonathan followed mama out of the front door. Big Mama went out the back door passed the laundry room leaving me, and Alley alone at the table.

"Where have you been? I haven't seen you since Sunday."

Alley had a mouth full of cereal when she looked back at me. She swallowed hard then spoke with a very thick southern accent. "Well on Monday after school, the social worker came by our house. Her name was Mrs. Green. She was a nice black lady, but I could tell she didn't like what my dad had to say to the principal. She asked me a lot of questions like, how did I get the bruise on my arm, and what did I hit when I fell."

"What did you tell her?"

Alley looked down at the bowl of cereal, and began stirring it with her spoon. She never looked up at me when she said, "I told her what dad told me to say. That I fell down the steps." Her melancholy eyes looked back at me as she continued, "--He said I better not tell her anything except that I fell down the steps hitting my shoulder on the rail. If I said anything else, he would make the other arm look worse than this one."

I leaned back in my chair, and sighed deeply. Saddened by this news, I still had to know more.

"What happened next?"

"Dad showed Mrs. Green the steps where he said I fell, and pointed out where I hit my shoulder. Mrs. Green told dad that if anything happens like this again that he needs to take me to a hospital. She said I could have been really hurt more seriously than he knows. Then they talked for a while at the front door. After that, she left." Alley began to eat her cereal again.

"Do you think that she will come back again?"

With a mouth full of cereal, Alley mumbled, "I… don't know."

Alley finished breakfast, and we went outside.

Since Big Mama has been living with us for the last five days, the yard is looking better than before. Big Mama has planted flowers by the walkway to the house. She has put potted flowers on the porch and patio. She got June-Bug, who lives down the street, to mow the grass, and trim the hedges. The garden plants have grown bigger. Alley and I helped Big

Mama plant herbs by the garden. Then we dressed Pee-Pee in a hat, and plastic beads. When Big Mama saw what we had done to Pee-Pee, she made us take it off of him. Alley and I played most of the day until mama came home.

"Alley," I said, "tonight we have to go to work with mama. Big Mama can't stay with us tonight. She has a meeting."

I could tell Alley didn't want to leave. "Can I come too?" She asked.

"I don't see why not, but I better ask mama first."

I turned to mama looking as pitiful as I could and asked, "Mama, can Alley come with us, please?" I thought for a minute that she was going to say no.

Then she said, "Alley, will your father mind if you come with us tonight?"

"No ma'am! I don't think he'll even come home tonight."

Mama's face grew with concern. "Alley, how long has he been gone?"

"Since yesterday."

"Yesterday?" Mama said in surprise.

"Yes ma'am."

"Alley, who takes care of you when your dad is gone?"

"Sometimes my dad's girlfriend will come by, but most of the time I take care of myself."

Mama was shocked. "Alley, I want you to call your father and ask first, okay."

Alley nodded her head, and picked up the phone. She dialed the number twice, and both times it just rang. "There's nobody there," she said.

"Does your dad have a cell phone?" Mama asked.

"Yeah, but I don't know the number."

Mama just shook her head. "I can't believe this." Then she said to Alley, "Well, I guess you will have to come with us. I can't let you just stay at home alone, but when we get to Mrs. Jenkins's house, I want you to call home, and tell your father where you are."

Alley said okay, and then we all left the house.

As my brothers, Alley, and I got into the van with mama, Big Mama came out of the house in a blue suit, and blue hat. She waved goodbye to us from the steps as she got into her car. Then a shadowy glow appeared from the steps where Big Mama was standing.

I saw the angel appear in the midst of the light saying to me, "You have to help her," she said. Then we drove away.

Now, mama hated her first job at the office. She said she hated all the office drama. She told Big Mama that the women were gossipy, jealous, competitive, and self absorbed. She loved working for Mrs. Jenkins. Working for Mrs. Jenkins made mama feel needed, and really appreciated. They were really good friends too.

We drove for about fifteen minutes until we came to this lovely old southern mansion that stood a fair distance from the road. Mrs. Smith was the morning sitter. She met us at the door. She was a chubby black woman who was dressed in a white uniform. When she spoke, her voice sounded like a small child.

"Hey Michelle," Mrs. Smith said. "Who are these darlin children?"

"Well, these two boys are my sons Jonathan and Jordan. This is my daughter Jasmine, and her friend Alley."

"Well, aren't y'all just darlin," Mrs. Smith said. "Now, Mrs. Jenkins is waiting on y'all, so y'all go on inside, and say hello. I've got to go. See you later Michelle. Nice to meet y'all."

We all said goodbye as Mrs. Smith left. As we walked inside of the grand foyer, we saw a dining room with some of the most beautiful dark wood antiques that I have ever seen. The living room was huge with a grand piano in the center. These rooms were so clean, and untouched that I could tell that no one had been in them in years. We walked down the hall that was lined with pictures of distant relatives. Some of the pictures were so old that they were turning brown. We entered the den where Mrs. Jenkins was sitting in an electric reclining chair watching TV. She pushed a button on the chair to sit up.

"Good evening, everyone," Mrs. Jenkins said with a toothless smile.

Mrs. Jenkins was a frail lady with thin white hair that looked like cotton blowing in the wind. The wrinkles on her pale white face gave away to years of emotion. Mama rushed over to Mrs. Jenkins to explain why we were there.

"I am sorry to bring them with me. My mother couldn't watch them for me tonight, and it was too late to call someone else."

Mrs. Jenkins turned to mama, and said, "Hush, hush child. I am happy to see children here again. I only get to see my own grandchildren on holidays. Sometimes they don't even come around then if they're too busy."

"Well, Mrs. Jenkins, they won't be in the way. They will be outside playing in the backyard until dinner." Then mama turned toward us, and said, "Guys go outside, but stay close. I'll call you when dinner is ready. Oh Alley, call your dad. There's a phone in the kitchen."

We all said yes ma'am, and left the room. I turned to see Mrs. Jenkins smiling at me.

As I walked out of the room, her eyes trailed down to the back of my leg to see my birthmark. She gasped when she saw it. Then she said, "Michelle, help me get into my wheel chair. I want to come into the kitchen with you."

Mama got the wheel chair from the corner, and helped Mrs. Jenkins into it. She wheeled Mrs. Jenkins to the kitchen table, and began to pull food out of the refrigerator for dinner. Mrs. Jenkins was looking out of the screen door at me and Alley playing *Jacks*.

"Your girl there," Mrs. Jenkins said. "She bears the mark."

Mama turned back to look at Mrs. Jenkins from behind the refrigerator door.

"What mark?" Mama asked.

Mrs. Jenkins looked at mama curiously, and said, "The *Ayin*. She is a descendant from the forty-four thousand tribes of the Israelites. Your daughter is a Seer."

Mama turned to look at me through the screen. Then she shut the refrigerator door, and put the food on the counter.

Mama turned back to Mrs. Jenkins. "That birthmark has been in my family for generation. Not all of us have this mark, but those that do are cursed with the madness that they can see things that aren't there. They feel that they alone have to fulfill some God given destiny. I know this is crazy, but many of the women in my family have died trying to fulfill it. My mother also bears this mark too. She has been seeing things for years. I had hoped this wouldn't pass on to my daughter, but I don't think that I'll be that fortunate. So far, she hasn't talked to me about any visions. Maybe this will pass us by."

Mrs. Jenkins sat there in shock with her mouth slightly open. "Michelle, this is a blessing, not a curse. She is here to lead the masses to Him at the end of time. It is her destiny, and an honor. Your child is blessed."

Mama looked back at me with a worried expression on her face. Then she noticed Jonathan and Jordan talking to a man. "Mrs. Jenkins," mama said as she moved toward the door, "who is that man?"

"Oh, that's Big Mike. I asked him to come here, and take a look at my car. It has been giving me trouble for the last two weeks. It almost stopped on me when Mrs. Smith took me to the doctor's office." Mrs. Jenkins looked back at mama with a devilish grin. "He's a nice-looking young man, isn't he? Why don't you go out there, and introduce yourself to Mike. He's really a nice young man. You'll like him. Go on."

Mama looked over her shoulder at Mrs. Jenkins from the screen door with a mischievous grin.

"Why Mrs. Jenkins, are you tying to play match maker?"

"No child! But I don't see anything wrong with the two of you getting to know one another."

Mama walked back to the counter. "Well, I just got rid of one man, and I am not trying to get another."

Mrs. Jenkins toothless mouth drew up as she turned her head. Then she said, "Aww shoot. Life is too short not to make new friends."

Still grinning mama said, "I have to finish dinner first. Remember, I still have a job to do. If he's still here when I finish, I'll invite him to dinner. Will that be friendly enough?"

Mrs. Jenkins laughed, and said, "That will do just fine. By the way Michelle, my lawyer told me that the stock you invested in is doing great. He said if you would have left that money in that terrible 401(k) you wouldn't be able to retire until you turned one hundred."

"What? What did you do? This 401(k) was consider the best option for me."

"Well honey, believe me when I say it was not," smirked Mrs. Jenkins. "Don't worry, you still have the money you left in that terrible investment, but I promise you will have wished you had invested it all."

"Mrs. Jenkins, how did you learn so much about the stock market?"

"Well, after my husband's first affair, I started to work in his firm. I learned there about all his investments and businesses. If those whores he was with thought that they were going get their hands on my husband's money, they had to come through me first. After my husband died, I continued running the companies for him until I got sick. Now, my boys control most of it." Mrs. Jenkins smiled.

"You're very smart Mrs. Jenkins and lucky too," said mama.

"You better know it. How else do you think I could stay here in this house by myself all these years? Lucky Hell! I didn't want to be homeless!"

Both Michelle and Mrs. Jenkins laughed. Mama finished cooking dinner, and came outside on the back porch to call us in. My brothers ran past mama into the house. Mama turned back to the screen door, and shouted, "Boys, wash your hands." Alley got up, and walked into the house while I sat there trying to gather my *Jacks* off the porch floor. When I stood up, a man started walking toward mama and me.

"Excuse me ma'am," he said. "Is that your van?"

"Yes, why?"

"Well, your van is leaking oil. And, who might this pretty young lady be?"

Mama gave him a warning look, and said, "Jasmine. For whom I am very protective of."

The man just smiled. "Well, ma'am, I can hardly blame you because she's a beauty, but I enjoy the ladies myself. Let me introduce myself. My name is Michael Raimond, and what is your name pretty lady?"

Now, mama was still staring at him suspiciously. I noticed he had a slight Creole accent. He had a tan colored complexion with dark soft curly hair. His dimpled smile could charm even the hardest heart. He was good looking, and big too. He's probably the biggest man that I have ever seen.

When mama finally spoke, she said, "My name is Michelle Patterson."

"Well, Mrs. Patterson I can fix that leak under your van for you if you like."

"Well, Mr. Raimond, I don't have any money, but thank you kindly."

"Oh, don't worry about the money. I think I might have some spare parts in my truck that will work."

Mama stopped looking so suspicious, and said, "Thank you Mr. Raimond."

"Just call me Mike. We don't have to be so formal, do we Michelle?" Mike never stopped smiling.

"Okay, Mike. If you think you can fix it, go ahead. Also, Mrs. Jenkins wants me to invite you to dinner."

"Sure!" His smile grew even larger. "When would you like to go?"

Mama's face flushed with embarrassment. "No, no. I meant she wanted you to eat here with us, today."

"Now, I will eat here with you today, but I'll hold you to your dinner invitation for another time. All right, let me go inside, and get washed up."

He walked passed us into the house with that same smile on his face. I looked up, and saw mama grinning too.

Everyone was sitting at the table, washed up, and ready to eat except for mama. Mama was busy chopping, and mashing Mrs. Jenkins food. Once she was finished, she put Mrs. Jenkins's plate in front of her, and then she put the rest of the food in the middle of the table. Mama pulled a big blue towel off the counter, and tied it around Mrs. Jenkins's neck. Mama said grace, and we all began to eat. Mrs. Jenkins always believed in doing as much for herself as she possibly could. When she tried to feed herself, her hand would shake so violently that she would have to use the other hand just to get the food to her mouth. At first, I wondered why mama put the towel around her neck, but now I knew. Any food that didn't make it to her mouth went down her chin, and onto the towel. Watching Mrs. Jenkins eat was like watching a two-year-old child learning to feed herself for the first time. Every now and then, mama would wipe Mrs. Jenkins's mouth with the towel. There was something strange about the way that Mrs. Jenkins chewed her food. Her mouth would move so fast that one would think that she had a mouth full of teeth. With every spoon full of mashed food, her jaw would work as fast as it could.

This was truly amazing to my brothers. I could hear Jordan whispering to Jonathan. I could see Alley covering her mouth trying not to giggle. To keep Jonathan and Jordan from whispering anything else, mama cleared her throat. Then she turned toward Mr. Raimond. "Mike, where are you from? I noticed that you have an accent."

"I'm originally from New Orleans, Louisiana in the lower Ninth Ward. I came here five years ago when I was hired for a contracting job. I have been here ever since. Now, I know you have a beautiful daughter over there, but who are the other beautiful children?"

Mama had completely forgotten to introduce everyone to Mr. Raimond. She gasped, and put her hand over her mouth.

"I am so sorry. These are my two sons Jonathan and Jordan and, this is my daughter's friend Alley."

"It's nice to meet y'all. Y'all can call me Big Mike. Everyone else does."

I could see the sparkle in Mrs. Jenkins eyes as she listened to this conversation.

"Do you have any kids Mike?" Mama asked

"No, I don't."

Suddenly, Mrs. Jenkins said, "but you do like kids don't you, Mike?"

"Yes ma'am. I've always wanted to have children, but my wife, and I didn't have any."

"So, you're married," mama replied.

Again, Mrs. Jenkins broke in their conversation. "No. He's not married. His wife passed away two years ago."

Mama turned her head from Mrs. Jenkins, and back to Big Mike. "I am sorry to hear this. My condolences."

"Thank you."

Mrs. Jenkins made another sudden outburst saying, "She's not married either."

Mama flashed a sharp look at Mrs. Jenkins before she turned back to Big Mike.

"No, I'm not married. I've just been recently divorced."

Mike gave mama a little grin, and said, "My condolences to you too."

Mrs. Jenkins burst out with laughter.

"So," Mike said turning towards my brothers. "Who likes baseball?"

Jordan and Jonathan both jumped in their seats saying, "I do, I do . . ." Jordan and Jonathan went on and on talking about what position they wanted to play. Jordan said that he could hit the ball over the left field fence at school.

"Uh un! Tell the truth Jordan," I said. "You hit the ball over the left fence in our backyard. When you went to get the ball, Mr. Davis dog chased you out of his yard, and bit you on the bottom."

Everyone laughed. Jordan gave me a sneer.

"So!" Jordan shouted, "I still hit it over the fence."

"I'm sure you've got a good arm Jordan. Now, how about you girls, what do you like to do?" Mike asked.

Alley and I looked at each other, and said, "*Double Dutch.*"

"I jump all the way through the song, and up to the count of three," Alley said.

"Our dog likes to jump rope too, but he can only jump one rope at a time," I said.

Big Mike turned looking at mama with a strange look. "Your dog jumps rope?"

"Apparently, the dog likes to play with them, but he is not our dog."

Mike just grinned. "Your family is as beautiful as their mother."

A huge smile was prominently displayed on Mrs. Jenkins face. We all talked, and ate until the food was gone.

"Well ladies and gentlemen. I am going to have to go, so I can have your van ready before y'all leave. Michelle, where are your keys?"

Mama pointed to the counter saying, "over there."

"I only need an hour to fix it. Is that okay?"

"Yeah, that will be fine."

"Good. Mrs. Jenkins, thank you for the dinner."

He put his plate in the sink, and walked outside. The rest of us got up, and cleared the table putting our dishes in the sink. Mama cleaned Mrs. Jenkins's face, and removed the towel.

The last thing I heard Mrs. Jenkins say before she left the room was, "He's a nice man, isn't he?"

Mama replied, "Yes ma'am."

"I know you like him. You can't fool me," said Mrs. Jenkins with a devilish grin.

"Come on Mrs. Jenkins." Mama rolled Mrs. Jenkins away from the table to the bathroom to take a bath. Alley, my brothers, and I went back into the den to watch TV.

After Mrs. Jenkins was dressed, and in bed, mama left the bedroom to clean the kitchen. I watched TV for a while, and then I got up to go to the bathroom.

When I came out, I could hear a small voice calling me. "Jasmine, Jasmine."

I turned to see Mrs. Jenkins waving for me to come to her. Her bedroom was just as big as the den. Her room was filled with beautiful antiques, and old pictures. Everything in the room was at least fifty years old except for the hospital bed. Mrs. Jenkins waved to me to come closer. I walked over, and stood by her bedside.

"Sit down," she said pointing toward the bed. "I ain't goin to bite yah."

Her bed was a little high off the floor. I had to hop up on the bottom half of the bed to keep from hitting the rail.

"Jasmine, isn't it?"

"Yes ma'am."

"Did you know that your mama just loves to talk about you, and your brothers? Now, I can see why. Y'all are just dear sweet children. You know, you remind me of my granddaughter when she was just your age. You see her in the picture over there."

Mrs. Jenkins pointed a thin shaky finger at a picture on the side table next to her bed. The little girl in the picture had curly blond hair with a pink bow on top of her head. Her nose and cheeks were covered with freckles, and her front tooth was missing when she smiled. I could tell from the sparkle in Mrs. Jenkins eyes that she simply adored her granddaughter.

"Where is she now?"

"Oh, she's in college. She's doing really well from what I heard. She says that she wants to be an accountant. I don't get to see her that much anymore. I know she's busy with school, and all, but she isn't as blessed to have what you have. I saw the mark on your leg there. You have the *eye*," Mrs. Jenkins said.

"Yes ma'am," I said then turned my face away from Mrs. Jenkins.

"Well, that's nothing to be ashamed of. You are blessed."

I turned back to Mrs. Jenkins, and said, "Big Mama told me not to say anything about it to anyone because mama wouldn't like it if I did."

Mrs. Jenkins shook her head. "No, no child. You are blessed. I know your mama is just scared about the task you must fulfill, but it is an honor to do God's work. Don't you ever be ashamed of who you are. You are a Seer." Mrs. Jenkins hesitated for a moment, and looked around the room. "Tell me child. Do you see any angels in here?"

I looked around, and said honestly, "no."

"Good, they haven't come for me yet, but I know they will be coming for me soon. I've left something for your mother when I pass on. You see, she doesn't just treat me like a patient. We are friends. Now, by some people's standards, this would be an unlikely friendship. But even though I don't know what is to be black, I do know what is to be a woman married to the wrong man. I like your mother a lot, and I will miss her. I know she could use what I'm going to give her."

The door opened so abruptly it startled me.

"Mrs. Jenkins," the lady said as she entered the room.

"Come on in Mrs. Fowler," said Mrs. Jenkins and then she turned back to me grabbing my hand. "Jasmine, you go on back into the room with the other children, but you remember what I said." She gave me another toothless smile. "You are blessed."

She let go of my hand, and I jumped down off the bed. Then I left the room. Mrs. Jenkins was a really nice lady. Now, I knew why mama likes working here.

When I came back into the den, mama said, "Where were you?"

"I was just talking to Mrs. Jenkins and--."

"Come on. It's time to go."

We all walked outside towards the van. Big Mike was leaning against the side of the van.

"*Madame*, your ride awaits you," he said. Then he pushed the lock to open the rear passenger door. Alley, my brothers, and I got in the back of the van. Mike shut the door, and handed mama the keys. "*Belles Madame*," Big Mike said with a grin, "what about our dinner date?"

Mama gave him a very strange look. "What did you call me?"

"Beautiful lady."

"Oh, is that what you said. The way you speak is very beautiful, but I can't understand a word of it."

"So sorry *Madame*," he said.

"Anyway," Mama continued, "I don't think I said anything about a date."

"We can talk about that later. Now, how about that dinner you owe me?"

Mama gave him another suspicious look. "First, let me see if my van will start."

Mike giggled. "Go ahead," he said. "Get inside, and crank up the motor. I promise you it won't leak anymore."

Mama walked around to the driver's side, and got into the van. When she started the van there was no smoke. Mama got out, and looked under the front end. There was no oil leaking from the engine, nor any oil on the ground. "Big Mike, you have done some really good work on the van."

Mike held his head down as his big brown eyes looked back up toward mama's face with an impish grin. "So, do I deserve dinner now?"

"I guess you do as long as you're not a criminal," mama said with her own impish grin.

"Darling, I don't even have a parking ticket."

"Well, why don't we have brunch this Sunday at my house? My mom just loves to cook."

"So, you're bringing your mother along to watch me?" He said with a raised brow.

"Yes, and my children too. My mother lives with us."

"Oh," Mikes said in relief, "then it's a date."

"No, it's dinner."

"Okay, okay. Here take this, and give me a call. You know, for directions, or if you want to talk." He gave mama the card, and said, "Call me." Mama got into the van, and Big Mike waved goodbye saying, "*au revoir*."

Whenever Creole people speak in the French language, it never quite sounds the same as it does when French people speak it. After we said goodbye, mama drove away.

Chapter 6
The Fiesta

The ride home was quiet. I could tell that everyone in the van was tired. Jordan had already fallen asleep. I sat there watching the stars trying to find the Big Dipper. Then I thought about what Mrs. Jenkins said to me. She said she had left something for mama, but what? I got the feeling that she didn't want me to tell mama this, so I just put it out of my mind. Soon the van turned a familiar corner, and we were back in our neighborhood. Mama drove the van to the front of Alley's house.

"Alley we're here. Jonathan opened the door, and let her out," mama said.

I looked up into the window of Alley's house, and saw a dark angel. He had an eerie glow around him.

I saw his mouth move, and in my head, I heard him say, "We will have her too." Then he gave me a sinister smile. I gasped and hit the lock on the door. "No mama! She can't go!"

Mama gave me a surprised look. "What are you doing Jasmine? Open the door."

Everyone was looking at me like I had just lost my mind.

Jordan woke up, and said, "Are we at home?"

"No Jordan," Mama replied. "Jasmine, open the door."

"No mama," I said frantically. "She can't stay there by herself with those dark angles. Please mama, they will hurt her. I just know they will."

Then I felt a tear roll down my cheek. Mama sat there for a moment unable to speak. I think she just realized that I could see angels just like Big Mama. "Jasmine, what did you say?"

"There is a dark angel in that house. Please, don't make her go. Please."

"How long have you seen these angels?"

"I don't know. I guess I've been seeing them since kindergarten."

"Why haven't you told me about this before?"

"Well . . ., Big Mama said I shouldn't talk about this around you. She said that you would get mad."

I could see that mama was holding the steering wheel tightly, and shaking her head in a fit of rage. She lifted her head abruptly as if she remembered something. "Alley, did you talk to your dad on the phone?"

Alley shook her head, and said, "No. The phone just rang."

Mama stopped talking, and noticed someone coming out of the front door.

"Alley, who is that man?" Mama asked.

A black man came out of the front door holding a bag. He walked passed the van, and got into a dark red car behind us.

"I don't know him, but he buys medicine from my dad."

Mama put the van in gear, and drove to our house. "Alley, I want you to call your dad again when we get home."

"Yes ma'am."

When we pulled up to our house, I could see Big Mama's car in the drive way. I was so glad she was at home because I wanted to go inside first to warn her before mama could say anything, but it was too late.

As soon as we walked into the house mama said, "Guys, go upstairs, and go to bed."

"What? But mama it's only 8:30. We don't even have to go to school tomorrow," Jordan pleaded.

"Now, Jordan."

He knew better than to push mama any further. So we all started slowly walking upstairs. Big Mama was sitting at the kitchen table listening to the TV in the den while she shelled the leftover peas.

"Well, hello everybody. How is Mrs. Jenkins?"

Nobody said anything. Mama walked past the den, and into the kitchen. "Michelle, what's wrong?" Big Mama asked with a very concerned voice.

Michelle paced for a moment, and then she said, "How long have you known that Jasmine could see the angels?"

Big Mama just sat back in the chair, and closed her eyes. When she opened them again, she said, "Michelle calm down. We all knew this would happen."

"Why didn't you tell me?"

"Michelle I was going to tell you, but I knew how you felt about this stuff, and I didn't want to upset you. So, I told Jasmine not to say anything."

"Mom, you told her to keep secrets from me. How could you do that?"

"Michelle, don't be upset with Jasmine."

"I'm not."

There was an odd silence for a moment then Big Mama continued, "I'm sorry. I had to know what her task would be before I said anything. Michelle, I would never try to keep secrets from you. I just thought that I could help her, or even do it for her. That's all."

Michelle closed her eyes, and said to herself, "This is insane." When she opened her eyes again, she asked, "What is her task?"

"Alley. Alley is her task. I've seen a lot of things about her, and even more in her father. She needs our help."

Mama gasped. "No. We can't get involved in that. Her father is a dangerous man."

"Tell me about her father," Big Mama asked. "What kind of man is he?"

"Well, I believe he is a drug dealer," Michelle replied. "He always has shady characters hanging around his house. He's not a very good parent either. That girl is always dirty, and under feed. I always feed her whenever she comes over. She is a sweet girl, but I don't want her father over here. I can't put my own kids in that kind of jeopardy."

"Have you tried to call the police?" Big Mama asked.

"Yes, but he's good at covering his tracks. I think someone is helping him." mama replied.

"What about the child's mother?" Big Mama asked.

Michelle walked to the refrigerator. She got a soda, and sat down at the table with Big Mama. She sighed deeply, and said, "I really don't know. I met her mother when James and I first moved into this house. She was a young girl, and quite attractive too. I don't know what she wanted with Billy. I guess some women like those bad boys. She came to my door a few times asking for money. She said she needed it for her kid, but at the time I never saw a child. I gave her some money, but I could tell she was being beaten by him. She was pregnant around the same time as I was. One night I passed their house looking through the window, and saw Billy punch her in the face. She had to be at least six months pregnant at that time. When I got home, I called the police."

"What did they do?"

"They took him away that night. I don't know what happened after that, but he didn't stay away for long. A few months later Mrs. Madison told me she saw Billy taking Jessie to the hospital. It was several weeks before she came home. When I finally saw her, she looked bad. It looked like she had aged several years. One day I was passing by her house, and I saw her on the front porch. She was sitting there in a rocker looking very dazed, and just plain out of it. I pulled over and got out of my car to congratulate her. I waved to her, and said, congratulations. She didn't say anything, but she did wave to me with her left hand. Her right hand was curled under, and her mouth drooped a little. She looked like she might have had a stroke, or something. Before I could get close enough to the gate to talk to her, Billy called her into the house. She walked to the door with a slight drag in her right foot. I got back in my car, and went home. After that, I didn't see very much of her anymore."

Big Mama took a deep breath, and said, "Does Alley have any other family?"

"Not that I know of," mama replied.

"Wait a minute. How did you find out Jasmine could see angels?" Big Mama asked.

"Jasmine said she saw a dark angel in the window of Alley's house," replied mama.

Big Mama gasped.

"What is a dark angel?"

"A dark angel is a fallen angel from heaven, a demon. Alley can't go back to that house tonight."

Michelle hesitated before she spoke. "I told her to call her father. What if he comes here to pick--?"

"He won't," Big Mama interrupted before mama could finish. "I don't think he's in this state right now."

Michelle knew that Big Mama was right, and that she could always sense things like this. She has never been wrong. "Okay, okay, but what should we do about Alley now?"

"Let her stay here," Big Mama replied. "Jasmine has to finish her task. It's her destiny. The angel said we have to help her. If we fail to do this task, the girl will be lost. There is no way around this. You know what I say is true, so let her stay here. Besides, I know her father won't be gone for too long. He doesn't like to lose anything."

"Mom, I can't afford to take care of another child. Also, summer camp starts on Monday. What is she going to do here all day?"

Big Mama looked up at Michelle, and said, "I'll take care of her."

"What?" Mama looked surprised.

"I'll pay for her to go to summer camp, and any other expenses she will need."

"Mom, are you sure about this?

"Yes, we have to help her."

"Okay, mom, but we can't keep her from her father if he comes back to get her. So, don't get too attached to her staying here, okay."

"I know Michelle," Big Mama said in a very melancholy voice.

"Cheer up. Maybe we can find her family before he comes back."

Big Mama shook her head in agreement.

"I'm going to bed," mama replied.

Mama left Big Mama at the kitchen table, and walked out of the room. Big Mama said a little prayer for Alley then she cleaned up the kitchen, and went to bed too.

*****

Today, mama and Alley got up early to go over to Alley's house, and get some of her things. They got back by the time Big Mama started making breakfast. Mama was carrying a big bag of her clothes. Just about everything Alley owned was dirty, but at least now she had a tooth brush although her tooth brush needed to be replaced. Big Mama took the bag of clothing to the laundry room, and Alley sat down at the table.

"Guys, I don't have time to eat this morning. I've got to get to work. Boys listen to Big Mama," mama said.

Jonathan and Jordan said in unison, "Yes ma'am."

Mama left the kitchen as we all said goodbye to her. Big Mama put a plate of eggs, bacon, and toast on the table in front of Alley and me. Big Mama told us all not to go wandering off today. She had to go to the store, and we were going with her. We finished breakfast, and went upstairs to get dressed. I was the first one to come back downstairs. Big Mama was feeding Pee-Pee. The dog was crunching the kibble so loudly it sounded like he was chewing rocks. Alley hadn't taken a bath when she left with mama this morning. She had on the same clothes she wore yesterday. When Alley came downstairs after she took a shower, she looked really nice today in my clothes. She could be a really pretty girl if she could just stay clean. When my brothers came downstairs, we all went outside. We played outside until lunch time. Alley and I walked into the backyard to find Big Mama. She was talking to our neighbor Mr. Davis over the fence. Mr. Davis was a widower that lives alone with his dog. His house was slightly smaller than ours, but his yard was identical in size to ours. Alley and I walked over to the patio table, and sat down without saying a word. Big Mama was so deep into her conversation with Mr. Davis that she hardly recognized that we were in the yard.

"Your yard is looking beautiful. You must have a green thumb," said Mr. Davis.

"Nah, I just put them in the ground, and let them do all the work," Big Mama replied with a grin.

"And, they are working too. Say, why don't you come by sometime, and give me some tips on redoing my landscaping. I would surely appreciate it," Mr. Davis said.

"Sure, anytime," replied Big Mama.

Then she turned to see us grinning. "Oh, I have to go make lunch. I'll talk to you later," Big mama said.

Mr. Davis waved goodbye to Big Mama as she walked over to us. "How long have y'all been there?"

"Long enough to hear you say that you are going to give Mr. Davis some tips on doing his yard," I said with a mischievous grin.

"It's impolite to listen to other people's conversations you know," Big Mama replied.

I looked back at Alley with that same grin.

"Come on," said Big Mama. "You two can help me make lunch."

We both got up, and walked into the kitchen with Big Mama. We made sandwiches, and soup for lunch. Alley went outside to call my brothers into the house for lunch. As soon as we finished, we all piled into Big Mama's old car. On the way to the store, Big Mama looked back in her rearview mirror, and caught Jordan making faces at her behind her head. "I see you, Jordan. You know if you don't stop doing that, your face will stay that way."

Jordan's eyes grew big, and his mouth fell open. Then Jordan looked in the rearview mirror to make sure his face hadn't changed.

"Did I ever tell y'all about Hanna?" Big Mama asked.

We all looked at Big Mama, and said, "No."

Big Mama continued. "Hanna was a young girl that lived in West Africa with her two brothers, mother, and father."

"Like me, Big Mama?" I asked.

"Well, not quite like you," replied Big Mama. "Her brothers are older than yours and bigger too. They didn't believe that a girl could be as strong, or as smart as a boy. She would argue with them all the time about this. So, one day they decided to form a competition to prove who was the strongest and smartest. Hanna said, 'I know how we can prove who is the strongest and smartest.'

Both brothers said, 'How?'

Hanna said, 'We can find a way to bring the water from the river without using a bucket to fill up every tub in the village.'

Her oldest brother Chaga said, 'This can't be done.'

Her youngest brother Sef said, 'Are we supposed to carry the water with our bare hands?'

Hanna said, 'Well, if you can't do it, then I won.'

They both said, 'We'll do it.'

'How long do we have to finish this?' Chaga asked.

Hanna said, 'Two weeks.' They agreed. For a week, her brothers were trying to figure out what to do. Hanna found two big wagon wheels, and a bunch of small pig troths in the barn.

Chaga asked, 'What are you doing with those wheels?'

She said, 'I'm trying to move them near the river.'

He said, 'You know a girl can't move those heavy wheels.' So, he called his brother Sef to move the wheels by the water. While they were moving the wheels, Hanna brought over some of the small old troths from the barn. She had a bag of nails with her as she began to hammer the troths to the wheel.

Her brother Sef said, 'Hanna, what are you doing?'

'Oh, I am trying to nail these troths between the wheels.'

Sef said, 'Give that to me. A girl can't use a hammer. You might get hurt.'

So, Sef took the hammer from Hanna, and nailed all of the troths between the wheels. Hanna made sure he nailed them all in the right direction. While Sef finished nailing the troths to the wheels, Hanna brought over a ladder, and a board. She opened the ladder next to the river, and nailed the board to the center of the ladder.

Before Hanna could finish nailing the spoke to the board, her brother, Chaga said, 'Hanna what are you doing?'

Hanna said, 'I am trying to nail this spoke to the board, and to put the wheel on it.'

Chaga said, 'A girl can't do that. Give it to me.'

So, Chaga hammered the spoke in the board, and both Chaga and Sef hung the wheel onto it. After they got the wheel on the spoke, they were amazed to see that the water forced the wheel to go around. Hanna walked back into the barn, and found a cow's troth with a broken leg, a barn hinge, and an old board. She nailed the hinge to the troth and board. Next, she knocked one end off the troth's sides with the hammer. Then she chopped the end of the board with an ax in a v-shape. Her brothers were still watching the wheel go around when she brought the board and troth to the river side.

She sat them down, and started to walk off again when her brother Sef said, 'Hanna where are you going?'

'To get the tub,' she said.

'No, no. A girl can't carry a heavy tub. I'll go get it.'

When he came back with the tub, Hanna put the open troth end into the tub, and stuck the pointed side of the board into the ground. When the water came over the wheel it poured into the troth, and ran down into the tub. Soon the tub was filled with water. Her brothers were amazed.

Hanna yelled, 'I won! I won!'

Sef said, 'You're not the strongest, or the smartest. We built it.'"
Big Mama looked back in her rearview mirror and said, "Do you know what Hanna said?"

We were just as amazed as Hanna's brothers. We said in unison, "No."

"Hanna said, 'I may not be the strongest, but I'm definitely the smartest. I figured out how to put water in a tub without using my hands or a bucket, and I got you two to do the work for me.'" Big Mama started to laugh hysterically.

Jonathan sat there with a very angry expression.

"Big Mama, are you saying girls are smarter than boys?" Jonathon asked.

"Ha, ha, ha! No child. But, we have different abilities, and if we work together, there is no telling what we can accomplish."

Jonathan still had an angry smirk on his face.

"We are here. No running in the store," said Big Mama.

Big Mama liked to shop at this huge super center because she could get everything she needed in one place. We went down the food aisle first. Alley and I were chatting behind Big Mama, but Jonathan and Jordan were on a mission. Anytime Big Mama would stop to look at something Jordan, or Jonathan would sneak some chips, or candy into the basket. Most of the stuff they put in the basket would be taken out by the time we got to the register.

Big Mama turned to us and said, "Every time I bring these boys to this store, I have to take half of the stuff out of the basket before I can pay for any of it."

After we got the food, Big Mama took us to the toy section. "Now, we have to get a present for Carlos's party on Saturday," she said. "So kids, look around, and tell me what you think he would like."

Alley picked up a toy race car to show Big Mama.

"He already has one of those," Jonathan said.

I grabbed a jump rope to show Big Mama.

"Jasmine, he's not a girl," Jonathan said with a smirk.

"Hey look at this," Jordan shouted.

It was a toy rocket designed to look like the *"Apollo 13"* rocket. This rocket could really blast off up to ten feet. It even had smoke coming from it when it blasted off. The rocket came with its own launch pad, and plug. The batteries were sold separately. My brothers were so captivated by the rocket that I just knew that they wanted one too.

Big Mama picked up the rocket, and looked at it from side to side.

"There are no small parts. The price is okay. I'll get it." Then Big Mama said, "Alley, you need a new toothbrush, and some clothes. Some of your shorts have holes in them."

As we went down the aisle, Big Mama put toothbrushes, soap, and shampoo into the cart. Then she turned to Alley and said, "You know when I was your age Alley, there were three girls at my school that would bully me around." Big Mama continued while my brothers talked amongst themselves. "Annie Mae, Betsy, and June. Yes, that was their names. Annie Mae was the main one that would start all the trouble. Every day she and a group of her friends would say something mean to me, or steal my things. One day at school in recess, we had a race. The girls were separated from the boys. We had to race from one side of the field, and back again. Only five kids in a group could run at given time. The winner of that group would race in the next group. The first race I ran in I won. The second race I ran in I beat Betsy, and June. Of course, this made me so happy that I beat two of the classroom bullies. The last race I was in was with Annie Mae. When we started to run down the field, she caught up with me. Once we got to the other side of the field I was gaining on her. Well, she wasn't going to let me win. She pushed me down into a ditch by the side of the field, and I split my pants when I fell. I stayed in the ditch while Annie Mae went on to win the race. Another group of kids ran past me, but I was too ashamed to come out of the ditch to ask for help. There were so many kids running that Mrs. Jackson didn't see me fall."

"How did you get out of the ditch?" Alley asked.

"After recess was over, Mrs. Jackson came over, and helped me out of the ditch. I tied my sweater around my waist, and walked home. I learned a valuable lesson that day," Big Mama said.

Alley looked up at Big Mama curiously with her big blue eyes glistening, and said, "What did you learn Big Mama?"

Big Mama leaned over to Alley, and whispered, "I learned not to be too ashamed to ask for help when you need it. Ah, look at this short-set Alley. Do you like it?"

Alley's eyes sparkled when she saw it. She said, "Yes!"

"Well, go on into the dressing room, and try it on. We'll wait for you here."

Alley tried on the outfit while we waited. Big Mama bought her two more outfits with a pairs of tennis shoes, and sandals too. After waiting in that long line at the super center we went home.

Friday, Alley and I played most of the day. We played with the crawfish in the creek behind our house. We dressed Pee-Pee up in the hat again, but Big Mama made us take it off him. I was so glad that Alley was here. Now, I wasn't the only girl in the house. Having her here felt like I really had a sister. When mama came home, she talked to us for a little while, and then she went straight to the kitchen. Mama started pulling food out of the refrigerator to eat, and I noticed that she had the cell phone to her ear. From the way mama was smiling, I knew she must be talking to Big Mike. Mama just laughed, and giggled the whole time she was on the phone. Now, mama has never been this happy before coming home from work. By the time she got off the phone it was almost time for us to go to bed. Big Mama cleared out my two bottom dresser drawers that held my collection of bubble gum machine prizes, and troll dolls. She put Alley's clothing into them. Her clothing was clean, and April fresh. When she opened the drawers, it gave the whole room a fresh scent. Alley fell asleep very quickly, but I said a little prayer for us.

"Now I lay me down to sleep.
I pray to the Lord that Alley's, and my soul He'll keep.
I pray that the Lord will send the dark angels away
And bless us all with a brighter day.
Amen."

*****

Carlos's birthday party had so many people in his backyard that it became a neighborhood party instead. When we entered the backyard, there was a big sign that hung over the gate. The sign read: *Feliz Cumpleanos Carlos*, which means happy birthday Carlos in Spanish." Mama and Big Mama entered the backyard first. To our surprise, Plump and Teach were standing there talking. We hadn't seen Plump all week. Alley and I ran over to her screaming, and we both hugged her at the same time.

Jonathan and Jordan gave Teach a high five and said, "What's up man?"

We all walked over to a table, and sat down. Big Mama saw Mr. Davis, and sat at the table with him. Mama started talking to Carlos's cousins. There was a huge table covered with a table cloth, and balloons tied to both ends of it. The table was covered with Mexican food. There were nachos, tacos, and some other Mexican foods that I have never seen before. Carlos's uncle was grilling chopped steak and chicken and putting it into a softshell taco wrap. Mama and Plump couldn't resist trying one of them. Soon everyone formed a line at the table, and started eating. There was another table covered with a table cloth piled with presents for Carlos on it. There were small tables, and benches set up in a semicircle around the patio. Carlos had so many relatives at the party and most of them I haven't seen before. Some of them would start speaking in English, and switch to Spanish within the same conversation. They went back and forth speaking English, and Spanish. For a while they only spoke in Spanish. Then they would suddenly start laughing.

Big Mama was having such a good time playing cards and eating chips with Mr. Davis. They both had on huge straw sombreros.

Suddenly, I heard Big Mama say, "I won! I won!" Then she leaned back on the bench laughing so hysterically that I thought her sombrero and wig were going to fall off. Carlos's cousins were flirting with mama. Some of his cousins were in a band that played Mexican music for the party. Carlos's older cousin pulled mama onto the edge of patio, and started samba dancing with her. They danced for about ten minutes until mama said she was tired, but I don't think he understood her. He kept trying to get mama up to dance again until Mrs. Sanchez, Carlos's mother, appeared on the patio. She said something in Spanish to the band, but they ignored her. Then she said it even louder.   Finally, the band stopped playing.

With a very strong Spanish accent, Mrs. Sanchez said, "Welcome everyone. Today is Carlos ninth birthday party, and we want to sing happy birthday to him."

Everyone clapped. Then Mrs. Sanchez told her husband, and brother-in-law to go inside and get the cake. Carlos was seated at the table in front with some of his relatives. His father and uncle brought out a huge cake with candles all around it. In the center of the cake, there was a candle in the shape of number nine. They put the huge cake on the table in front of Carlos who sat there in amazement. Carlos's mother lifted her hands up as if she was directing the band. His relatives begin to sing happy birthday to him in Spanish, and the band began playing the melody. At the end of the song everyone cheered. Carlos closed his eyes to make a wish, and tried to blow out the candles, but there was just too many.

So, his mother said, "Come on kids. Let's help Carlos blow them out: one . . . two . . . three."

All the kids blew the candles out, and everyone clapped. Mrs. Sanchez cut the first piece of cake for Carlo before cutting slices of cake for everyone else. Then everyone began eating cake including Big Mama and Mr. Davis. I tapped Alley on the shoulder, and pointed at Big Mama. Plump looked too. Mr. Davis was feeding Big Mama a piece of cake. Alley covered her mouth and giggled.

Plump said, "Yuck! There is nothing worse than seeing two old people feeding each other cake."

When we finished eating, Carlos began tearing through his presents. When he got to the rocket he gasped. After he opened all of the presents, he ran into the house, and found some batteries for the rocket. He plugged the rocket into an outside outlet, and the rocket began to count down. Once the countdown reached zero the rocket blasted off into the air.

All the kids yelled, "Wow!"

He played with the rocket while his mother took the rest of the presents into the house. Finally, Carlos's mother had to take the rocket from him, and tell him it was time to hit the piñata. Carlos's dad hung a piñata from a tree limb in the backyard. He put a bandana over Carlos's eyes, and gave him a bat. He spent Carlos around three times, and swung the piñata. All the kids gathered around Carlos, but Carlos was so disoriented that he swung the bat the wrong way. My brothers and Teach had to jump back to keep from getting hit. Carlos's father ran up to him, and was hit in the stomach with the bat.

Grabbing his stomach, he yelled, "Carlos! Stop swinging the bat!"

Carlos lifted the bandana, and saw his dad gripping his stomach. "Sorry dad," Carlos said.

His dad stopped the piñata from swinging, then said, "Let's take the bandana off, and try it again."

Carlo hit the piñata as hard as he could, and candy flew everywhere. All the kids rushed over to grab the candy off the ground. I grabbed as much as I could hold. Soon the band stopped playing. Someone turned on a stereo that played Spanish rap music. People begin to dance on the patio. Carlos's uncle started making margaritas for the adults. Now, it was starting to get dark. The longer this party went on, the more it turned into an adult party. Some of Carlos's cousins were shooting off fireworks in the front yard. Big Mama was laughing, and having such a good time with Mr. Davis, and Carlos's relatives that she didn't want to leave. Every time Big Mama would laugh, Carlos's uncle would pour her another margarita. Mama saw Big Mama drinking, and decided it was time to go.

Mama called all of us over to her, and said, "Let's go." Mama knew if she didn't get Big Mama off that bench right now, she would be too drunk to walk home. Big Mama wouldn't leave until Mr. Davis agreed to walk her to the house. As we walked across the street, Big Mama and Mr. Davis just giggled, and laughed all the way to the front door. Mr. Davis kissed Big Mama's hand, and told all of us good night. It was almost 7:00 o'clock at night. The party might have started at 2:00 o'clock in the afternoon, but we were all too full to eat dinner. We had been eating all day on some of the best Mexican food I've ever tasted. Big Mama went to bed early. She walked to her room still wearing the sombrero. Mama played a board game with us for a couple more hours, and then she sent us to bed. I got up to use the bathroom. When I came out, I heard mama on the phone. I heard mama tell someone to come by around 2:30 tomorrow afternoon. I just smiled, and went back to bed.

Chapter 7
Holey Panties

Big Mama was up early this morning cooking breakfast. The smell of the food woke me up. Alley was still asleep in my bed with her mouth wide open when I left her to go downstairs. When I walked into the kitchen, Big Mama turned to me, and said, "Good morning. Are you hungry?"

"Yes ma'am." I walked over to Big Mama, and looked up into her eyes. Her green eyes were slightly red. I was a little concerned, so I asked, "Big Mama, are you okay?"

She looked down into my own big green eyes and laughed. "Yes baby. I am fine. A little margarita can't get me down. You go on, and set the table for breakfast."

I got the dishes out of the cabinet, and began setting the table. Mama came downstairs and said good morning to both of us. She went into the refrigerator to get some juice and then she said to Big Mama, "I am shocked to see you up so early. I thought I would have to cook this morning. Are you still going to church?"

Big Mama laughed. "Yes, I'm going to church. I didn't drink that much."

Alley walked downstairs next in her pajamas. She sat down at the table next to me.

"Big Mama told me that I'm going to summer camp with y'all," Alley said. "I can't believe it. I've never been to camp before. This is going to be a great summer. I wish I could stay here forever."

Big Mama walked over to the table, and put a plate of eggs, bacon, toast, and bowl of grit in the middle of the table.

"Today we're going to eat buffet style," she said. Then she put a large spoon in the grits, and eggs. As Alley and I sat there piling food on our plates, I couldn't stop wondering how long she would stay with us. No one knew where her father was, or when he was coming back. I couldn't bear the thought of her staying in that house with those dark angels. Soon my brothers came downstairs. Both of them were giggling about something when they entered the kitchen. If I know my brothers like I think I do, they are up to no good. Soon mama and Big Mama sat down to eat with us. Big Mama said a prayer, and then we all began to eat.

"I'm not going to church today. I need to clean the house, and go to the store. Also, I'm going to cook today, and we will be having a guest this afternoon," mama said.

Big Mama turned suddenly towards mama, and gave her a surprising look. "Who is this guest?" She asked.

"His name is Michael Raimond."

"Big Mike?" Jordan asked.

Mama turned to Jordan, and said, "That's Mr. Mike to you Jordan."

"But mama, he said to call him Big Mike."

"Wait a minute," Big Mama interrupted. "Who is this Mike person, and where did you meet him?"

"I met him at Mrs. Jenkins house the night the kids came with me. He was outside fixing Mrs. Jenkins's car. And, Mrs. Jenkins wanted me to invite him in to eat dinner with us that night."

"Yeah, and he talks funny too," Jonathan giggled.

Mama looked at Jonathan, and turned back to Big Mama and said, "He's from New Orleans. He is a Creole."

"Well," Big Mama continued, "does he just fix cars on the side for people, or does he have another job?"

"He works for a construction company most of the time. He just fixes cars when business is slow."

"So, that's who you've been talking to all night. I can hear you giggling all the way to my room," Big Mama said with a grin.

"Just like you giggling at Mr. Davis next door," mama said with her own grin.

"Okay, okay. I deserved that, but what time is he coming by?"

"By 2:30 p.m."

"Just make sure Jasmine doesn't pass gas on him while he's here!" Jordan said in a very loud outburst. "She kept me up all night passing gas. Alley, I don't see how you can sleep in her room."

"I did not, Jordan!" I said enraged.

"Yes you did," He laughed. "Hey Alley, check out her underwear. I'll bet she has holes in them."

Jordan began to laugh again. Alley gave him a curious look.

"Holes in her panties? Why would she have holes in her panties?" Alley asked.

"Because when she passes gas, it blows a hole right through them."
Jordan started laughing hysterically. Alley and Jonathan began to laugh
too.

I was so humiliated. I yelled, "You're a liar Jordan!" Before I
started to cry, I ran to my room.

"Jasmine!" Mama called for me as I ran up the stairs. I ran into my
room, and lay across the bed sobbing. I soon sat up on the side of the bed,
and started to wonder why Jordan wanted Alley to check my underwear
for holes. Then I thought that they must have been in my room. I opened
my dresser draw, and gasped. One by one, I pulled my underwear out of
my drawer. Every single pair had a hole in it. My two demon brothers
came into my room after Alley had left, and cut holes in my panties. I
grabbed as many pairs as I could, and ran downstairs. Mama was pouring
a cup of coffee by the sink.

"Mama! Look at what Jordan has done!" I held a pair of underwear
up with a huge hole in the back, and everybody at the table gasped except
for Jordan. Jordan was looking around for a way out of the kitchen. Mama
picked up a dish towel, and popped Jordan over the head.

"Jordan, how could you do this!" Mama shouted.

He gave her a pitiful look, and said, "She can still wear them."

"I can't wear them like this!" I said infuriated.

"After you finish breakfast Jordan, I want you to go, and get a
clean pair of your underwear for Jasmine. And, I mean a clean pair,
Jordan," mama demanded.

Both Jordan and I yelled at the same time, "What?"

"Jasmine, I'll buy you some more when I go to the store, so you
can change when you get out of church."

"Mama, I have to wear Jordan's underwear to church?" I was
enraged again.

"Jasmine, I don't have time to get you anymore before church
starts."

"But Mama, I don't want her to stink up my underwear. Besides, I
wear boys' underwear," Jordan pleaded.

"Well Jordan, you shouldn't have cut holes in her underwear. She
will wear yours until I can get her some more, understand?" Mama said in
a very stern voice.

"Yes ma'am," Jordan replied.

"And, you apologize to your sister now, Jordan."

Jordan gave me a mean look, and said very quickly, "sorry."

I looked back down at my underwear, and I wanted to cry all over again.

"Come on Jasmine. Sit down, and finish your breakfast. Give them to me, and I'll throw them away," Big Mama said.

I gave the underwear to Big Mama, and sat down.

"Jordan, I won't forget this today. You will have something to do around here when you get back," mama replied.

"Michelle," Big Mama paused, "why don't you let me find something for him to do?"

"Like what?" Jordan said in fear of what Big Mama might say.

"Like, help me make dinner in the afternoons," Big Mama replied.

"What!" Jordan was in shock. "I can't cook!"

"But you will learn. Everyday when you get home, for two weeks, you will help me cook, and clean the kitchen."

I could tell Jordan was so angry with me he could spit nails, but he said in a very monotone voice, "Yes ma'am."

"Good," Big Mama said, "Now, let bygones be bygones you two."

We finished breakfast, and went upstairs to get ready for church. I let Alley wear my baby blue dress. I thought it would look good with her eyes. Then Jordan knocked on the door. He handed me a pair of his *Spiderman* underwear. "I don't want them back," he said.

I snatched the underwear from him, and shouted, "This better be clean."

Then I slammed the door in his face. I put on my yellow dress, and the ugly "*Spiderman*" underwear. Alley and I went downstairs. Soon my two brothers came downstairs looking like "*Twiddle Dumb and Twiddle Dumber*" again. Big Mama wore a peach dress, and a peach hat. I don't know where she finds these hats, but this hat matched the dress she wore right down to the lace. We all piled into Big Mama's old car, and then she drove us to church.

As usual, everyone at church was singing, and clapping with the choir. Alley and I sat on the opposite sides of Big Mama from my brothers. I was still mad at my brothers. I hated sitting there in my beautiful yellow dress wearing "*Spiderman*" underwear. Today, Mrs. Percy was sitting behind us. Every time the preacher said something that she liked she would stand up, and say 'preach,' or 'amen.' She would shout so loudly that she could be heard at the back of the church. Today Reverend Howard preached his sermon on loving your neighbor, loving yourself, and loving God.

Reverend Howard said, "If you don't love yourself, then you can't love God because you hate what God has created. Also, you will have the sin of jealousy because you will envy anyone you feel that has what you don't. Which means you can't love others if you're always putting other people down, or gossiping. Can I get an Amen?" He asked the audience.

Everyone shouted, amen, but Mrs. Percy was the loudest. I turned to my left, and saw Mrs. Leola sitting there with her arms folded. She had a smirk on her face. It seemed like she felt that the preacher was speaking to her directly. On our way out of the church, Big Mama saw Mrs. Leola standing by a group of ladies in the foyer.

Big Mama walked over to Mrs. Leola, and said, "Leola, might I have a word with you for a moment? Kids, y'all wait for me over there." Big Mama and Mrs. Leola walked over toward the church office. "I saw you talking to my daughter last Sunday, and I was wondering what you said to her," Big Mama asked sternly.

"Well Bertha, I hardly think that is any of your business, now is it?" Mrs. Leola said with an ultra sweet smile.

Big Mama wasn't smiling. "She is my daughter, so I'm making it my business."

"I don't have to tell you anything, Bertha," Mrs. Leola replied sternly.

"My daughter is going through too much right now and she can't deal with you too, but I can."

After Big Mama said this, the two stood silently staring at one another.

"She has been coming to this church too long to stop coming here because of you. So, you will apologize to her for whatever you said Leola." Big Mama replied.

"I will not!" Mrs. Leola glared at Big Mama.

"You will, or I'll tell that nice group of ladies over there about your husband coming out of young Shantel's house this passed Wednesday night." Mrs. Leola gasped. "Yes," Big Mama continued, "I saw him on my way to my club meeting. He was kissing that young lady, and everything right there in the front yard for everyone to see. Or, should I tell them about your outlaw son who has been breaking into people's cars downtown. I also heard he robbed two people last week."

"Are you threatening me Bertha?" Leola asked enraged.

"No, I don't make threats. Next Sunday Leola, or I'll top your record for spreading the news, okay."

"Okay, okay." Mrs. Leola replied gritting her teeth.

Big Mama gave Mrs. Leola a condescending smirk.

"There's nothing like common decency. I guess some people just can't keep a man either, can they, Leola," Big Mama said as she walked away.

Mrs. Leola's face looked like it was about to explode. She was furious. Big Mama walked back to us with a mischievous grin. "Come on kids let's go home."

When we got home, the house was clean as a whistle, and the smell of good food was in the air. Mama had on a pretty sun dress that was trimmed in yellow ribbon with a white background, and yellow flowers. Mama also had on some white flip flops that were about two inches high. We went upstairs to change our clothes. Normally, mama doesn't pick out our clothes on Sunday. Sunday was the day we relaxed, and she didn't care what we had on, but not today. On my bed, she laid out an outfit for me and Alley's new short set for her. After we all got dressed, everyone came downstairs except for Big Mama.

"Y'all please try to stay clean. Play a game in the house until Mike gets here," mama asked.

Soon Big Mama came out of her room in her regular house dress with the pink flowers. Big Mama walked around the couch, and sat down.

"Mom, can you find something else to wear today?" Mama asked.

"Why? This dress has never bothered anyone before. Besides, I am comfortable, and this is who I am. I suggest that you be yourself too." Big Mama replied.

"Okay, okay," mama reluctantly replied.

Alley, my brothers, and I played cards on the floor then the door bell rang. The first one to the door was Pee-Pee. He barked twice then sat down wagging his tail. Mama answered the door. Big Mike stood at the door with the same big smile on his face he had at Mrs. Jenkins house.

"*Belle dame bonsoir,*" he said.

Mama gave him a strange look. "What?"

"Good evening beautiful lady." Big Mike replied.

"Oh, is that what you said. Mike, I still haven't gotten used to the way you talk. Come in. Mom, I want you to meet Michael Raimond. Michael this is my mother, Bertha Thomas."

"Call me Big Mike. Everybody does."

"Well, nice to meet you Big Mike. Michelle has told me a lot about you, but she didn't tell me that you were so handsome." Big Mama said with a mischievous grin.

Mike's dimples started to show as he blushed and chuckled. "And, the same can be said for you too ma'am."

Big Mama laughed along with Mike. Mike stopped laughing abruptly and said, "Oh, I forgot something. Excuse me for a moment. I left something outside."

Mike walked back outside on the porch, and walked back into the house with a beautiful bouquet of roses. Big Mama, Alley, and I gasped.

"How beautiful," Mama replied. "Please, put them on the coffee table."

Alley walked to the coffee table with Big Mike saying, "Wow!"

"Now that's romantic," Big Mama said turning to mama.

"Come on everyone. Let's go to the table," mama replied.

Now mama and Big Mama had different styles of cooking. Mama always chose a lighter menu. Mama cooked asparagus, beef tenderloin with vegetables, salad, and mashed cauliflower that looked like mashed potatoes. Big Mama asked Big Mike to say grace. Mike said a little prayer thanking God for the food, and then we all started to eat.

"This is a delicious meal. Who prepared this meal today?" Mike asked.

"I did. I thought we should eat a little lighter today. Sometimes when I eat a heavy meal it puts me to sleep every time," mama replied.

"Yes, but after eating this Mike you might be hungry in an hour. Say Mike, do you cook?" Big Mama asked.

"Yes ma'am, but I love Creole foods. I love the spices, and flavors of the Creole cuisine."

"I heard that Creole folks eat gator meat. Is that true?" Big Mama looked at Mike with a raised brow.

Alley, my brothers, and I said in unison, "Yuck!"

Mike looked around at everyone and said, "Don't knock it until you've tried it. It's good."

"I'm sorry Mike, but that's one thing I won't try. I can't eat reptiles," mama replied.

Mike laughed. "So, Michelle, do you cook meals like this every day?"

"No. Most of the time, I don't cook at all. My mom does most of the cooking, and she's a great cook."

"Thank you, baby." Big Mama interrupted.

"Why?" Mama asked. Mama looked at him curiously. "Do you like women that cook every day?"

Mike just grinned. "I don't care if a woman cooks everyday, nor do I need a woman to cook for me. If I waited for a woman to cook for me, I would starve to death." Mike grinned again.

Big Mama stared at him intently for a moment and said, "Your wife, Tracy, passed away didn't she Mike?"

Mike stared at Big Mama in shock. "Yes, but how did you know her name. I don't think I told Michelle her name."

"Mom is a really good guesser. Mom, stop it." Mama said with a stern look and a loud whisper.

"Wait a minute, Michelle." Then he looked back at Big Mama. "How did you know her name?"

Big Mama gave him a slight grin. "I can sense a lot about you like, you want to start your own business, and I believe you will be successful too. I know you don't have any children, but you would like to have a family someday."

Mike put his fork down, and sat back in shock. "Wow. Is your mother psychic?"

"Something like that," Mama replied. "Mom, stop it. Let's change the subject."

Mike stared at Big Mama like she grew another head.

"So, Mike, you want to start your own business?" Mama asked.

"Yes. Construction can be unsteady at times. During the off seasons, I fix cars on the side. I want to open my own shop. I've seen how some mechanics rip off women, and I want to give them an alternative."

"Wow! I wish I could fix cars. I would build a race car if I knew how." Jordan said.

"Maybe I could show you a thing or two if your mother doesn't mind. Well guys, are you going to play baseball this summer?"

"Can we mama, please?" Jordan pleaded.

"That depends on how the two of you behave," said mama.

Mike turned to Alley and me. "How about you girls? What are you going to do this summer?"

Before I could speak Alley said, "I'm going to summer camp. I have never been before."

Mike looked at Alley very curiously. "Really, then what do you do in the summer?"

Alley stopped smiling. "I just stayed at my house with my dad."

Mike could tell that talking about her father upset her, so he changed the subject.

"Mrs. Thomas, you have a beautiful family here, and especially your daughter." Mike winked at mama.

"Big Mike, what part of New Orleans are you from?" Big Mama asked.

"I'm from the lower Ninth Ward."

"I haven't been to Louisiana since my husband died, but that is such a romantic city with the beautiful iron work on the buildings, and the jazz music that plays all night long. Michelle you should go there one day," Big Mama said with a smile.

"Yeah," Mike agreed. "Maybe you should come with me sometime. My aunt still lives there. We can visit her."

Mama looked at Big Mama like she wanted to say stop it again. Then mama turned to Mike.

"Why don't we eat dinner first?" She replied with a smile.

"Yes, dinner first," Mike said, "and later I have something in the truck for the kids."

We all talked, and laughed until everyone was finished eating. Jordan was the first to get up from the table when Big Mama stopped him. "Jordan, stop! Just where do you think you're going? Remember you are going to help me in the kitchen today."

Jordan slowly walked back to the table saying, "yes ma'am."

"Jordan, you clean the table off, and I'll put the food up." Big Mama said. Everyone else went outside to the backyard.

"I have to get something from my truck. I'll be right back."

When Mike came back, he had a baseball and mitt. Mama sat in the chair by the patio table, and watched us.

Big Mike walked over to Jonathan, Alley, and me saying, "Let's play catch. Jonathan, do you know how to hold the glove?"

"Not really," Jonathan replied

"Well let me show you." Big Mike demonstrated to Jonathan how to hold a mitt, and how to catch the ball with it. "Okay," Mike continued, "Jasmine threw the ball to Jonathan under handed. Now, don't throw it hard. Jonathan, you catch it, and throw it back to Alley. You girls toss the ball back and forth to Jonathan. Y'all understand?" Big Mike asked.

We nodded our heads. I threw the ball to Jonathan a little high, but he still caught it.

"Jasmine, that's too high!" Jonathan shouted.

"That's okay because when you play a real game, you might get a ball like that. Now, you guys keep playing, and I'll watch over here," Mike said.

He walked over, and sat in a chair beside mama. Big Mike shouted directions from the patio as we continued to play.

Soon Alley and I got bored with this game, and I said, "Let make this a real game. I'll go inside, and get my bat."

I went into the house, and brought the bat outside. We played a three man baseball game. You could only strike out once. If you hit the ball, you had to run to home to get a point. If you strike out before you got to home, you would be out. Mike watched us play this game for a little while. I think he liked this better than catch.

Mike turned to mama saying, "So, what did Jordan do?"

"He cut holes in the back of Jasmine's panties this morning." Mama said flatly.

Mike laughed so hard that we all stopped playing to see what was going on.

"Y'all keep playing! Mama shouted. "Mike, it's not funny."

"It may not be funny to you because you're his mother, but believe me, that will be funny to anyone else you tell it to." Mike continued to laugh.

"Well, now he has to cook, and clean the kitchen for two weeks," replied mama.

"Poor kid," Big Mike said. "Hey, why do you say that's not your dog?"

Mama looked down at Pee-Pee who was lying at her feet wagging his tail. "I don't know who he belongs to."

Mike reached across the table, and grabbed mama's hand and said, "You can buy a dog that will never belong to you if that dog doesn't choose you. But, when a dog comes to your house to live and keeps coming back, that dog has chosen you. That dog belongs to you, no matter what. Anyway, how long have you had this dog?"

"For about two weeks." Mama replied.

"Would you give the dog back if the owner shows up to claim him?" Big Mike asked with a raised brow.

"Only if he or she can prove that this is their dog," replied mama.

Mike just smiled and grabbed mama's hand. "Your hands are so soft. With all the work you do for Mrs. Jenkins, how do you keep your hands looking so good? And, your feet are beautiful too," he asked.

"I get my nails, and feet manicured once every two weeks. This is just about the only luxury I have time to give myself."

"You like working for Mrs. Jenkins, don't you?"

"Yes, I do," mama confessed. "I know that I shouldn't get involved with the patients, but Mrs. Jenkins is my friend. I hate my other job."

Mike looked at mama curiously. "Why?"

"I am the only black person in my department, and some people don't like this. Not everyone feels this way, but too many do. I worked really hard to get what I have, but some people think that I am here because someone gave me something. Can you believe that? Who in that department would give me anything?"

"Why don't you quit, and just do the kind of work you do for Mrs. Jenkins if that's what you like?"

"I do love the work I do for her, but that kind of work doesn't pay very much. As you see, I am the only one working here. I am a single parent, and I need my jobs. Besides, it's not the job that bothers me. It's the people."

Mike gave mama a look like he didn't believe her. "I don't know about that. It doesn't seem like this job fulfills you very much even if no one bothered you. I can tell you like helping others. One good example is this dog here. He makes you feel that what you are doing for him is appreciated, and that you have made a difference in his life. You can't fool me."

Mama gave him a little smile. "Maybe you're right."

"Just don't forget you have to take care of yourself too."

"Okay," mama said smiling again.

Mike looked slowly up into mama's eyes. "Did I ever tell you how beautiful you look in that dress today?"

"It's just a sundress," replied mama.

"Maybe it just a sundress to you, but to me this dress reveals your beautiful skin, and those gorgeous legs." Mama started to blush. "Don't be shy," Mike said. "You are a beautiful lady. I know guys must hit on you all the time."

"Well, not all the time," mama admitted.

Mike lifted mama's hand, and kissed her knuckles before he released it.

"Tell me about your kids. The boys resemble you, but that girl looks just like your mother."

"Yes, I know," mama replied. "I thank God none of them look like their father. Now, Jasmine is the most curious child. She will question you about everything. Jonathan is a quiet child, but he has a sharp mind. On the other hand, Jordan is my active child. He's always into something. Be careful around him. He likes to play practical jokes."

Mike looked at Alley. "What about Alley? Is she just visiting?"

"Yes, she is staying with us until her father comes back," mama replied.

Mike gave mama an odd look. "Where is her father?" He asked.

"We don't know."

Mike looked back at Alley. "I knew there was something more to her story because she didn't want to talk about her father."

"Yeah, he's not a very good man," mama replied.

"How long will she stay here with you?" He asked.

"Until we find her family or until her father comes back," mama replied.

"Michelle, I really admire you for taking in this child like that."

"Well, don't be too proud. It was my mother's idea. Now, you see why I can't quit my job."

"Yes, I do," said Big Mike. "Why don't we go out to eat at this place I know that is near the lake? Just you, and me this time, okay."

"Okay," mama replied.

Big Mama and Jordan came outside with two glasses of tea, and two plates of chocolate cake.

"We thought you two would like to try a piece of Jordan's chocolate cake. Michelle, I know chocolate is your favorite. This is the first time he has ever made a cake. Isn't that right Jordan?" Big Mama said proudly.

"Yes ma'am." He replied.

"I made y'all some of my famous mint ice tea. Go on. Try it. Tell us what you think," replied Big Mama.

Mike took a bite out of the cake. "Man, this is good, really good. Jordan, you made this from scratch?"

"No," Big Mama interrupted, "I didn't want to start him off with something that complicated. This is from a box."

"Well Jordan," mama replied, "This is great, and the tea is delicious too mom."

"Thank you. Guys, come inside, and get some cake," said Big Mama

Alley, Jonathan, and I ran up the back steps, and into the house. Before we all enter the house, Big Mama yelled, "Wash your hands!"

"Come on Jordan. Let's go inside," Big Mama replied.

Jordan and Big Mama left the patio to let mama and Big Mike enjoy their cake.

Once Big Mike and mama finished the cake, Big Mike said, "I have to go. Let's go inside, so I can tell everyone goodbye."

Mama and Big Mike walked back into the house, and put the dishes into the sink. Alley, my brothers, and I were all sitting at the table enjoying our piece of cake. Big Mama was standing by the refrigerator pouring each of us some juice.

"I want to thank you for inviting me today, and for that delicious meal. Hopefully, I'll be seeing y'all soon," said Big Mike as he waved to us. Then mama and Mike walked to the front door.

"Michelle, walk with me to my truck."

"All right," she replied.

The sun had begun to set in the west giving the sky a beautiful hue of color. Michelle's face looked more childlike in the dim light of the sun. Mike grabbed her hand, and kissed her knuckles again. "Will you call me tonight? I just want to hear your voice before I go to sleep," he said.

"Okay," Michelle replied.

This was the first time Mike stopped smiling. He traced Michelle's lips with his fingers. "You have a beautiful mouth."

Before Michelle could say anything, he pulled her by the waist towards him. Holding the small of her back, he kissed her deeply. She could feel his lean muscled chest pressed against hers and his firm thighs rubbing against her own. His kiss was so intoxicating that for a moment she forgot where she was. His tongue probed the inner corners of her mouth. With each flick of his tongue, she began to moan. She could feel him becoming erect. This sensation was becoming too much for her to handle. Michelle tried to step back from his grasp, but Mike held the back of her head firmly. Gently, he stroked the back of her neck. When he released her, she stepped back touching her swollen lips with her finger tips.

"That felt like we just made love." Michelle was so swept up with emotion that she didn't realize what she had just said. She quickly dropped her head in embarrassment.

Mike gently lifted her chin with his finger, and said, "Oh, it's much better than that."

Michelle stepped back from his hand. "Look. This conversation is moving a little too fast for me. I just got out of a relationship, and I need a little more time before I rush back into a new one."

Mike leaned against the truck with his arms folded across his chest. With a big grin on his face he said, "I know. I am not trying to pressure you. I will slow down as slowly as you want me to, okay. But, I had to kiss you. I've wanted to kiss you since the first day I saw you at Mrs. Jenkins's house. Your mouth is so beautiful, and you taste so sweet." Mike took a step forward towards her.

"Mike." Michelle said timidly.

"Okay. I'll slow down, but I want to kiss you again," he said. He lifted Michelle's hand, and kissed her palm. "*Bonne nuit belle dame*," he said as he got into the truck.

"What did you say?"

"Goodnight beautiful lady, and call me."

Then he left the driveway. Michelle was watching him drive away when she noticed that Mrs. Madison had been on her front porch watching them the whole time. Michelle waved to Mrs. Madison as she went into the house. Mrs. Madison waved back to her with a huge grin on her face.

Chapter 8
Pine Mountain

Summer is always the best time of the year for me because of summer camp. Going to summer camp was like going on a mini vacation each week. Alley loved every minute of summer camp. I don't think that I've ever seen Alley this happy all year. The first day at "*Lee Community Center*" began with orientation. We were separated into four different groups by our ages. I was glad that Plump, Teach, and Alley stayed in my group. The second day was a day for arts, and crafts. We made papier-mâché masks, and I made two red devil masks for my little brothers. Mama loved the mask so much she said she was going to put them in her office at work. Today we were going to *Pine Mountain Park* for a hike through their wild life reserve. All the kids in my group piled into an old school bus as the director drove us away. Plump sat between me and Alley on the bus.

Plump was the kind of person who could talk to herself if she had no one else to talk to. She talked to us about her stay with her grandmother this passed week. She told us all about her grandmother's Chihuahua, named Pepie, whom just hated her little brother. She said the dog bit her brother on the ankle. Without taking another breath, Plump began talking to us about her grandmother taking her, and her brother to the park. She said, "Grandma took us to the park, and had the nerve to come down the slide in a skirt. As soon as she came down the slide, her skirt flew up. Oh, I was so embarrassed. Can you believe that? She just sat on the ground laughing like it was funny."

Alley was giggling as Plump continued to talk. I started to stare outside the bus window as the bus rode out of the city. The bus drove across a long suspension bridge over a beautiful lake.

I heard Teach shout, "Look at that!" All the kids looked out of the other side of the bus's window to see about ten fishing boats headed towards the bridge.

All the kids yelled, "ooh," or "cool," as the boats passed underneath the bridge. Soon the bus drove passed the lake to a road that was surrounded by a thick forest on both sides. There was a sign with an arrow that read: *Spotted Buck Hunt Club* one mile. Someone must have shot at some wild ducks because a few miles down the road a flock of wild ducks flew in every direction. Some flew so close to the bus it looked like they were going to hit it. When I looked back at the trees again, there was the lady. This was the same lady that I saw in my dreams weeks ago. Her hand was still turned inward, and she had on the same bloody gown. She just stood there, and waved at me with her left hand.

I turned to Alley and Plump and said, "Do y'all see that lady over there?" I pointed towards the small group of trees by the embankment.

"See what? There's nothing out there," Plump replied.

I turned back to see if she had left, but she hadn't. I could see her just as well as I could see Alley and Plump. I didn't say anything about it anymore, so Plump continued talking. As we approached a sign that stretched across the entire street that read: *Pine Mountain Park*, the bus pulled over to the camp ground rest area, and we all got out.

By the rest area there was a beautiful lake surrounded by majestic mountains. The mountains were covered with tall trees that gave a subtle sent of pine as the wind blew. Our camp director was a short stocky black woman named Sadie Mays. She made sure that everyone had a good time, but she was tough. There was no horse playing around her. We gathered around her as she spoke.

"Listen up everybody. I want everyone to stay together, and stay on the path. Do not pick any of the flowers, or plants while you are out here. Now, if you fall, or something bites you, notify your camp leaders."

The camp leaders were the teenage kids that worked for the camp during the summer. They would chaperone us through the trail. Mrs. Mays continued saying, "We'll be seeing different wildlife along the way, so don't wander off. This is a big forest, and you can be lost for days before anyone finds you. Everyone understand?"

We all said, "Yes ma'am." Then we started up the trail. Two of the camp leaders were in the back of the line, and two were on the sides of us. Mrs. Mays led us up front. Alley, Teach, Plump, and I walked through the woods chatting along the trail. The first animal on exhibit was a black turkey vulture.

The care taker said, "The turkey vulture was one of three vultures in the United States. This vulture is native to this area, and commonly called a buzzard."

I thought to myself that this was a good name for such an ugly bird. Then the care taker threw the bird a rat. "Yuck," I yelled as loud as I could when I saw the bird rip the rat's head off. We left this animal pretty quickly, and continued up the red sandy path. The next exhibit was a skunk. As soon as the kids gathered around this exhibit we gasped, and stepped back.

The lady pulled the skunk out of the cage, and said, "Don't worry. It can't spray you." We all gave a sigh of relief. The care taker said, "A skunk is about the size of a cat." As she continued to talk, I thought to myself, this is one cat I don't want to find around the house. This skunk also brought to my mind the images of *"Pepe Le Pew."* I don't think that I was the only one with this idea.

Teach grabbed Plump's arm, and tried to imitate *"Pepe Le Pew"* saying, "My little lover, *Mew, Mew. . ."*

Plump pulled her arm back, and punched Teach in the shoulder. As we walked deeper into the forest, I could hear Mrs. Mays yelling at the kids to stop chasing the peacocks, and chickens that crossed our path. We saw several more exhibits of snakes, owls, and deer. We walked almost an hour before we stopped for lunch. We ate outside on the picnic tables. For lunch we had boxed sandwiches, fruit, chips, and a juice box. There was a concession stand there for anyone who wanted to buy anything extra like water, or food. Of course, Plump couldn't pass up the hot dogs on the rotisserie. Plump was trying to talk Alley out of eating her potato chips, but Alley wasn't giving in. Then I noticed there was a small red fox standing by one of the tables. It was a beautiful animal with a long fluffy tail. I threw a piece of bread from my sandwich to the fox. He sniffed it and he picked it up, and trotted away. He stopped by the trash cans. I got up, and followed him. The more I tried to feed him, the faster he would run into the woods. The fox just stayed far enough out of my distance, so I couldn't reach him. By the time I stopped following him, I noticed I was near a cliff. The sky was clear with only a few birds passing by. It was quiet. Suddenly, the angel that was on my grandmother's porch was standing next to me. "Who are you," I asked.

"My name is Gabriel. I am here to help you find your path," she replied.

I looked at her very strangely, and said, "I'm not lost. The camp is just back that way."

She smiled at me saying, "No, you may not be lost sweet *Ayin*, but Alexandria is. She will need you very soon, and you must not let her hurt herself. Fulfill your destiny sweet *Ayin*. Bring her mother home."

I turned to hear Alley calling for me. When I turned back, the angel was gone, but the lady was there. Before I could step back from her, the lady possessed my thoughts. My mind went blank.

Alley walked towards me, and touched my arm. "Come on. We have been calling you."

Without facing her, a voice spoke from my body. "Hello Alexandria. I've have missed you so much. You have grown into such a beautiful young lady. I am sorry you've suffered because of my mistakes. I only have a little time to tell you this, so I want you to be brave. He's coming back soon, v . . . very soon. Stay with the *Ayin*. She will protect you."

"Jasmine!" Alley said.

I heard a voice say as I turned around. "What?"

Alley looked at me like she was terrified. "Your eyes!"

"What about them?" I asked.

"They turned blue, and your voice changed. I've heard that voice before."

"That's not possible Alley. Come on. Let's go."

We turned, and walked back down the hill. When I looked back, I saw the lady staring at us as we left. When we got back down the hill, Plump and Teach were standing in line with the other kids.

"Where have y'all been?" Plump asked.

"I saw a fox and I--," I said.

"Come on. Get in line before Mrs. Mays comes back here."

Alley and I got in line, but Alley didn't say very much to me after leaving the hill. We started back down the trail again. There were more wild bird exhibits than any other animal exhibit down the rest of the trail. There was this one exhibit where ten kids could go into it at a time, and feed the birds. The birds have a bright display of red, green, and yellow patterns on their feathers. They were flying erratically over our heads as we entered the exhibit. Some birds would land on the kid's shoulders, or heads. The care taker gave us a little cup to feed the birds, but she said we couldn't pick up any birds.

I sat on the bench holding my cup when a small bird landed on my hand. "Teach, Alley, Plump! Look!" I said as the bird began to drink out of the cup. They were still trying to get a bird to land on their hands when I called them, but all they managed to do was chase the birds away. I sat still as the bird continued to drink.

"Guys look!" I said. I held out my hand with the bird on it. Teach, Alley, and Plump finally stopped chasing the birds to look at me. The bird stopped drinking. He cocked his head to the side, and looked at me. Then the bird pooped right beside me on the bench where I was sitting. I gasped. Teach, Alley, and Plump laughed hysterically when they saw this. I tried to get the bird off my hand, but the bird wouldn't leave. The bird cocked his head looking at me blinking his eyes. It seems to me that the bird didn't understand what was wrong with me. Finally, I had to go get the care taker to take the bird off my hand. She gently removed the bird from my hand, and I got out of there. We continued down the trail talking, and laughing until we came back to the bus. All the kids got on the bus one by one as the director called out our name. Once we all were accounted for, the bus pulled out of the parking lot, and drove away. On the way back to the center, Plump sat next to the window this time. She started to talk to Alley and me, but soon she fell asleep. Alley hadn't said very much to me until now.

"Jasmine, on the top of the hill today when I came to get you, your voice changed. It sounded like my mother's."

"What?" I looked at her with a little bit of shock.

"Don't you remember? "Alley asked.

"No." I truly didn't remember anything. For a moment on that hill my mind went blank."

"Who is coming back Jasmine? Is it my father?"

"Alley, I don't remember saying this. Are you worried that he might come back?"

She looked down, and said softly, "Yes. I've had so much fun here with you, and your family that I don't want to go home."

"If he comes back, I'll still see you at summer camp."

Her big blue eyes were filled with a kind of sadness that I hadn't seen in a while when she looked at me. "He won't let me stay at the camp. I know he won't."

"Alley, let's not talk about him now," I said because I knew talking about him would upset her. "He may stay gone until summer camp is over, and remember what I told you. If you ever need a place to hide, you can come to my house, okay."

Alley smiled, and gave me a big hug. We continued to talk while Plump began to snore. When we got back to "*Lee Community Center*," it was time to go home. The community center was only eight blocks from our house, so we all walked home. My brothers were just getting out of baseball practice when we got off the bus. On the way home, we stopped by Mr. Muhammad's corner store. You would think that Plump would be full after all the food she consumed today, but she wasn't. She bought a big bag of candy, soda, and bubble gum.

Alley tapped me on the shoulder saying, "I don't have any money."

"That's okay Alley. I'll buy you something. What do you want?"

Alley grabbed a soda, and two pieces of gum. I walked up to the counter and put the items down.

"Hi Mr. Muhammad," I said.

"Salaam little one. What can I do for you today?"

"Can I get a pickle?"

"Yes, and would your friend like a pickle too?"

Alley shook her head, and said, no. I paid for our snacks, and waited outside the store for everyone else. Everyone decided to come to our house. As I turned the corner of my block, Big Mama was playing cards with Mr. Davis on his porch. Mr. Davis was looking bewildered while Big Mama had a huge grin on her face.

Suddenly, Big Mama said, "GIN! Ha, ha, ha!" She started laughing loudly as Mr. Davis sat there scratching his head. "Oh Ben, the kids are home. I have to go."

Big Mama left the porch as Mr. Davis said, "Same time tomorrow?"

Big Mama waved her hand, and shook her head in agreement. "How was the park today?" She asked.

"It was great Mrs. Thomas," Plump replied. "We saw vultures, snakes, an owl, and a bird that almost pooped on Jasmine." Big Mama laughed.

"Well, I was going to offer y'all a snack, but it seems like everybody has one. I am going to water my garden. I'm glad y'all had a good time."

Big Mama grabbed the garden hose from the side of the house, and opened the back fence to go into the backyard. I finished my pickle, and left everyone talking on the front porch. I needed to speak to Big Mama about what happened today. When I walked into the backyard, Big Mama was watering the garden, and pulling weeds.

I sat down onto the patio chair, and said, "Big Mama, I want to tell you something."

"What is it baby?" She spoke without looking at me.

"I talked to the angel today."

She stopped watering for a second. "What did she say?"

"She said that she was here to help me find my path."

"Is that all she said?" Big Mama asked with a smile.

"No. She said not to let Alley hurt herself, and to bring her mother home. Big Mama, I don't know where her mother is. How am I supposed to bring her home?"

Big Mama stood there for a second. She hesitated before she said anything. "Don't worry Jasmine. Your mother and I are looking for her family. You make sure she stays safe. We don't want her to get hurt while she is here." Big Mama began to pull weeds again.

"There is something else. On the hill I saw the lady that was in my dream, and for a minute everything went black. The next thing I heard was Alley calling my name."

Big Mama stood still and gasped slightly.

"Alley said I spoke in another voice, and that my eyes changed colors. She said I told her that her father is coming back."

"I know her father will come back for her, but not very soon. That's why your mother and I are looking for her family. Don't worry Jasmine, we will help her. Now you go back up front with your friends. The best thing we can give her now is a little bit of happiness and peace before he comes back. In life problems are going to come. We choose to cry, or laugh, but remember we always have a choice. Now go on."

I gave Big Mama a little smile, and left the backyard. When I walked around to the front yard, I saw my brothers, and Teach playing soccer with an old beach ball.

Plump saw me coming and yelled, "Jasmine, go get the *Jacks*!"

I ran inside the house, and got them. We played outside for an hour before Plump saw her mother's car pull into their driveway. "Guys, I have to go. I'll see you tomorrow," she said. Alley and I continued to play Jacks.

Then Big Mama came outside on the porch, and shouted, "Jordan, it's time to make dinner!" Then she turned around, and walked back into the house.

"Why does she have to say that so loud out here?" said Jordan with a bit of embarrassment. "It's embarrassing enough to have to cook, but now she's telling everybody."

Pouting, Jordan folded his arms, and marched into the house. Teach decided to leave too now that the game they were playing was a player short. Finally, the rest of us decided to go into the house. Big Mama was on the phone, but Jordan was mixing something red in a big bowl.

Big Mama hung up the phone, and said, "Everybody, come here for a minute." We gathered around Big Mama in the kitchen. "That was your mother on the phone. She said that your father will be picking y'all up this Saturday. He's going to take all you to *Water World*. Alley you are going too." Alley was in shock.

"But, I don't have a swim suit," Alley replied.

"Don't worry about that. I'll get you one tomorrow."

We all started cheering. Jordan was cheering with the bowl full of red dough in his hand.

"Jordan, what is that red stuff in that bowl?" I asked.

"That's a red velvet cake," Big Mama answered. "Now, y'all go back in the den until we finish cooking."

Dinner was really good. Jordan was starting to become a really good cook. When we finished dinner, Big Mama and Jordan cleaned up the kitchen while the rest of us watched TV. Big Mama took the cakes out of the oven to cool. Jordan mixed the frosting with nuts and fruit.

"Why don't you go into the den, and play with everyone else. I'll finish up here," Big Mama insisted. Jordan gave the frosting to Big Mama, and left the kitchen. The smell of the cake filled the house. "Who wants cake," Big Mama asked.

Was she kidding? We all wanted a piece. While Big Mama cut the cake, Jordan turned the TV to a rap video. Jordan and Jonathan sat on the floor bobbing their heads to the beat. Big Mama walked out of the kitchen with two slices of cake on two saucers she handed to Alley and me. She stopped in her tracks when she turned toward the TV. "What on Earth is this?"

"You don't like rap music Big Mama?" Jordan replied.

"No! All that gyrating, and what is that they have on? Jordan, turn something else on. This hippity hop music is the worst mess I ever heard. I hear more bad language in these videos than I did marching in the sixties. Let's get the cards out, and play a game. Just turn that mess off."

Big Mama walked back in the kitchen, and brought out two more pieces of cake for Jonathan and Jordan.

"I am going to sit this one out today, and watch you guys play," she replied.

Big Mama walked into the kitchen, and came out with a piece of cake for herself. Then she sat on the couch to watch us play cards. Soon mama came home. We all greeted her as she walked into the kitchen.

"Mom, you have those kids' playing cards again like old prison buddies," mama replied.

Big Mama gave mama a smirk. "It's better than listening to that hippity hop music. Have you heard what they are saying in that music?"

"I agree," mama said with a smile.

Suddenly there was a knock on the door. Pee-Pee gave a little bark, and walked to the front door first. When mama answered the door, Big Mike was standing there.

"Hey, I was just passing by, and I thought that I might stop." He hesitated. "I know it's late, and you probably just got off, so if you want me to leave."

"No, come in," mama insisted.

Big Mike spoke to everybody as he entered the room.

"Mike, would you like a piece of cake?" Big Mama asked.

"Yes ma'am," he replied.

"Good, because Jordan helped me make it."

"Mom, you stay seated, and I'll cut us a piece," mama said.

Mama went into the kitchen, and came out with two slices of cake on two saucers. Both mama and Big Mike took a bite of the cake.

"Jordan, you can cook!" Big Mike said.

"This is delicious," Mama agreed.

"Thank you, thank you," said Jordan. Then he stood up and took a bow.

Mama and Mike laughed. Mike turned to mama and said, "Your yard is beautiful."

"Well, thank mom for that. Since she's been here, everything is blooming."

"Thank you," Big Mama said smiling proudly.

"I've noticed that your siding needs a little paint, and I could fix that shutter for you."

"Mike, like I said before, I don't have the money."

"Don't worry about that. I know some guys that could do this for hardly anything. You just buy the paint, and they will do the rest."

"Go on Michelle. What do you have to lose?" Big Mama asked.

"My pride, besides, I can't let you do all that work without paying you."

"I tell you what I can do," Mike paused. "I'll fix the shutter for you at no charge, and I think I still have some paint from an old job I did that you can have if you like it. At least you won't have to buy any paint, and you can talk the guys into accepting payments. What do you say?"

Big Mama answered before mama said a word. "We accept!"

Mike laughed. Then mama turned to Big Mike and said, "Okay."

"This house has needed a paint job for years. Come on kids. It's time for us to go to bed. Y'all tell Big Mike good night," Big Mama replied. They all got up and said good night then left the room.

Looking into Mike's beautiful brown eyes and his dimpled smile made Michelle's heart melt. This man was truly gorgeous, but he was dangerous too. She didn't want to give her heart to another man, so soon after her first love crushed it. But Mike was like a bad habit she just couldn't quit. Having him this close to her made her want him even more. She kept telling herself that they would just stay friends, and nothing more. But in her heart, she wanted this man.

"I'm sorry for coming over so late," Mike said. "I just wanted to see you."

"I'm glad you stopped by" Michelle replied. "I don't go to bed this early anyway." Mike reached for her hand, and kissed her palm.

"I don't want you to feel that I'm moving too fast, but I can't resist you."

Michelle stared at him without saying a word. She thought to herself, *I know the feeling.*

"Why are you staring at me?" He asked.

"You have the most beautiful eyes."

Mike grinned. "Not as beautiful as your mouth. You know that I want to kiss you again."

Mike lifted Michelle's chin with his finger as he leaned toward her.

Michelle turned away from him. "Let's get to know each other a little better first."

"What do you want to know?" He asked.

"I know you have an aunt in Louisiana, but do you have any family here?"

"No," Mike replied. "My brother, and his wife visit me sometimes, but I have no family here."

"What about your parents?"

"They're deceased. Now pretty lady, can I have that kiss?" He asked with a smile.

When Mike spoke these words, the heat in Michelle's chest rose to her cheeks, and burned her face as she blushed. This same heat that was building inside of her also made her nipples tighten, and erect. There was no denying it. She wanted this man, and it showed. Mike noticed this too.

"Come here," Mike asked her as he pulled her in his arms cradling her. Pulling her in his arms like this was a bold move. This made Michelle a little nervous, and very vulnerable. "Now you can't get away."

"Mike--."

"Shh . . .," he said putting his finger over her lips as he gently traced them. He pulled her to his lips, and gently kissed her lower lip. He finally took her mouth kissing her fervently. His tongue teased her own sending shock waves down her spine as she arched her back. Soon she matched the thrusting of his tongue with her own as she began to moan. Mike gently stroked her face, and shoulders before his hands cuffed her firm breast. His hands began to massage her tender breast, and gently squeeze the erect nipples between his fingers. She moaned louder, and finally withdrew from his kiss.

"Your hand," she said.

"What about it?"

"You're touching my breast," Michelle said slightly out of breath.

Mike grinned. "I know, and you feel really good too." Michelle was startled by the door opening in the upstairs bathroom. She sat up abruptly.

"Mike, it's getting late, and I have to get up early tomorrow."

Mike touched her cheek with hand. "I am way ahead of you. Come on. Walk me to the door."

Michelle and Mike walked to the door, and Pee-Pee was at Mike's heels wagging his tail.

"You've come to say goodbye to me boy." Mike patted the dog's head.

"No Mike. He wants to go outside."

Michelle opened the door, and let the dog out.

"I'll be here Saturday morning to fix that shutter." Then he lifted her chin, and kissed her deeply. She was still dazed by his kiss when he released her.

"Until Saturday," he stated gently. Then he kissed her gently on the brow, and left. Pee-Pee walked back on the porch wagging his tail. The happy face dog looked like he was smiling. Michelle let the dog in, and went upstairs.

*****

The first week of summer camp, and baseball practice was over. We all came downstairs dressed, and ready to go because dad was coming soon to pick us up. Big Mama was up early cooking breakfast. By nine o'clock the doorbell rang. Mama answered the door with Pee-Pee at her side.

"Good morning." It was Big Mike, but this time he gave mama a kiss before she could reply. Alley, my brothers, and I sat at the table, and said in unison, "ooh!" Then we all started giggling when Big Mama turned around to see who it was.

"Oh, good morning, Mike," Big Mama greeted him.

"Good morning," Mike replied. "I see that y'all are up early this morning."

"Their father is coming by this morning to take them to *Water World*," mama explained.

"Mike, would you like to have breakfast with us?" Big Mama asked.

"No ma'am, but I will have some of that coffee." Mike walked into the kitchen, and sat at the table. Big Mama poured him a cup of coffee, and sat it on the table in front of him. The doorbell rang, and Pee-Pee barked again. Pee-Pee followed mama to the door wagging his tail. It was daddy. My brothers and I left the table to run, and give daddy a hug. Mama shut the door behind him.

"Well, who do we have here," daddy asked. Then he saw Big Mama. "Good morning Mrs. Thomas."

"Good morning," she replied.

"James," mama said, "This is my friend Mike Raimond."

"Your friend? Hmm?" Daddy turning to mama with a surprised look, "Well, nice to meet you Mr. Raimond." Daddy walked into the kitchen, and shook Mike's hand.

"Nice to meet you too," Mike replied.

"And, who is this," daddy asked.

"Daddy this is Alley. She's coming with us," I replied.

"Yes, that's right. Now, why are you here so early, Bertha? Did you come to greet me?"

"No. I live here now," Big Mama replied.

Pee-Pee walked over to daddy, and sniffed his shoe. "What is this?" He asked.

"That is a dog," mama said sarcastically.

"Does he live here now?"

"Yes James."

"Well, things have certainly changed around here."

Mama rolled her eyes at him. "Yes, they have, and for the better. Kids, go get your bags."

We all went upstairs.

"When will you bring them back James," mama asked.

"Tomorrow around two o'clock."

Alley, my brothers, and I came back downstairs with our duffle bags. We put our swim suits on underneath our clothes, so we wouldn't have to change once we got there. We gave mama a hug, and waved goodbye to Big Mama, and Mike. Daddy left right behind us. Tammy was in the SUV waving at mama.

"Good morning," she said to mama, but mama didn't respond.

We all got into the truck and daddy drove away. Mama shut the door, and walked back into the kitchen.

"If y'all want anything else, have at it. I'm going outside to work in the garden," said Big Mama. "Since the kids aren't going to be here, Ben and I are going to play bingo tonight." Big Mama turned, and left the kitchen. Pee-Pee followed her outside the back door.

Michelle got a cup of coffee, and sat at the table with Big Mike. With Big Mama and the kids gone, suddenly the house felt empty to Michelle. She stared at the cup of coffee as if it was the only friend she had left.

"Hey, I'm still here," Mike said softly.

Michelle looked up. "I know, and I'm glad that you are here too. Without the kids around the house, it's just too quiet. The dog has even deserted me."

Mike laughed. "Why didn't you tell me that their father was coming today?"

"I'm sorry. I just didn't think about it. We haven't seen each other since Wednesday."

"Oh yeah, that's right. I'm going outside to get started on the shutters. What are you going to do today?" He asked.

"I am going shopping."

"Will you be here for lunch?" Mike asked.

"Yes."

"Good," Mike stood up, and kissed her hand. "Until lunch, *belle dame*," he said then he left the kitchen.

*****

Water World was the only amusement park in our town. It was famous for the water slides, and bucket waterfalls. There was a wave pool on one side, a floating lagoon on the other, and the kid's adventure island was in the middle. There was also a baby pool near the front, but we never went in there. The smell of cotton candy, hot dogs, and pizza filled our noses as we entered the park. Daddy took our clothing, and put it into a locker for us.

"Now kids, stay together in here. This is a big place. I don't want to have to search for anyone before we leave," daddy warned.

"Yeah, you better listen," Tammy replied, "because I'm not looking for anybody."

We looked at each other, and then we looked back at her. We said in unison, okay. Then we took off. We ran straight for the kid's adventure island. Tammy asked daddy to get something for her to drink while she found two lounge chairs for them. As soon as daddy walked away, two guys walked over to Tammy. Alley and I were in the pool watching her the whole time. One of the guys asked, "Who is that old man you are with?"

"Oh, he's nobody, just my sugar daddy for now."

Then she gave him her phone number. I turned to Alley, and whispered, "Let's get her."

I climbed up the tower to the top the canopy, and told my brothers to spray her with the fire hose when she got close enough. I got down, and walked over to Alley.

"Tammy, I can't find my ring. Will you help me look for it?" I pleaded.

"Okay," she said, "but don't splash me. I don't want to get my hair wet. Where do you think it might have fallen?"

I walked near the tower, and pointed down. "I think it's over here somewhere."

Alley stood back giggling. As soon as she got close enough, my brothers opened fire on her with the fire hose. They hit her right in the face knocking her on her back. She tried to grab me, but before she could I took off yelling, "Daddy! Daddy!"

Daddy came back to the lounge chairs holding two drinks. By the time Tammy got to her feet, a big bucket of about sixty gallons of water came crashing down on her. Jordan and Jonathan laughed so hard they started to cry. Alley stood there giggling so hard she couldn't move. But once Tammy got up again, I ran behind my daddy.

"Daddy, daddy, she's trying to hurt me!"

Daddy sat the drinks down, and grabbed Tammy by the shoulders. "What is going on?"

"Your daughter deliberately got me out here, so that the water would dump on me!"

"I did not daddy! I lost my ring, and I asked her to help me find it. I didn't know that the water was going to come down on her like that." I looked up at daddy with my big green eyes, and with the most pitiful expression I could make.

"Tammy this is a water park. We came here to get wet."

"But, look at my hair," Tammy said as she stomped her feet like a small child.

"I'll pay to have it fixed for you, okay. Don't get so mad. They are just children."

Tammy gave me a mean look. She grabbed a towel. "I'll be back. I'm going to the bathroom to fix my hair."

I grinned" as she walked away.

"Jasmine, that was not very nice," daddy replied.

"But daddy, she was talking--."

"I want you to be nice to her, okay."

"Yes sir." Daddy looked at me, and started laughing. "I miss you pumpkin."

"I missed you too daddy."

"Give me a hug."

I gave daddy a big hug, and said, "I love you daddy."

"I love you too pumpkin. Now, let's have some fun." Daddy held my hand as we jumped into the pool together.

Chapter 9
Jamaican Man

When Michelle came back from the store, the shutters were fixed, and the front of the house had been scraped of loose pant. Mike was sitting on a swing that wasn't there before. Michelle got out of the car carrying bags as she walked on the front porch.

"Well, you've been busy," she said.

"What do you think?" He asked.

"The shutters look great, but I can't say that much for the siding though," Michelle said as she touched the wood panel siding.

"The loose paint has to be scraped off first, and then the siding has to be pressure washed before it can be painted."

"I thought someone else was going to do the work."

"You see, I had to do some of the prep work to get the price down. The guys are going to do the actual painting," Mike replied.

Michelle walked over to the swing. "Where did this come from?"

"There is no place to sit out here, so I hung this swing up. I thought that your mother and the kids would like it, but if you want me to take it down I will."

"Are you kidding? It's beautiful."

"Go, and put those things in the house and come back out here."

Michelle took the bags into the house along with a few others she had in the van. Once she put them away, she came back outside on the porch, and sat down on the swing with Mike. Mike had two buckets of paint sitting on the porch by the swing.

"Since we have enough of this color paint, I thought we'd paint the siding this pale grayish blue color and the trim would be painted in white. I'll paint the door myself a crimson red color. So, what do you think?"

Michelle's eyes were filled with excitement. "I love it. I can't wait to see it finished."

"Good," Mike said with a smile. "Your mother is already planning on putting some rocking chairs out here. I am going to paint them the same color as the trim."

"I am sure we will have some flowers out here too before my mom is finished. Mike, I can't thank you enough for what you've done. I've been so involved with my own problems, and I've been just too busy to do anything about this house. This house was starting to fall apart around me, just like my life."

Mike put his arm around her shoulders, and whispered, "We are going to change that too."

He brushed the hair away from her shoulders, and kissed her gently on the back of her neck. Then he kissed, and nibbled on her earlobe whispering in her ear, "You are a beautiful lady." He kissed her cheek as she began to smile. When she looked up, Pee-Pee was sitting on the porch panting very loudly. Soon Big Mama walked around the side of the house.

"Woo!" Big Mama sighed as she walked onto the porch. "Mike, you have done a beautiful job with this house. I can tell that it is going to look great. Why don't y'all come into the house, and have some lunch with me. It's getting hotter than my skillet out here."

Big Mama, Mike, Pee-Pee, and Michelle walked into the kitchen. Mike sat at the table, and Michelle waited behind Big Mama to get into the refrigerator.

"Let's see," Big Mama said as she began looking inside the refrigerator. "Mike, do you mind if we eat leftovers, or would you like a sandwich?"

"I'll have the leftovers. I'm hungry. What do you have?" He asked.

"We have some fried chicken, collard greens, macaroni and cheese, and corn bread," Big Mama replied.

"Woo wee! I'll take some of that."

Michelle looked at both of them, and said, "I'll just have a sandwich."

"You see Mike, that's why this dog is getting so big. She doesn't eat anything. I have to give it to the dog to keep from throwing it away."

"Mom, I'm always rushing from one place to another. I don't always have time to sit down, and eat a big meal. Also, mom, you know what the doctor said," Michelle warned.

"Oh, here we go," Big Mama said with an exaggerated sigh. "Doctor Michelle is always getting on to me about what I eat. I thought I was your mother."

"Okay mom, just remember I told you so."

"Well Mike, how does it taste today?" Big Mama asked.

"It's great. Leftovers are always better the second day."

"Well, I'm glad that somebody enjoys it," Big Mama said as she turned to stare at Michelle. They all talked, and laughed for an hour before they finished eating lunch.

"Oh, look at the time," Mike said. "I have to go home, and get changed if you want me ready to go out tonight. Thank you, Mrs. Thomas, for this wonderful meal I had today. I haven't had a meal like that since I left my aunt's house in Louisiana."

"Anytime Mike. Anytime," said Big Mama.

"I'll be here around four o'clock."

"Four o'clock?" Michelle said a little surprised. "Do you normally eat that early?"

"No, no. I thought with the kids gone, that maybe you would like to go see a movie too."

"Yeah, go on Michelle," Big Mama interrupted. "There's no reason to sit around here being lonely."

"Okay, I'll be ready."

Mike kissed Michelle on her brow, and said goodbye to Big Mama. Then he left.

"Mom, what do you think of him?" Michelle asked.

"Well Michelle, I like him. Not many men would work on your house for free like this, but what matters is that you like him."

Michelle didn't respond to her. She liked this man all right, but she didn't want to be heartbroken again.

*****

Mike came back right at four o'clock to pick Michelle up. When Michelle answered the door Mike was looking good, and smelling good too.

"*Belle dame bonsoir*," Mike said to her as she opened the door.

"Now Mike, I'm sure you said beautiful lady, but what else did you say?" Michelle asked.

"I said good evening beautiful lady," Mike said with a dimpled grin. "Where is your mother?"

"Oh, she left with Mr. Davis about an hour ago."

Mike laughed. "I think that old man Davis is trying to put the moves on your mother."

"Mr. Davis? Oh no. That man can't move anything anymore. They are just friends," Michelle explained, but Mike didn't look so convinced. "Come on," she said. "Let's go."

Once they got outside there was a beautiful red sports car in the driveway. "Where is your truck?"

"I work in that truck Michelle. I didn't want to take you out in that. I think you will enjoy being seen in this one better."

"I think you're right," she replied. Mike held the door open for Michelle to get into the car. Then he got into the car, and drove away.

Michelle was glad Mike picked a comedy to go see at the movies. She didn't want to see anything sad or scary today.

Walking out of the theater Mike asked, "How did you like this movie?"

"I thought it was great. I think you, and I have similar taste."

"I am glad you feel that way because I'm taking you to a Jamaican club near the lake."

"Wow! Caribbean food, that sounds great. I've never eaten Caribbean food before."

"Then you are in for a real treat. Come on. Let's go."

Mike drove through the city past the lake front where there was a beautiful park, and walking trail surrounding the lake. Once Mike parked the car, they walked into a carnival like atmosphere outside of the club. There was a blues singer sitting on an old bucket peddling for money. The jugglers were entertaining the crowd of people as they passed by and there were a few street artist painting pictures of the beautiful scenery of the lake. Inside of the dimly lit club doors, stood two large palm trees, and a water fall. As they got closer to the waterfall's pond, Michelle saw some beautiful Koi swimming in the shallow water. Steel drum music gave the club a lively atmosphere of the tropics. After paying the hostess at the door, they entered the club. Downstairs reggae music was playing. There was a big dance floor where people were dancing, and a huge bar in the corner of the room. Michelle and Mike walked upstairs to the dining room. The tables were decorated in a tropical theme. More palm trees lined the entrance, and the kitchen had an open grill. The hostess seated them at a table by the balcony.

"Michelle, do you like it so far?" Mike asked.

"This place is wonderful. I feel like we are in Jamaica." Soon the waitress came to their table. She had on a *Jamaican Man* t-shirt, which was the name of the club, with a pair of black pants. Her hair was in dreadlocks.

"Good evening. My name is Stacy, and I'll be your server today. What will you be having today?" She asked with a very strong West Indies accent.

"I'll have the jerk chicken with the grilled vegetables, and a salad," Mike said.

"And, for you ma'am," the waitress asked.

"I'll have the Conch Salad, and fritters," replied Michelle.

"Great. Would you like to try one of our rum specialties?" The waitress asked.

"Wow, that sounds good," said Michelle. "Give me a glass of water, and a *Bahama Mama*."

"How about you, sir?"

"I'll have a glass of water, and a beer."

"Good," the waitress replied. "Would you like to try the house appetizers?"

"Yes," Mike agreed.

The waitress took the menus, and said, "Your appetizers will be out soon," and then she left.

Mike reached across the table, and grabbed Michelle's hand. "You know what the Jamaican's say about eating Conch Salad, don't you?"

"No, what do they say?" Michelle asked curiously.

"They say it's an aphrodisiac."

Michelle laughed. "Don't worry Mike. I won't take advantage of you tonight," Michelle replied with an impish grin.

Mike snapped his fingers. "Darn," he said,

Soon the waitress came back with their drinks.

"This *Bahama Mama* is great," Michelle replied.

Then the waitress brought the appetizer tray to the table. The tray was covered with tropical fruit, and grilled pork shish kabobs. The appetizers really complemented the drink Michelle had. Once they finished the appetizers, the waitress brought out the main course.

"Michelle, have you ever tried jerk chicken before?" Mike asked.

"No, I haven't."

"Here, try this." He cut her a small piece of chicken, and said, "I warn you, this maybe a little hot."

Then he fed her the chicken from his fork. At first, the chicken put a wonderful flavor in Michelle's mouth, but soon that flavor became hot.

"Oh Mike, this is hot. Really hot!" Then Michelle grabbed the glass of water, and drank half of it before she put it back down. "How can you eat that?"

Mike dimpled grin became mischievous. "I guess some like hot."

They continued eating, and talking for about twenty minutes before they had enough.

"Michelle, would you like some Rum Cake for dessert?" Mike asked.

"No thank you. I am full. I still have so much food here that I don't think I can eat it all."

She looked over the balcony onto the dance floor. All the people on the dance floor were dancing to the reggae music. "Come on Mike. Let's dance."

Mike paid the waitress and left a big tip. Then they left the table, and went downstairs to the dance floor. People were dancing, and jumping to the reggae music. Mike and Michelle walked onto the middle of the dance floor blending in with the other dancers. They danced together for the next three songs. Then a slow reggae song started to play. Michelle started to leave the floor, but Mike grabbed her hand.

"*Madame*," he said as he led her back onto the dance floor wrapping his hand around her waist sending shivers tingling up her spine. Soon they began to sway to the rhythm of the tropical beat. Leaning against Mike's firm chest was becoming very erotic for Michelle. Mike's hand slowly began to message her lower back sending more shiver from her back to her breast. Her nipples were becoming perky, and erect. They could be visibly seen through the front of her black backless dress. She wasn't the only one becoming erect in this dance. The more Mike stroked her spine the harder his manhood became. The dance was becoming primal, and intoxicating under the tropical beat. Mike felt that if the song didn't end soon, he would have to take her right here, right now. Finally, the music did end.

"Mike," Michelle said. "It's getting really hot in here. Why don't we go outside?"

Mike kissed her hand, and said, "Lead the way."

They walked outside past the jugglers and the street artist to the lake front. They crossed the walking trail where joggers were running, and lovers were holding hands. They walked across a long bridge to a gazebo on the lake, and sat on a bench watching the ducks, and swans going by.

"It's really beautiful out here," Michelle said.

"Have you stopped missing your kids yet?" Mike asked.

"I stopped missing them after I went to the store this morning. I love them, but it's nice to have a break."

Mike stroked her cheek with his finger. "You know all about me, but you haven't told me anything about yourself."

"What would you like to know?"

"Well, do you have any brothers, or sisters?" Mike asked.

"Yes, I have a brother with a bit of a drinking problem. He's a happy drunk though. We tried to get him some help once, but he told us he didn't have a problem. He said he had a habit, and drinking was it." Mike laughed. "He comes by my house all the time. You'll see him sooner, or later."

"He sounds interesting," Mike paused. "What about your ex-husband."

"What about him?"

"I was curious," Mike replied. "I just can't believe a man would leave such a beautiful woman like you, but if you don't want to talk about it, I'll understand."

Michelle looked up at Mike for a moment, and hesitated before she spoke. "It's okay Mike. I don't mind talking about it now. It's old news anyway. James and I were married for twelve years. We met in high school. He cheated on me once before we got married, but I took him back, and married him anyway. Now that I think about it, he might have cheated on me more than once when we were married, but I just didn't want to accept the truth. I think I was more afraid of being alone than of him cheating. I finally had to accept it when it was thrown in my face. Do you remember the young girl he had in his truck when he came to pick up the kids?"

"Yeah."

"Well, I caught them upstairs in my bedroom together, if you know what I mean."

"Oh no." Mike replied.

"Yes Mike, in my bed. He left with her that night, and he has never come back to live with us again. For the first month after he left, I slept on the couch. I could not stand going back into that room. Then I decided that it was my house now, and I wasn't going to let them put me out of my bedroom. I got a new bedroom suit, and re-did everything in that room. I donated my old things. Now, there is nothing left to even remind me of James in that room."

"Well, good for you."

"Yeah, but I am still paying for that bedroom suit. I should have sold that furniture. It was only a year old, but it had to go so I could keep my sanity."

"If you ever need any help Michelle, don't be too proud to ask for it. What I give to you I won't ask for it back," Mike stated with a concerned look.

"Thank you, Mike, but I think I'll be okay."

"And, you were never alone," he said. "Your mother is there for you, and you have three beautiful children with you. Most importantly, you can still handle your business. You won't take a dime from any one, and still, you've managed to support your family. I am proud of you. Just don't be too proud to ask for help. I am here if you need me."

"Okay," she replied.

Mike reached for Michelle's hand, and kissed her knuckles. "Now, you aren't going to push me away because of what he has done, are you?"

"No Mike," Michelle said as she looked away from him. "But, I can't say that I'm not a little scared."

"Of what?"

"Of you." She turned back to Mike. "I'm forty years old, and getting older. So, if you decide to find someone younger, well I just can't go through this again. It hurts too much."

Mike kissed her hand again. "If I wanted someone younger, I would be with someone younger. You are a beautiful woman, and you don't need to compete with younger girls. Like I said when I met you, I like the ladies. I don't want a little girl. Just give me a chance, okay. I promise to take things as slowly as you like."

Michelle gave him a little smile and said, okay. Then she leaned toward him, and kissed him passionately. When she released him, his eyes were a bit dazed. "Now, you know that I will definitely give you a chance."

"Answer this question for me," Mike asked. "Do you still love him?"

"No," Michelle replied. "I care for him, but I stopped loving him years ago. He has hurt me too many times."

"Good," Mike replied with a dimpled smile. "Now, can I have another kiss?"

This time he didn't wait for her to kiss him. Before she could speak again, he kissed her fervently under the gazebo. He raised his hand to gently caress her face. Then his hand moved to the back of her neck. When his hand slid to her shoulders, Michelle held his hand right there, and pulled away from his lips.

She looked around, and said, "Come on. We better go before someone calls the cops on us."

Mike smiled as they got up holding hands, and walking back over the bridge to the car.

The ride home was a quiet one. Michelle found herself staring at this gentle, but also beautiful man that she was afraid of. She knew there was no way of telling what the future would be, but for now, she would just enjoy the time they had together. This was one of the best first dates she had ever been on. Michelle never thought that she would enjoy Caribbean food so much. Soon Mike's car turned onto her street. He parked the car, and got out to open her door.

As they walked onto the porch, Michelle said, "It's only a little after nine o'clock. Would you like to sit on the swing for a little while?"

Michelle enjoyed the time they had spent together so much that she didn't want it to end. Mike agreed. They both walked to the porch, and sat down on the swing. Mike put his arm around Michelle's shoulders, and kissed the side of her cheek.

"I want to ask you something a little personal," he said.

"Just a little personal?" She asked with a mischievous grin.

"Yes. You told me that you stopped loving your husband years ago. Is that right?"

Michelle shook her head.

"Well, how long has it been since you had? You know." Mike said curiously.

"Sex?" Michelle asked.

"Yes."

Michelle thought to herself for a moment. Then she said, "I think it has been more than two years."

Mike was in shock. "You're telling me you haven't made love in more than two years?"

"Yes Mike," she replied with a little embarrassment. "I've just been recently divorced."

Mike kissed her cheek again. "I'm sorry. I wasn't trying to embarrass you. Do you forgive me?" He said as he looked down at her with his big brown eyes.

"Yes, but what does this mean?" She asked.

Mike gave her a strange look. "It means nothing."

"Then you won't pressure me for sex."

"Michelle, I'm not going to pressure you for anything that you don't want to do. Remember, I said I'll go as slowly as you want."

Michelle shook her head, and said, okay.

"So, what are you doing tomorrow?" He asked.

"I'm going to church with mom tomorrow."

"Do you care if I come along with y'all?"

"No," she replied. "You can ride with us if you like."

"Good. What time should I be there?"

"By eleven a.m."

"I'll be here." Mike carefully removed her hair from her shoulders, and kissed the back of her neck when Big Mama's big old car pulled into the driveway. Mike stopped kissing Michelle's neck to see who was coming up the drive way. Big Mama and Mr. Davis got out of the car together laughing, and giggling all the way onto the front porch.

"Hey y'all," Big Mama said.

"Good evening," greeted Mr. Davis. Mike and Michelle returned their greetings as they approached them on the swing.

"Guess what?" Big Mama said. "Ben here has finally found something he can beat me at. He won eight hundred dollars playing bingo tonight."

"I certainly did," Ben replied.

Then he pulled the money out of his pocket to show Mike and Michelle. They gasped.

"I wouldn't go waving that around if I were you," Mike replied.

"I know, I know," said Mr. Davis.

When Michelle saw all the money he had won, she said, "Maybe Mike and I should play bingo sometime."

"I'm not the bingo type," Mike said with a little giggle.

"Well, we are going again," Mr. Davis insisted. "Isn't that right Bertha?"

"That's right," Big Mama agreed.

"Well Bertha, I'll see you again for our next card game," Mr. Davis said. "I believe my luck is about to change. Y'all have a good night."

Everyone told Mr. Davis good night as he left the porch.

"It's getting cool out here. Are y'all going to come inside?" Big Mama asked

"I'll come inside in a minute mom."

"Well, suit yourself. I'm going to bed. Good night." Then Big Mama went inside the house.

Mike kissed Michelle on the side of the head, and gave her a hug. "I had better go too if I'm going to make it to church tomorrow. I hope you don't feel pressured by me asking that question earlier."

"No Mike. I don't."

Mike stood up, and grabbed Michelle's hands helping her off the swing. Then he wrapped his arms around her waist.

"Don't misunderstand me because I would give anything to make love to you right now. But, when we do make love for the first time, believe me, you will want to do it again, and again, and again." Then he kissed her lasciviously. His tongue set off a flame inside her causing her to moan deeply. When he released her, his passionate kiss left her wanting more, but he gave her another kiss on the brow, and left the porch. She watched him drive away before she went into the house.

When she got to her bedroom, she laid back on the bed saying to herself, "If he feels even half as good as he does when he kisses me, I know he must be great in bed."

*****

This Sunday everyone was dressed in blue. Big Mama wore a blue suit and hat. Michelle had on a baby blue dress that was sheer across her shoulders and a baby blue belt that tied at her waist. Mike had on a navy suit with cream colored shirt, and striped tie that complemented his tan skin, and beautiful eyes. They hadn't planned on wearing shades of blue, but they all looked great together. As they walked into the church service, Mike seemed to grab the attention of the young ladies in the audience. Michelle just smiled at all the attention they received, and they found a seat near the front. For most of the service Mike couldn't keep his eyes off Michelle. She was simply beautiful today, and her lovely dress just accented every inch of her curves. After the service, Michelle introduced Mike to her friend Sharon, and Sharon's husband Greg. Mike greeted them, and shook their hands.

"I have heard so much about you. I'm glad we finally met," Sharon said.

"I am glad we finally met too," Mike replied, "but I hope everything you heard was good."

"Oh yes, really good." Mike began to grin.

"Oh no. Mrs. Leola is headed this way," Sharon said with a sigh.

Michelle turned to see her coming, but it was too late to walk away.

"I can't stand her," Michelle whispered to Mike under her breath.

"Well hello Michelle," Leola said. "I just wanted to come by, and apologize for my bad behavior the other Sunday. You know how it is darling. Now, who do we have here?"

"This is Michael Raimond. Mike, this is Leola Nickels," said Michelle.

"Well, nice to meet you," Leola extending her hand.

"And, you too," Mike replied shaking her hand.

"Well now, he's a cute one Michelle, but whatever does he see in you?" Leola grinned. Michelle glared at her, and then she rolled her eyes. "Mike, you have to come back to our church again sometime. I am just dying to get to know you better," she said with an evil grin.

"This is a wonderful church, and I would love to come back. But, there are some people I would like to get to know better here," he said as he turned to Sharon and Greg, "and there are some people I don't care to see again," he said as he turned back to Mrs. Leola.

Soon the evil grin left Leola's face as she stood there glaring at Mike.

"Come on Michelle. I'm getting hungry. Let's find your mother, and go get something to eat. Nice to meet y'all." Mike grabbed Michelle's hand, and they walked away.

Mike drove Michelle's van back to her house. He walked to his truck, and got out a bag of clothes to change into. Everyone changed out of their dress attire into something more comfortable. Michelle and Mike had on shorts and t-shirts, but Big Mama had on her standard house dress. Mike, Michelle, Big Mama, and Pee-Pee walked into the kitchen.

"Have you cooked for today already?" Mike asked as he sat at the table watching Big Mama pulling dishes out of the refrigerator.

"We cooked most of this when you left yesterday," Michelle replied.

"All we have to do now is heat it up," Big Mama said.

"Great. What are we having?" Mike asked.

Michelle replied, "Squash casserole, baked chicken, green beans, and rolls."

"Wow. That sounds good. Do y'all always cook like this?"

"Yes," Big Mama interjected, "but now we only cook large meals on Sundays."

Mike's dimpled smile grew wide as he leaned back in his chair. "I guess this is my lucky day."

Michelle and Big Mama laughed. Suddenly there was a knock at the door. Pee-Pee barked loudly as Michelle answered the door.

"Hey Pete," she said.

"What's up little sis?" He replied. He grabbed his sister, and kissed her on the cheek.

"Oh!" Michelle said very loud. She could smell the alcohol on his breath.

"What's cooking?" Pete asked. "I'm looking, and feeling like an anorexic." Hey mama!"

Pete walked over to Big Mama, and gave her a hug and kiss.

"Ugh Pete! It too early," said Big Mama.

"And, who might you be sir?" Pete asked.

Michelle walked into the kitchen, and put her hands on Mike's shoulders saying, "Pete, this is Michael Raimond. He's a friend of mine."

"Well now!" Pete said with surprised look. "How do you do Mr. Raimond." He extended his hand.

"Just fine," Mike shook Pete's hand. "Call me Mike."

"Okay, Mike. Are you the one responsible for fixing this monstrosity of a house?" Pete asked.

"My house isn't a monstrosity Pete," Michelle snapped.

Pete gave Michelle a smirk, and looked back at Mike.

"Yes, I'm the one," Mike said calmly, "but this house isn't in that bad of a condition. All I did was nail the shutters back up, and scrapped the loose paint off the siding.

"Who put the swing up," Pete asked.

"That would be me too." Mike replied.

"Oh, how romantic," Pete winked at Michelle. "Speaking of what happens with romance," Pete paused, "Where are the kids?"

Big Mama answered saying, "James has them this weekend. They will be back this afternoon. Pete, why don't you have a seat, and I'll fix you a plate."

Pete sat down at the table, and began telling Mike how he built a bridge in the war. Big Mama and Michelle prepared a plate of food for Pete, and Mike. Pete went on and on telling Mike one of the most unbelievable stories about the first gulf war that he had ever heard before.

"Now Pete, there is no way you could have built a sand castle big enough for you to hide in, in that amount of time without the enemy seeing you," Mike said.

"I sure did," Pete replied with a mouth full of food. "--and, the sand protected me from the bullets too."

Both Michelle and Big Mama shook their heads. Pete kept telling this unbelievable tale until everyone finished eating.

"Would y'all like a piece of apple pie," Big Mama asked.

"Mama, you don't even have to ask. I've never turned a piece of your pie down, even when I was sick. Mike, you've got to try this. It will make you slap your mama, oops."

"Watch your mouth, Pete." Big Mama said sternly.

"Sorry Mama."

Everyone agreed with Pete. The pie was delicious. Before they finished eating the pie, the door bell rang. Michelle answered the door with Pee-Pee at her side. She was greeted, and hugged by all four kids. Jasmine's and Alley's hair was curled, and looked beautiful. It looked like they had been to a salon.

"Who did your hair Jasmine?" Michelle asked. "It's beautiful."

"Tammy took us to her salon," Jasmine replied. "Hey Uncle Pete!" All the kids ran into the kitchen to greet Big Mama and Mike too. Soon James came inside with the kids' bags. He put them down by the door, and greeted everybody.

"Did you have any trouble with anyone James?" Michelle asked.

"They were on their best behavior most of the time," James commented. "Can I talk to you outside for a moment?"

Michelle walked outside on the porch, and said, "What's wrong James?"

"What do you know about this Mike person anyway and why is he always here?"

"James, I know enough about him to know that he's welcome here, but you're not," Michelle stated as she became enraged. "How dare you tell me who I can bring to my own home! You don't live here anymore, remember."

"Well, my children live here, and I have a right to say something if this man is going to be around them."

"James, do you think I would have my kids around someone who might hurt them? Besides, Mike hasn't been around the kids this weekend. He's only been around me, and don't you dare tell me who I can be with after you brought that trash into my house." Mama pointed to Tammy in the truck.

"This isn't over Michelle," James replied.

"It is if you want to pick the kids up here again, or would you like me to tell the attorney that you have been harassing me."

"Fine Michelle, but he better not lay a hand on my kids, or I'll--."

"Do what?" Michelle snapped back at him. "Mike isn't into children like you. It's time for you to go."

"Yes, I believe it is," James agreed as he walked back to his truck and sped away.

Michelle walked back into the house. She was visibly shaken by something James said to her on the porch.

"Kids, take your bags to your rooms," Michelle said.

Michelle tried to pretend that nothing was wrong. She walked back into the kitchen, and sat down at the table. She picked up the fork, and played with the crust on the remaining piece of pie. Mike reached over, and grabbed her wrist. He looked up into her melancholy eyes that couldn't hold back the pain she felt.

"I'll come by tomorrow and Tuesday to finish scraping the house. On Wednesday the painters are going to start painting, okay," he said. "Well, thank you again Mrs. Thomas for the meal, and nice to meet you Pete."

Pete said something that no one understood. Mike stood up.

"Anytime," Big Mama replied.

"I'll see y'all tomorrow. Michelle, do you mind walking me out," Mike asked.

"No, come on."

Michelle and Mike walked outside to his truck. He leaned against the truck and said, "Michelle, I'm concerned about you. What did James say to you?"

Michelle slowly looked up at him. "He doesn't like you being around the children. He threatened that if you laid a hand on them, but I didn't let him finish his threat."

Mike lifted Michelle's chin with his finger, and grinned. "I had a feeling that is what you were upset about. Darling, he doesn't want you anymore, but he doesn't want another man moving in on his territory either. This house, you, and the kids are still his territory in his mind. You've only been divorced for a month. He hasn't gotten used to the fact that this is not his house anymore. Believe me. I'm not afraid of that little man. Little men always threaten women to make themselves feel strong. I bet yah he won't say anything to my face," Mike replied.

Michelle started to smile. Mike pulled her towards him. "Good, I'm glad to see you smile again." He kissed her gently. Then he touched her brow to his. "I have to go. Call me tonight," he said as he got into the truck. "I'll see you tomorrow."

He backed the truck out of the driveway. Once he drove away, Michelle saw Mrs. Madison rocking in her rocking chair on her front porch. She waved to her and she nodded back in response. As Michelle walked back to the front porch, she wondered if Mrs. Madison saw her, and Mike last night on the swing. Mama thought to herself, we'll have to be more careful about what we do out here on this swing. Then she walked inside the house.

Chapter 10
A Whale of a Tale

Mike worked really hard scraping the paint off the siding most of the day on Monday. Big Mama would bring him a glass of lemonade, or water whenever he wanted to take a break. Tuesday, Mike pressure washed the siding. Alley and I watched him for a little while. He washed away spider webs, and mold from the side of the house. Then he even washed away a big spider. Alley and I ran when we saw him do that. Later on in the evening, Mike would spend time eating, or talking to mama when she got home. Last night before Mike left, he said the painters would finish the work, but he would be here Friday to paint the front door.

"Mike, the rocking chairs and table will be here by Tuesday, and they don't need to be painted because they are already painted white. Can I put them on the porch by Thursday?" Big Mama asked.

"Well, just wait for the paint to dry first. It shouldn't take more than a day to dry. Also, y'all may want to use the back door until the porch is dry. I have to go now. Y'all have a good night." He got up, and mama walked him to the door. "What are you doing on Saturday?" He asked her.

"The boys are playing their first baseball game on Saturday."

"I would love to go to the game. I haven't seen a little league game in years. That is if you would like me to go of course, or are you getting tired of seeing me?"

"I could never get tired of looking at that those gorgeous eyes," mama said with a mischievous smile.

Mike gave mama a kiss on the cheek. "What time should I be here?"

"By nine a.m."

"Man. That's early."

"I know." Mama replied.

"I'll see you later." Mike kissed mama on the brow, and left.

*****

Today was Wednesday, and we were going to Pine Mountain Lake today. Alley and I put our swim suits on under our clothes so we wouldn't have to change at the lake. Mrs. Mays told us yesterday that we were going straight to the lake first thing this morning, so we had to be ready when we got there. We walked downstairs to the kitchen to eat breakfast. Big Mama had the table set, and a bowl of cereal for us to eat when we got to the table. When Alley sat down, I noticed that she looked different. She is cleaner now than she was in school, and she looks healthier. The biggest change I've noticed is how happy she is now. She seems to be happy all the time. She loves summer camp unlike school. In summer camp, Toad and Stool weren't there to harass her. She enjoyed doing arts, and crafts at the center on Monday and the movie we saw on Tuesday. When I see her now, she always has a little smile on her face. I don't think she's conscious of it, but she is smiling all the time.

"Now that I have you here alone, Alley, tell me something?" Big Mama asked. "Do you have any family around here?"

"No ma'am," Alley replied.

"Have you tried to call your dad?"

"Yes ma'am, but no one answers the phone."

"Do you remember your daddy saying anything to you, or anyone else before he left?"

"He didn't say anything to me, but he was talking to Officer Daniel Smith before he left."

"He was talking to a police officer Alley?" Big Mama asked with a little curiosity.

"Yes ma'am."

"Did you hear what they said?" Big Mama asked.

"Officer Smith said somebody saw him, and that he better lay low for a while. The next day when I got up, he was gone. His girlfriend stayed with me for a day then she left."

Big Mama stood there shaking her head. Soon my brothers came running downstairs. Jordan raced Jonathan to the table, but Jordan fell, and Jonathan fell on top of him.

"Boys, stop running in this house before you break something," Big Mama shouted.

Mama walked downstairs next. Since Mike has been coming around more often, mama's mood has changed too.

"Good morning my beautiful family," she said. Then she gave me a kiss on top of the head.

"Mom, I don't have time to eat this morning, but I'll get something on the way to work."

"Suit yourself," Big Mama replied.

"Oh Jordan, your baseball coach left a message for me last night saying you put a frog down a little boy's shirt, and you filled another boy's pants with dirt," mama said sternly.

"What!" Big Mama shrieked. "Jordan, this means you will have another week of cooking and cleaning."

"No!" Jordan cried.

"Jordan, if I hear about anything else bad from your coach, you are off the team," mama said sternly.

"Yes ma'am." Jordan began to pout.

"Jasmine and Alley, y'all need to get going before y'all miss the bus," said Big Mama.

Alley and I got up grabbing our bags, and ran outside.

*****

On the bus, I sat next to the window, and Alley sat next to me. Plump sat near the aisle across from Teach and a boy we nicknamed Pookie. Of course, Plump started talking constantly again. She continued to talk until we left the city. I was glad I sat by the window.

"Alley, you are going to love this lake," Plump said. "There are all kinds of fish in this water and they have a concession stand where you can buy cotton candy, hot dogs, or pizza if you want that. I've even heard that there is a whale in this lake. He's a friendly whale, but don't kick him, or he'll swallow you whole."

"Plump, that's not true," Teach said. "Whales live in the ocean."

"Yeah, I've been out here before, and I have never seen a whale," said Pookie.

"Whales don't like boys," Plump stated flatly. "Whales think boys stink!"

"You stink!" Teach shouted.

"You stink!" Plump snapped back.

This went back and forth for a while before Pookie interrupted them. "Anyway, who every heard of a whale living in a lake?"

"I have," Plump demanded. "They lay on the bottom of the lake so you can't see them when you look at the lake."

"That's because they aren't there," Teach replied.

"Yes, they are, Teach! You don't know anything!" Plump shouted.

"Okay Plump," Teach paused, "if there is a whale in the lake, I'll buy you an ice cream cone at the concession stand today, but if there is no whale, you owe me an ice cream cone. Do we have a deal?" He said holding his hand up.

"Deal!" Plump slapped his hand in a high five.

"An ice cream cone?!" Pookie shouted. "Man, you know an ice cream cone won't satisfy Plump. You should have said a *Fat Burger.*" She would have made sure it was a whale in that lake then."

"Shut up Pookie!" Plump shouted as everybody on the bus continued to laugh. "Maybe he should have bought you some mints. I can smell your breath over here."

"That's your feet you smell," Pookie replied. "Hey Plump, I heard that your mama is so fat that if she was a brick, she would be a project."

All the kids on the bus started laughing hysterical again.

"Well, I heard that your mama is so ugly that she could put her face in some dough, and make some monster cookies," Plump shouted back.

The kids on the bus laughed again.

"That's enough," Mrs. Mays said as she continued to drive the bus. "No more talking about each other's mamas, understand."

"Yes ma'am," Pookie and Plump said in unison.

"Look!" Alley shouted.

All the kids looked out of the right side of the bus window and said, wow, when they saw the five hot air balloons floating over the lake. These balloons had a rainbow of colors. We could see the people inside of them firing them up, so they could go higher to cross the bridge. Soon, we passed the bridge, and came near the sign that read: *Spotted Buck Hunt Club* one mile. Passing this sign gave me the creeps, but I couldn't turn away from the forest. Then a small deer with a white tail, and spotted flank was eating wild flowers by the embankment.

"Alley look," I said pointing toward the fawn.

"Cool." Plump whispered.

Then I looked up, and I saw the lady. She was so close to the bus that I thought the bus was going to hit her. "Watch out!" I yelled.

Then I ducked down in my seat. Plump and Alley stared at me as if I had lost my mind.

"What's wrong with you Jay-Jay?" Alley asked.

I sat back up in my seat, and slowly looked out of the window. I saw the lady standing there as the bus drove down the road.

"Are you all right?" Alley asked.

"Yeah, I thought we hit something," I replied.

"Jay-Jay, you are crazy," Plump said sitting back down, and then she started talking to Alley again.

Finally, the bus arrived at the park. There were some people on the lake in paddle boats, and in the corner of the lake, fishermen were fishing. Coming off the bus there was hardly a cloud in the crystal clear blue sky as the sun warmed our skin.

"Listen up everyone," Mrs. Mays said. "Enjoy the lake until lunch time. Then we'll meet at the picnic area for lunch. There will be no horse playing in the water, and no running on the beach. After lunch, we are going to play water volley ball, and I don't think I have to remind everyone to not wander off. Everyone understands me!"

We all said, "Yes ma'am."

"Good, go change."

The girl's locker room was on one side of the concession stand, and the boys were on the other side. We walked in the locker room, changed out of our clothes, and then we put the bags in the lockers.

We walked to the beach together when Teach and Pookie walked up behind us. "Hey, where is that whale?" Teach asked.

"Shut up Teach! You're going to scare him away," Plump shouted.

"Yeah right," he said with a smirk.

"Let me get in the water first Teach!" Plump demanded.

"Okay, but I'll be back." Teach reminded her.

Teach and Pookie walked off. Plump, Alley, and I walked into the water that was amazingly warm.

"Now Plump, is there really a whale in this water?" Alley asked.

"You'll see," she said with a grin.

"Hey guys, look at this," I said. There was a school of spotted brim about three feet away from us. The fish had an iridescent bluish green color with a hug spot on their flank by their eyes. The fish seemed to be watching us, but as soon as Plump got closer to them, they took off in every direction.

"Plump, you scared them away," I said sadly.

"No, I didn't. They heard the whale coming."

"You really think there is a whale out here."

"Yes, come on!" Plump replied.

We spent most of the day chasing fish away, and digging up the small shells that lined the sandy man-made beach. Alley walked about a yard into the water, and stood there for a moment staring down at the water.

"Alley, whatcha doing?" I asked.

Alley put her finger to her lips, and said, "Shh!"

Plump and I looked at each other, and wondered what in the world was she doing. Then Alley jumped in the water, and grabbed a big cat fish that was almost half her size. Plump and I sat there with our mouths slightly opened, and our eyes bucked.

Alley held the fish up high in her arms, and said, "Look at this!"

The fish didn't wiggle much at first, but the mouth of the fish looked like it was gasping for air.

"Alexandria, you put that fish down before his fins stick you!" Mrs. Mays yelled at her from across the beach.

Alley lowered the fish down into the water. As soon as the fish touched the water, he took off splashing water into Alley's face with his tail. Plump and I rolled back on the beach laughing. We had been playing in the water for about two hours now when suddenly Teach and Pookie appeared behind us.

"Okay Plump," Teach said with his arms folded across his chest. "You've had two hours to find this whale. Now, where is this whale?"

Plump put her hands on her rather large hips, and shouted, "I don't have to prove anything to you Teach!"

"See, I know there was no whale out here," he shouted.

"You want to see a whale Teach? I'll show you a whale," Plump said with a smirk. "Come on!"

Pookie, Teach, Alley, and I followed Plump to the side of the lake.

"Gather around me. I don't want everyone to see. They'll scare him away." She walked out into the water about a yard feeling the bottom of the lake with her feet. "I found him!" Plump dove into the water head first. For a moment we didn't see her anymore. We looked at each other, and we were scared. Then we all took a step forward to see if this creature was in the water, or if Plump had been eaten. Without any warning, Plump's big naked butt burst from the water. She passed gas creating a water spout just like a whale. We were utterly amazed. Then she stood up, and pulled up her Tankini bottoms. "Did y'all see the whale spout?"

We all looked at each other, and then everyone broke out in hysterically laughter. That is, everyone except Mrs. Mays.

"Bernadette, you come here this instance!"

Plump looked scared. She knew she was in trouble. Plump walked slowly over to Mrs. Mays. We could hear Plump begging Mrs. Mays not to call her parents. Mrs. May decided not to call her parents, but Plump had to sit in time out until lunchtime. Plump was lucky because she only had to stay in time out for an hour before we went to lunch. The center provided us with box lunches. Of course, this wasn't enough for Plump, but this time Teach went to the concession stand with her. True to her word, Plump bought Teach an ice cream cone. She also bought a hot dog for herself. Teach bought two big slices of pizza to eat along with his lunch. When they got back to the table, I couldn't believe all the food Teach had to eat.

"Teach, man that's a lot of food. You know we are playing volley ball after lunch," I said.

"So, I can handle this." Teach ate the two slices of pizza, and his boxed lunch. Plump finished her hot dog, and lunch too. We all walked back to the beach, and sat on the sand while Mrs. Mays and the camp leaders set up the valley ball net in the water.

"I don't feel so good," Teach moaned.

"I told you Teach! You can't eat all that stuff out here in this heat. Now you can't play volley ball," I said shaking my head.

"Yes, I can," he demanded.

Mrs. Mayes blew the whistle, and we all walked back into the water. Mrs. Mays divided the group into two equal size teams. Plump and Teach were on my team, but Alley was on the other side. Mrs. Mays blew the whistle, and we began to play. Plump was really good at this game. She would hit the ball so hard that it would shoot across the net causing the other team to duck out of the way. Alley made a few good hits across the net, but Teach just swayed in the water trying not to fall over.

"Teach, why don't you go sit down? You're sick!" I said.

"No, I'm not!"

"Yes, you are Teach! Go on before you fall out in the water."

"No. I'm okay."

"Okay Teach, you're going to be sick," I replied.

The game went on for fifteen minutes more before Teach caught the ball.

"Teach hit it back across the net!" I shouted.

Teach just held the ball saying, "Ugh." Then he threw up on the ball, and in the water. Kids were running and jumping out of the water like someone threw a bomb in it. Mrs. Mays ran into the water towards Teach.

"Derrick, come here!" She yelled.

Teach slowly walked to Mrs. Mays still trying to stand up in the water. Mrs. Mays caught him before he got to the shore, and sat him down on the beach.

"Camp leaders, take the net down. We are going back to the center. Everyone else, back on the bus!"

Once we all were accounted for, she drove the bus out of the park. We got back to the center earlier than expected. Mrs. Mays called Teach's mother, and told her to come pick him up. For the rest of the afternoon, we made arts, and crafts.

We always took the longer route home away from the big kids. We know if we walked by them, we would have to pay them, or they would take our money. We made our usual stop at Mr. Muhammad's store for snacks and then we went home. Plump didn't come by our house today. She was afraid her mother might have found out what she had done at the beach today, and embarrassed her in front of everybody. When we turned the corner to our house, the front, and the side of the house had been painted. The house looked brand new. Well, at least it did on two sides. Big Mama was sitting on Mr. Davis front porch talking when we walked up.

"Kids, don't touch that porch. It has to dry before y'all can walk on it. Y'all will have to go around to the back door if you want to go into the house. I'll be home in a minute, and let the dog out."

We walked around to the backyard. I opened the back door, and let Pee-Pee outside. We all played in the backyard until Big Mama called Jordan in to help make dinner. Once Jordan left, we all went inside the house too.

For the next two days of summer camp, we didn't go anywhere outside of the center. Thursday, we had more arts and crafts. We also played games at the center. On Friday, we watched movies. Alley and Plump didn't care that we didn't go anywhere. Alley was just happy to be there, and Plump was glad she didn't get into any trouble when she went home Wednesday. I wanted to go somewhere, but I guess Mrs. Mays was too embarrassed to take us anywhere else after Teach threw up at the lake. The last two days at home weren't any better either. Big Mama and Jordan stayed so busy in the kitchen that Big Mama didn't have time to tell us any of her usual stories. Alley and I watched TV, and played cards the rest of the day. But when mama got home, I knew there was something wrong. Mama told Big Mama that Mrs. Jenkins was really sick yesterday. Mama said that she had to take her to the hospital last night, but she was back at home today. Big Mama tried to console mama, but mama knew that Mrs. Jenkins would probably not get any better.

Friday afternoon Big Mike came by to paint the door. That night he gave mama some beautiful flowers to cheer her up, but I don't think it worked. The only good thing that happened in the last two days is that our house looked great. The paint made our house look brand new. Big Mama put two rocking chairs, and table on the front porch. She also put a beautiful pot of velvet red petunias on the table. Our house was once the eye sore of the block, but has now become the beauty of the block. The flowers Big Mama planted by the front walkway were getting bigger, and the garden vegetables were getting big enough to harvest. I picked a tomato when Big Mama wasn't looking to eat, and it was good too. I plan on trying the cucumbers when they get a little bigger.

*****

Today was Saturday, and we all were going to Jordan's and Jonathan's first baseball game. Mr. Davis and Big Mike were coming to the game too. We all got dressed before we came downstairs for breakfast. Big Mama was the first one up, and ready this morning. She prepared eggs, bacon, and grits with cinnamon raisin toast for breakfast this morning. The scent of the cinnamon, and coffee filled the whole house. Soon my brothers came downstairs wearing their uniforms. Alley and I ran downstairs after them.

"Eat up boys. Y'all need your energy for the big game," Big Mama said as she brought them two big plates of food.

Big Mama walked back over to the stove, and brought Alley and me a plate of food too. Mama came downstairs wearing a tank top, and some Capri pants that matched. She had on some new sandals too.

"Wow mama, is that outfit new?" I asked.

"Yeah, do you like it?"

"Yeah, it's cute."

"I think Mike will like it too," said Big Mama with a grin.

"I didn't wear this for him, mom."

"Yeah, right."

Then the doorbell rang, and Pee-Pee stopped eating long enough to bark. Next, Pee-Pee walked to the door with mama.

"Good morning Mr. Davis. Would you like to have some breakfast with us?" Mama asked.

"Sure I would. Thank you very much. Morning everybody!"

"Good morning," we all said in unison.

Mr. Davis walked into the kitchen, and sat down at the table. Big Mama fixed him a plate of food, and sat it in front of him.

"Ben, would you like some coffee?" Big Mama asked.

"Don't mind if I do." He tasted the food and said, "This is wonderful Bertha."

"Thank you."

Mama started to make her plate when the doorbell rang. As usual Pee-Pee walked with mama to the front door.

"Well, hello handsome," mama said. Mike kissed mama on the cheek.

Mr. Davis looked at Big Mama and said, "Why didn't I get a greeting like that?"

"Ben, you've got to be special to get that kind of greeting in the morning," Big Mama said with a smile. "Michelle, let Mike come in the house. Mike, would you like some breakfast?"

"No thank you. I've already eaten," Mike replied, "but I'll have some of that coffee."

Big Mama poured Mike a cup of coffee as he entered the kitchen.

"Okay boys, who are y'all playing against today?" Mike asked.

"The Blue Devils," Jonathan said.

"You mean to tell me that the Blue Devils are playing against the Saints?" Mr. Davis asked. "Well, with a name like Saints, y'all have to win."

"Guys, just remember to have fun," Mike replied.

Soon all the adults were talking about the news. Jordan made faces trying to imitate them talking. Mama was loading the dishwasher at the same time.

"Come on everybody. It's time to go," mama said.

All the kids got into the van with mama and Big Mike. Mr. Davis and Big Mama drove to the game in her big old car. At the game, mama and Mike sat next to Big Mama and Mr. Davis. Alley and I sat in front of them. Mike brought Alley and me a couple of sodas, and chips. Big Mama had a sun visor on with a blue plastic brim. When the light hit it, it made her face look blue. When I looked out into the crowd, I saw daddy and Tammy walking towards the stands.

"Hey Daddy!" I shouted really loud as I waved to him.

Everyone turned to see daddy entering the stands. Tammy had on a really short mini skirt, and a tub top.

Big Mama whispered to mama, "Did she know she was going to a kid's game?"

"Hello everybody," greeted daddy.

Everyone said hello.

"Well, nice to see you again Mike. I didn't think I would see you here today," daddy said.

"I wouldn't miss it for the anything in the world," Mike replied.

Mama interrupted them saying, "Why don't y'all have a seat. The game is about to start."

All the players came out on the field as we all stood, and said the *"Pledge of Allegiance to the Flag."* Then the announcer shouted, "Play ball!"

Big Mama and Mr. Davis loved the game. They were cheering so loud it seemed like they wanted to be on the field playing too. The first inning had begun, and Jonathan was pitching. Jordan played center fielder. Player twenty-four from the Blue Devil's team was up to bat. The first two pitches were strikes. But the third pitch was a hit. Player twenty-four ran to first base, but before he got there, he tripped over his shoe strings, and landed face down.

A fat kid at first base yelled, "Wipe out!"

The right fielder threw the ball to the first baseman, and twenty-four was out. When the next person got up to bat, the left fielder, and Jordan were tossing a rock back and forth to each other. I don't think they even noticed the other player make it to first base. Jonathan struck one of the players out from the other team, but three of the Blue Devil's players made it to first, second, and third base. The next batter hit the ball towards the left fielder. The left fielder saw the ball coming towards him, but he was too scared to catch it. The ball hit the ground. Jordan picked the ball up, and tried to throw the ball to second base, but two players made it home. The score stayed the same for the next two innings, but the third inning changed the game. Jordan was up to bat. The first pitch across the plate was a strike. Then Jordan got another strike after that. The last pitch Jordan hit the ball to the left fielder, and ran to first base. The boys in the outfield were fighting over the ball, so Jordan stole second base too. When he got there, he celebrated. He started break dancing.

The crowd cheered and shouted, "Go Jordan, Go Jordan!"

Finally, the official had to stop Jordan from dancing. The pitcher from the Blue Devil's team struck out two more of the Saint's players. But, two players from the Saints made it to first and second base while Jordan ran to third base. He barely made it to third base. He had to slide into third base before the official called it safe. The bases were loaded, and the fat kid was up to bat.

A player from the Blue Devil's team turned to Jordan and said, "You will never make it. That kid is too fat to run to first base, and we are going to throw the ball to home plate before you can even get there."

"Don't be so sure of that," Jordan replied.

The first ball the pitcher threw to the fat kid was a strike, but the second ball was a hit. He hit the ball so hard it sailed over the outfield fence. The fat kid barely jogged around the bases. When he got to home base, he didn't break dance like Jordan. He did the twist. He shook his hips all around home plate. The crowd just roared. The Saints were beating the Blue Devils by four to two. The score didn't change for the next two innings.

"Does anybody want anything? I'm going to get something to drink," Mike asked.

We all said, no. Mike got up, and left the stands. Soon I noticed that daddy got up too. Mike was on his way back when my daddy confronted him. "I hope you're enjoying the game," daddy said.

"I'm enjoying the game, and everything else," Mike replied.

"Yeah, I've been there myself. Look Mike, I don't know anything about you, and you don't know anything about me, but those kids out there are all I care about. I'll do anything to protect them if you know what I mean."

Mike walked up to daddy very close, looking him up and down. "I understand your meaning, and I don't hurt kids myself, but I don't take kindly to threats either. And, I don't like my lady to be threatened if you know what I mean."

Daddy looked him in the eyes, and said slowly, "I don't make threats."

"Good. Now, you enjoy the game." Mike left bumping daddy's shoulder out of his way as he walked back to his seat. Daddy turned around glaring at Mike as he walked away. By the time Mike and daddy came back, the game was in the bottom of the sixth, and the bases were loaded.

Jonathan pitched the ball, and the umpire said, "Strike one."

Jonathan looked at the catcher, and he gave him a signal for a fast ball. Jonathan pitched, and the umpire said, "Strike two."

The catcher signaled Jonathan to pitch another fast ball, but this time the batter hit the ball up center field. Jordan ran for the ball, but when he got close enough to catch it he realized he was stepping in dog poop. The ball fell right in front of him while Jordan tried to wipe the poop off his shoe in the grass. The second baseman ran for the ball, and so did the other two out fielders. When they all tried to go for the ball, all three players crashed into Jordan. All four of the other team's players made it to home base. The Blue Devils won the game six to four. The coach tried to calm the Saints down at the same time the Blue Devils were celebrating. Finally, when the Saint's player stopped being mad at Jordan, they shook the other team's hands. I looked back into the stands to see daddy and Tammy getting up, and walking towards the dugout. We all got up, and were headed in the same direction. The other kids were leaving with their parents while the coach was washing the back of Jordan's shoes off with a hose. When the coach finished, Jordan and Jonathan walked over to us waving goodbye to the coach.

We all said, good game, to Jordan and Jonathan, but not daddy. He said, "Son, you can't worry about a little dog doo-doo on your shoe. You have to catch that ball."

"You played a really good game. You will catch that ball next time. Y'all tell your father goodbye," mama interrupted.

Jordan, Jonathan, and I hugged daddy and said goodbye. After the game, we all went to a pizza restaurant.

Chapter 11
Independence Day

After we got back from the restaurant, everyone came to our house. Even though mama made Jordan and Jonathan washed their hands at the restaurant, they were so dirty that they had to take a bath when they got home. Big Mama and Mr. Davis spent most of the evening sitting outside on the newly painted front porch. They sat there playing cards, and drinking tea most of the afternoon before Mr. Davis decided to go home. Mike left shortly after we got home. Alley and I played with Pee-Pee for a little while before we went over to Plump's house. Mrs. Madison gave us some lollipops as Plump, Alley, and I walked back to my house. We played jump rope, Jacks, and cards before Plump said she had to go home too.

Sunday after church, Mr. Davis came by to eat dinner with us. I could tell that Mr. Davis and Big Mama were becoming really good friends. Since Big Mama has been living with us, I've seen more of Mr. Davis than I have seen all year. He also bought Pee-Pee a treat today. I think Pee-Pee is starting to like Mr. Davis too. Mama and Big Mike went to a barbecue at Sharon's house today. Mama said Sharon's husband had to work tomorrow, so they had to have their barbecue today. I looked out of my window to see mama and Mike coming up the driveway. Then I saw mama and Mike kissing on the front steps. Yuck! I was so ashamed. Don't they know that the neighbors might see them? I turned from the window to see Alley asleep in my bed. She had become the sister I have never had. It will be hard to see her go back home. I left the window and went to bed too.

*****

Today was the Fourth of July, and it was also my brother's birthday. The Fourth was on a Friday, and mama didn't have to go to work. She didn't have to work at Mrs. Jenkins house either. Mama asked Sharon to sit with Mrs. Jenkins, so that she could give my little brothers a party. The party didn't begin until three o'clock in the afternoon. Mama decided to have the party at the park by the lake front. The lake was crystal clear, and beautiful as the sky. The park was full of people riding bikes, walking, and just celebrating Independence Day. There were street artist painting portraits of the lake, and venders selling carnival style foods to the pedestrians walking by. The lake was filled with paddle boats, and some of the native water fowl migrated to a small island to get away from the crowds of people in the park. A few birds were being fed by the people at the picnic tables. We all got to the park early to set up everything for the party. Mama rented the covered grill picnic area which was close to the bathrooms, and soda machines. This picnic area looked like a large dinning room with a huge grill in the front of it. There was a small kitchen behind the grill that had a refrigerator, and a huge sink. Big Mike and mama brought out an extra table from his truck to set the food on. The table was covered with a red, white, and blue banner. There were little flags tied to the poles that held the roof up, and a big banner that read: *Happy Birthday Jonathan and Jordan*! The multitude of grills in the park filled the air with the smell of grilled meat. Mike was grilling ribs, chicken, hotdogs, and hamburgers on the big grill under the covered picnic area. Mama was putting covered dishes of sliced fruit, vegetables, different kinds of chips, and hamburger and hotdog buns on the table. She put a large cooler full of juices, and sodas at the end of the table. I saw Uncle Pete slip a case of beer into the cooler when mama wasn't looking.

"We'll just cover those with ice. No one will ever know they're there," Uncle Pete said to Alley and me when we passed by.

Mama put three empty trays on the table for the meats. Soon people started to arrive. Our usual friends, Plump, Teach, Carlos, and their parents were there, but soon it seemed like the whole neighborhood showed up. Mama gave out hats and horns to the kids at the party. Mr. Davis was sitting by the grill with Big Mike, and Uncle Pete. Of course, Uncle Pete was trying to get Mr. Davis to drink a beer. Even Mr. Muhammad came to the party. He gave out candy to all the kids. Big Mama tried to fix him a plate of ribs, but he said he doesn't eat pork. June-Bug and a couple of big kids from down the street were setting off bottle rockets which sent the ducks flying off in all directions. The park official lady came over, and stopped them. She said if they didn't stop, they would have to pay a fine. There were so many people at the party that a few of them were sitting on the ground on blankets. When people slowly stopped coming to the table to graze, mama tried to get everyone's attention.

"Listen up everybody," mama said. "Today is the ninth birthday of my two sons, Jordan and Jonathan."

The crowd began to clap.

"If you please, we would like for everyone to sing *Happy Birthday* to Jordan and Jonathan."

Jordan and Jonathan sat at the front table with Alley, Plump, Teach, Carlos, and I looking *Twiddle Dumb and Twiddle Dumber* again. Jordan and Jonathan started singing louder than anyone else at the party.

Mama brought out the cake, but before she could say, make a wish, Jordan blew out the candles.

"Jordan!" Jonathan yelled.

Big Mama served the cake on *"Spider Man"* plates to the guests. Uncle Pete went back to Big Mama's big old car, and pulled out one of the biggest portable stereos that I've ever seen. Uncle Pete turned the stereo on to some R&B music.

Then he turned to Big Mike, and said, "Let's get this party started right."

Soon people gathered on the grass, and started dancing. Even Big Mama and Mr. Davis started to dance. Uncle Pete grabbed some lady that I have never seen before, and pulled her out onto the grass to dance. She had the biggest hips that I have ever seen. When she danced, her hips seemed to dance all by themselves. I think my uncle noticed that too. Mama and Big Mike burst out in laughter when they saw them. Soon mama and Mike walked out onto the grass to dance. When mama and Mike came back to the table, I saw daddy walking toward us.

"Daddy!" I shouted as I ran to give him a hug.

When my brothers saw daddy, they ran over to give him a hug too. Soon Tammy followed behind daddy. She had on some unbelievable short shorts, and a tank top. Even I was shocked by this outfit.

"Good evening, James," mama said. "You are late."

"Better late than never," daddy replied. "Hello Mike. Looks like I'm seeing more of you all the time."

"Yes," Mike said, "and it's going to stay that way too."

"James, would you like some cake?" Big Mama asked as she walked up behind daddy.

"Yes, thank you," he replied.

"Hey everyone," Tammy said as she stood beside daddy.

Mama didn't speak to her.

"This is for the boys." Tammy held out two gift boxes in her hands.

"Thank you," Big Mama replied. "I'll take them. Why don't y'all have a seat, and enjoy the party."

James and Tammy found a seat near mama and Big Mike.

"So," Mike said to mama, "I still can't believe he left you for that hood rat. You are a beautiful woman, and don't you ever forget that."

"Do you want something to drink?" Mama asked smiling at Mike.

"Yeah," Mike said, but when mama stood up Mike pulled her back down into his lap, and kissed her deeply. The passionate kiss made her moan softly. When he released her, she was a bit dazed.

"I'll have a cola," he replied.

Mama smiled at him, and got up. Mike leaned back in the chair grinning. He could sense someone was staring at him. Mike turned to see James glaring at him from behind. He just smiled, and continued to watch the party. When mama got to the cooler, she pulled out what she thought was a cola, but when she turned the bottle to see the label it was a beer.

"Pete!" Mama yelled.

Big Mike got up, and tried to calm her down. Soon Mike pulled mama back out on the grass to dance again. Mike whispered in mama's ear, and pointed toward Tammy. Tammy was flirting with some young guys by the food table. Mama just laughed as Mike grabbed her, and gave her a hug. Daddy didn't even notice Tammy. Daddy was talking to Mr. Davis and Big Mama. He also got up to visit with a few neighbors he hadn't seen in a long time. The party lasted about another hour. Mama started taking down the decorations, and within twenty minutes all the food was put back in the coolers. The picnic area looked like the party never happened.

"Come on guys. Tell everyone goodbye, and thank y'all for the gifts. It's time to go see the fireworks," said mama.

We all said goodbye to the remaining people at the party, but most of the people had left earlier to go to the fireworks show too.

Uncle Pete unplugged the stereo, and said to everyone, "This thrill is gone," then he left the picnic area.

Jordan, Jonathan, and I ran over to daddy to tell him goodbye. Once all of the remaining food, drinks, and gifts were loaded into the van, we were ready to go. Big Mike loaded the table on the back of his truck before we left. Mama drove home first, but we didn't get out of the van. She took the food into the house. Mike drove up behind her, and unloaded the table taking it to the backyard to put it into the shed. Once Mama came back to the van, Big Mike got into the van with her. Mama drove the van through the city, and up a hill across from "*Vulcan Park*." She parked the van, and everyone got out. We walked to a large opening that was surrounded by a rail. The area looked over a cliff of dark red iron ore boulders. When we walked out onto the opening, we could see the huge backside of the statue of *"Vulcan."* The size of this statue seemed to be magnified in the night sky. It was utterly beautiful.

"Hey," Uncle Pete shouted waving to us to come over. Big Mama and Mr. Davis were sitting near the curb in some folding lawn chairs.

"You made it," he said. "I thought I might have to send a search party after you."

"We had to take the food home first Pete," mama said.

"Well, y'all come on over here. Sorry, all of the chairs have been taken," Uncle Pete motioned towards Big Mama and Mr. Davis.

Mama was carrying a blanket, and said, "That's okay Pete. We'll use this."

Mama and Big Mike spread the blanket over the grass. My brothers, Alley, and I sat in front of mama and Big Mike. Uncle Pete stayed seated on the curve drinking a beer. Soon the fireworks show began. The burst of colorful lights, and the booming sounds made the crowd gasp. Some of the rockets came so close to *"Vulcan"* I thought it was going to hit his naked backside. A few of the rockets looked like giant spiders, and others rockets burst into shades of blue and purple with sparkles dancing at the end. There were so many rockets going off at the end of the show that if you closed your eyes, you'd think you're in a war zone. The fireworks made the statue of *"Vulcan"* light up in the night sky, but I don't think mama or Big Mike saw a thing. When I looked back at them, they were kissing. I mean really kissing. I gave Alley a nudge to turn around. She just giggled when she saw them. Mama and Big Mike continued to kiss under the stars and fireworks until the show was over.

I didn't think Big Mama noticed them until she said, "Now that y'all have decided to come up for a little air, let's go home."

*****

On the way home from summer camp today, I could sense that something strange had just happened. We all made our regular stop at Mr. Muhammad's store, but I knew something would be different when we got home today. When we turned the familiar corner towards our house, Mike's truck and Sharon's car was parked in our driveway. My brothers and Alley walked into the house, but I stopped when I saw the angel on the porch.

"Hello sweet *Ayin*," the angel said. "Today is a wonderful day. Your mother's friend has come home. No longer will she suffer a decaying body, or the evil forces that can influence the hearts of men. But, you must be prepared sweet *Ayin* because the events that follow her death will change your life forever."

The angel walked towards me, and I stepped back.

"Don't be afraid, sweet *Ayin*, for He is always with us. Fulfill your destiny, and bring her mother home."

The angel kissed me on the head, and disappeared. Suddenly, I could hear Pee-Pee howling at the front door. The dog sat at the door, and howled continuously until I walked inside. Big Mama, Mr. Davis, Mike, and Sharon were sitting at the kitchen table when I walked into the house.

"Big Mama what is going on?" I asked.

"Jasmine, I need to tell you something and then I want you to go upstairs with your brothers and Alley. There's no easy way to say this, so I'm just going to say it. Mrs. Jenkins died last night. Your mother maybe upset for a little while, so we all have to be supportive of her right now. Jasmine, are you okay?"

I put my hand over my mouth as the tears rolled down my cheeks. I backed away from them, and ran upstairs. I slowly walked into my room, and sat on the bed. I put my face in my hands, and cried. Alley was crying too. Alley walked from the window and sat on the bed beside me. She put her arm around me without saying a word. Then we heard a car pull into the driveway.

"Alley, that's mama," I said.

I heard mama walking into the house saying, "What is going on? Why is everybody here?"

"Alley, I've got to find out what has happened," I demanded.

We snuck out of my room, and walked to the edge of the steps. I could hear Big Mama talking in the kitchen.

"Michelle, sit down. We want to tell you something," Big Mama said calmly.

"Did something happen to the kids? Why didn't you call me at work?" Mama asked frantically.

"Michelle, Mrs. Jenkins passed away last night," Sharon said.

"What?"

"I took her to the hospital myself, but the doctors couldn't revive her. I'm sorry Michelle," Sharon said tearfully.

"What? No!" Mama replied. "I saw her Thursday, and she was okay. I don't believe this! Why are you saying this, Sharon?" Soon mama's shock turned to rage. "I don't believe you! I'm going over there!"

Mama grabbed her keys, and Mike stood up, and said, "Let me take you." Mike ran behind mama as she left the house.

*****

Mike and Michelle drove to Mrs. Jenkins house without saying a word. When they got to the house, Michelle ran out of the van before Mike could get out. When she got to the door, John, Mrs. Jenkins's son, answered the door.

"John, where is she?" Michelle asked frantically.

"I thought that you would have been told by now," he said. "I am sorry, but her body has been moved from the hospital, and sent to *Smith Funeral Home*. But you can't see her before the funeral on Thursday."

Michelle started to feel faint. Luckily, Mike walked up behind her as soon as she staggered backward.

"Why don't y'all come in, and sit down," John said.

"Thank you," Mike replied holding Michelle up by the waist.

Michelle sat there in the untouched living room chair still in shock.

"Would y'all like something to drink?" John asked.

"Some water please," Mike replied.

John went to the kitchen, and came back with a glass of water.

"Thank you," Mike replied as he handed the glass to Michelle.

"How did she die?" Michelle asked after taking a sip of the water.

John hesitated before he spoke. He didn't want to cause her any more pain. "She had a massive stroke, and stopped breathing. Once Sharon got her to the hospital, the doctors tried to revive her, but her brain was without oxygen for too long. She was technically brain dead when she got there."

Michelle's eyes filled with tears as she began to cry silently.

"She didn't suffer. It all happened really fast." John said.

Michelle closed her eyes, and gave a sigh of relief. "What time will her funeral start John? I want to be there," Michelle said.

"The service will be held at *Smith's Funeral Home* Friday at two o'clock, and followed by the grave-side service."

"Thank you, John," Michelle replied. "I'm sorry for coming here like this. I can't imagine your pain right now and my condolences to you, and your family. Come on Mike. Let's go."

Michelle stood up, and started to walk out of the door when John grabbed her arm.

"Thank you for being her friend," he said. "I know that I haven't been around as often as I should have, but I'm glad that you were here. She really liked you. Thank you for making her last day's happy ones."

He released Michelle's arm, and she left without saying a word. Mike said goodbye to John, and took Michelle home.

*****

Michelle didn't go work on Wednesday. She didn't eat breakfast with her family either. All that day, she either cried in her room, or sat on the porch staring with red swollen eyes looking at the traffic going by. Big Mama tried to get her to eat lunch, but she wouldn't eat. Later on, Mike came by, and sat on the porch swing with Michelle. She put her head on Mike's shoulder, and cried for thirty minutes before Mike walked her back into the house. He took Michelle upstairs to her bedroom, and asked her to lie down for a while. Soon Mike came back with a sandwich for her. She didn't want to eat, but Mike convinced her that she needed to. Once Michelle was asleep for the night, Mike said goodbye to everyone, and left.

The day of the funeral Mike got to our house early. Big Mama tried to get Michelle to eat lunch, but she refused. Mike had on a tailored black suit that fit him handsomely. Michelle wore a simple black dress with her hair pulled back in that same ponytail that she hadn't done this way in a long time. Michelle's downcast face held nothing more than listlessness, and despair when she said goodbye to her family. They all said goodbye to Mike and Michelle at the doorway and then they were gone.

On the way to the funeral, Mike put his hand on Michelle's knee.

"You will need to be strong now. This won't be easy, but maybe it will give you a sense of closure," he said.

Michelle shook her head in agreement without saying a word. Even though she didn't speak, her melancholy eyes spoke volumes. Mike parked the car at the funeral home, and helped her out of the car. They walked into the small funeral home chapel, and found a seat near Mrs. Smith, the morning sitter. Michelle didn't know anyone there besides Mrs. Smith and Mrs. Jenkins's sons, nor did she care. The service was nice, and short. Michelle left the graveyard with Mike's arm around her shoulders.

Once they were in the car, Mike said, "Let's go some place quiet for a while."

Mike called Big Mama on his cell phone, and asked her to watch the kids just a little while longer. He drove Michelle to the lake front. They got out of the car and walked to the gazebo. Because today was a weekday, the park had very few people in it.

"It's beautiful out here today isn't it," Mike said. "You know if you need to talk to someone, I am here."

"I know Mike," Michelle said, "but I just can't help feeling . . ."

"Feeling what?"

"I know you will probably think I'm crazy," she said.

"No, I won't. Please tell me."

Michelle hesitated then she looked away. "I should have been there that night," she said as tears rolled down her cheeks. "Maybe if I was there, she would still be here."

Soon Michelle started to cry hysterically again. Mike put his arms around her shoulders, and pulled her to his chest. He kissed her on the head and said, "Sweet heart, it is normal to feel guilty when someone you loves dies. Everyone goes through this, but it's not your fault. Even if you were there, she would have still died, but your children are your first priority. What would you have told the boys if you couldn't be with them on their birthday? They are only nine years old once in their life times. You don't want to miss out on that, do you?"

Michelle continued to cry on Mike's shoulder. He reached in his pocket to give her a tissue. "Michelle, people die every day. It would be selfish of you to only think about the way she died."

Michelle lifted her head up, and stared at him with swollen eyes. "What?" She asked.

"Michelle, she was your friend. Do you think she would have wanted you to sit here feeling guilty about not being with her on your twin boy's birthday? Think about it this way. The reason you were there is because her own sons didn't have time to spend with her. What would she have given to have spent time with them if she could have? Never feel guilty for spending time with your children no matter what happens. They won't be with you forever, and you can't get this time back. Do the right thing, and honor her memory by remembering the funny and happy moments you spent together. The one fact that is true for all of us is, one day we too will die, but remember that you gave her the best gift anyone could have given her."

Michelle gave Mike a strange look. "What?"

"You gave her your friendship," Mike replied. "She didn't die lonely, or sad because she had you, Michelle."

Michelle stopped crying, and looked out over the lake. She hadn't thought of this before. She knew Mrs. Jenkins wanted her to be off for her kid's party. She even told her to go. Mike was right. If she could have spent this time with her family, she would have given anything to do so.

Michelle smiled slightly, and said, "She was funny. She wanted me to meet you. I think she liked you."

"Yes, Mrs. Jenkins was a sweet old lady," Mike said. "She gave me a twenty dollar tip after she paid me for fixing her car."

"I miss her Mike."

"I know."

Mike kissed Michelle on the side of the head, and held her close on the park bench under the gazebo. Michelle and Mike sat there watching the ducks, and wild water birds float by on the water. Soon the sun began to set.

"Mike, what time is it?" Michelle asked. "I am getting hungry."

"It is almost six o'clock," he replied.

"Let's get something to eat. I'm starving."

Mike smiled as he stood up, and followed her to the car. Somehow, Mike knew that Michelle would be okay now. They drove through the city to a nice restaurant downtown. Mike and Michelle talked about everything except the funeral over dinner. When Michelle got home, the children were already in bed. Big Mama was up waiting when Michelle walked in. Pee-Pee walked over to Michelle, and licked her on the knee. Michelle patted the dog on the head as she entered the room.

"Hey Mom," she said. "Thank you for watching the kids for me."

"Honey, you know I didn't mind. Are you okay baby?"

"I will be."

"God has her now," Big Mama said, "and she is happier than she has ever been. Thank you for being here with my daughter today, Mike. I thought I was going to have to get Mr. Davis to watch the kids, so I could go with her."

"Oh, there's no need to thank me. I would have been there anyway," Mike replied

"Well, I guess I'll just go to bed now," Big Mama said. "Good night y'all."

Michelle and Mike said goodnight to Big Mama, and then they sat down on the couch in the den.

"Thank you for being here with me Mike. I don't know what I would have done these past few days without you." Michelle said. "I feel like you have been here all the time, but we have only known each other for a month."

Mike smiled, and said, "I feel the same way too, and don't thank me so quickly. I wanted to be here to support you through this, but I wanted to be with you for my own selfish reason too. Michelle, I am falling for you very fast, but I know you have just come out of a relationship. So, you probably don't want to get too serious with anyone right now, but I am hoping you will change your mind when you get to know me better."

"You are such a good looking man, Mike," Michelle said looking up into Mike's eyes. Mike started to grin. "No, I mean it. You have gorgeous eyes, beautiful wavy hair, and a dimpled smile that would melt any woman's heart. To top it all, you have a decent job, and you want to start your own business. You could have any woman you want, so why are you here with me?"

"Didn't you hear me?" Mike said. "I think I'm falling for you."

"But Mike, I'm not a young thing anymore. I see how the girls looked at you at church. So, what made you even look at me in the first place?"

Mike stared at Michelle intensely for a moment. "Your ex-husband has really done a number on you."

Michelle gasped a little, and looked away.

"He's got you believing that you aren't beautiful, or that nobody would want you," Mike said as he lifted Michelle's chin with his finger to look her into her eyes. "He even knows this is a lie. You should have seen how he looked at me when I kissed you in the park. If his eyes were bullets, I would be dead right now."

"He was looking at us?" Michelle asked with a little surprise.

"Oh yes," Mike said, "and he is jealous too, now that he sees that another man appreciates what he has taken for granted for so long. When I said you are beautiful Michelle, I meant it. You are a forty year old woman with a figure of a twenty year old. Your breasts are still firm, and your ass just speaks to me."

"That's enough Mike," Michelle said as she started to blush. Mike just grinned.

"Michelle, you have everything I want in a woman. You are beautiful, and smart. You just have to believe it yourself."

"I am a very lucky woman to have you, Mike."

"Yes, you are," he replied. Then he leaned over to Michelle and kissed her. The amorous kiss seemed to take her breath away.

"I've got to go," he said finally, "but I'll be here tomorrow, okay."

Mike stood up, and helped Michelle off the couch. They walked to the door. Mike kissed Michelle's brow, and left.

Michelle went to work on Monday, but she and Mike spent most of the evening and night together with the whole family before he went home.

Chapter 12
Caught in the Act

This was the first week that mama didn't have to go to Mrs. Jenkins house. Even though she had more time for herself and family, she still missed her friend. Today was Saturday and my brothers had another baseball game. When mama came downstairs, we all sat at the table eating breakfast.

"Good morning," Big Mama said. "I didn't think we would see you up this early."

"I was already up anyway. I couldn't sleep last night," mama said as she poured herself a cup of coffee.

"Are you going to eat breakfast with us today?" Big Mama asked.

She looked at the adorable faces of her family, and said, "Yeah."

Mama fixed her plate, and Pee-Pee walked over to her licking her on the knee. The dog sat at her feet panting, and seemed to have a smile on his face. The smile on the silly dog's face touched mama's heart in some way. She couldn't resist the temptation to feed him any longer. She gave the begging dog a piece of bacon from the pan. Pee-Pee took the bacon, and ran to his bed to eat it.

"Michelle, if you start feeding that dog from the table, he will start to beg," Big Mama warned.

"It just one piece of bacon and I couldn't resist him," mama said smiling at the dog. Then she looked back up, and said, "mom--?"

"You don't even have to ask," Big Mama interrupted. "I'm taking the kids to the game today, but I will need to use your van. Ben is coming with me, and there isn't enough room in my car."

"Sure, you can take it. Thank you."

Big Mama patted mama on the shoulder, and smiled at her. Soon the doorbell rang Pee-Pee gave a bark. Mama answered the door with Pee-Pee at her side.

"Good morning Mr. Davis. Would you like to have some breakfast with us?" Mama asked.

"Don't mind if I do," Mr. Davis replied.

Mr. Davis walked into the kitchen saying good morning to everyone. Mama found another chair for Mr. Davis to sit on at the table with the rest of us. She fixed Mr. Davis plate, and he said, "Okay boys, who are y'all playing today?"

"The Hawks," Jonathan replied.

"Good, so y'all are just going to send them off flying today." We all laughed.

"We hope so Ben," Big Mama replied.

We finished eating, and everyone said goodbye to mama as she waved to us from the front door.

Michelle cleaned the kitchen, and went upstairs to take a shower. When she got dressed, she came back downstairs to watch TV. Pee-Pee lay down on the rug at her feet with his eyes closed. An hour and a half had passed and she knew the kids would be home soon. Michelle still felt a certain amount of emptiness inside as she sat there. She didn't even watch the TV that was on. She just stared outside of the window. Then she realized that she had an even bigger problem. The second job she had come to rely on was now gone. She didn't have a clue about what she was going to do next, but right now she couldn't think about that. Suddenly, there was a knock at the door. Michelle answered the door with reliable Pee-Pee at her side.

"*Belle dame bonjour,*" Mike said as he entered the front door.

"Well, good morning to you too," Michelle replied.

"Your mother said you would be here today, so I thought that I might stop by. But, if you want to be alone, I'll . . .," Mike waited for her answer.

"No, I am glad that you're here," Michelle replied.

"I have something for your dog."

"He's not my dog." Michelle replied.

"Yeah right. Well, anyway, here boy." Mike bounced the ball to Pee-Pee. The dog's ears stood up on top of his head, and he took off chasing the ball into the corner of the room. Pee-Pee rolled around on the floor with the ball in his mouth. Then he took the ball back to his bed, and began chewing on it. Michelle stood there in shock. Then she just laughed. "I've never seen him do that before," she said.

"It's good to see you smile."

"And it's good to just see you. Let's sit down. Do you want something to drink?" She asked.

"No," Mike said. "How are you doing today?"

"Okay I guess, but now I have a bigger problem."

"What?" Mike asked with a concerned look.

"I don't have a second job now. I relied on that second income to help me pay my bills. I'm going to look for another job, but it takes time to find one. I don't know what I am going to do right now."

"Michelle, you know I said that I would help you."

"I know Mike, but . . ."

"No buts, Michelle. Your family needs a roof over their heads. Don't be too proud to accept help. I will help you out until you find something else."

"How can I thank you Mike?"

"We'll talk about that later," he said with a grin.

Michelle started to laugh. "You're crazy Mike." She laughed again. "Tell me something, how long do you think it will take you to open up your own business?"

"Right now, I'm to busy with my construction job to start on that, but by the fall I will have enough money to put a down payment on a building I've been looking at."

"Who are you going to finance it with?" Michelle asked.

"Well, I'm not sure," he replied.

"I work with some people who could help you, and I know someone who could even help you with your bookkeeping."

"I think I may need your help after all," Mike replied.

"I would be glad to help."

"You know something," Mike said. "I think you could run your own business."

"Really?" Michelle said with a raised brow.

"Yeah. That's what you do everyday at your job for someone else. You do the finances for other companies, so why can't you do the same for yourself? Tell me Michelle, if you could run your own business, what would it be?"

"I don't know." Then Michelle thought for a moment. "I would like to open an elderly sitting service. There are so many people who don't want to put their family members in a nursing home, but they have to work. Someone has to stay with these people because they can't be left alone anymore. I think it would be a good alternative to having a sitter come to their homes. The cost would be cheaper than a home sitter because of the volume of people we would serve. I've been sitting for two years with Mrs. Jenkins, so I don't see why I can't do the same thing at a central location. I couldn't take the really ill or severely disabled patients though. We could only accept the patients that needed a little help in their daily routine."

Mike sat there amazed. "You should really consider doing this," he said. "I think you would do a great job. I mean it. You should go into business for yourself. You told me you didn't like your first job, so you should really consider this."

"Mike, where would I get the money to start my own business?"

"Borrow it."

"With what? I don't have that kind of collateral," Michelle replied. "You've saved some money up for your business already, but I have nothing. Banks won't just give you a loan without some kind of collateral."

"What about your house," Mike asked.

"No. I won't risk losing my house, Mike. This may be something I might do in the future, but not now. I'm glad you believe in me. My ex said he could survive without me, but I couldn't survive without him. He didn't even believe I could take care of this house. Now, it looks like he might be right."

"So, that is why you won't accept my help," Mike realized.

"Mike, I don't want to depend on another man to come to my rescue every time I get into trouble. I need to stand on my own two feet now. Please understand that."

Mike kissed Michelle on the head, and said, "Michelle, I do believe in you, but you have to believe in yourself no matter what anyone says. Think about this. Who put you through school?"

"I did," she said.

"When did James stop paying bills around here?"

Michelle thought about this for a moment and then she said, "His paycheck would be short sometimes. This went on for two months. I got a second job, so that our lights wouldn't get cut off."

"I'll bet he wasn't coming home as much either during this time."

"How did you know?" Michelle asked.

Mike looked up at Michelle, and said, "It's hard trying to take care of two households unless you're rich."

"I guess you're right."

"Michelle, are you telling me that you put yourself through school, you're taking care of your house by yourself for over six months, and you've even moved your mother in here, but you don't believe that you can survive without him?"

"Well, when you put it that way, I guess I am surviving without him, or at least I was. What am I going to do now?"

"First, you are going to stop listening to your ex-husband," Mike said. "He just said those things to hurt you. I know men like him. As long as they can make you feel like nothing, you will never think that you can do any better. Don't allow him to keep hurting you now that he's gone. Allow me to help you. We all need some help sometimes, and this doesn't mean that you are incapable of doing things on your own either. Because I believe in you, I want to help you. Don't shut me out."

Michelle leaned her head on Mike's chest. "They're not many men like you anymore Mike. How did I get to be so lucky?"

"I think I'm the lucky one." He replied softly.

He lifted her chin, and began kissing her. Mike leaned Michelle back on the couch kissing her deeply. His kisses were passionate, but his hands were gentle. He released her mouth to cover her jaw with warm soft kisses. Michelle's hand stroked Mike's back, and caressed his tense shoulders. He started to nibble on her ear, and whispered something in her ear in French. Hearing the French Creole whispers in her ear sent shivers down her spine. She knew at this moment she wanted this man. These feelings were new to her. The first time she made love to her ex-husband she was a young girl, and scared. Now, she was a woman with desires. She had no resistance to deny him anything. Even the smell of this man was intoxicating. Mike's hands slide from her shoulder, and moved slowly over the hardened peeks of her firm breast. He didn't want to move too fast with her. He didn't want her to feel like he was out to get one thing, but he had to touch her, to taste her. The thought of this made his manhood ache with desire. He propped himself up on his forearms, and peered into Michelle's dazed eyes.

"Let me touch you," he whispered in her ear.

His hands slid to the hem of her t-shirt pulling it above her breast. Mike's eyes feasted upon her chocolate brown skin, and firm breast.

"Wait a minute," Michelle said. "Let me undo it." Michelle unhooked the bra from the front. Mike slid down between her thighs to her chest saying, "*Votre corps est si parfait*," which means, your body is perfect, but Michelle didn't understand a word of it. Still, the French speaking Creole aroused her. Then he lowered his head to the harden nipple, and took it into his mouth. Michelle arched her back, and gave into a deep moan. Mike's tongue flick, and teased the swollen peek sending little shock waves to her groin. After he paid such loving attention to the first nipple, he soon surrounded the other with his warm lips, and playful tongue. Michelle shamelessly moaned even louder as he sucked the swollen peak. His hand cupped the other breast, and soon his finger tips began to massage her perky swollen nipple. He released the nipple from his lips, but allowed his hand to enjoy the other breast. He kissed the side of her neck sending the familiar shivers down her spine.

"Let me touch you Michelle," he pleaded with sweet whispers in her ear.

Michelle's breathing increased rapidly as Mike's hand slid down her stomach disappearing underneath her shorts. She grabbed his wrist, but his hand stayed firmly in place. Michelle turned to see Mike's eyes staring into hers. Then he began teasing the little knob. Michelle turned her head from Mike moaning loudly as she gripped his wrist harder. Mike placed loving kisses on her brow as he continued to tease, and heighten her arousal.

"Don't hold back Michelle," he whispered into her ear.

She couldn't even if she wanted too. Her moans grew louder, and louder. Her head tossed back and forth like a mad man. Finally, she arched her back, and screamed her released. Mike's finger plunged into her little tight canal feeling the little contraction before he let her go completely. Michelle lay there gasping for breath still gripping Mike's wrist. Mike slid down, and kissed Michelle's stomach causing her stomach to tremble. Then he sat up, and turned away from her. Michelle sat up on her forearms.

"What's wrong?" She asked.

"Michelle, I can't do this anymore. I want you so badly it hurts. This teasing is driving me insane. I want to make love to you, but not just this once. Your very presence is like a drug to me, and I just can't seem to get enough of you. But--," Mike paused. Then he turned to face her. "I don't want you to think that I'm running some kind of game on you. Michelle, I can wait to make love to you for as long as you would like me to, but when you're ready, I promise you won't be disappointed, or unsatisfied."

"Mike, I want you now," Michelle said. Michelle's sudden aggressiveness took Mike by surprise. "Come on. Let's go upstairs."

Soon as they stood up, and turned to walk upstairs. Suddenly, the front door opened. Michelle realized her bra was still unhooked, and her t-shirt was above her breast. She could hear the voices of her screaming kids celebrating on the porch. Mike turned to Michelle as she dashed off into the laundry room. Mike realized his clothing was a little disheveled too. He turned around quickly to tuck his shirt back in his shorts.

Suddenly, the boys ran into the den shouting, "We won! We won!"

Then they grabbed Mike around the waist hugging him on either side. Mike hugged them around the shoulders, and said, "That's great guys!"

Soon Big Mama walked into the door after Alley and me.

Michelle walked back into the room from the kitchen. "Hey guys," she said.

"We won! We won!" Jordan and Jonathan shouted as they grabbed Michelle around the waist almost knocking her down.

"Great guys," she said.

Big Mama walked into the room looking around very suspiciously. She looked down at the disheveled couch and then turned to Mr. Davis giving him a mischievous grin.

"Well, hello Mike," Big Mama said mischievously.

"Hello," Mike said with a smile.

"Hey y'all. How was the game?" Michelle asked.

Big Mama nudged Mr. Davis saying, "Oh the game was really good. Looks like you're in a good mood Michelle." Then Big Mama turned to Mr. Davis smiling.

"Michelle," Mike said putting his arm around her waist, "why don't we take the kids to the skating rink this afternoon to celebrate, so your mother can have the day off."

Jordan, Jonathan, Alley and Jasmine started jumping up, and down cheering.

"Boys go upstairs, and take a shower. We'll wait on the porch for y'all when you're ready," said Michelle.

Then Michelle and Mike walked outside the front door to the swing.

"Ben, would you like a glass of tea?" Big Mama asked.

"Don't mind if I do," he said.

Mr. Davis and Big Mama walked to the kitchen. Mr. Davis sat at the table while Big Mama poured him a glass of tea. Once Big Mama sat down with Mr. Davis, Jasmine walked into the kitchen.

Alley followed behind her when Jasmine said, "Big Mama, Mike is coming around a lot now, isn't he?"

"I guess so," Big Mama replied.

"Big Mama, do you think daddy will ever come back?"

"Jasmine, your mama and daddy have separated. I don't think he will be coming back here anytime soon, but even though they have separated from each other, they will never separate from you Jasmine. Your parents love you, and your brothers. They will always be there for you all."

"Why did they separate, Big Mama? When mama came to pick us up from your house, daddy was already gone when we got home and he never came back."

Big Mama sighed, and said, "Jasmine, sit down. You too Alley."

Alley and Jasmine sat down at the table with Big Mama and Mr. Davis.

"Jasmine, sometimes people change over time, and want to move on. Your daddy wanted to move on in a different direction in his life than your mother. So that's what he did."

"He wanted to move on with Tammy," Jasmine said but Big Mama didn't respond. "Big Mama, we don't see him as much anymore. Did he want to move on from us too? What did we do to make him want to leave us?"

"No child," Big Mama said shaking her head. "The problems your mom and dad are having are their problems, not yours. You didn't do anything. You don't see your daddy as much anymore because he doesn't live here anymore. How can I make you understand? Jasmine let me tell you a story about Tamu. Tamu was a young girl in West Africa who lived with her mother, father, and older brother Bem. Bem grew tired of living in his small village where he was known, and loved. He thought that the only way out of the village was to take a horse that belongs to his sister Tamu. Tamu loved her brother. She would have done anything for him, even given him the horse if he had asked her too.

One night Bem snuck out of his house, and took the horse leaving the village. Well, Tamu was heart broken. Not only was her beloved brother gone, but he also took her horse that helped the family on the small farm. Tamu's parents were heart broken too. Bem did finally get to the other village, but it wasn't what he had hoped for. He thought this place would be exciting, but as soon as his money ran out, the excitement just seemed to run out too. Bem came back home penniless, and without the horse. He sold Tamu's horse to buy some food to eat. When his father and mother saw him, they ran to him and hugged him. They were happy he was alive, and home. Tamu was angry. She wondered how could a brother she loved do this to her. She wouldn't talk to him when she saw him.

Bem's father sat down with him after dinner, and said, 'You are a man now, Bem. Whatever you were searching for out there you need to find it. You can not stay here, but you are always welcome home to visit. The next time you return to us you will have a new horse for your sister.'

Bem agreed. The next day he packed up his things, and left. By the time he reached the field Tamu ran behind him crying. She gave him a big hug. Do you know what she realized that day?" Big Mama asked.

Alley and I shook our heads, and said, "No."

"She learned that even when someone makes a mistake you can still love them, and love doesn't end because that person is far away," Big Mama said.

Soon my brothers ran downstairs all fresh and clean.

"Come on y'all!" Jordan shouted. "Let's go!" They told Big Mama and Mr. Davis goodbye, and they ran outside on the porch.

After everyone ate lunch, Big Mike drove the van to "*Wally's Skate Palace.*" Jasmine's brothers jumped out of the van racing Alley, and Jasmine to the ticket booth. Jonathan beat them. After we rented our skates, we all got onto the floor. The flashing neon lights changed with every beat of the music. Even the music changed from rock, rap, R&B, to country. Mama held hands with Alley and me. We begin spinning around in a circle together in the middle of the rink. Then we skated off together holding hands. Jordan and Jonathan were racing to catch up to Mike. When Jordan got to Mike, Mike picked him up high in the air spinning him around.

Soon as Mike put Jordan down, he shouted, "Spin me again Mike!"

Then Jonathan wanted to spin around. They were spinning so much I got sick just looking at them.

"That's enough guys," Mike said. Mike skated off the floor, and sat on a carpet covered bench. Soon mama joined him.

"I am having so much fun here," Mike said. "You know something, I feel like I'm apart of your family now. Since my wife died, I've been alone up here. It's nice to have a family again."

Michelle just smiled. "Will I have to adopt you too?" She asked.

"Please," he pleaded.

"I don't need anymore mouths to feed." She said with a grin.

"Oh, don't worry *belle dame*. I will take care of everyone." Then he kissed mama on the cheek. "Are you thirsty?"

"Yeah," she replied.

"I'll get some drinks for everyone."

"Let me help you," mama said.

Mike and mama walked over to the concession stand, and brought back the drinks to a small table near the skating rink's floor. She waved to us to come over to the table. Alley and I got to the table first, but we slowed down before they actually got there. My brothers came toward the table at full speed. Mike caught Jonathan before he hit the table, but Jordan slammed right into it.

"Jordan!" Mama shouted.

Alley and I grabbed our drinks just in time, but mama had to hold the others steady on the table. Some of the drinks spilled, but the majority of the drink stayed in the cups.

"Okay Jordan," Mike said. "If you spill mine, you'll owe me a drink."

Jordan's eyes were really big when he looked at his mother. Then he slowly turned, and sat at the table.

"I still beat you Jordan," Jonathan said. Then he stuck his tongue out at Jordan.

"Stop it guys," mama said sternly.

"Hey guys, are y'all going to be in the races?" Mike asked.

"No, I'm going to dance," Jordan said.

"Sounds like fun. I might try this dance myself," Mike said.

"Come on Jonathan. It's time to go."

Jordan grabbed his cup, and drained it. He stood up with the cup skating behind Big Mike. Jordan poured the cup of ice down the back of Mike's shirt.

"Got yah sucker!" Jordan shouted as he skated away laughing.

Jonathan was laughing so hard he almost fell off the bench. After watching Mike struggle to get the ice out of his shirt, Jonathan skated off the meet Jordan. Mama started to go after Jordan, but Mike stopped her.

"I got this," he said. Mike snuck up behind Jordan while he was still bragging to Jonathan about what he just did. Mike grabbed Jordan by the back of the pants, and dumped his cup of ice in the back of Jordan's pants. Jordan ran to the bathroom holding his bottom, and yelling.

Mike came back to the table, and said, "I think he learned his lesson."

Mama gave him a grin, and shook her head. "Now, I think I have three boys instead of two."

"I'll go in, and check on them." Mike left the table, and went in to the bathroom. A few minutes later he came out with Jordan and Jonathan. They were laughing again, so mama figured there were no hard feelings. When they came back to the table Jordan's pants had a small wet spot on the back, and so did Mike's shirt. Soon the DJ started to play the music, and called all the dancers to the dance floor. They got on the dance floor, and danced.

After we left the skating rink, Mike didn't drive them home. Instead, he drove them to Sharon's house.

"Why are we here Mike?" Mama asked.

Mike parked the van, and turned to Michelle. "Michelle, Sharon is your friend, and where I come from that's a hard thing to find. Anytime you've called her, she has been there for you. She was there the night Mrs. Jenkins died. You were pretty hard on her when she tried to tell you about Mrs. Jenkins. I think you should talk to her. Come on Michelle. You owe her that much."

"I know Mike, but I don't know what to say to her."

"Just say, I'm sorry."

Mike pushed the locks, and opened the van doors. They all got out of the van, and walked to the front door. Mike rang the door bell, and Mr. Greg, Sharon's husband, answered the door. Mr. Greg shook Mike's hand, and gave mama a hug.

Mr. Greg greeted the children, and said, "It's so nice to see y'all this evening. Sharon didn't tell me that y'all were coming by. I would have prepared something for you."

"She didn't know we were coming by," Mike said. "Michelle wanted to speak to Sharon. Is she here?"

"Oh yeah. She's in the den. Y'all want to come in?" Mr. Greg asked.

"No, no," Mike said, "but if you aren't busy, I thought we could sit out here on the porch, and talk for a while so the girls can be alone."

"Sure, sure." Mr. Greg agreed. "Michelle, you go on inside. You know where she is."

Big Mike and Mr. Greg sat on the porch talking like two little old men. We played with a ball we found in the yard as mama walked into the house.

"Hi Sharon," mama said as she entered the den.

"Hey! I didn't think I would see you for a while. How are you doing anyway?" Sharon asked.

"I'll be okay I guess, but Sharon I want to say that I'm sorry for the way I acted."

"Michelle, I understand. It can't be easy to hear news like that. Come over here, and sit down."

"Sharon, how are you?"

"I'm okay, but I've never been through anything like that before."

"Sharon, I'm sorry to put you in that situation. I knew she was sick, but I never though this would happen. Are you mad at me?" Mama tried to anticipate her answer.

"I'm not mad at you. You couldn't have known she was going to die, and don't worry about what you said to me either. I probably would have said the same thing to you. But, I have to say, I was getting a little jealous of your friendship with her. For a minute it looked like Mrs. Jenkins had taken my place."

"Sharon, no one could take your place. Give me a hug."

Michelle and Sharon hugged each other on the couch and then Sharon said, "Now, tell me about that pretty man you have out there. Girl, he is fine, and you said he wants to start his own business."

"Yeah. He has the money saved, and he has even picked out a location."

"Michelle, he is going into business for himself, and he likes kids too. Girl, I think he is the one."

"Sharon, we haven't known each other but a month."

"Michelle, girl, don't you let that good looking man go. Believe me, ain't nothing out there."

"I'm not looking to get married again, okay. I've only been divorced for a month, and one week."

"Michelle, get real," Sharon said. "Your ex was dating Tammy for at least eight months, if not more, before you got a divorced. You hardly saw him during that time. For two months he stayed gone before the divorce was finalized. Honey, you hadn't had a man in almost two years. Michelle, it's time to move on."

"I just don't want to get hurt again," she said with her eyes cased down.

"I know, but you're going to have to take a chance sometime, and he's a pretty one."

"He is good looking, isn't he," mama replied giggling.

"Uh huh," Sharon agreed.

"I think I'll play with him for a little while."

"Play! I wish I could play like that." Sharon said with a giggle.

Sharon and mama started to laugh. Then they talked about everything that had been going on in their life since they parted. They continued to talk until it was time to go home.

Chapter 13
Mr. McBeavie

Monday after summer camp, we were in the kitchen with Big Mama. She was baking some chocolate chip cookies for us and telling us one of her stories. Mama came into the kitchen, and sat down to listen too.

Suddenly, the doorbell rang. Mama and Pee-Pee answered the door.

"Hey beautiful," Mike said as he entered the room.

"What, no French?" Mama replied.

"*Madame*, the day isn't over." Then he kissed mama on the hand.

"Hey Mike. Would you like to have a cookie?" Big Mama asked.

"Sure," Mike said. He walked into the kitchen with mama behind him.

"How was work today, Mike?" Mama asked.

"Today, I hung off the side of a building for two hours, and then I stayed in the mud the rest of the day," he replied.

"You're very clean for a man that plays in the mud all day and what kind of mud smells that good?" Big Mama asked mischievously.

"I've been off work since two o'clock today. I go to work very early in the morning. When I get home, I take a shower, and work on my next job. That is if I have one at the time," Mike said.

Big Mama looked out of the corner of her eye giving Mike a mischievous grin saying, "That still doesn't explain that sweet smell." Then she winked at us.

"Oh, it's just a little something I thought I'd put on. Do you like it?"

"Oh yes Mike. How about you Michelle, do you like it?" Big Mama asked with a little grin.

"Mike always smells good," Mama said.

Suddenly, there was another knock at the door.

"Who could this be?" Big Mama asked. "I know it isn't Ben. He went to visit his daughter today."

"Mom, I'll get it," Mama said.

"No. You stay here with Mike, and have a cookie. I'll get it." Big Mama walked to the door, and said, "Who is it?"

"Ma'am my name is Mr. McBeavie. I'm the lawyer for the late Mrs. Jenkins."

The man had a thick southern accent when he approached Big Mama at the front door. He was a rather large white man with big belly, and one of the worst comb-over hair do's I have seen in this whole creation. His suit was a size too small, and his tie was hanging loosely around his neck. His whole appearance was a bit disheveled. He was carrying a briefcase, but the worst thing he was carrying was a cigarette in his mouth. When he talked, the cigarette would jump to every movement of his lips.

"Ma'am is Michelle Patterson here?" He asked.

"Yes sir," Big Mama replied. "But, ain't no smoking in this house."

"Oh, excuse me," he said.

He took a long drawl on the cigarette, and flicked the bud into the grass. Big Mama gasped.

"Man, my grass ain't no ashtray!" Shouted Big Mama.

"Well, where would you like for me to put it?" He asked.

"Put it in those trash cans out there."

Mr. McBeavie walked off the porch saying something under his breath which I believe was a curse word. He stepped on the bud to put it out, and then he picked up, and put it in the trash can. When he came back to the door, he said slightly out of breath and a little annoyed, "May I speak to Mrs. Patterson now?"

"Yes, come on in," Big Mama said very sweetly. "Michelle, someone is here to see you."

All of us walked out of the kitchen to see who it was. Pee-Pee walked over to the man, and sniffed his pants legs.

"Ma'am, will that dog bite?" He asked.

"Nah, he's just trying to figure out who you are," mama replied. "Come here Pee-Pee."

Pee-Pee left the man, and sat down at mama's side.

"Ma'am, may I have a seat?" Mr. McBeavie asked.

"Sure. Everyone let's go into the den."

After everyone found a seat, Mr. McBeavie said, "My name is Jim McBeavie. I've been Mrs. Jenkins's attorney for more than thirty years."

He reached into his pocket, and handed mama his card. "Ma'am, have you been Mrs. Jenkins's sitter for the last two years?" He asked.

"Yes sir," mama replied.

"Well ma'am, I don't doubt that you were, but my office requires me to see some kind of identification before I can go any further with this conversation," Mr. McBeavie continued.

"Hold on I'll go get my license out of my purse." Mama walked upstairs while we curiously waited to find out what this mysterious man was here for. When mama got back downstairs, she handed Mr. McBeavie her license. "Here. See, it's me," mama replied.

"Thanks ma'am," he said. "Last Friday was the reading of Mrs. Jenkins's final Will and Testament. Most of her belongs, and money was divided between her two sons, but she left you something too."

"Really?" Mama said in shock. "She didn't say anything to me about it."

"She didn't say anything to her sons either. If they had any idea of what she was doing, well let's just say that I wouldn't be here right now. Mrs. Jenkins wanted me to keep this quiet until she passed." Then he began to chuckle. "You should have seen the looks on those boy's faces. Man, I though I was going to have to take a pill. That was priceless."

He continued to laugh. We stared at each other then looked back at him.

"Sir," mama interrupted, "I don't mean to rush you, but what did she leave me?"

"Oh yes." Mr. McBeavie opened his briefcase to take out an envelope, his glasses and some papers. Then he put his glasses on.

"Mrs. Jenkins wanted to make sure all her sitters were paid up to the end of the year, so here is a check for that amount. But, she also wanted to offer you a chance to vacation in her rental home in Gulf Shores. You will have at least a week vacation that you will have to schedule with her son John before you go. She said you work so hard everyday and she knew you needed a vacation." Then Mr. McBeavie pulled out a laptop from his briefcase and put his glasses on. He typed something into the computer and said, "Now about the stock you owned. Have you been checking it online lately?"

"No. I haven't thought about it," replied mama.

"Look here," he said as he looked over his spectacles. Mama gasped when she saw the six figure amount. "Is this right?"

Mr. McBeavie chuckled. "Yeah, that's right. Those Wall Street investors are as crocked as a politician, but they know how to make money. Normally, those guys don't do anything for the average person, but Mrs. Jenkins didn't tell them it was for you at first."

Everybody in the room just sat astounded by what he just said. No one said a thing for a moment.

Mr. McBeavie handed mama the papers containing the information on her stocks. "Well, now that I see that I have everyone's attention, Mrs. Patterson if you will just sign this paper saying you have received the check, and I'll be on my way."

Mama took the pin he handed to her, and signed the papers. Then he put them in his briefcase and handed mama the check. Mr. McBeavie struggled to get off the couch.

Mike walked over to him, and said, "Let me help you."

"No, no. I got it. Just make sure you deposit that check within ninety days, or it won't be any good."

Big Mama walked him to the door, and we all said goodbye. But mama didn't say anything. She held onto the papers, and just stared at them. Suddenly, she started to jump up and down screaming with the papers in her hands. When she stopped jumping, she flopped on the couch saying, "God is good!"

"Baby, are you all right?" Big Mama asked.

"I don't think I could possibly get any better," mama replied. "Let's go out to eat, and I'm paying. I can't believe this! Now, I know what it feels like to win the lottery. Come on guys!"

Mama ran upstairs with the papers in her hands, and came back down with her purse.

"Let's go," she said.

Mike drove us to a new steak house restaurant that mama wanted to try. When we walked inside of the foyer, we could smell the scent of grilled meat throughout the restaurant.

The hostess greeted us saying, "Welcome to *Season*. How many are in your party?"

"Three adults, and four children," Mike replied.

"Okay, please have a seat. Your table will be ready shortly," said the hostess. Then she walked away.

Big Mama leaned towards mama saying, "This is such a fancy place. Are you sure you don't need a little help paying the bill?"

"No Mom. Don't worry I got it."

The hostess came back to us, and said, "Follow me."

The lights in the dinning room were low. The sound of the grill, and people chatting filled the air in the restaurant. The booths were covered with white linen table cloths, shiny silver ware, and beautiful glasses. The center two aisles had rows of tables covered in the same table cloth. The restaurant's walls were filled with memorabilia of the movie stars both past, and present. The hostess found a booth for us in the corner of the restaurant. The waitress was a small lady with her blonde hair pulled back in a pony tail.

She passed the menus out to everyone, and said, "What can I get for y'all to drink this evening?"

Jordan shouted, "I want a soda!"

"Absolutely not," mama said quickly. "You are hyper enough. No caffeine Jordan. Ma'am do you have any juices?"

"Yes, we have fruit juice, and orange juice," she said.

Jonathan, Alley, and I got the fruit juice. Jordan wanted to be different so he got the orange juice. Mama and Big Mike ordered water, but Big Mama had to have her old faithful, ice tea.

"Ma'am, I would also like to order a bottle of wine," mama added. "Mom? Mike? Would you care to have some wine with me?"

"I can't," Mike said, "I'm driving the family."

"How about you Mom?" Mama pleaded. "I need to toast with somebody."

"Okay, but I don't like red wine. That stuff tasted like vinegar," Big Mama said with a disgusted look.

"Okay, we'll have a white zinfandel then," mama said, and Big Mama agreed.

After the waitress came back with our drinks, we placed our orders. Alley and I got the grilled chicken, but my brothers got hamburgers. I couldn't believe that they would come to a nice restaurant like this, and order hamburgers? Of course, mama, Mike, and Big Mama ordered steaks. They called it prime rib. I guess that's good. The waitress brought out some hot rolls, and a large bowl of salad for us to share. Soon we all began to eat.

"Well Michelle, have you given any thought to what we talked about earlier?" Mike asked. "Now would be a great time."

"Time to do what, Mike?" Big Mama asked.

"Time for Michelle to start her own business," he replied.

"Michelle, that would be a great idea," Big Mama said. "Honey, let this money make some money for you. What kind of business do you want to open?"

"A senior care sitting service," mama replied. "I think I could really do this now."

"And, I know exactly what you should name it," Big Mama said. "*Jenkins Senior Care Center*. After all, she gave you the idea."

"Mom, that sounds really good, but we have to pay off our bills first. I want to be free of debt for a little while."

Mike looked concerned. "Paying off all your debt won't take up to much of your money, will it," Mike asked.

"No Mike," mama said. "It shouldn't take that much to pay off my debts, and my mother's debts too."

"You are going to take care of my debts too, Michelle?" Big Mama asked.

"Of course, mom, why wouldn't I?"

Big Mama kissed mama on the cheek. "Thank you, baby, I couldn't have a better daughter."

"Well, let's toast to that," mama said. We raised our glasses in the air. All the wine, juice, and water glasses chimed in the air at once.

"Mike, I will need your help if I'm going to open my own business."

"You've got it," he said. "First thing you need is a lawyer to help you with the contracts, and regulations for opening a center like this. Then you will need a business plan."

"Now, this is getting to be too much for me right now," mama replied raising her hand. "Let's take this one step at a time, okay?"

"Okay. Let's just eat first," Mike replied with a smile.

"Thank you," mama replied.

Mike leaned over, and gave mama a kiss on the cheek.

"Oh good. The food is here. Let's eat," she said.

We finished eating, and mama left a huge tip for the waitress. Then we went home.

******

Today was Wednesday, and we were going on a trip to a large aquarium somewhere in Tennessee. The bus ride was long, and Plump talked the whole way there. I was glad we got there early because waiting in the line under the hot Tennessee sun can be grueling. Once we were inside, we walked up a long flight of stairs. By the time we got to the top of stairs, Plump wanted to sit down. We came to an exhibit where we could pet the baby sharks.

The lady at the aquarium said, "Don't touch the heads of the sharks. Even though they are small they can still bite."

Teach leaned over to me, and said, "Who would stick their hand in a shark's face? That would be stupid."

"Yeah Teach," I said, "but she wouldn't be saying this if someone hadn't tried it before."

With all those little hands in the water, I'm shocked the sharks didn't make a meal of us all. The shark's skin felt like sand paper, but the body of the shark wasn't gray like I thought it would be. This shark had big brown spots on his tan body. Next, we moved onto the butterfly exhibit.

I think butterflies are pretty, but I hate bugs. And, these bugs were trying to land on me. I got out of there as fast as I could. The next exhibit we came to was the sea horses.

"Look! They're in love!" Plump shouted.

There were two sea horses that had their tails hooked together. We left the exhibit, and rode up a long elevator that stopped at a wild snapping turtle exhibit. Around the corner of the glass enclosure there was a large alligator with his mouth opened, and next to that tank was a big catfish in a tank. This catfish was bigger than the one Alley caught.

"Wow! That fish is bigger than Buster," Alley shouted.

"Who is Buster?" I asked.

"Oh, he is the fish I caught at the lake," she replied.

We walked down a ramp facing a huge aquarium of salt water fish. There was a shark, barracudas, coral, and some other fish I didn't know the names of. Plump and Alley sat on the side of the salt water aquarium. They were talking when a huge sting ray swam up, and landed flat against the glass. The underside of it this creature was flat, and white. He was two feet taller, and wider than Plump and Alley sitting there together. His mouth was moving along the glass, and his gills moved to the rhythm of his mouth. I was so amazed I couldn't speak. I just backed away, and pointed at the ray. Alley and Plump sat there staring at me.

"What's wrong with you?" Plump asked.

Finally, I managed to say, "Look!"

When Alley and Plump turned around, and saw the huge ray behind them laying flat against the glass. They took off screaming, and running.

"Alexandria and Bernadette, stop screaming in here," Mrs. Mays said. "Use your inside voices, and that goes for everyone else too."

"Yes ma'am," Alley and Plump said in unison.

The exhibits were full of places kids could crawl into, and look under the glass. I crawled into this cave, and stood up under a glass dome of the tank. When I looked out, I felt like I was inside of the aquarium. I put my finger on the glass and a pretty purple and yellow fish followed it. I waved to Plump and Alley. They started to run towards the cave. The first person to stand up in the cave with me was Alley.

"Cool," she said as she looked around.

Soon Teach came in. He made an ugly face, and scared the purple fish away. Now, there were three of us in the cave, and the space was getting pretty tight. The last person to enter the cave was Plump. When she stood up, she squeezed the rest of us up against the glass.

We yelled, "Plump, get out!"

"I want to see too," she said.

I shifted my way toward the opening, and got out. Alley soon followed behind me. Teach and Plump stayed inside making faces at us before they decided to come out of the cave. We saw the jellyfish exhibits before we left the aquarium. Instead of box lunches today, we ate at a fast food hamburger restaurant for lunch. We all had toys that came with our meals, and Mrs. Mays let us play on the fenced in playground area until it was time to go. Plump was quiet on the way back to the center. I think she was tired, but Alley didn't stop talking. I just smiled and nodded when she said something to me, but I really didn't hear most of what she was saying.

After we left summer camp, I didn't have enough money to stop at Mr. Muhammad's store today. We left Plump and Teach at the store, and went home. When Alley, my brothers, and I got home, Big Mama and Mr. Davis were playing cards on the front porch, and drinking ice tea. As usual, I could tell that Big Mama was winning from the way Mr. Davis was looking. Pee-Pee was sitting on the porch panting very loudly.

"Hey guys," Big Mama said. We all said hey back to her.

"Now that I've beaten Ben here twice, I'll go inside, and get y'all some cookies." Big Mama stood up abruptly, and said, "Woo, it's a little hot out here. I'm a bit dizzy."

She took two steps forward then she passed out cold hitting the porch floor hard. Pee-Pee jumped back as Mr. Davis ran toward her.

"Big Mama!" I screamed as my brothers, Alley, and I ran toward her.

"Jasmine, go in the house, and call 911," Mr. Davis said.

I ran into the house as fast as I could with tears streaming down my face searching for the phone. When I picked it up, my hand was shaking so hard I could barely dial the numbers.

The operator said, "911 emergencies. May I help you?"

"My grandmother has passed out on the front porch. Please send someone here quick. We live at 1717 Divinement Lane," I said with tears rolling down my cheeks.

"How old are you honey?" The operator asked.

"Ten." I replied.

"What is your name?"

"Jasmine."

"Jasmine, can you take the phone with you, and see if she's breathing?" The operator asked.

"Okay, hold on," I said. I walked out onto the porch, and said, "Mr. Davis the operator wants to know if Big Mama is still breathing."

"Yes," he said, "but her breathing is really shallow."

I told the operator what he said, and she said, "Good. Stay on the phone with me until the paramedics get there, okay."

I agreed. Soon the ambulance arrived. They started asking Mr. Davis a lot of questions. I called mama at work, and asked her to come home. The men put Big Mama on a stretcher, and rolled her to the back of the ambulance. When they got her on the back of the truck, I saw them putting an oxygen mask on her. The man talked with Mr. Davis for a while, and then gave him a card. When they left with Big Mama, we all stayed on the porch with Mr. Davis. We were still frightened, and worried about Big Mama. Ten minutes later, Mama drove up and parked in the driveway. She jumped out of the van, and ran up the path to the front porch.

"What's happened guys?" Mama asked.

"Big Mama passed out," Jonathan said.

Mr. Davis walked over to mama, and gave her the card that the paramedic handed him. "They took her to Baptist Hospital's emergency room," he said.

"Thank you for calling the paramedics, and staying here with my children. I am lucky to have you for a neighbor."

"I didn't mind staying here until you got home, but don't thank me. Thank Jasmine. She called 911. She even called you."

Mama walked over to me, and gave me a big hug. "Come on guys. Let's go." Mama said.

We got in the van while mama let Pee-Pee in the house, and locked the doors.

"Do you mind if I come along," Mr. Davis asked.

"Oh no," mama replied. "I wasn't going to leave without you anyway."

Mr. Davis smiled, and they both got into the van. Then mama drove away.

Mama parked the van in the emergency room's parking lot. We got out of the van, and walked into the emergency unit. Mama talked to the lady at the help desk while we waited with Mr. Davis. When I looked around, I could see angels everywhere. There were some dark ones there too. When I turned to my right, I saw a man the paramedics were bringing in through the emergency room doors. They were trying to resuscitate him, but I saw his soul step out of his body as the angel walked toward him. They talked for a little while then they disappeared. The medics continued trying to resuscitate him as they rolled the man on the stretcher through the back door.

"Guys, they have moved mom to a room on the fifth floor. Let's go," mama said.

As we walked down the hall, I saw more angels standing around. Some were standing by people praying. Some angels were watching over sick people sleeping. But the dark angels were dragging souls off, and disappearing. We got on the elevator that took us to the fifth floor. It was quiet on this floor, and Big Mama's room was at the end of the hall. When we got close enough to see inside the room, I saw an angel talking to Big Mama.

I ran into the room and said, "No, no! You can't take my grandma!"

The angel smiled at me, and disappeared before I got too close to her.

"Baby, lower your voice. I'm not going anywhere," Big Mama said. "She just came to talk to me."

Soon everyone else entered the room.

"Mom, I'm glad that you are all right. What happened?"

"Oh, my sugar got a little too high, and the doctors want to keep me here to make sure I have no other problems. I will be able to go home tomorrow. They are bringing a dietitian in here tomorrow to talk to me before I leave. You can pick me up after you get off work."

"Mom, please listen to the dietitian. We don't want this to happen again," mama replied.

I could tell that mama was really upset. She didn't want to show it in front of us, but she was scared too.

"Don't worry Michelle," Big Mama replied. "I've had a long talk with the angels, and she told me it wasn't my time now, but if I don't take care of my body, I won't be here to help Jasmine. She said my body is a temple, and I've been treating it like a trash can. Ha, Ha! She even said if I wanted to go to glory now, I could continue to eat this way after I helped Jasmine with her destiny, but not now. Can you believe that? Like I am ready to go at anytime, Angels," Big Mama said as she shook her head. "They don't know about death, so it's like going home to them."

"Mom, you have to take care of yourself. We can't lose you."

"I know baby and I promise to do better. Don't worry. You aren't going to lose me yet," Big Mama said with a smile.

Mr. Davis stood there with his mouth open.

"Mama, what are y'all talking about?" Jordan asked. "I don't see any angels."

"Oh, it's nothing Jordan, I'll tell you about it later," mama replied.

Alley leaned over to Jordan, and said, "Jordan, your family can see some weird things."

We stayed in the hospital for another hour. Soon the nurse told us visiting hours were over, so we had to leave. Mama drove us home. I could tell she was still upset, but she didn't say anything to us about it.

On the way out of the van, I grabbed mama's hand, and said, "Mama, don't worry. The angels are watching over her now. Believe me, she isn't going anywhere. I saw her myself. She won't take her until He is ready."

Mama gave me a strange look. Then she put her arm around me as we walked into the house.

Chapter 14
The Storm

After Big Mama got out of the hospital on Thursday, she was back to being her old self again. But, this time she promised to change the way she had been eating. This also meant that everyone in the house was going to eat healthier too. Jordan made a face when Big Mama told him she wasn't going to buy anymore chips. He wasn't too happy about the healthy eating thing, but mama loved the idea. I think she was surprised by the drastic change in Big Mama's attitude towards healthy living. Maybe it takes an angel to come down from heaven to get some people to change their ways. Mama decided to cook today since Big Mama had just gotten out of the hospital. She made a big salad, grilled chicken, and corn on the cob.

The doorbell rang and Big Mama answered it. It was Big Mike.

"Hey Mike. Wow! Those are some beautiful flowers. She's in the kitchen. Go on and take them to her. I want to see her expression."

"These aren't for her. These are for you," Mike said.

"For me?" Big Mama replied with a bit of surprise. "Thank you, Mike. Come on in. Michelle, look at what Mike has bought me."

Big Mama and Mike walked into the den. Big Mama sat the flowers down on the coffee table.

"They are beautiful Mike," said mama.

Alley and I saw the flowers and gasped.

"Mrs. Thomas you gave us quite a scare," Mike said.

"I'm sorry about that Mike, but you don't have to call me Mrs. Thomas. Just call me Bertha," Big Mama replied.

"Okay, Bertha," he said.

"Mike, would you like to eat dinner with us?" Mama asked.

"I thought you'd never ask. Hey guys, whatcha doing?"

"We're playing cards," Alley answered.

"Deal me in a hand after dinner," Mike replied.

"Okay."

Mike walked into the kitchen, and kissed mama on the cheek.

"What's cookin?" He asked.

"In honor of mom's first day out of the hospital, we will be eating lighter. We are eating grilled chicken, salad, and boiled corn. For dessert, we are having some no sugar added mint chocolate chip ice cream."

"That sounds good to me." Mike replied.

"Now Mike, you know when she cooks, you'll be hungry again one hour later," Big Mama said.

"Mom, this is what the dietitian told you to eat."

"I know baby, but Mike's a man. He needs more than this."

"This will be plenty for me. I need to cut back too," replied Mike.

"Well, welcome to the club," Big Mama said.

"Dinner is ready." Mama called us to the table.

We all went to the table, and Big Mama said grace. Then we begin eating.

"Mom, do you think you are will be strong enough to come to Gulf Shores with me this weekend?" Mama asked. "This is the first week I can take my vacation from work. Do you want to come with me?"

"Mama, are we going too?" I asked.

"Of course, I can't leave y'all here," she said. Alley, my brothers, and I started cheering in our seats.

"I'll go with you, but weren't you planning on going to Gulf Shores later?" Big Mama asked.

"Yes, but I won't have time to do that now. Soon I'll be starting my business, and this is the only chance I will have to go anywhere for a while."

"Well, count me in."

"How about you Mike? After all, you said you would help me," mama asked.

"Sweet heart, I can't this weekend. The work I am doing is running behind, so we have to work overtime this weekend to catch up. I'm sorry," he said.

Mama's face was full of disappointment.

"Will you call me?" She asked.

"Everyday. When will you get back home, Michelle?"

"Monday night, and would you mind doing a little dog sitting? I don't want to leave him in a kennel.

"Of course, I'll take care of your dog."

"He's not my dog," mama replied.

Big Mama just smirked when she heard what mama said.

"Guys, we have to pack tonight. We're leaving first thing tomorrow morning."

Once we finished eating dinner, everyone went into the den except for mama. Mama cleaned off the table, and started loading the dish washer. My brothers, Alley, and I played cards with Big Mike.

"Now, guys don't expect me to take it easy on you. I play to win," Mike said.

We played four games. Alley won once, Jonathan won one game, but Big Mike won twice. Mama finished cleaning the kitchen, and walked out to the den.

"Okay guys, y'all need to go upstairs and pack. Get your swimsuits and at least seven outfits to change into. Also, pack plenty of underwear," she said.

"Why so much underwear?" Mike asked.

"Mike, believe me, it's better to have too much than not enough." Mike laughed.

Big Mama stood up, and said, "I'll go upstairs and help them. I have to pack too. Come on kids. Let's get to packing."

Alley, my brothers, and I walked upstairs with Big Mama. Mama sat down on the couch with Mike.

"Are you sure you can't go?" Michelle asked.

"No darling. We've been behind on this project for weeks. My boss won't let me off for anything right now.

"Okay, but I'll miss you."

"I'm shocked you aren't tired of me coming around here so often."

"Believe it or not Mike, I'm happy to have you here. Don't ever feel like I'm getting tired of you. I would ask you to stay over tonight, but my mother would have a fit. I may not always be able to entertain you, but you are always welcome. I'll let you know if I need my space. Don't worry about coming by so much. I would be disappointed if you stopped," she said.

"I'm going to miss you too," he said. Then Mike kissed Michelle's cheek.

"Mike, you know all about me, but I need to know more about you."

"Okay, what would you like to know?" He asked.

Michelle looked away from him. Then she started to grin. When she turned back to him, she said, "I want to know more about your sex life."

Mike laughed. "All you have to do is ask. I'll be glad to show you if you like."

"That won't be necessary. You asked me about my sex life, or the lack there of, so I think it is only fair that you tell me about yours."

"What do you want to know?"

"I'm surprised that a man like you didn't have somebody when I met you. I know you've been dating since your wife passed, so what happened?"

"I've dated a few times, but nothing serious happened with any of them."

"Mike, you've never been serious with any of them?"

"Okay, one, but I don't believe in sharing. She was dating another man at the same time she was with me. I had to let her go."

"So, the same thing happened to you as it did with me."

"Not quite. I didn't love her. It bothered me that she did that, but I got over her very quickly."

"Did you worry that she might have given you a STD or something? Because I did when I found out what James did to me. I got tested for everything they could think of when I found out my husband had cheated on me."

"I didn't get tested, but I have always protected myself."

"Mike, you are a very responsible man, but not enough men in our community are. If you hadn't come along, I probably would have never dated anyone. My family can't afford for anything to happen to me. They all depend on me. I can't risk my health to anyone."

"Michelle, I promise you I am healthy." Mike said.

"How do you know?" Michelle asked with a raised brow.

"I guess I will have to make an appointment with my doctor to prove it to you."

"You don't have to prove anything to me. I'm just glad you were willing to talk about this with me."

"Now, does this mean I can't have a kiss anymore?" Mike said with a grin.

"Of course, you can. That's one chance I am willing to take," Michelle said.

Mike lifted her chin with his finger, and kissed her softly. Suddenly, Jordan ran down the stairs.

"Ma, I can't find my swim trunks, ooh!" Jordan said putting his hand over his mouth. Then he ran back upstairs. Mike and Michelle stopped kissing, and turned to see Jordan running up the stairs.

"Well, I guess I'll be going home now," Mike said smiling.

"Okay. Let me get Pee-Pee's bowl, and chain," Michelle replied. She walked into the laundry room and got Pee-Pee's things, and gave them to Mike.

"Hold on, I forgot his food." Michelle walked back out to the laundry room, and came back with the dog food.

"Why don't I carry this out to the truck for you? Here Pee-Pee," she said.

The dog followed her outside to Mike's truck. Mike opened the door, and the big yellow dog jumped inside. Mike took Pee-Pee's things, and put them in the back of the truck.

"You know I think you should come to my house sometime," Mike said.

"Yeah, I've never been to your house before, and it's about time you asked too."

"You'd like it there, and there are fewer distractions," he said grinning.

He grabbed Michelle by the waist, and pulled her towards him. He kissed her softly at first, but soon his kisses became more passionate. When he released her from his kiss, he put his brow to hers.

"Call me when you get there," he said.

"I will."

"Please be careful," he said.

Then he kissed her brow, and got into the truck and drove away.

*****

The drive down to Gulf Shores took a long time. After a few hours in the van, I, or one of my brothers would yell, "I have to pee!" Mama would pull over to a rest stop, and we would jump out of the van running to the bathrooms. We finally got to the house. Mama parked the van, and we all got out. The house was two stories high. It had peach siding, and it was trimmed in white. The house looked like it was on stilts. We had to walk up a long flight of steps to get to the deck. The deck wrapped around the entire house.

"Hold on guys. Let me get the key," mama said.

"When did you get the key?" Big Mama asked.

"Oh, Mr. McBeavie came by my office, and gave it to me yesterday. I got it."

When we entered the house, we all were amazed. It was beautiful. The large great room had beautiful terracotta tile floors. The area rug near the fire place and a sixty five inch screen TV sat by two beautiful beige slip covered couches. There were two big arm chairs covered in the same fabric as the couches on the other side. A glass table was in the center of the rug, and two round glass end tables on either side of the couch. The huge glass lamps sitting on the table held sea shells inside of them. The kitchen was huge with stainless steel appliances. In the middle of the large room there was a staircase that led to the bedrooms on the second floor.

"Mr. McBeavie said there are three bedrooms upstairs with one master bathroom. There is a bathroom in the center of the hall, and one bedroom down here," mama said as she pointed pass the staircase.

"I'll take the one down here," Big Mama replied. "I don't want to climb those stairs while I am here."

"I'll take the master bathroom!" Jordan yelled.

"No, you won't," mama demanded. "You and Jonathan will room together. Alley and Jasmine will share a room. Y'all go put your things down, and let's go outside."

We ran upstairs to put our bags in the rooms. The rooms were just as beautiful as the rest of the house. Alley and I put our things down, and ran down the steps. We walked through a set of French doors to the back deck. Mama was already outside sitting on the bench and talking on her cell phone.

She stopped talking on the phone, and said to us, "Girls don't go far. Wait on the rest of us."

Alley and I walked down to the patio area which was fenced in. The patio had two lounge chairs, and a six chairs table set covered with an umbrella. There was a hot tub and a barbecue grill there too. Alley and I sat on the side of the hot tub, and put our legs into it.

"Alley what does this button do?" I pushed the button. The water started to bubble.

"Cool," Alley said as she kicked her feet in the water.

Alley was giggling and splashing water everywhere. I just noticed her front tooth was growing in. When I looked up, my brothers were running full speed down the steps. Jordan and Jonathan jumped into the hot tub cannon ball style. Both of them jumped in the water with their clothes on. They splashed so much water on us we both got wet from head to toe.

"Jordan! Jonathan! Get out of there!" Mama shouted.

"Mama, look what they did to us!" I yelled.

"It's okay Jasmine. You will dry."

"I see someone found the hot tub," Big Mama said as she approached us.

Jordan and Jonathan were sitting on the side of the tub soaking wet. Both of them were grinning like two "Cheshire" cats.

"Alley, I bought something for you," Big Mama said. She handed a bottle of sunscreen to Alley.

"I don't want you to get burned while you're out here with us." Big Mama gave Alley a floppy denim hat. "This might keep your nose from getting sun burned too."

"Come on guys. Let's go to the beach," mama said.

Mama opened the back gate, and we all walked out of it. We walked down a sandy stone path to the white sand that lined the shores. The gulf waters were as blue as the sky. The sound of sea gulls, and waves crashing against the beach filled the air. My brothers chased small crabs along the shore until they escaped into their burrows underneath the sand. When Alley and I got close enough to the shore, we ran towards the water.

"Guys, don't go too far. Alley! Jasmine! That's far enough," mama yelled. Big Mama and mama sat down on the sand, and watched us play.

"I am glad we have a washer and dryer in the house. I'm sure we might have to use it at least once before we leave," mama said.

"Honey, I'm glad we got to see it before it's gone. It's a beautiful house."

"I heard her sons are going to put the house on the market as soon as we get back," mama replied.

Then mama hesitated for a moment. She looked out over the gulf, and said, "Mom, do you think Mike is really a good man? I know you can see things in people that no one else can see, so tell me. Should I trust him?"

"Michelle, Mike is a good man, and I believe he is falling in love with you."

Michelle was shocked by what she had just heard. She knew her mother had never been wrong before. She turned to her mother, and stared with her mouth slightly opened.

"Michelle, don't act so surprised. You don't have to be physic to see how he feels about you. He's always around, and he's very supportive of you. But, if you're asking me about the future, I can't say. Nothing is certain. God has given us all free will, and Mike has to make his own choices. I can't say what he will do, but it is up to you to give him a chance."

"You like him, don't you mom?"

"I guess I do," she replied.

"Come on. Let's go for a walk." Mama stood up, and held her hand out to Big Mama to help her up. Big Mama grabbed her hand, and stood up beside her.

"Guys let's go for a walk!" Mama shouted.

We all walked down the shoreline headed towards the pier. Mama and Big mama chatted while my brothers, Alley, and I found interesting stuff on the beach.

"Look!" Alley said.

She had a clam in her hand that was the size of her palm. The clam had blue and tan rings on its shell. Jordan was chasing a huge crab that was bigger than his hands.

Mama shouted, "Jordan, if that crab pinches you, I don't want to hear about it, so leave it along!"

By the time we got to the pier a huge fish jumped out of the water. The fishermen gathered on both sides of the pier casting their hooks into the ocean, and telling tall tales of their catch of the day. We walked to the end of the pier, and looked down at the waves lapping against the pillars. There was a huge grouper swimming in the water around the pillars waiting for scraps the fishermen threw out. I saw a flounder swim to the surface of the water then dive back down. A large sting ray stayed out far enough from the pier, so that the fisherman's hooks wouldn't reach him. The sun was starting to set sending out a hue of orange and red colors across the Southern sky. Mama said it was time to go back to the house so we could get ready to go to dinner. On the way back to the house, three pelicans passed us flying in a straight line. We got back to the house, and changed our clothes. Mama washed my hair, and combed it up in one curly frizzy ball. She drove us to a small seafood restaurant down the street where we ate dinner.

The next day we went to an amusement park. I know Big Mama must have been tempted to eat the delicious pizzas or hot dogs that were sold at the park, but she resisted. The smell of the cotton candy, and caramel covered apples was too much temptation for me. I just had to have one. Mama bought each kid a candy apple. Big Mama decided to get a diet soda with mama. My brothers, Alley, and I rode on just about every ride in the park, and I was so tired that I fell asleep in the van on the way back to the house.

Sunday, mama and Big Mama got into the hot tub. They chatted about everything from books to men. When mama and Big Mama got out of the tub, we all went to the beach again. Later on, we decided to go shopping. Each of us got a t-shirt, and a hat. Monday seemed to come by too soon. We were having such a good time that none of us wanted to go home.

When she got back to the rental house mama said, "Come on guys. Let's pack. It's time to go."

We all packed our things. Mama and Big Mama checked behind us and then we left. I felt a little sad leaving the beautiful house on the beach, but I wanted to get home to see my dog Pee-Pee. We got home about nine o'clock at night. Everybody unloaded their luggage from the van, and entered the house. I unpacked most of my things, and threw them into the hamper. Alley put on her pajamas and fell asleep on top of the covers. I took everything out of my bag and changed into my pajamas. Then I got into bed too. It was fun going to Gulf Shores for the weekend, but it was good to be home.

*****

Tuesday, summer camp ended early. There was a storm headed towards our county. Mrs. Mays called all the parents to come, and pick up their kids early. Mama got off work early too. Mama parked the van, and moved the trash cans to the shed in the backyard. She walked back to the front door, and opened it. She put the two rocking chairs, and table that were on the front porch in the hallway next to the den. Big Mama and the rest of us were sitting down on the couch watching the news. The news was on every channel broadcasting the weather that was approaching.

"Hey guys. What did the weatherman say about the storm?" She asked.

Big Mama turned her head to look over the couch, and said, "The storm is in Tuscaloosa County, and it's headed this way."

Mama walked into the den to listen to the weather report on the TV when the door bell rang.

"Who would be out in this weather?" Big Mama asked.

Mama answered the door. It was Mike. Mike was carrying Pee-Pee's chain and bowl. Pee-Pee ran inside the house, and jumped up putting his front paws on mama's thighs. Then he gave her an excited bark, and wagged his tail. Mama patted him on the head, and backed away so the dog could walk further inside the house.

"Come on in, Mike. It's starting to rain," mama said.

"Hold on. Let me get the dog food, and take down the swing."

Mike ran back to the truck when a big clap of thunder roared outside. Mike ran back onto the porch, and handed mama the bag of dog food. Then he took down the swing. When he walked inside the house, Mike was drenched from head to toe.

Mama put the bag dog food down on the floor, and said, "Let me get you a towel." She walked to the downstairs bathroom, and came back with a towel for him.

"Thank you," he said.

Mama closed the door behind him. They walked into the den, and Mike greeted everyone.

"I would sit down, but I'm a little wet," he said.

"I bought you a t-shirt and shorts when we were in Gulf Shores. I was going to surprise you, but now is as good a time as any," mama said. "I'll go get them."

She went upstairs, and came back down with the t-shirt and shorts. "The bathroom is right down the hall."

Mike went to the bathroom to change.

"Michelle, we might all have to stay down here tonight," Big Mama stated. "The storm is getting worse, and this is the lowest floor."

"Okay mom. Kids y'all go upstairs, and get your pillows, and a blanket and come back down here."

Mama went upstairs, and brought two blankets for each couch and some two pillows from her room. Mama moved the coffee table, so that Alley, my brothers, and I could lie on the floor. Big Mama walked back to her room, and got a flash light. She also put candles on the coffee tables, and fire place mantel. When Mike came back to the den, we were all sitting under the blankets.

"Y'all look comfortable," he said with a grin.

Mama and Big Mama were sitting on the couch.

"Come over here Mike," said mama.

"Who brought out the candles?" Mike asked.

"I did, and I have a flash light too. Just in case the power goes out, and someone has to use the bathroom," Big Mama said.

With each hour that passed the rain grew even harder, and the lights in house began to flicker for a moment. The meteorologist warned people in our area to go to their place of safety. I was getting scared. It was about eight o'clock now, and the sky was pitched black. Big Mama put the cards on the coffee table to give us something to do. I think she was trying to distract us from the storm, but it didn't work. The flash of lighting outside lit the night sky. We could hear the winds howling, and shaking the house. By nine o'clock the power went out. Big Mama lit the candles on the coffee tables, and fire place mantel.

"Mama, I'm scared," I said as I laid my head on mama's knee.

"It's just a storm. It will pass," she said.

But, I know she was nervous too. Mike put his arm around her shoulder to calm her fears.

Jordan went to the window, and said, "Ooh! There's ice on the ground."

"Jordan, that is called hail, and come away from that window. It's not safe to be near a window during a storm," mama demanded.

Big Mama got up. "I've got a pocket radio in my room. Let me go get it, so we can hear about weather," she said.

Big Mama took the flash light to her room. After a few minutes had passed, she came back with a portable radio. The weather man said that a tornado had been spotted south of us. He said there might be considerable damage, and power outages throughout the county. Big Mama sat the radio on the coffee table, and sat down on the other couch.

"I am going to sit over here," Big Mama said. "Two is company, but three is a crowd."

I climbed on the couch with Big Mama, and wrapped the blanket around both of us. "Big Mama, I am scared. I know this is a bad storm, but I feel something bigger is coming."

Big Mama put her arm around me. "I feel it too baby, but don't worry, He will protect us," she said.

"I know Big Mama, but I feel that so many people will die. I see people wandering in the streets trying to get out of the water. Others will plead for help, but no one will come." Tears filled my eyes, and I could say no more.

"I see it too baby. They will think He has forgotten them, but He has not. Those that are lost will be found in his hands. Despair will spread, but hope remains. Jasmine, don't be afraid because He is always with us."

Then Big Mama began saying the *Lord's Prayer*. The storm outside grew louder. The lighting was flashing so fast it looked like someone was shooting off multiple fireworks at once. There was a loud crash outside that sounded like a bomb just exploded. Then the winds grew. There was a sound outside that sounded like a train approaching. The house began to shake. Big Mama continued to pray. Alley and my brothers were sitting on the other couch with mama and Mike. The rumbling and flashing lights grew louder, and closer. I screamed. I thought the house was going to cave in. Then suddenly it stopped. The rain was tapping on the window panes. Mike got up to look outside the front door.

"Oh no," he said as he walked to the front door, and opened it.

"Mike, what's wrong?" Mama asked.

"A huge tree has fallen across the street. The branches are blocking the driveway. I think another tree fell down the street, but it's too dark to tell. All the street lights are out, and I'll have to wait until morning to see the extent of the damage," he said.

"Kids, I think the worst is over. Take the flash light upstairs, and go to bed," mama said.

"Take your blankets and pillows too," Big Mama said, "Well, I guess I'll be going to bed too. I think I've had enough excitement for one night. Good night y'all." Big Mama took a candle, and went to bed.

"Mike, what time is it?" Mama asked as she walked over to him.

Mike pushed the button on his watch which made it illuminate. "It's 11:45 p.m."

"No wonder I'm so sleepy. Where do you want to sleep?" She asked.

Mike's dimpled smile grew broad. "Well darling, if I go upstairs to your room, I won't be getting any sleep. I think it would be safer if I slept on the couch. Let's continue to let your mother think I'm an honorable man."

"Mike, I didn't mean it like that, but I could sleep down here and you can take my room."

"No Michelle. I'm not going to put anybody out of their rooms. I'll just sleep on the couch. You can sit with me for a little while," he said.

Mike lay back on the couch with two pillows behind his head, and mama lay in front of him with her head against his chest. They talked for a while before mama fell asleep. Mike loved the idea of having her so close to him. He laid there with her in his arms, and fell asleep too.

*****

The light from the window woke Michelle. Soon she realized where she had slept last night. Sleeping here on Mike's chest was as comfortable as her bed. His arms felt as warm as the morning sun shining through the windows.

"Good morning beautiful." Michelle looked up to see Mike's beautiful eyes staring back at her.

"Good morning to you too," she said. "Has anybody else gotten up yet?"

"No, but I'm getting hungry," he replied.

"Well, breakfast maybe a little complicated since we have no power."

"You have a grill outside with a burner, don't you?" Mike asked.

"Yes."

"Why don't I cook breakfast for everyone, and we can eat outside on the patio. I'll have a look around the house to see if there's any damage while I am out there," Mike said.

"I hope the power comes on soon, or I'll have to throw everything out of the refrigerator again," Michelle said with a sigh.

"Come on," he said, "Let's clean up."

Michelle and Mike put the furniture back in place, and threw the burned out candles away. Michelle folded the blankets, and took the pillows upstairs. Mike put the cards back in the box, and went to the kitchen. When Mike opened the refrigerator door, Pee-Pee walked over to look inside of it with him.

"Well, boy, let's see what we have here." Mike found a few things he could put on the grill. Then he shut the refrigerator, and walked outside with Pee-Pee.

Chapter 15
He's back

Once mama got to her room, she called the office on her cell phone, but a recording played on the phone that said, "Due to the power outages in our area, this office will be closed today." All employees please call the office Thursday no later than eight a.m. for further instructions."

Mama turned the phone off, and she went in the bathroom to take a shower. Once she was dressed, she walked down the hall into each bedroom telling everyone to get dressed, and come outside. Then she walked downstairs, and outside to the patio. Big Mama was already dressed and sitting at the table with her breakfast, and a cup of coffee.

"Good morning," Big Mama said. "Would you like a cup of coffee? It's instant, but it's still good."

Mama walked to the table, and got a cup. Big Mike had the coffee pot on top of the grill warming. Mike was grilling sausage, ham, toast, and he fried some eggs in a pan on the side burner. The smell of the food made mama hungry.

"Mike, this is a great idea and you're a good cook," she said.

"I've been on many camping trips where I would have to make breakfast outside. Sometimes I would have to start a fire in the ground to cook, and breakfast was anything that I could catch. You make do with what you've have when you have to. Maybe later on Michelle you should have a generator installed. You know that living in the South a generator is a necessity, not a luxury."

Mama made a cup of coffee, and sat back down at the table. Mike put a stack of silverware, a bag of paper plates, foam coffee cups in the middle of the table. He even brought out Pee-Pee's water, and food dish outside.

"Mike, would you like to go upstairs, and take a shower? I took your clothes out of the dryer, and hung them on the back of the kitchen chairs. They dried a little last night before the power went out. I think they're okay now. You can use my bathroom. I have an extra tooth brush I just bought in the drawer under the sink," mama said.

"I will in a minute, but I want to finish here first," he replied. "I've looked around the house, and it weathered the storm well. I swept the patio, but there is trash, tree limbs, and leaves scattered everywhere in the front yard. The old lady across the street fence was broken when the tree fell, but she is okay. She spoke to me this morning. I am going to take her a plate of food over to her house later on. Another tree did fall over into your other neighbor's yard across from Mrs. Madison's house last night, but no one got hurt. I guess we're all pretty lucky. The storm looks like it passed us."

"Oh, I think it was more than luck," Big Mama replied.

Jordan and Jonathan came outside. Mama got up to let them sit down. Then she made them a plate of sausage, eggs, and grilled toast.

"Mama, may we have something to drink?" Jordan asked.

"I couldn't bring the juice out here," Mike said. "And, the ice melted. I cleaned the water up on the floor, and threw the water out of the tray."

"They have some juice boxes they can drink," mama said. "The juice won't be cold, but it's either that, or water."

"I'll take the juice boxes," Jordan replied.

Jasmine came downstairs dressed in a nice short set, but her hair was a mess. Her hair looked like it did when she slept on it last night.

"Jasmine, come with me, and let me fix your hair. It will only take a minute. I promise," said mama.

Mama and I went back into the house as Alley came outside dressed.

"Good morning, Alley. Do you want something to eat?" Big Mama asked.

"Yes ma'am," Alley replied.

Big Mama got up, and prepared a plate of food for Alley.

"Mike, I'll go take Mrs. Madison's breakfast to her, but do you think there is enough for Ben?"

"Sure," Mike said. "We've got to use this stuff before it goes bad anyway."

"Thanks Mike. I'll go get him." Big Mama made a plate of food for Mrs. Madison and then she walked out of the side gate. Mama and I came back outside. Mama had my hair combed neatly into two pony tails. She prepared a plate of food for me, and sat it on the table. I sat down by my brothers to eat.

"Where is mom?" Mama asked.

"She took a plate over to Mrs. Madison's house. Then she said she was going to ask Ben to come over," Mike said.

"Mike, why don't you sit down, and I'll finish cooking for you."

"Okay." Mike sat down, and started to sip his coffee. Pee-Pee walked over to him, and Mike patted the dog's head.

"Mike, are you ready to eat now?" Mama asked.

"Yeah." Mike watched mama putting food on the plate. His eyes lingered over the back of her calves, and up to her thighs. Then his eyes seemed to stop at her backside. He sipped his coffee, and swallowed hard.

"Mike, what are you looking at?" Jordan asked.

Mama turned around suddenly.

"Oh, nothing," Mike said with a grin.

Mama brought Mike his breakfast when the side gate swung open.

"What's up? What's up? I could smell the food all the way down the street."

"Uncle Pete!" I screamed, and ran over to give him a hug.

"Oh no," mama said under her breath. "Hey Pete."

"Little sis, give me a hug." Pete grabbed mama, and squeezed her tight.

"Ugh Pete! That's too hard!"

"I'm just glad to see that my baby sister is all right."

He walked over to the table, and greeted everyone else. Uncle Pete also shook hands with Mike.

"Morning!" Uncle Pete said to Big Mike. "You're here real early this morning."

"I never left," Mike said.

Uncle Pete's eyes grew wide. Then he turned to look at mama. "Now little sis, that's one of my moves."

"Pete, the tree fell across the street, and blocked the driveway. Didn't you see it when you came in? He couldn't leave because he couldn't move his truck Pete," mama said.

"Uh hmm," Pete replied with a smirk. "Well, I hope you got enough sleep last night because I'm hungry."

Mike started to grin. Mama piled Pete's plate with food, and sat it on the table in front of him. Big Mama and Mr. Davis entered the backyard. Mr. Davis exchanged greetings with us, but Uncle Pete gave his standard greeting.

"Kids, if y'all are finished, get up, and let Big Mama and Mr. Davis sit down."

Alley, my brothers, and I got up, and put our plates in the trash cans. We walked around to the front yard to play.

"Little sis, it looks like you're about to have a party," Pete said.

"Michelle, why don't you sit down, and eat. You haven't had a thing," Big Mama said.

"Yeah sis. You're getting so skinny that you're starting to look like a neck bone with hips."

"You're not funny, Pete," she said.

"Now, now children," Big Mama replied. "We have guests. Ben, when they get together you would think I still have two kids."

Mama made a plate of food, and sat down by Mike. Big Mama prepared Ben's breakfast, and sat down by him. "Ben, we are eating on paper plates because the power is out, and no one wants to wash dishes."

"Yeah Ben," Pete said. "They just don't make women like they used to."

Mama gave Pete a mean look. "Mike, did you call your foreman?" She asked.

"Yes. He told me not to come in today. The site is too muddy. The heavy equipment could get stuck. It's just too dangerous right now, but I'll have to go in early tomorrow."

"I'm glad those days are over," Ben said. "Aren't you Bertha?"

"Oh yes. Ain't nothing like getting up when you want to," Big Mama replied.

"Mr. Davis, did you have any damage at your house?" Mama asked.

"Two of my pots on the porch broke, but that was all."

Soon the sound of chainsaws could be heard from the front yard.

"Oh good," Pete said. "The city finally got here. Maybe they'll have the power back on before you have to cook everything in your refrigerator out here on this grill today."

"I hope so too Pete," mama replied. "One year I had to throw everything away. Three hundred dollars worth of food was ruined."

"Has anybody heard anything on the radio about the storm last night?" Pete asked.

"Not since last night," mama said.

"Let me go get the radio," said Big Mama. Big Mama got up, and went into the house.

"Guys, if you're finished, I'll take your plates." Mama took up the paper plates, and threw them in the trash can. She cleaned off the table and gave the leftover scraps to Pee-Pee. Big Mama came back outside with a radio. Both mama and Big Mama sat down at the table to hear the news report. The reporter said two tornados touched down last night in our county. Several buildings and homes were damaged, but the storm seemed to skip our area. He also said there were a few minor injuries, but no one was killed. The reporter said the power crews will probably be working late into the night to restore power.

After the news ended, Big Mama said, "Well guys, it's time for me to get into my garden. I bet there are vegetables everywhere."

"Bertha, I'll help you," Mr. Davis said.

"Okay Pete. Are you willing to get a rake, and help me clean up?" Mike asked.

"Okay. I guess I got to work for food today," replied Pete.

Both Pete and Mike swept the driveway, front porch, and walkway. The city workers had most of the limbs cleared out of the driveway by noon. Mike and Uncle Pete put the rocking chairs, and table back outside on the porch. Mama cleaned the house, and washed the few remaining dishes left in the sink. When she walked outside, the yard looked like it did before it stormed. Mike and Uncle Pete were hanging the swing back up too.

"Guys, y'all have done a great job out here, and the power just came back on," mama said.

"Good," Uncle Pete said. "I got to go to the bathroom."

Pete opened the front door, and ran inside the house. Mike and mama sat down on the swing.

"Sorry Mike. My brother can give you too much information sometimes," she said. Big Mama and Mr. Davis walked onto the porch, and sat down in the rockers.

"Woo! It's really starting to get hot out here. Hey, were did the kids go to?" Big Mama asked.

"Alley and Jasmine left the house earlier, and said they wanted to go over to Plump's house. Jordan and Jonathan said they were going to walk to the store with Carlos and Teach," mama replied.

Soon the boys came back from the store, and sat on the steps drinking their sodas, and eating their snacks from Mr. Muhammad's store. Everyone exchanged polite greetings.

Then Big Mama said, "Boys, did y'all get any damage at your house?"

"No," Carlos said.

"We had to pick up some branches in our front yard, but the house is okay," Teach replied.

"Good," Big Mama replied.

Plump, Alley, and I walked back across the street dodging broken limbs, debris, and city workers as we entered the front yard.

Plump said in a very excited voice, "Hey everybody! I saw where y'all had a tree to fall across your driveway. We had a tree that fell in our backyard too. I was scared to death. It sounded like a bomb going off. The tree broke our back fence, and it is lying in the alley. No one can drive back there. Do y'all think that the city workers will come, and clean it up?"

Everybody was silent for a moment. None of us could believe that she could say all of that with what seemed like one breath.

"Yes baby," Big Mama said slowly. "Y'all go on, and play."

Mr. Davis leaned over to Big Mama, and said, "Does she talk that fast all the time?"

"I'm afraid so," Big Mama replied.

Pete stepped out of the front door, and onto the porch. "Who is that?" He asked.

Mama's heart sank. Then she slowly stood up. It was Alley's father.

In a very thick Southern accent he said, "Afternoon folks. I saw were y'all had a tree to fall down out here, but it's good to see your house didn't get any damage."

No one said anything.

"Your neighbor across the street told me Alley was here," Billy said with a grin.

"Hi daddy," Alley said somberly. She greeted him, but I could tell she wasn't happy to see him. Her face had the same melancholy look as it did months ago.

"We tried to call you several times. No one seemed to know where you were. The lady you left Alley with just disappeared. We have been taking care of her for two months now," mama said.

"Oh, the lady was my girlfriend. She was supposed to stay with Alley until I came back, but I guess she just ain't no damn good," Billy said grinning.

Mama's eyes narrowed. I could tell Mike didn't like this man either.

"Who was the black man coming out of your house?" Mama asked. "When I drove to your house, I saw a black man leaving out of your house, and getting into a red car. Who was he?"

"That man thinks I owe him some money. He ain't the nicest sort of fellow either. He's been in and out of jail, and he's the one that robbed me. My whole house is a mess," Billy said with the same smile, but no one responded. "Thank you for looking after her for me like this. I really do appreciate it." Then he turned to Alley. "Alley, you look nice, and it looks like you have a tan. Where did you get those clothes?"

"I bought them for her," Big Mama answered.

"She went on vacation to Gulf Shores with us," mama replied.

"Well, tell them thank you, and you go get your stuff. It's time to go," Billy replied.

"Jasmine, you go inside, and help her pack," said mama.

"Mama no!" I cried.

"Jasmine, go on now! This is her father, and she has to go. We can't keep her here. Go on now." I turned to Alley with tears in my eyes.

"Y'all see her again. She's right around the corner. You can come by, and see her anytime," Billy said.

"Jasmine! Alley! Go get your things." Mama demanded softly.

Alley and I walked into the house.

"Does Alley have anymore family?" Big Mama asked Billy.

"Now, I don't see how any of that is your concern, but if you must know, I am all she's got."

"Where is her mother?" Mama asked.

"Oh, she is taking care of her aunt who was in a car accident," Billy said with a grin.

"That's strange. She could barely take care of herself."

The smile soon faded from Billy's face. "I said that's where she is."

Alley and I walked back out onto the porch.

"Come on Alley. Tell your friends goodbye."

Alley walked down the steps, and looked over her shoulder. Then she waved goodbye to us. Her father took the bag she was carrying. They walked to the end of the corner. Then she was gone. With tears in my eyes, I ran back into the house.

"Plump, go on into the house with her. Maybe you can calm her down. Boys, why don't y'all go around back, and play," Big Mama said.

Mike grabbed mama's hand, and said, "Sit down Michelle." She was visibly shaken and angry when Billy left.

"I can tell he's no good," Mike said.

"We think he hurts Alley, but every time we try to call the authorities some how he always has a good excuse for why she's hurt," mama said. "I think he has someone helping him."

"Alley told me the night her father left he was talking to a police officer. I think his name was Officer Daniel Smith. Alley told me the officer said he needed to lay low for a while because someone had seen him," Big Mama said.

"I think this situation might be worse than we think it is," Mike replied. "I'll talk to my brother. Maybe he will be able to help us."

"Does your brother work in law enforcement?" Mama asked.

"Something like that," he replied. "Hey, I want y'all to meet him. He will be here this weekend."

"We'll be here," Big Mama said.

"Good, now I am going upstairs to take a shower," he replied. "I'll see y'all in a minute." He kissed mama on the head, and walked inside the house.

"Michelle, we have to get that man away from that child. He will hurt her. I know it," Big Mama said.

"I know," mama replied.

"I know a few shady characters that can help you out with this problem," Pete interrupted.

"No Pete. We don't need anymore shady characters coming to our house. You are enough," mama replied.

Big Mama and Mr. Davis laughed.

When Mike got out of the shower, Pete, Big Mama, and Mr. Davis were gone. Mama was sitting in the den watching TV. The boys were still outside playing, and Jasmine and Plump were still upstairs in Jasmine's room.

"Where did everyone go to?" Mike asked.

"Pete left to get something to drink, and mama is repotting Mr. Davis's flowers at his house."

Mike walked into the den, and sat on the couch next to her. "I'm glad I got you alone. What are you doing tomorrow?" He asked.

"Tomorrow, I will be at work. When I get off I have to stay with the kids. Mom has a club meeting. They changed the date because of the storm. On Friday after work, Sharon and I are going to look for a building with the real estate agent for my new business. Saturday, James is picking up the kids, so I'll be all alone," she said.

"Good, so you can go out with me, my brother and sister-in-law for dinner."

"Okay." She agreed to go out, but she was a little nervous about meeting his family for the first time. "I wish you could have come with us to Gulf Shores. You would have loved it."

"Then I'll have to make it up to you by taking you somewhere even more exciting," Mike replied.

He kissed her fervently. She was so taken aback by his sudden move she instinctively moaned. When he released her from his kiss, he said, "I have to go."

"Now?" She asked.

"Yes. I have to check on my house, and make sure it hasn't blown away. Come on. Walk me to the door." He kissed her softly, and left.

*****

I hadn't seen Alley in the last two days. Yesterday I went by her house, and called her, but she never came outside. This Friday was our last day in summer camp. We had a big party at the park. There were clowns there, and some people doing magic tricks. Plump didn't mind the people doing the magic tricks, but she hated the clowns. The first time she saw a clown she started screaming, and ran to Mrs. Mays. I told her he was just here to make us laugh, but she didn't care.

"He's not funny. He's a monster! Look at that Face!" Said Plump.

The only way I could get Plump to leave Mrs. Mays's side was to tell her that the other table was giving out cup cakes. We walked over to the table and got a cup cake. Then we sat under a tree by Teach.

"Guys, have any of you seen Alley?" I asked.

"No. I haven't seen her since she left your house," Plump replied.

"I haven't seen her either," Teach said.

"Guys, do y'all remember seeing those bruises on her legs? You know her father hurts her."

"Jay-Jay, we know, but what can we do? We're just kids. Who is going to listen to us?" Plump replied sadly.

"And, I heard that her daddy is a drug dealer," Teach whispered rather loudly.

"How do you know that," I asked.

"Because June-Bug told me her daddy sells meth to kids at the clubs downtown. Also, he saw him driving downtown selling drugs to people from his car."

"I heard that too Jay-Jay," Plump replied, "--and I would be careful about going around his house. He likes kids if you know what I mean."

"Hey, here comes the clown!" Teach shouted.

"Where Teach?" Plump yelled.

"Ha, ha, ha! You're scared of clowns." Teach laughed so hard he rolled over in the grass.

"You're not funny Teach!" Plump yelled. Then she kicked some rocks on him, and walked off.

After summer camp, Teach apologized to Plump. Baseball camp was over too, so my brothers met us at the center earlier than usual. Big Mama was outside waiting on us. I can really see a change in Big Mama since she changed her eating habits. She has also been walking with us to and from summer camp these last two days. Her skin even looks healthier. We would normally take the long route home, but Big Mama didn't want to go that way today.

"Big Mama, let's go this way," I said.

"Why?" She asked.

"Because those big kids are over there, and they are mean to us. Sometimes they'll take our money."

"Not today," Big Mama said. "You're with me now. I'm not going to let those bullies pick on you, or me either. Let's go," she said.

We walked around the corner, and started to approach the boys standing there. As we got closer to them, one of the boys said, "Ma'am would you like to donate some money to help some poor boys out?"

"No, I would not," Big Mama said, "--and may I suggest that if you need some money, you seek employment."

"Ah shoot lady," the boy replied. "We ain't working for the man."

"Then work for yourself, but remember this. You can't earn a retirement from hanging out on the corner. Come on kids."

We all walked passed them. I was shocked. The boys looked like they'd just been hit with a bat. Soon we approached Mr. Muhammad's store.

"Big Mama, let's stop here."

We walked inside the store, and Mr. Muhammad said, "Salaam little ones, and Salaam dear lady."

"And, Peace be unto you too," Big Mama replied.

"Big Mama, you know what he said?" I asked with a bit of surprise.

"Yes baby. He said peace to y'all."

Plump and I looked at each other, and said, "Oh," in unison.

We got our snacks, and said goodbye to Mr. Muhammad. When we turned the corner to our house, I saw Alley sitting on the steps. I ran to her and hugged her.

"Ouch Jay-Jay! Don't squeeze me that hard," Alley said in pain.

"I'm sorry. Are you okay?"

She shook her head, and said she was all right. I knew she wasn't. I could see little bruises, and whelps on her legs, but I didn't say anything about it. Big Mama approached us along with everybody else.

"Hey baby! Give me a hug," Big Mama said. Alley stood up, and gave Big Mama a hug. Big Mama lifted her chin, and said, "Are you all right?"

"Yes ma'am." Alley replied.

I looked at Big Mama. I could tell that Big Mama didn't believe her either.

"Okay," Big Mama said. "Would you like something to eat?"

"Yes ma'am," she replied.

"I'll go, and make you a sandwich. Later, if you want to, you can eat dinner with us."

"Okay," replied Alley.

Big Mama gave Alley a concerned smile, and went in the house. Teach and my brothers ate their snacks on the steps. Then they started kicking a ball around the yard. Plump told Alley about the party that we had at the center today, and about the scary clowns we saw. I didn't think they were scary, but I didn't want to interrupt her story. Plump's mother came home early, and Plump said she would see us later. Then she left. After Plump left, I wanted to know how Alley really was, but I didn't want to say anything in front of Plump.

"Alley, I don't want to upset you, but where have you been? Why didn't you come to summer camp?"

"My dad wouldn't let me go. He said I had to stay home, and clean the mess up."

"Is that why you have all those bruises?"

"He got mad at me when he found out that I stayed with y'all. He said I shouldn't have stayed with niggers. He beat me so badly I couldn't come outside to play with you yesterday when you came by." Alley's voice began to shake. She was about to cry.

"Alley let me tell Big Mama. She will help you."

"No. If another social worker comes to our house, he will know that I told. Besides, he makes me lie to them anyway. I'm afraid of what he will do to me if I tell."

"Alley, you can hide here. I won't tell anybody."

"I know Jay-Jay, but he knows I've come here before. This will be the first place he will look."

"We will protect you, Alley." I said softly.

"I don't want your family to be hurt by him. He can be very mean."

"Let us help you."

"I told you Jay-Jay. No one can help me, but there may come a time when I will have no choice. Then I will need your help."

"Alley, if you need to hide here, you can. If you're hungry we will feed you. And, if you want our help, we will help you. All you have to do is ask, okay."

With tears in her eyes, Alley gave me a hug, and said, "Jay-Jay you are my sister, and I love you."

Big Mama came back outside with the sandwich. Alley quickly wiped the tears from her eyes.

"Thank you," she said.

Alley ate dinner with us, and then I walked her home.

Chapter 16
Meet the family

Today was Saturday, and daddy was coming by this morning to pick me, and my brothers up. Big Mama was up early in the kitchen making breakfast for us all. I got dressed, and came downstairs. My brothers were already sitting at the kitchen table when I got there. Mama walked into the kitchen shortly after I did.

Mama said, "Today, I'm going to do nothing. Well, that is until Mike picks me up for dinner tonight. I'm just going to catch up on cooking shows and read one of my romantic novels, or something."

"Baby, you don't need a romantic novel. Your real life is getting romantic enough," Big Mama said with a grin.

My brothers were sitting at the table talking about vomiting, and other gross stuff.

I yelled, "Mama, Jordan and Jonathan are talking about vomiting at the table!"

"Boys stop it before I have to separate you two," said mama sternly.

Right at this point I realized how much I missed Alley. I had no one on my side to help me counteract my brother's comments. Alley lived with us for two months, and now she was gone. I missed seeing her here. The door bell rang, and it abruptly changed the focus of my mind.

"Kids, that must be your father," mama said. "Hurry up, and finish. Then go get your bags."

Mama answered the door, and it was daddy. He was early today.

"Hello everybody," daddy said as he entered the room.

"James you're early. They haven't finished their breakfast," said mama.

"That's okay. I wanted to talk to you anyway. Can we go outside onto the porch for a minute?"

"James, I don't think I like the way this sounds."

"I promise I'm not here to start any trouble."

"Okay James. Come on."

Mama stepped outside, and daddy shut the door behind them. She looked at James's truck, and Tammy wasn't there.

"James, where is Tammy?" Mama asked

"Oh, we broke up. She wasn't into the family life," he replied.

"Let me guess," mama said with a grin. "She went to the highest bidder"

"What?" Daddy said curiously.

"She found another man who could give her more than you." James looked down for a moment and grinned.

"I guess so," he said. "Michelle, I know I've made some mistakes. Also, I realized that I never apologized to you like the judge told me to. Well, I just wanted to say I'm sorry."

"Now, that's big of you James. Is that all?"

"No. We have three kids Michelle that need to have their parents together under the same roof. I think maybe we should try it again."

"What?" Mama looked at James as if he said something crazy. "Are you kidding James?"

"No Michelle. We've been together for twelve years. Are you really ready to throw that all away?"

Suddenly, the fury that mama had buried away in her heart was about to burst through her mouth.

"I didn't throw this marriage away James! You did! Do you really think I would want to come back to you after you brought that hood rat into our house, our bed? Man, you have one Hell of a nerve!"

"You forgave me before. So, why can't you forgive me now?"

"Because James, I know it's a lie. I have finally woken up. You've been telling me for years you would never do it again, and like a fool I would take you back. Not anymore. You've made a fool of me for too long, and now it is going to stop."

"Michelle, I promise you that I won't hurt you again. I care about you, and-."

"Just shut up James. Nothing you say to me means anything anymore. You don't care about me, or your children. You left us for two months before we even got divorced. You didn't even come back to see if your kids still had a roof over their heads. We both know you wouldn't be here now if Tammy hadn't left you."

"Do you think you'll ever forgive me?" He asked.

"James, maybe some day, but this isn't about forgiveness. I feel good about myself now for the first time. When I was with you, you made me feel like I couldn't take care of myself unless you were here. Now, I'm about to start my own business."

"What?" James said in shock.

"Yes. I'm going to start my own business. Also, you told me that nobody wants an old bitch like me, but I found somebody that does. And, guess what James, he believes in me too. He's here for me when I need him, and not when it's convenient for him. Do you think I would throw all this away for you? James, you're just selfish. You don't care about me. That's why you left with Tammy in the first place. You just think you can sweet talk me into going back with you, so you can do this to me all over again. Do you really think you can come back just like that?"

"Michelle, I know I was selfish, but--."

"And, you still are! James, you really hurt me this time. Some days it was all I could do to get up off the couch because I couldn't sleep in that bedroom. I cried for months. If you wanted to leave, then you should have left. You didn't have to hurt me like that. James, what if one of our children saw you like that the night I came home from work?"

"Michelle, I know it's only been few months since we been divorced, but I hope in time you'll forgive me."

Maybe James, but I have somebody now, and no matter what, I'm not coming back to you."

"So, how long do you think this 'Mike' person will stick around?" James asked with a lot of emphases on Mike's name.

"I don't know, but it doesn't matter anyway. I'm not coming back to you no matter what," Michelle said. "Let me go get the kids. It's time for you to go."

Mama stood up to walk towards the house when she turned to James, and said, "Don't worry James. There are plenty more hood rats where that one came from. You will find someone else."

Then she walked into the house. My brothers and I were ready when mama came back into the house. We all heard mama and daddy arguing, but no one said anything.

"Guys, are you ready to go?" We all said yes. "Come on."

Mama gave us a hug, and we left the house. My brothers and I got into the truck with daddy and then he drove us away.

"Michelle," Big Mama said. "Are you all right?"

"Yes. I'm okay."

"I knew he would try to come back, but I'm proud of you. You've finally stood up to him. It's about time too."

"Mom, have I ever told you how much I love you?" Mama asked.

"Not lately, baby," Big Mama replied.

"Well, I do, and I'm glad you are here."

Big Mama smiled, and stood up. "Now, I'm about to leave. Pee-Pee and I are headed outside. I've got to fix my petunias, and the garden. The storm tore through my plants, and now I have to replace a few of them. If you need something, just let me know. Come on Pee-Pee, we have some work to do."

Pee-Pee followed Big Mama outside the back door. Mama lay down on the couch, and stayed there for most of the day.

*****

Michelle was asleep on the couch when the phone rang. It was Mike. He told her he would be coming by a few minutes earlier before dinner. She ran upstairs to take a shower. When she got out of the shower, she decided to wear her conservative navy-blue pants suit. She didn't want to look too provocative when she met Mike's brother, and sister in-law for the first time. Michelle walked downstairs to find Big Mama and Mr. Davis playing cards in the den.

"Now, don't you look lovely," Big Mama said.

"Thank you. So, who's winning?" Michelle asked.

"Me, of course, but Ben is getting better."

"Yeah, and soon I'll be good enough to give her a real challenge."

Michelle grinned. The door bell rang, and Michelle answered the door with Pee-Pee at her side.

"Hi beautiful," Mike said. Then he kissed Michelle on the cheek. "This is my brother Trey, and his wife Lisa."

"It's nice to finally meet you," Michelle said. "Y'all come on in."

Mike, his brother, and sister in-law walked inside as Michelle closed the door behind them. They followed Michelle to the den.

"Mr. Davis, mom, this is Mike's brother Trey, and his wife Lisa. They are here visiting from Mississippi. Trey, Lisa, this is my mother, Bertha Thomas, and my neighbor, Benjamin Davis."

Mike's brother and sister in-law exchanged greetings with Mr. Davis and Big Mama.

"Y'all have a seat," Big Mama said. After everyone was seated, Big Mama said, "Trey, what part of Mississippi are you from?"

"We live in a small town called Bay St. Louis that is not too far from Biloxi. We live very close to the gulf."

"I'll bet it is beautiful looking over that Gulf water. I don't think I've ever been there before. The only part of Mississippi I've ever been to is Biloxi," Big Mama said with a laugh. "I went down there on a bus trip one year with some of my club members. Man, I had the best time. We stayed at this big hotel near the river boats. The hotel played live music, and put on concerts. My group went on a gambling boat. I tell you, if I had more money I'd still be down there."

Everybody laughed.

"I think Ben would love those river boats. Ben is good at playing bingo, and I think he would really love it. Ben, have you ever been to the casinos?" Big Mama asked.

"Nah, I can't say that I have, but we may have to take a bus ride down there one day, and try our luck," Ben replied.

"Okay Ben, you've got a date," Big Mama said as she laughed. "Trey, we didn't mean to take over this conversation. Why don't you tell us a little bit about yourself?"

"I moved to Mississippi after I served in the military. Then we got married, and found a home in Bay St. Louis."

"Lisa, what do you do?" Michelle asked.

"I'm a fifth grade teacher," she replied.

"Now, I admire your profession. We need more smart people to pass on what they have learned to the next generation. A good teacher is worth more than gold," Big Mama said.

"Lisa, do y'all have any kids?" Michelle asked.

"No, they don't have any kids right now," Big Mama interrupted. "But, I don't think it will be long before there's a new arrival though."

Trey and Lisa looked at Big Mama strangely.

"Stop Mom," Michelle said through a toothy smile.

"Oh Michelle, they like kids, but y'all are just too young now to deal with children. Enjoy this time you have together before you have to find a reliable baby sitter."

"Michelle, do you have any kids?" Lisa asked.

"Oh yes. I have three." Michelle got up. She walked to the mantel, and got the picture of her three kids posing together.

"This is my daughter Jasmine, and these are my twin boys Jordan and Jonathan."

Lisa began to smile, and sighed when she saw the picture.

"They are beautiful. The girl looks like your mother, and the boys look like you. Where are they now?" Lisa asked.

"Oh, they are with their father," replied Michelle.

"Good, now you will have more time to spend with us," Lisa said with a smile.

"Speaking of time," Mike said, "I think we had better be going."

"Well, y'all have a good time," Big Mama said. "It was nice to meet y'all."

They all said goodnight to Big Mama and Mr. Davis. Then they left.

Michelle and Mike rode in Mike's red sport car, and Mike's brother followed them in his car.

"Mike, I thought we all were going to ride in the same car together," Michelle said.

"No. My car is a little too small for four adults. He's going to meet us there. This gives me a little time to be alone with you."

"Mike, I want to tell you something," Michelle said with a bit of hesitation.

"What? You're pregnant!" Mike said with a big grin.

"What? No Mike. Why would you ask me that question?"

"I thought if it wasn't anything that important then maybe you could go on, and just tell me. Although, if you want to get pregnant, I would love to practice with you," Mike said grinning.

"Stop being silly, I want to tell you something."

"What?" Mike asked with a raised brow.

"I think James is jealous of you."

"I knew that," Mike said.

"How did you know?"

"Any man that confronts me at his son's baseball game about me hurting his kids he hasn't cared to visit in months must be jealous. He left his kids for two months without saying a word to you, or them. I know this man isn't worried about his children's well being. He is worried about me."

"He confronted you at the game?" Michelle asked looking a bit shocked.

"Oh yes. He thought he could intimidate me, but I believe we have an understanding now."

"You know he wants to get me back." Michelle said turning to look at Mike.

"Really," Mike said looking at Michelle out of the corner of his eye.

"You know why, don't you?"

"I've got a hunch," he said.

"He broke up with Tammy. She found another man who could pay more," Michelle said with a grin.

"Michelle, he might have broken up with her, but that's not why he wants you back. He didn't really care about Tammy anyway. Don't you remember how she flirted with every man at Jordan's and Jonathan's birthday party? Everybody saw that, so I know he had to, but he didn't care. When I kissed you that day, I saw him staring at us. He was more worried about what I was doing with you than about Tammy. Tammy was something different for him. She was young, and he liked being seen with her. I believe he thought maybe he could sweet talk you back someday, but he didn't expect me to be here," Mike said with a grin.

"Mike, I'm not going back to him. Maybe it's my fault that he thinks he can come back because I have allowed him to do that to me so many times in the past, but I have changed. I feel more confident now, and I actually believe in myself for the first time now. He made me feel like I was nothing. I felt so bad about myself that I thought I couldn't have anyone else in my life that would care about me. So, that's why I kept taking him back, but not anymore. I'm not going back to that no matter what."

Mike was approaching a red light. When he stopped, he said, "Come here."

Michelle leaned over to him, and kissed him. He placed his hand on the back of her head drawing her closer to him. His warm lips and probing tongue sent shivers down her spine. Suddenly, they were startled by a horn blowing. Mike looked up to see that the light had changed. He released her head, and started driving again.

"I'm proud of you," he said.

"You know, my mother said the same thing." Michelle replied.

"Then your mother and I have something in common."

"Mike, where are we going?"

"I thought we could try this little Italian place called, *Buon Consumo*."

"Sounds really good to me, I'm hungry."

Mike drove to the south side of town. Most of the buildings were on the main stretch of the highway. Mike pulled into the parking lot, and parked next to his brother's car. Mike and Michelle met Mike's brother and sister in-law in the foyer of the restaurant. The restaurant had light stucco covered walls, and little round glass tables near the bar area. The bar was in the middle of the restaurant. The over hang above the bar was covered with the flags of Italy. The dinning sections were on either side of the bar. There was beautiful Italian art work on the walls, and solid wood tables that were scattered throughout the dinning room. The waiter seated the group near a window over looking the red checkered board covered tables on the patio. The waiter took their orders and Mike decided to buy a bottle of wine for all of them to share.

"Mike, this is a beautiful place," Lisa said.

"Mike seems to know all the great restaurants around town. I've lived here all my life and I've never been to some of these places before," Michelle said.

"When you live alone, and you don't want to cook, believe me, you will get to know who has the best restaurants in town," Mike said. "Isn't that right *belle dame*?"

"Now Mike, where did you learn to speak French?" Michelle asked.

"We are Creoles," Trey replied.

"Come on Trey. Every Creole in Louisiana can't speak French. How did you learn the language?" She asked.

"Our grandmother was of French and African descent. My *grandme're* taught us to speak a type of language that combined French and Spanish," Trey said.

"I took a French course in high school because I thought it would be easy. I soon realized that not all of the words we spoke were French. I had to work my butt off to pass that class," Mike said.

Michelle laughed.

"I joined the military, but unlike your brother, I have never been to war. Because I spoke fluently in French, I was sent off to France. I was stationed near Paris for three years. I stayed there most of my term."

"Trey, what part of the military did you serve in?" Michelle asked.

"I was in the Marines," he replied.

"Is that where you met Lisa?" Michelle asked. Lisa and Trey smiled at each other.

"No. I met Lisa in college. She was in my Human Sexuality class."

Everybody laughed.

"I'm not kidding, she sat behind me."

"Well, I guess y'all learned a lot in that class," Mike said with a laugh.

"But," Lisa interrupted him, "he signed up for the G.I. Bill, so he had to serve his country after he graduated. I waited until he was out of the military before we got married."

"How sweet," Michelle said. "She waited for you."

"Oh, she knew I was coming back," Trey replied.

Soon the waiter came back with the salad and left plates with some silverware for them to serve themselves.

Once they all prepared their plates, Trey said, "Michelle, Mike tells me that you are trying to open your own business."

"Oh yes. I am trying to open an elderly sitting service. We don't have one in our area, and I think the community needs one. Besides that, I am ready to leave my old job."

"What kind of work do you do?" Trey asked.

"I work for a finance company." Michelle replied.

"So, I can come to you for a loan?" He asked.

"Oh, I don't approve loans. I only process them," she replied.

The waiter came back to the table with their entrées. The Italian food and the wine complemented each other.

"Now that you know what I do for a living, tell me Trey, what you do? Mike was a little vague about telling me about your career." Michelle asked.

Mike and Lisa turned to look at Trey.

"What? Is it a secret?" Michelle asked.

"No, no. I work for the FBI," Trey said. "We just don't go around telling everybody now that our country is at war. Somebody might want to make a target of us, if you know what I mean."

"The FBI," Michelle said in a whispered voice. "No wonder."

"I was recruited by them before I left the Marines."

"How fascinating," Michelle said. "Lisa, I know you must worry about him."

"I do, but he is good at what he does, so I try not to think about it," Lisa replied.

"Mike, do you think he could help us find Alley's mother?" Michelle asked.

"What?" Trey asked.

"I'll tell you about it later after dinner tonight," Mike said.

"Tell me Mike, how'd you ever find such a beautiful woman?" Trey asked.

"I was working on a car for Mrs. Jenkins when Michelle came outside on the back porch. She was calling her kids in to eat dinner when she asked me to join them."

"Now Mike, I can't take credit for that. Mrs. Jenkins is the one who wanted me to invite you," Michelle said.

"I wish I could thank her for that." Mike said as he winked at Michelle.

"Why can't you?" Trey asked.

"She passed away not too long ago," Michelle said solemnly. She took a sip of her wine when Mike reached over, and grabbed her wrist. He wanted to console her, but the look in her eyes made it known that the pain in her heart was still there.

"We're sorry for your loss," Lisa said. "Why don't we talk about your business?"

"Oh yeah, I almost forgot. Sharon and I found a building. It's an old retirement home. It has ten bedrooms, a kitchen, dinning room, and a large recreational area. The owner is willing to include any leftover equipment if we accept his asking price," Michelle said. "It does need a little bit of work, but it could be a great place. The realtor wants to show me more buildings, but I'm really hoping we could get this one."

"Now guys, that deserves a toast," Mike said. Everyone raised their glasses and Mike said, "To your success."

The glasses chimed in the air and then everybody took a sip.

After dinner, Mike told Michelle he was going to finally take her back to his house, but it was only to talk about Alley. They drove about twenty minutes before they arrived at Mike's house. Mike had a modern two story house that was simply beautiful. His front lawn had been recently cut, and the front door was made of a thick smoky glass. There were huge glass panels beside the door. The front over hang also functioned as a balcony for the upstairs bedroom.

"Mike, I didn't think a man as rugged as you are would have such a beautiful place," Michelle said.

"Oh really," he said lifting one eye brow. "What did you expect?"

"I guess I expected more of a bachelor pad. You know something not as neat."

"Well, I might have picked something out like that when I first came here, but I wasn't alone. My wife found this place."

"Mike, where is your brother?" Michelle asked.

"Oh, he'll be here in a little while. He said he had to stop by the store. Lisa needed some things. They should be here soon."

"You know you, and your brother could pass for twins."

"Yeah, but he's older and I'm prettier," Mike said with a grin.

Michelle laughed as Mike opened the door. His living room was made on an opened floor plan. His house was as modern and beautiful on the inside as it was on the outside. The floors were made of large wooden panels. He had a large shaggy area rug by the fireplace, and a huge leather sectional sofa surrounding it. A glass table was in the middle of the rug, and two modern floor lamps hung over the back of the couch.

"When I bought this house, it didn't have a second floor. A few of my friends and I built the second floor," he said.

"Mike, you have done such a great job on this house. I'm curious, why would you want to own a repair shop? I would think you would want to start your own construction business."

"Construction can be a seasonal business. When the season is low, I won't have any money coming in. I need something that is steadier in revenue than construction. And, as long as people make cars, they will break down, so I know I will always have a steady income. Even if the auto repair business is slow, I can always do some construction work on the side to make some extra money. Come on. Let me show you the upstairs." Suddenly, the door bell rang. "Damn," Mike said.

"It's okay," Michelle replied calmly. "You'll have to show me later. Don't keep your brother waiting."

Mike answered the door. Trey and Lisa sat down on the couch next to Michelle.

"Sorry guys. Lisa had to stop by the store first. So, what did y'all want to talk to me about?" Trey asked. Mike sat down on the sectional by Michelle.

"My daughter has a friend that lives around the corner from us. We think that she is being abused by her father. We've called the authorities twice, but her father always finds a way of not getting caught. I know he's a drug dealer, and he left his daughter in their house alone for two months before he came back. I've been taking care of her up until now. Mike and I think he's getting help from the police," Michelle said.

"What makes you think the police are involved?" Trey asked.

"Because, Michelle's mother said that he was talking to a police officer named Daniel Smith before he left, and I don't believe an officer would be at a known drug dealer's house to talk unless he was putting him in jail," Mike replied.

"Also," Michelle continued, "Alexandria's mother is missing. It's been several years since I've seen her. We would also like to know if Alley has anymore family members around that would be willing to take her from that monster. Do you think you can help us?"

"Oh yes, I've investigated many cases like this one before. Let me make a few phone calls tonight, and I'll let you know something tomorrow," Trey replied.

"Thank you, Trey. Maybe now we can get this monster away from that little girl," Michelle replied.

Michelle talked with Mike's brother for a little while longer before she decided that it was time to go home.

"Well, it was nice to meet y'all, and I hope y'all have a safe trip home," Michelle said.

Trey hugged Michelle, and so did Lisa.

"I know we'll be seeing you again," Trey said. "Mike has never brought anybody else by to see us before."

Michelle looked at Mike with a bit of shock.

"You must be very special." Trey said.

"She is," Mike replied. "Come on. Let's go." Mike drove Michelle home.

When Mike parked his car in Michelle's driveway, he said, "Tomorrow I'll come by your house around three o'clock, and tell you what my bother has found out. Will you be home by then?"

"Yes," she replied.

"Good. I would walk you to the door, but I want to hurry back to see what my brother has found out so far. Come here."

Mike kissed Michelle softly on the lips and on the brow.

"I think we may have disappointed your neighbor by not kissing on the porch," Mike said grinning. "Go on inside, I'll see you tomorrow." Michelle left the car, and went into the house.

*****

After church, Big Mama and Michelle were sitting outside on the patio drinking tea.

"Mom, Mike's brother is an investigator for the FBI." Michelle said. Big Mama's eyes grew big. "I told him about Alley's father. I'm hoping he can help us."

"An FBI agent, isn't that something," Big Mama said shaking her head in shock. "Baby, I think we're all lucky you're with Mike now."

"Did I hear my name?" Mike walked toward them from the side yard.

"Hey sweetie, have a seat. Do you want some of mom's tea? She used a sugar substitute, but it's still good," Michelle said.

"No thanks." Mike replied.

"Mike, what did you find out from your brother?" Big Mama asked.

"He told me that the police department that Officer Smith works for is under an investigation for money laundering. There are five police officers involved that started this phony internet business as a way of making their money seem legit. The Feds believe they are getting payoffs from local drug dealers. The drug dealers that paid the officers loved this deal because they have police protection, and they can do their business without the risk of going to jail. But, the drug dealers that don't want to pay, well they get the shake down. The police would harass them every time they were caught on the street. These officers were making so much money from this scam that some of the other officers got suspicious. They got so greedy that they would steal from each other. Someone made an anonymous phone call that tipped off Internal Affairs. That's when the officers started this phony internet scam. And, because they are using the internet and the accounts are overseas. The Feds can't seize the money."

"Mike, why did the Feds get involved if it was an IAD problem?" Michelle asked.

"The cops are using the internet, and foreign banks to deposit the money. Once they started this, their crimes became a federal offence. Thanks to your tip the Feds will be able to stop them."

"How?" Michelle asked.

"They needed a way to connect the officers with the drug dealers. Before, all they had on the officers was a service through the internet that the customers would pay a fee by a wire, or direct deposit. And of course, no drug dealers that got beat down were going to come forward. They would risk going to jail too. Until now, there was no connection, or witnesses between the cops, and the drug dealers, but now you've given them a suspect. Tell me, what's Alley's father's last name?" Mike asked.

"Hope," Michelle said.

"I told Trey where she lived, and he has her father's first name already, but this will definitely help. Now, don't tell anyone about this. We don't want to tip him off in any way, okay?"

"Of course, we won't," Michelle said.

"Mike, we won't tell anyone," Big Mama said.

Michelle heard the back gate open. It was James. He was followed by Jordan, Jonathan and Jasmine.

"Well, hello Mike. I see that you're here again."

Chapter 17
The Sins of the Father

"Hi James," Michelle said. "Guys, go put your bags in the house."

"I rang the doorbell, but no one answered the door," James said.

"I'm sorry James, I didn't think you would be here this early," replied Michelle.

"Hi Mrs. Thomas," said James. "How are you enjoying living here?"

"I'm enjoying myself just fine James," replied Big Mama.

"I like this old house myself, but it wasn't as nice back then as it is now. I guess you've had a lot to do with that, Mike."

Mike glared at James for a moment. "A lot of things are nicer around here now," Mike replied.

Before James could say anything else, Michelle interrupted them. "James, thank you for bringing the kids back early, but now I think it's time for you to go."

"Yes, I believe it is. We'll talk later Michelle. See yah Mrs. Thomas, Mike." James walked back to the front yard and then he left.

"Mike, don't pay any attention to that man. He's just trying to beat a dead horse," Big Mama said with a grin.

Mike smiled at Big Mama, but Michelle could tell that he was annoyed. Big Mike stayed until dinner. Then he went home too.

*****

This was the first week after summer camp ended, and school was going to start next week. On Monday, I wanted to play with Plump, but she had to stay with her grandma until her mother got home. I decided to help Big Mama in the garden. We picked vegetables, and pulled weeds. Big Mama even let me help her plant an herb garden. We planted the herbs in a row that she dug next to the garden. Big Mama told me the stories of the destinies faced by the *Ayins* in my family. The tails of sacrifice, honor, and bravery from mysterious distant lands gave my mind images of my family's rich history. It was getting close to noon now. Big

Mama and I walked to the front yard where my brothers were playing soccer with an old ball they had found in the yard. Pee-Pee was barking, and running back and forth between them when Big Mama and I walked onto the porch.

"Jasmine, do you want something to drink?" Big Mama asked.

"No, I'll get something later." I replied.

Big Mama went into the house while I watched my brothers playing, and I noticed Pee-Pee's eyes never left the ball. Every time one of my brothers kicked the ball, Pee-Pee would chase the ball in whatever direction it went. Jordan stopped the ball with his foot. Pee-Pee put his head down and his backside up. Jordan kicked the ball, and Pee-Pee took off. The dog jumped in the air hitting the ball with his nose. The ball sailed across the sidewalk, and rolled down the street. The dog ran after it and so did my brothers. My brothers were screaming. Pee-Pee was barking. I was laughing. I laughed so hard I almost fell out of the swing. When I looked up again, I saw Alley coming around the corner. Her clothes looked like she had slept in them. As she approached the porch, I could see that some of the bruises on her legs had faded, but today she had red marks across her face.

"Hey Alley," I said softly.

"Hi," she replied.

Then she walked over, and sat by me on the swing. I could see the images of finger prints that left their red marks across her beautiful face. It was hard for me to believe that anyone would harm such a sweet girl. I wanted to ask her how she got the marks, but I knew better. She was in enough pain, and I didn't want her to re-live the memories by asking too many questions.

"Do you want to eat lunch with us?" I asked.

"Sure," she replied.

Big Mama walked back onto the porch. "Alley, hey honey. Are you okay," she asked.

Alley put her head down, and said, "Yes ma'am."

"Big Mama, can Alley eat lunch with us today?" I asked.

"Of course, she can. Alley, I want to take a picture of you."

"No Big Mama! I look awful right now. Please, don't take my picture," Alley pleaded.

"Come here baby," Big Mama said. Big Mama gave Alley a hug. "You are beautiful, and everybody here knows it."

"But, look at my face." Alley lifted her head, so that Big Mama could see it. Big Mama put her finger under Alley's chin, and looked at her face from side to side. Then Big Mama stepped back, and folded her arms.

"Yeah, I see your face, and it is as beautiful as it has ever been. You should never be ashamed of your face, but the person who did this to you should be. Alley you're with us now, and we all love you no matter what," Big Mama said.

"You love me, Big Mama?" Alley asked with big blue eyes looking up into Big Mama's.

"Very much, but I need to be honest with you. I wanted to take your picture, so I can show it to someone who will help us. We really need his help Alley, so please take the picture. If you like, you can take the picture with Jasmine. Jasmine, you don't mine, do you?"

"No ma'am," I said.

"You see Alley," replied Big Mama. "We'll all love you just the way you are."

Alley hugged Big Mama and then she sat down on the swing beside me. Big Mama went into the house, and got the camera. When she came back, she took the picture of Alley and me. Believe it or not, Alley even smiled.

"Now, that's a beautiful picture," Big Mama replied. "Boys, y'all stop chasing that dog, and come inside. It's time to eat lunch."

Later on, that afternoon, Big Mama and Mr. Davis sat in the rocking chairs sipping a glass of ice tea, and talking about the weather. Alley, my brothers, and I played a game of *Jacks* on the porch until Teach and Carlos walked into our yard.

"Jordan, Jonathan, do y'all want to walk to the store with us?" Carlos asked with a very thick Spanish accent.

"Yeah," Jordan and Jonathan said in unison. "Big Mama, can we go with them?" Jordan asked.

"Okay, but come straight back here when you leave the store," Big Mama said. "You know something Ben. When I was their age, I would walk about a mile to the store. I would always take my friend Lucy with me. We played kick the can all the way to the store and back. Most of the time we just wanted to talk alone without grown folks hanging around us. When we got to the store, we didn't have any money to buy any candy like these kids today. Oh no Ben, mama would give us a grocery list, and just enough money to buy what we needed. Lucy always helped me carry the bags home. One day we were walking home carrying the groceries, and giggling all the way, when an old truck was speeding down the road. There were three young white boys in the truck just a hooping, and hollering. We ran as fast as we could. The truck was approaching fast. The boys in the truck yelled, 'Run you little niggers, run!' Lucy couldn't run as fast as I could. I yelled, 'Lucy, come on!'

"She yelled back saying, 'I can't.'"

"There was a creek beside the dirt road we walked on. I turned to Lucy, and said, 'Jump!'"

"'What?' She yelled back."

"'Jump Lucy! Jump!' I shouted. I jumped into the creek with the bag still in my hands, but Lucy didn't make it. The truck hit the side of Lucy's leg, and she slide down the hill into the creek. I ran back to Lucy with tears in my eyes. I was terrified that she might be dead. She was laying face down on the rocks when I turned her over. "I said, 'Lucy, are you all right?'

"She just moaned for a moment as her eyes rolled back. Then she grabbed my arm, and said, 'Why?'"

"I shook my head, and said truthfully, 'I don't know.' I tried to get her up, but her leg was badly broken. I crawled up towards the edge of the road to see if the truck was gone and it was. When I came back to Lucy, she was crying hysterically. I tried to move her again, but she screamed. I told her I had to find someone to help us. She told me to go get Papa. I told her that her house was too far away, but she didn't want me to get anyone else. I said okay, but stay down here, and keep quiet. I ran for thirty minutes before I got to her house. Her father put me in his truck, and we drove to where she was. I called her name, but she didn't answer me."

"Her daddy yelled, 'Lucy!'"

"Then we heard a faint voice saying, 'Papa?' Her father picked her up, and put her in the truck. I got in on the other side. We both were dirty, and scratched up. I told mama, papa, and Lucy's father what happened. They told the local sheriff, but of course, he didn't do anything. The doctor fixed Lucy's leg, but she walked with a limp from that day on. You know something Ben. The more I see how things have changed, the more I realized how much has stayed the same," Big Mama said with a little sadness in her voice.

"I know what you mean Bertha, I know what you mean," replied Ben.

Soon we saw Plump walking towards our yard. "Hey guys? Whatcha doing?" She asked.

"Playing *Jacks*," I said.

"I want to play." Plump sat down on the porch to play with us when the boys walked into the yard. The boys sat on the steps eating their snacks, and blowing huge bubbles with their bubble gum. While I watched Alley playing Jacks, I thought about what Alley's father had called us. I also thought about what Big Mama said in her story.

"Big Mama, what does 'nigger' mean?" I asked. Big Mama and Mr. Davis turned to me, and gasped. I was a little scared. I thought I was really going to get it this time, but Big Mama said, "I will tell you what it means, but I don't want to ever hear you say that again. It is a very old word used to describe African people. It is a bad word. It is used to belittle us, or to somehow make us seem less than human. The word has been given many meanings over time, but none of the meanings are any good. It pains me to hear our own people use this word to describe one another. How can a black person call another person this without the meaning applying to them too? We are African Americans Jasmine. We should not use words that were made to bring us down, and accept them into our culture. Use your words to build our people up instead of tearing each other down. You will never be a nigger. This is the word used by the slave owners to make our people feel like we were inhuman. If you accept this word, then you will not only believe you are nothing, but you will become what you believe. Who you say you are Jasmine is what you will become.

Kids, listen to me. Please remember the friendships you have now, and when you grow older think like the child you once were that didn't see race, religion, or gender. This world would be a wonderful place if we all accepted our differences, and understood that God is the only Supreme Being that dominates us all. It is blasphemy for a human to dominate another human. Also, we are stewards of this earth. We are here to protect His planet. We are not sent here to kill, and destroy His people, or the Earth, but to have life eternal. If we destroy this planet, where will we live? The earth will survive without us, but we can't survive without it. Think of your futures. Fight the people who would poison the air, water, and earth for profits that benefit their own greed. The future is in your hands. Be a part of the light, or wallow in darkness forever."

Big Mama paused for a moment. I thought she was about to cry. Then she said, "Ben, I am going inside for some more tea. Would you care to join me?"

"Oh yes Bertha. I would love to," Ben replied.

Big Mama and Mr. Davis walked into the house together. I could tell that Big Mama's memories of her friend brought back painful feelings from the past, and I don't think it helped the situation when I asked this question either. Now, I realized why Big Mama doesn't want us to curse, or call each other bad names. She understands that if we say these things long enough about ourselves, we will start to believe them. But, I believe we are all God's flowers. We are multicolored, and beautiful in His sight. We must take care of his flowers too. Nothing anyone calls me will change my opinion.

*****

Today was Thursday, and we had to register for school. Big Mama took my brothers to their classes and mama took me to mine. My homeroom teacher looked like a young lady in old lady's clothing. She even wore pointed rimmed glasses. Her name was Mrs. Ranch. Mrs. Ranch passed out all the important papers to our parents including our schedules. I looked around the room, and the only person in my first class that I knew was Teach. He was waving at me from two rows back. I waved back to him. After orientation, we all met back at the van. Jordan was upset that the only class that he had with Jonathan was P.E. Big Mama said it was getting too hard for the teachers to tell them apart now.

"Mom, I am closing on the building that Sharon and I saw last week," mama said. "Will you bring their papers back here on Friday for me?"

"Of course, I will. Michelle this is great news. Have you told Mike the news yet?"

"I'll tell him tonight. I am turning in my notice in on Monday. I'm nervous. This is such a big move."

"I know baby, but it will all work out. You will see," Big Mama said with a smile.

Later on that night, mama called Big Mike. I could hear him yelling with excitement over the phone. They talked until nine thirty that night, or at least until I fell asleep.

Monday seemed to come too soon. I hated getting up so early. It was hard to believe the summer was gone so fast. At school today, Toad and Stool started bullying the younger students in the hallways earlier this year. They never missed a chance to pick on Alley either. Alley walked by

Toad carrying a bunch of books, and papers. Toad put his foot out in front of Alley tripping her. She tripped falling face forward to the floor. Her books and papers were scattered everywhere. Alley scrambled to pick them up before anyone walked on them.

"Ha, ha, ha, you stupid girl! What's wrong with you? You can't hold your books without falling down?" Toad said as he continued to laugh.

I helped Alley pick up her books. Then I turned to Toad and Stool, and said, "You Jerks! She could have hurt herself. Why don't you pick on somebody your own size?"

"Oh yeah?" Toad yelled. "What are you going to do about it?"

"Do about what?" Principal Whitaker was standing right behind him.

"Todd tripped Alley, and threatened me," I said.

"Todd, come with me," Principal Whitaker said. Toad gave me a mean look before he walked down the hall with the principal.

I touched Alley's shoulder, and whispered in her ear, "Don't worry Alley. We're going to get them."

Wednesday after school, Big Mama picked us up. When Big Mama's big old car turned the corner onto our street, I saw Mike fixing Mrs. Madison's white picket fence. The angel was standing behind him. When she saw me staring at her, she smiled at me, and disappeared. Big Mama parked her car in the driveway. We all got out. Big Mike waved to us, and said he would come by later. Big Mama gave us some granola bars for a snack today. We normally would go outside to play, but Big Mama said things had to change now that she was living with mama. We had to have our homework done by the time mama came home from work. Jordan hated doing his homework first. He felt that most of the daylight would be gone before he could get outside to play. An hour had passed. Even though Jordan complained the whole time, we all finished our homework, and went outside. Big Mama walked outside with us as we played in the front yard. Mike repaired, and painted Mrs. Madison's fence. Mrs. Madison tried to pay him, but Mike wouldn't take it. Mike walked into our yard, and sat down in the rocker by Big Mama.

"Mike, you have done a beautiful job on Mrs. Madison's fence," Big Mama said.

"Thank you," Mike replied.

"I know you must be hot working out there in the hot sun. Would you like some tea?" She asked.

"Yes ma'am. Thank you," Mike replied.

Big Mama got up, and walked into the house. When she came back, she had two glasses of tea. She gave Mike his and then she took a sip of her own.

"Mike, I want to give you something." Big Mama reached in the pocket of her dress, and pulled out the picture of Alley and me.

"If you can give this to your brother, it may help to prove that Alley is being abused."

Mike took the picture, and said, "What kind of man could do this to his own child?"

"A man that was abused himself," Big Mama replied. "The little boy that felt helpless as a child has grown up to feel powerful releasing his fury against his own daughter."

"I will give this to my brother. He will be up here soon. Maybe we can find her a good foster family to take care of her until then."

"No Mike!" Big Mama shouted. This was the first time Big Mama realized what would happen to Alley once the police caught up with her father. "She has to stay with us. We are all she has known. It would be terrible to put this child with strangers after all she has been through. Please Mike, talk to him. Don't put her through anymore pain."

"Bertha, I will talk to him," Mike said. "Don't worry."

I was getting bored playing with my brothers, and I wanted to go see Alley. So, I ran onto the porch, and said, "Big Mama, can I go see if Alley's at home?"

"Okay, but y'all come back here. I don't want you to go into that house."

"Yes ma'am," I said as I left the yard.

"Bertha," Mike said, "I talked to my brother yesterday. He said that one of the police officers was followed. They found a bag of money, and drugs in a storage unit he rented. The officer made a deal with the Feds, and he told them where Billy kept the drugs. Once they get a warrant, they are going to raid his house."

"Mike, is it possible to have you, or your brother to contact me before they do this? I really don't want Alley there when this happens."

"I'll try, but I can't promise you that. I don't know when all this is going to happen."

"Mike, I know you will do what you can. I am glad you are willing to help us." Big Mama said sadly.

Mike smiled, and sipped his tea.

"Mike, I know you love my daughter. She doesn't know that yet. Both of you are holding onto the past. You can't dishonor your wife's memory by loving again. Tracy is happy now, and it's time for you to be happy too. You don't have to forget what you had, but just be open to the possibility of what you can have. Don't live in fear Mike."

Mike stared at Big Mama for a moment. "There is something different about you. Michelle won't tell me, but I believe you are physic."

"Oh Mike, you don't have to be physic to see how you feel about her." Big Mama laughed as she looked down the street. "Mike, Jasmine should have been back by now. If you don't mind, would you go get her for me? Alley's house is a block down that way."

"I don't mind at all," Mike said.

"Thank you, Mike, something's not right. I can feel it," Big Mama said with a sudden seriousness.

Mike looked at Big Mama curiously. He knew something was wrong, so he left immediately.

*****

Once I reached Alley's house, I saw a dark angel standing on the porch. I gasped, and stepped back from the fence. The angel smiled at me, and went into the house vanishing through the front door.

I yelled, "Alley," but she didn't come outside.

So, I called her again, and still there was no sign of Alley. Then I saw the door open. It was Billy. He walked outside to the end of his driveway, and down by the fence where I was standing. When I saw him coming near, I stepped back away from the gate.

"Hey Jasmine, Alley is in the house. Why don't you come inside?" Billy asked.

"I can't. I was told to come straight back home," I said truthfully with some apprehension. "Can Alley come outside, and play?"

"Sure, she can, but she's always going to your house. I think it's only neighborly for you to come to her house sometimes," Billy said with a smile. "You sure are a pretty little thing with those green cat eyes. Now, how do you suppose you got those eyes?"

"My grandma's eyes are this color." I said cautiously.

"Are they really?" Billy continued to smile as he looked me up and down. "Have you ever been with a boy before?" He asked.

I wasn't sure of what he meant by this, so I just stared at him.

"Why don't you come on inside, and let me talk to you." Billy started to open the gate when I backed up again.

"I ain't gonna hurt yah. Come here." He demanded.

I started to run when he grabbed me by the arm.

"I told yah I wasn't gonna hurt yah! Come on!" He said still smiling at me.

Then I heard a loud voice behind us saying, "Let her go!" It was Big Mike. Billy released my arm so fast that I stumbled backward.

"Hold on a minute. This ain't what it looks like. I just wanted to invite her into the house to see Alley, that's all." Billy said with an evil grin.

Mike glared at Billy for a moment. I thought Mike was going to hit him. "So, what did you need to talk to her about?" Mike asked.

"Now, I don't appreciate your tone," Billy said. His smile was gone. His voice held the same sinister Southern accent as the monster in my dreams.

"I don't appreciate you," Mike replied. "I may not be her father, but if you put your hands on her again, I guarantee you won't be using those hands for a long time."

"Mister, are you threatening me?" Billy asked with a glare in his eyes.

Mike walked up to Billy with his hands clinched in a fist. Billy must have thought Mike was going to hit him because he stepped back.

"Mister," Mike said with a long pause, "I don't threaten. You've got this whole neighborhood afraid of you. I know men like you. You prey on these people making them too afraid to speak out, but I'm not afraid of you. I know you are a coward. There aren't enough men in this community to stand up against you. You intimidate the women, and elderly in this neighborhood, so they won't tell the authorities what you are doing here. What I can't stand the most is a man that would harm is own child."

"What?" Billy said in fury.

"You heard me! Everybody knows how you hurt that little girl. You are one sick ass man," Big Mike said. "We are going now. Just remember what I said. I ain't afraid of you. Come on Jasmine."

Mike grabbed my hand, and we turned to leave.

"You think you can come around here, and talk to me like that! If I put a bullet in the back of your head you want be so big then, will you," Billy said with his fist clinched.

Mike held my hand, but he didn't turn around. "Mister, I've been in the Army for three years fighting on missions without a bullet in my gun. Believe me. I've learned how to kill a man with my bare hands. I promise you this, if you leave that spot before I am gone, I will kill you before you get to that gate," Mike said with sincerity. "Come on Jasmine. Let's go."

Mike held my hand as we walked down the street. He never looked back, but I did. Billy was fuming mad. His face was red as crimson and his fists were still clinched when we turned the corner. When we got home, Big Mama was standing on the porch. Mama had just driven up when Mike and I walked into the yard. Mama got out of the van, and I ran up to her. Then I hugged her around the waist. Mama looked at Big Mama and Mike.

"What's wrong?" She asked.

"Mike, is she all right?" Big Mama asked.

"Yes," Mike said, "She's just scared."

"Mom, what's going on?" Mama said sternly.

"Michelle, come here and sit down. Boys, y'all go into the house, you too Jasmine."

My brothers and I walked into the house quietly. Mama sat down in the rocker, and Mike sat in the swing.

"Mom, what's going on?" She asked again.

"Michelle, Jasmine went to see Alley. Your mother thought she was gone too long, so I went looking for her. When I got there, Billy grabbed Jasmine by the arm. We got into a little argument for a moment, and then I warned him," Mike said.

"Mom, I warned you about bringing that girl into our house. He's dangerous," mama said.

"Michelle, he's got to be stopped. If we don't stop him, who will?" Mike asked.

"I know Mike," mama replied.

"We can't leave Alley with that monster," Big Mama demanded.

"Mom, what if he comes here tonight?" Michelle asked.

"I'll stay here tonight, if that is okay," Mike said. "I really don't think he wants to see me again. I'll stay on the couch, and keep watch."

Big Mama turned to mama, and said, "Would that be okay?"

"Yes," mama agreed, "but Mike can't stay here forever mom. What will we do when he leaves?"

"Don't worry Michelle. My brother told me Billy's house will be raided soon, and there is a warrant for his arrest," Mike replied.

"Thank God," mama said with a sigh. Now maybe this will all be over soon. Y'all let's go into the house."

Mike ate dinner with us, and he was here when mama told us to go to bed. My brothers were still playing with Mike when I went upstairs. They didn't want to leave. I loved having my own room. Sometimes it was nice coming up here to just be alone. I was looking through my drawer to find my favorite pajamas when I came across Alley's floppy denim hat Big Mama bought her at the beach. When I picked the hat up, my mind instantly saw a vision of Alley. She was screaming and crying in pain. I saw her father slap her across the face knocking her into the corner of the room. He grabbed her by the back of her shirt, and threw her on the bed.

I could hear her screaming in my head saying, "No daddy! Please don't do this!"

"Shut up," he said as he raised his hand to slap her again.

She screamed as her daddy pulled her pants off. Her father's eyes were red, and he fumbled a little when he took his pants off. I could tell he had been drinking. I could hear Alley screams in my ears. I could even smell the vile stench of this man. I thought I was going to be sick as he climbed on top of her. Her screams rang in my ears. I still had the hat clinched in my hand when I covered my ears to drown out her screams. I could see the agony, and pain in her face.

I ran to the window with my hands still covering my ears and screamed, "Alley! Alley!"

I felt helpless. I would have done anything to make him stop even if it meant I would have to take his life. I sat down behind the window sill with my hands still covering my ears. She never stopped screaming. She never stopped crying. She cried out for her mama, but no one came. I had to make her screams in my head stop. I banged my head against the window sill yelling, "Make it stop! Make it stop! Please make it stop!" Big Mama opened my door, and ran to me on the floor. She struggled to sit on the floor beside me. When she sat down, she held me as I screamed.

"Jasmine, stop it! What wrong!" She shouted.

I cried hysterically. "Big Mama, he's hurting her! He's hurting her!" I screamed. "I can hear her screaming in my head! Make it stop! Please, make it stop!"

Big Mama took the hat out of my hands, and suddenly everything was quiet. I continued crying hysterically. When Big Mama touched the hat, she was taken aback.

"Oh no," she said softly.

"Why Big Mama, why would he do this to her?" I asked.

"He's listening to demons, and now he's become a monster." Big Mama closed her eyes for a moment then she opened them again. "He's gone now Jasmine."

I leaned my head against Big Mama's chest, and cried. Big Mama began to pray.

"Dear Father, forgive us of our sins, and please hear our prayer. Father, please send your angel Gabriel to guide us on this path."

Then a wondrous light appeared in my room. The angel Gabriel turned around, and walked out of the light. Big Mama said, "Please, help us free this child from that man that is possessed by demons. Tell us what He would have us to do."

"You must get Alexandria out of that house tonight. Bring her here," said the angel.

"What about her father?" Big Mama asked.

"Don't worry, we will protect you. Take care of the little girl." Then the angel walked towards me. "Sweet *Ayin*, I have a message for you."

The angel's eyes abruptly turned blue. She spoke with a familiar voice I have only heard in my dreams. There was a bright light that glowed around her when she said:

> *"Upon His rock through shifting sand*
> *You will follow me to this shallow land.*
> *Look for me with thy heavenly eye.*
> *Upon this ground they'll be surprised.*
> *I'll be below you waiting to go home.*
> *So, find me sweet Ayin,*
> *And tell my daughter she'll never be alone."*

Then the angel disappeared. Big Mama held me for a moment, and said, "Jasmine, go wash your face, and get into bed. I have to talk to your mama, and tell her that you are all right. I am going to get Alley."

Big Mama got up, and left the room. I sat there for a while. I was still in shock. Then I decided it was time for me to get up too.

Chapter 18
Hope

Big Mama walked downstairs to the den where Michelle and Mike were sitting alone.

"Mom, why was Jasmine screaming?" Michelle asked.

"She saw a vision of Alley," Big Mama said as she walked into the den, and sat on the other couch.

"I knew there was something about your mother that made her a little different, but I didn't know that your daughter has this same ability too," Mike said.

"Mike, my mother is an *Ayin,* or what you call a Seer. I don't go around telling people because most people would think I am crazy."

"Not if they talked to her," replied Mike.

"Well, my daughter was born with this ability too. This trait runs in my family."

"Michelle, I have to go get Alley, and bring her back here," said Big Mama.

Michelle knew her mother couldn't be talked out of this. "Mom, you can't go over there tonight. That man will kill you."

"No, he won't. He's not there. The angel of the Lord appeared to us in Jasmine's room. She said I had to go get her, and bring her back here. She told me I would be safe."

"Why does the angel want you to go over there now?" Michelle asked.

"Because I believe Alley's father has molested her. That's why Jasmine was screaming. She could hear Alley's cries and she saw what happened. I saw it too when I touched Alley's hat."

"Mom, you can't go over there by yourself!"

"I'll go with her," Mike said, "but this time I will have to take my gun I have in the truck just in case we run into trouble."

"Mike, you're going to take a gun with you?" Michelle asked. She was surprised to find out Mike had a gun.

"Michelle, this ain't the kind of man that wants to talk."

"I think we should call the police," Michelle said.

"And, tell them what, that I had a vision? They will think I'm crazy," Big Mama said. "No, there will be no need to call the police, or bring a gun. The angels will protect us. I am going to get a bag for some of her clothes. Then I'll be ready to go." Big Mama left the room quickly, and soon returned with a duffle bag.

"Come on Mike. Let's go," Big Mama said as they walked out of the house, and got into his truck.

Thirty minutes had passed while Michelle sat on the couch waiting for Mike, and Big Mama return. Michelle heard the truck drive up and she ran to open the front door. When Big Mama and Mike walked into the house, Alley slowly peeked from behind Big Mama. Alley's melancholy face was bruised by her father's hand. Her beautiful blue eyes were red, and swollen. She held her head down, and didn't speak.

"Baby, go sit down on the couch, we'll be in there in a minute," Big Mama said. Alley walked slowly past them, and sat down on the couch.

"Mom, how is she?" Michelle asked.

"I don't know. She won't talk. I want to take her to the police department tomorrow, but if she won't tell them what happened, then there's nothing I can do to keep her here. She's not my child, so I can't even take her to the doctor. I'm hoping that she will want to talk in the morning."

"I'll take her bag," Mike said.

"Okay Mike. Take it to Jasmine's room, and tell her I need to talk to her. She's not sleeping."

"What? No Mom. I don't want her involved," Michelle said in shock.

"Honey, she has already seen more than a child her age should see anyway. I won't keep her up too long. Please, let me talk to her," Big Mama pleaded.

"Okay Mom, but don't upset her."

Mike walked upstairs, and knocked on Jasmine's door. He put Alley's bag down by the foot of her bed, and said, "Your grandmother wants to see you." Jasmine's eyes were so swollen from crying she could barely see when she walked downstairs with Mike.

Mama put her hand on my shoulder, and said, "Are you okay, honey?" I shook my head, but I didn't say anything.

"I'll be upstairs if you need me. Come on Mike." Michelle and Mike walked upstairs. Jasmine turned to walk into the den when she saw Alley sitting on the couch with her head down.

"Alley? Alley, are you okay?" Jasmine asked as she walked towards her.

"Jasmine, sit down honey, I want to tell you something." Big Mama said. "Jasmine, Alley, I need you two to be strong because what you've been through tonight will not end quickly. Alley, what your father has done to you is not your fault, and there was nothing you could do. Jasmine, I know you are just as upset by this because you saw it too. Right now, you both will need to depend on each other. Alley, tomorrow I want to take you to the police department and then to the doctor."

"No!" Alley shouted. This was the first time she had spoken all night.

"Honey, if you don't tell the police, we can't stop him from hurting you, or another child again."

Alley hesitated for a moment. Then she said, "I need to go to the bathroom." Alley quickly left the room.

"Big Mama, why would her father do this? Y'all told us not to talk to strangers, but her father isn't a stranger."

"I know Jasmine. Sometimes it's the ones we know, and love that can hurt us the most. Lord, I hope this man pays for what he has done here tonight."

"Big Mama, Alley doesn't believe in God." Jasmine said.

"Honey, I understand. Right now, she thinks God has abandoned her, but he hasn't. So many people say they love the Lord, but they refuse to obey his commandments. There will be a lot of weeping, and wailing in the end. Jasmine, you must let her know this was not God's doing, but her father's. Also, you must give her the courage to talk to the police."

"How Big Mama?"

"She won't talk to me, but she will talk to you," Big Mama said. "Let her cry if she needs to cry. Let her tell you what happened, and encourage her to tell the police. Don't let this monster hurt another child."

Big Mama and Jasmine turned abruptly to look upstairs when we heard the sound of water.

"Alley must be taking a shower," Jasmine said. "Big Mama, what do we do now?"

"We will fulfill our destinies, Jasmine. I've never told you this, but the birth mark on your leg is called, *Elohim's Ayin*. This is a Hebrew word that means *God's eye*. This name was given to the ones that bear this mark by the Hebrew slaves that left Africa in search of the Holy Land. We all have a destiny to fulfill. My destiny is to take care of Alley until she can reunite with her family. Your destiny is to find her mother Jasmine. Together we must bring God's people to the light. There will be many more evil things you will see in the future. I'm afraid most people will be so deceived by this evil, and they will not listen to you. Look for the signs of His coming. Man will cause so much destruction on the earth from wars, and pollution that many of our planet's animals will die. When this happens, people will starve. Pestilence and disease will take over the earth. Many will die. There will be a great country to rise from the east to rule the earth, and anyone that calls out God's name will be put to death. But, don't worry Jasmine, for you have been chosen. You will not face the evil of this world. If you are to see this day, you will be taken up in His second coming, and you will forever live in peace no matter what as long as you never forget your destiny."

"Big Mama, is my destiny to find Alley's mother, or to bring people to the light?"

"Baby, when you find her mother, you will be doing God's will. His will, will lead them to the light. You may have a different destiny in the future, or you may just have this one. Just lead the people to the light of God, and your destiny will be fulfilled. Now Jasmine, it's time to go to bed. Don't wake Alley if she's sleeping, but be there when she wakes."

I hugged Big Mama, and went upstairs. Alley was asleep in my pajamas when I got into the room. Her hair was slightly wet, and her face was still swollen. Jasmine did as Big Mama told her, and went to bed.

*****

When I woke this morning, Alley wasn't there. I ran downstairs where Mike was sleeping on the couch. I ran over to him, and said, "Have you seen Alley?"

His eyes were still groggy from sleep when he turned over to look at me.

"What?" He asked.

"Have you seen Alley?" I asked with a bit of panic in my voice.

"No," Mike said. "Maybe she went to the bathroom?"

I left Mike on the couch, and ran upstairs to check the bathroom. Alley wasn't there. I checked my brother's room and she wasn't there either. I opened mama's door. She was still asleep.

"Mama, have you seen Alley?" I asked.

"What?" Mama said as she rubbed her eyes.

"Mama, Alley is gone."

"Are you sure? She might have gone downstairs."

"I'll go see," I said.

I checked the bathroom downstairs and the kitchen too. She wasn't in either room. I put on my shoes, and walked outside. Pee-Pee followed me outside. I looked all around the house. She was no where to be found. I walked back into the house with Pee-Pee and Big Mama was standing in the den with Big Mike.

"Jasmine, did you find her?" Big Mama asked.

"No ma'am," I said.

"I'll go look for her," Mike said.

"Hold on Mike. I'll go with you," Big Mama replied.

Big Mama left the room and then mama came downstairs. "What's going on? It's not even six a.m. yet," said mama.

"Alley is missing Michelle," Mike said. "Your mother and I are going to look for her."

"Mike, please don't go back into his house. I don't want any trouble."

"Don't worry Michelle. If she went back home, we will call her later. I'm not going into his house. We are just going to look around the neighborhood."

Big Mama changed out of her nightgown into a pair of jeans and t-shirt.

"Let's go Mike," Big Mama said. "Michelle, we'll be back before you have to go to work."

Big Mama and Mike left the house. Mama told me to go upstairs, and get dressed. I took a shower, and put on my clothes. I sat on the edge of my bed to tie my shoe strings when I saw Alley's hat on the floor. I picked it up. My mind saw Alley down by the creek behind our house in the woods. She sat on her knees peering into the water and poking the ground with a knife. Suddenly, the angel of the Lord appeared in front of me.

"Jasmine, go to her. Stop her from hurting herself before it is too late. Go now!" The angel said.

I ran downstairs, and outside the back door. I opened the back gate, and saw the angel pointing in the direction down the hill. I ran down the hill slightly out of breath when I saw Alley sitting by the creek.

"Alley!" I said startling her. "Alley why are you down here? Come back home."

"No Jasmine!" Alley said. "I'm trash now. I don't deserve to be around your family."

"Alley, we love you. Come back."

"No one can love me now. I'm so ashamed. I can't go to school today."

"Alley, I won't tell anyone. I promise, but you have to tell the police."

"No Jasmine! You don't know what my dad did to me?"

"Yes, I do! Last night I touched your hat, and I saw everything. I could hear you screaming so loud in my head that I banged the back of my head on the window sill trying to make it stop. Now I have a huge knot on the back of my head, see."

Jasmine sat down beside Alley, and put her hand on the back of her head to feel the lump.

"You saw?" Alley asked.

"Yes." I said as I started to cry. Alley put her head on my shoulder, and cried too.

When she could speak again, she lifted her head, and said, "Last night when I went upstairs to pee, I found blood in my underwear. I took a shower, and put on one of your mother's pads that were under the sink. I was too ashamed to go back downstairs, so I went to bed."

"Alley, my mama told me that sometime women bleed once a month. She called it a period. She said it happens to all women, so you don't have to be ashamed of that."

"Jay-Jay, I heard about a period before. Plump told me. That's why I know what pads are for, but I've never had a period before. I don't think that is why I'm bleeding. I think he hurt me. Don't you?"

"I know he hurt you, but I don't know why you're bleeding. Alley, I think you should go to the doctor with Big Mama, so the doctor can make sure that you are all right."

"It doesn't matter. I don't want to live like this anymore. My mother left me alone with this man. No one loves me. Not even God."

"No Alley. God loves you."

"No, he doesn't!" Alley said with fury. "I prayed to stay with y'all, and He let my daddy come back to take me away."

"Alley, God didn't do this to you. Your father did this, and you should blame him."

"Jasmine, I'm not going back!" Alley said firmly. "That's why I came out here."

I looked at Alley strangely. "Why did you come out here?"

"Jay-Jay, I came out here to die."

Alley showed me the knife she had down at her side.

"No Alley! If you die then I have to die too."

"Jay-Jay, I can't go back to him!"

"Alley, Big Mama said if you talk to the police you won't have to go back, and even if you did die, he won't stop hurting kids. After school yesterday, I came by your house. I called your name, but your father came outside. He said I had pretty eyes, and he asked me if I had ever been with a boy before. Then he tried to pull me into your house, but Big Mike stopped him. I don't think I've ever been so happy to see Big Mike in my life. If Big Mike hadn't gotten there when he did, I would have been hurt too. Alley, you have to stop him before he tries to hurt me or another kid again."

"Jasmine, I'm too ashamed to talk about it to anyone."

"I'll go with you Alley. I'll tell them what he tried to do to me too."

"You'll go with me?" Alley's bright blue eyes were full of hope.

"Yes, I'll go," Jasmine said. "We will be ashamed together."

A tear fell from Alley's bright blue eyes as she gave me a slight smile. I held my hand out, and Alley gave me the knife. We stood up, and dusted ourselves off. I put my arm around Alley's shoulders as we walked back to the house.

Mama walked downstairs to the kitchen, and saw the back door open. She opened the screen door, and yelled, "Jasmine!" But, there was no answer. She walked back through the kitchen, and she started to go upstairs when the doorbell rang. Mama thought it might be Alley, so she opened the door without checking first.

"Good morning." Billy said stand there with a big smile.

Mama gasped, and stepped back.

"I just came by to see if my daughter might have come by here".

"Why would she come by here this early? What have you done to her?" Mama asked.

Billy stopped smiling, and looked at mama curiously. "So, you haven't seen her? How about your mother? She might have seen her."

"My mother isn't here," mama said quickly as she glared at Billy.

"Well, if you see her, let me know." Then he paused looking mama up and down. "I'll be back to ask your mother later," Billy said with a grin.

Then he walked away. When Alley and I walked into the kitchen, I put the knife in the sink. Mama shut the front door, and locked it. She ran to us and hugged us.

"Where have y'all been?" She asked.

"I went to look for Alley," I replied.

"Jasmine, next time you tell me where you are going first." Mama hugged me again. Then she turned to Alley. "Alley, are you okay sweetie?" She asked.

Alley shook her head, and said, "Yes ma'am."

"Good, let me call Mike and mom."

Mama called Mike and Big Mama on her cell phone to tell them we were at home.

"Mama, Alley can't go to school today," I said.

"I know honey," mama replied. "You go on upstairs, and get your stuff."

"No mama! I can't go either. We have to talk to the police," I said.

"What?" Mama said looking confused.

"Mama, I have to talk to the police too." Soon as I said this, Big Mama and Big Mike walked into the house.

"Alley, why did you leave baby?" Big Mama asked.

"Because she can't go back there," I said.

"What's going on?" Jonathan asked from the top of the steps as Jordan walked up behind him.

"Boys y'all go get dressed for school," mama said. "Why don't the rest of us go into the den? I don't want the boys involved in this."

We all walked into the den, and sat down on the couches.

"Big Mama, I have to go to the police, and tell them what Billy tried to do to me yesterday. Besides, Alley won't go without me."

Mama put her hand over her mouth, and gasped. "What did he do to you, Jasmine?" Mama asked.

"Before Mike got there, Alley's father asked me if I had ever been with a boy. Then he tried to pull me into his house."

"Why didn't you tell me this Mike?" Mama asked.

"Mama, Mike didn't know. Mike got there just when Billy was trying to pull me into his house. Mama, I have to go with Alley. She won't go if I don't go with her."

"Okay Jasmine, I am going too," mama said.

"You and Alley get dressed. Mom, I'm going to take the boys to school. Then I'll be back to take y'all to the police department."

"Michelle, I called my brother yesterday, and he should be here by this afternoon. Alley, will you talk to him?" Mike asked.

"Yes," she said softly.

"Good, after tonight I don't think, you will ever have to see him again," Mike assured her. "I better go. I've got a lot to do."

Mike stood up, and kissed mama's brow. Then he left.

"Alley, go upstairs and get ready. Jasmine, you go with her," mama said.

Both Alley and I stood up, and left the room.

"Mom, Billy came by here looking for Alley earlier. He said he was going to come by again to see you. If he comes by when I'm gone, lock the doors, and call the police."

"Michelle, I don't think he will come back again today, but he will come back soon," Big Mama replied.

"Mom, please be careful. I'm going upstairs to call my boss to tell him I won't be in today."

Mama went upstairs leaving Big Mama on the couch. Big Mama said a silent prayer. When she finished, she walked to her room too.

*****

Mama parked the van by a huge police department with big glass front double doors. I turned to Alley, and grabbed her hand. I know she was scared because I was too. Big Mama opened the van door, and we got out.

"Guys, I know you're scared, but I promise you that mom and I will be with you the whole time. Just tell them what you know, okay," mama said.

We all walked up a small flight of steps, and entered the building. The lobby of the building was covered with a dark wood paneling. There were two glass doors on either side of the room. In the middle of the precinct, was a large bay area and glass windows that surrounded it. The police officers were coming in and out of the left door using their badge card key. People going through the right door were usually buzzed in, and in hand cuffs escorted by the police.

Mama walked up to the front desk, and said, "Officer, my name is Michelle Patterson, and I want to report a crime. Can we talk to someone in private?"

"Oh yes. We were expecting you. Just walk through that door."

The officer buzzed the door open, and we walked in. There were two large metal detectors on either side of us. Mama's and Big Mama's purses were checked before they could go back. Detective Mike Fisher met us at the door. The detective looked too young to be a police officer. He had short brown hair, and he had the shadow of a beard peeking through his white ivory skin. We followed him to his office. Detective Fisher told us that Mike's brother called him, and told him we were coming. He also knew about the other investigation. Once we all found a seat, I told Detective Fisher what Alley's father said, and did to me first. When the detective asked Alley what happened to her, she didn't want to speak.

Big Mama said, "Detective Fisher, we think she has been molested by her father."

Detective Fisher stood up, and kneeled down beside Alley. "Is this true?" He asked.

Alley put her head down, and said, "Yes sir."

Detective Fisher put his hand on her shoulder, and said, "Its okay honey. I'm going to get someone for you to talk to."

Detective Fisher left the room. When he came back, there was a black woman with him. She was wearing a navy-blue suit, and she had short dark hair.

"This is Mrs. Green. She will be the social worker on this case," said Detective Fisher.

"I know you," Alley replied.

"Yes, I've been to your house before when you fell down the steps."

"I didn't fall down the steps. That's what daddy made me say." Alley put her head down, and didn't look up again.

"Alley, why don't you come with me and Detective Fisher for a moment?"

Alley looked up abruptly at me, and began to panic.

"Can Jasmine come with me?" She asked.

"No. We need to talk to you alone, but they will be here when you get back," Mrs. Green promised. "All we are going to do is talk. I promise. Come on honey."

Alley got up, and looked back at me before she left the room. They were gone about forty five minutes before they came back.

Mrs. Green gave Big Mama a piece of paper, and said, "I want to take Alley to be examined by a pediatrician at St. John's Children's hospital. They specialize in these kinds of cases. If you like, you can meet us there."

Alley looked at Big Mama, and said, "No! Don't leave me! I don't want to go with them!"

"It's okay Alley. We won't leave you. We will go there, but you have to be brave, okay. What happens after we leave the hospital?" Big Mama asked.

"Well, normally she would be in our custody if she has no other relatives, but Agent Trey Raimond said that you made a request to have custody of her."

"Yes ma'am. We have been taking care of her for the last two months, and we would like to keep taking care of her until you find her family," Big Mama said.

"Okay, you will have temporary custody, but tomorrow you will have to come downtown to my office, and fill out a form to be her foster parent."

Alley ran over to Big Mama, and hugged her. She looked up with her wide big blue eyes, and said, "Does this mean I don't have to go back to him?"

"Yes, it does," Big Mama said with a smile.

"And, that I can come, and live with you?"

"Yes."

"I love you Big Mama," Alley said with tears in her eyes as she hugged Big Mama.

"I love you too, baby," Big Mama replied caressing her head.

"Come on Alley. We have to go," Mrs. Green said.

Alley, Mrs. Green, and Detective Fisher left the room.

Mama drove us to the hospital. She parked the van in the parking deck, and we all walked across a high covered cross walk that was high above the street. We walked to a small office suite which had a label on the door that read: *Dr. Peters Suite 208*. We entered the room, and the small office resembled a child's playroom. The room was painted in bright colors of red, yellow, and blue. The chairs lined the walls, but there was a toy box in the center of the floor. When I looked up, I saw a picture on the wall. The little girl in the picture was looking up at a rainbow. In the center of the picture was a poem. The poem was titled, *"Hope,"* the poem read:

"When the rain is all around you, and there is no happiness in sight,
Just remember, a rainbow of hope can bring you through the darkest of nights."

Big Mama walked up to the desk, and asked for Alley. The receptionist said Alley was there, and in a little while someone would come out to speak to Big Mama.

That little while we waited became an hour. I was getting bored. Then Mrs. Green opened the door to the waiting room, and said, "Mrs. Thomas, will you come with me."

Big Mama followed Mrs. Green and Detective Fisher to a small office. Once everyone was seated Mrs. Green said, "Mrs. Thomas we have evidence that Alexandria has been molested. The hospital will run some test on the samples they've collected, and we will let you know the results shortly after we have conducted our own investigation. The doctor will be here in a minute to talk to you about her condition."

"Detective, Alley's father is a dangerous man. We think he is a drug dealer. Earlier today he came by our house looking for Alley, and he said he would be back. We need some protection from this man." Big Mama said.

"We will increase our patrols in your neighborhood, and if you see him call us immediately."

Big Mama was worried. She knew this man could be capable of much more than drug dealing.

"Don't worry Mrs. Thomas, this will all be over soon," Detective Fisher replied.

Big Mama looked at the detective curiously. She knew he wasn't talking about the time. Suddenly, there was a knock at the door. Dr. Peters walked into the room. She was a small white lady with wire rimmed glasses. Her hair was pulled back into a ponytail.

"Mrs. Thomas my name is Dr. Peters. I work with the DA on many cases like this one. Are you Alexandria's guardian?" She asked.

"Yes, she is," Mrs. Green answered.

"I have given Alexandria a complete physical. She has a few old injures that have healed, but the bruising on her back, and hip will take a longer time to go away because of their size. She also had some vaginal tearing, and bruises. She told me she got a pad from under your bathroom sink last night. I gave her a few more, but the bleeding should stop after today. Here are two prescriptions I want her to take. One is for pain. It might make her a little sleepy, and the other one is an antibiotic. She has a little bit of an infection. Also, you will need this." Dr. Peters handed Big Mama the prescriptions, and some papers.

"What's this?" Big Mama asked.

"Alley will need to see a therapist. Dr. Joyce is a wonderful psychologist, and rape counselor. She has helped kids for over twenty years. Alley needs to see her at least twice a week."

"Okay," Big Mama said, and she sighed deeply. "No one has told her about sex yet, and now she going to a rape counselor." Big Mama sat there shaking her head.

"Don't worry about that, I've already told her," Dr. Peters replied.

"Mrs. Thomas, here's my card. Come see me by ten a.m. tomorrow to fill out the papers. Do you have anymore questions?" Mrs. Green asked.

"No," Big Mama replied.

"Okay then, Alley is waiting right outside. I'll see you tomorrow."

Big Mama stood up, and walked out of the room carrying the papers. Alley was sitting on a bench right outside of the office doors. Alley sat there with the bag in her hands, and her head down. Big Mama walked over to Alley, and sat down on the bench.

"You know something Alley, long before I had my first child my mama told me that sometimes a woman has to go to the doctor. It's a humiliating experience the first time, but it is necessary to make sure that we are healthy. The first time I went to the doctor I was scared and when I tried to get off that doctor's table, I fell flat on my face. Do you know what I did?" Big Mama asked with a grin.

Alley's bright blue eyes looked back up at Big Mama, and she said, "No."

"I got back up. Sometimes when you fall down Alley, you can't just stay there being ashamed. No, you've got to get back up again."

Big Mama stood up, and put her hand out to help Alley up from the bench. Big Mama and Alley met us in the lobby. Then we went home.

Later on that evening after dinner, Alley's father's house was raided. The lights flashing from the police cars lit the night sky. The police officers looked like men in the army. They wore black suits with bullet proof vest, and helmets. People started to gather in the street. Mama walked around the corner to see what was going on. I was curious, so I followed mama around the corner too. She was a little upset that I followed her, but she let me stay anyway. The police that were dressed in regular clothes were searching Billy's car with gloves on.

One officer said, "We found it. It's in the trunk." In the trunk of Alley's father's car, the detective found bottles of liquid, and buckets. The detective held up a bunch of little bags. These were the same bags I saw Alley's father with in my vision. Mike and his brother Trey walked up to us. Mike's brother had on a bullet proof vest on over his shirt.

"Guys, it not safe for y'all to be out here. Y'all go back home. Mike will walk home with you, and explain everything to you when you get there. I'll see you later," Trey said.

Mike walked back to the house with us. Mama opened the door, and we walked into the den.

"Kids, why don't y'all go upstairs, and play a game while we talk," mama said.

"Every time something happens, we have to leave so they can talk. Next time I think y'all should leave so the kids can talk," Jordan said walking out of the room.

"Jordan!" Mama yelled as Jordan ran up the steps.

"Alley's father wasn't at home when they raided his house. They found a meth lab in the trunk of his car. He had bags of meth in his room, and a few stolen guns in the closet. They didn't find any money. Trey said he believes another officer might have tipped him off. They are going to stake out his house tonight to see if he will come back," Mike said.

"He won't," Big Mama replied without looking up. "He's not in this state." Then she turned to Mike. "But, he will be back."

"Alley gave them enough information to put him away for a long time," Mike said.

"Let's just hope they find him quickly. That poor girl has been through enough," mama said.

Mike stayed with mama until his brother knocked on the door. The police were gone from Alley's house, and soon the people were gone from the street too. Mike's brother talked to mama for a few minutes longer than Mike and Trey left together. That night I prayed that we all would be safe through the night, but Alley was already sleeping peacefully before I ended my prayer. I guess from now on her days, and nights could only get better.

Chapter 19
Old Ghost

Today was Friday, and thank God it was. Mama had taken off today to go get her business license downtown. Big Mama was up early today cooking breakfast for us. Big Mama told Alley and me that we didn't have to go to school today. My brothers tried to get out of going to school too, but mama said they had to go. Mama told Jordan and Jonathan to go to our homeroom teachers, and get our homework today because she didn't want us to get behind.

Then mama turned to Big Mama, and said, "Mike asked a few people he knew to come by the center on Monday to fix the place up. The guys should be finished within a week."

Big Mama was surprised that the center would be up, and running so fast. Mama took Jordan and Jonathan to school while Big Mama gave Alley two pills to take after breakfast this morning. Alley slept most of the afternoon. When mama got back, we went outside onto the patio. Then Big Mama went downtown to the Department of Human Resources. It was almost lunch time before Alley woke up. Mama made lunch for us, and Big Mama came back around the time we started to eat.

"Mrs. Green will come by on Tuesday, and Alley had to meet the counselor on Monday at four thirty p.m.," Big Mama said.

Mama and Big Mama talked a little while longer and then mama had to leave. When mama came back, my brothers were with her. They brought tons of homework for Alley and me with them too. It took almost the whole afternoon to finish it all. When Alley and I finally finished, we went outside. We played until Alley saw Big Mike's truck coming down the street. Mama stepped outside onto the porch. She greeted Big Mike and his brother as they stepped out of Mike's truck. Mike called Alley into the house. Trey asked Alley if she knew where her father might have gone, but Alley said she didn't know. But, she said he would go the Atlanta sometimes on business. Then Trey asked Alley what her father was wearing when he left.

Mama interrupted them, and said, "I saw him last, and he was wearing a pair of jeans. He had on a t-shirt printed with the words, '*Cowboy up*' on it."

Trey told them if they could think of anything else, to give him a call. Mama asked when she could get Alley's things out of the house.

"Anytime," Trey said. "The police were done with their investigation, but you would need to call the police department to have an officer to go inside the house with you."

Mama said she would call one tomorrow. Soon Mike told mama they had to go, but he would call her later. Mike kissed mama's cheek, and they left.

Alley touched mama's arm, and asked, "Do I have to go back to that house?"

"No Alley, you don't have to, but we need to get your things out of there. It would help us if you came along with us just this one time. I don't want to leave anything you might want to keep."

"What if my father is there?" Alley asked.

"The police will take him to jail. Don't worry. We have legal custody of you now, and the police will be coming with us."

"Can Jasmine come too?" Alley asked with a pleading look.

"Okay," Michelle replied.

Alley hugged mama and ran outside.

*****

Saturday, mama took me and Alley to Alley's dad's house. We met a police officer name Officer Larry Lucky at the gate. He was a big black man with a very happy face. Mama got a big suitcase and some bags out of the van for Alley's clothes. Officer Lucy walked us up to the house, and opened the front door. The front door was broken. We opened the door, and the front room was a mess. I could tell that the investigators searched every inch of this house. Every drawer in the kitchen was opened, and the cushions on the couch were turned over. We walked back to Alley's room, and everything was opened in there too. Mama opened the suitcase on the bed. Alley grabbed all of the shoes from the bottom of the closet. Then she put them into the suitcase. Next, she pulled out all of the clothes from the closet, and put them into the suitcase. Soon the entire closet was empty. Alley had one dresser in her room. When she started unloading the drawers, I saw a shinny silver locket hidden under some clothes. I picked it up.

"Alley, this is pretty. You have never worn it," I said.

"I know. It was my mother's," she replied.

I handed the necklace to her, and she put it around her neck. When Alley and mama finished packing, the room seemed as empty as the entire house. I could tell that Alley's daddy hadn't been there since the raid. Mama made Alley check the rest of the house to make sure everything was out of the house before we left because she said we were not coming back here again. Alley got her things out of the bathroom and then we finally left. The rest of the afternoon Alley, and I played outside. Alley's facial bruises were getting better. By Sunday the bruises were barely noticeable.

Monday seemed to come too soon. Big Mama took us to school today. She gave us both absentee excuses, and told us to give the notes to our homeroom teachers. We both took a note, and walked inside the school. After I gave Mrs. Ranch the note, the day seemed to slow down. My English class was so boring I don't think I heard a thing in that class because the teacher was putting me to sleep. My history class was a bit more exciting because my teacher was so animated in his description of history. The bell rang again, and I was off to my favorite class of the day, P.E. I saw Alley and Plump walking down the hallway, but before I could get close to them, Toad tripped Alley again.

"Ha, ha, ha! That's what you get for getting me in trouble last week," Toad shouted as he quickly ran off. Plump helped Alley up, and I picked up her books.

"Plump, Alley, let's get them. I have a plan," I said.

I whispered my plan to Alley and Plump as we walked down the hall. When Alley, Plump, and I got to the girl's locker room, we changed our clothes quickly, so that we would be the first ones in the gym. We found Teach, and told him our plan. Teach laughed so hard we thought Toad might have heard us.

"Shh, Teach," I said. "Go on. Tell him."

Then Alley, Plump, and I ran back into the girl's locker room. Toad and Stool walked out of the boy's locker room chatting about something twisted, and evil they had done to another student in the hallway when Teach walked up behind them.

"Todd, Coach Jody wants you and your brother to take those balls outside onto the field," Teach said.

"What?" Toad replied.

"Why?" Stool asked.

"I don't know. That's what he said," Teach said as he walked away.

Toad and Stool could barely carry the balls as they walked to the door. Stool was yelling at Toad saying, "Watch it Todd! You're bumping into me!"

"I am not!"

"You are too!"

This went on until they got in front of the girl's locker room. Alley and I ran out of the locker room behind them. I pulled Toad's shorts down, and Alley pulled Stool's shorts down. Then I found one of Coach Jody's old whistles, and I blew it as loud as I could. All the girls and boys ran into the gym to find Toad and Stool with their shorts down, and bottoms showing. Toad and Stool couldn't grab us because their hands were full. Stool dropped his balls trying to pull up his shorts, but Toad tripped on the balls. They both fell down on the gym floor with their butts showing. The kids in the gym were laughing so hard that some of them were crying. Teach was laying on the floor laughing.

Coach Jody ran into the gym and shouting, "What going on?"

Toad and Stool stood up pulling their shorts up, and ran to the boy's locker room. Coach Jody saw them running, and he started to grin too.

"Guys, I don't know what happened here, but I don't want to see this again." Coach Jody said.

"I don't want to see it either!" Plump shouted.

Coach laughed, and said, "Guys, let's pick up these balls, and get started."

While we picked up the balls, Coach Jody went into the boy's locker room to get Toad and Stool. Once Coach Jody convinced Toad and Stool to come out of the locker room, we all giggled when we saw them.

"Kids, we aren't going to laugh anymore. We are going onto the field to play kick ball."

Alley, Plump, and I walked ahead of Toad and Stool giggling all the way. When we turned back to look at them, they were so angry with us that their faces were red. They looked like they were about to explode. We didn't care because it felt so good to finally get back at these two evil bullies. My team lost the kick ball game, but we were happy the rest of the day.

After school, Big Mama took Alley to see a counselor. My brothers and I went to aftercare. I hated going to aftercare. We stayed in the room with the babies. Mrs. Johnson made us do our homework while we were there. Jordan hated this, but Jonathan always finished his homework first, so he didn't care. We all finished our homework by the time mama came to pick us up. On Tuesday Mrs. Green came by our house, but the rest of the day was boring. Wednesday, Big Mama had to go to her club meeting so mama said Big Mike was coming over, and he was bringing dinner. My brothers, Alley, and I were playing cards on the coffee table when the doorbell rang. Mama walked from the kitchen to the front door with Pee-Pee at her side.

"*Bonjour belle dame,*" Mike said as he kissed mama's hand.

"Wow! You're speaking French again. How romantic," she said.

"Just for you," he replied. Then he kissed mama on the brow. "Oh, let me go get the food."

Mike walked to his truck, and came back with two bags of food. The smell of barbecue filled the air in the den. Mike walked into the den, and said, "Hey kids! I hope you're hungry because tonight we are having ribs."

My brothers, Alley, and I cheered as Big Mike followed mama to the kitchen. Mike put the food on the table. When mama reached for some plates, Mike turned her around, and kissed her. The kiss was so passionate mama almost stumbled back, but Mike caught her. He massaged her back, and ran his fingers through her hair. My brothers, Alley, and I sat there on couch looking at them with our mouths slightly opened. When Mike released her, mama was out of breath.

"What was that for?" Mama asked.

"I know this passed week hasn't been easy for you, but you stayed strong through it all. Also, I just wanted to kiss you," he said with a dimpled grin.

Everyone on the couch said, "Ugh," in unison.

Mama turned abruptly. "The show is over guys. Go upstairs, and wash your hands."

Mama got the plates down, and began to set the table. Once she put the glasses on the table, Mike hugged her again. "It feels so good to have you in my arms again."

"Mike, they'll be down here in a minute. Do you want them to catch us again?" Mama asked looking up at him with a grin.

"Okay," Mike said. "Let me help you."

Mike and mama finished setting the table. Soon we all came downstairs, and sat down at the table. Mama said grace, and we began to eat.

"Mike, this is good. Where did you buy these ribs?" Mama asked.

"I made them myself."

"Wow Mike! You can cook!" Jordan said.

"Maybe one day I can show you how to make ribs," Mike said.

Jonathan looked at Jordan, and said, "Jordan is too short. He'll burn himself up trying to reach the grill, but I can do it. I'm taller than him."

"You are not!" Jordan said glaring at Jonathan.

"Yes, I am!"

Alley and I just shook our heads.

"Boys stop it. You're the same size," mama demanded. Jordan stuck his tongue out at Jonathan. Mike laughed.

"Guys, I can teach both of you how to cook on the grill," Mike said with a smile.

My brothers continued their antics at the table until dinner was over. After dinner, Big Mike helped mama clean the kitchen and the rest of us cleared the table. When mama and Big Mike finished cleaning the kitchen, Big Mike played the spin the dial game with us. He wasn't any good at this game. Mike fell twice hitting the floor each time with a loud crash. Each time Mike fell, Jonathan would laugh so hard he could barely stand up to play the game.

With Mike's last crash on the floor, mama said, "Okay guys, go upstairs, and get ready for school tomorrow."

Alley, my brothers, and I didn't want to leave, but mama wouldn't take no for an answer. So, we all left the room.

Once the kids were gone Mike said, "Michelle, I think you have some barbecue sauce on your lips. Here, let me get it off."

Mike put his finger under Michelle's chin, and kissed her. Mike leaned forward coaxing Michelle to lie down on the couch. Once she lay down, Mike was on top of her. His tongue teased the corners of her mouth while his hand slowly went under her shirt. She moaned as his heavy hands cupped her breast. Mike withdrew his kiss which left her lips swollen, and hot. Then he stared deeply into her eyes as he lifted her shirt and bra over her breast. Michelle was slightly out of breath and her eyes were dilated. Mike's smell, taste, and touch were heightening her arousal almost to the point of completion. She could feel the firmness of his arousal pressing against the crouch of her shorts. Then Mike lowered his head taking the harden peek into his mouth. Michelle tried to control her moans. She didn't want to alert the children, but she felt like screaming. She bit her lip, and held back the moans. With every flick of Mike's tongue, Michelle's groin ached with desire for him. She could no longer hold back the moans. Then Mike suddenly stopped. Michelle heard the key turning in the front door. Mike sat up quickly and so did Michelle. Michelle rushed to put her clothes back in place before Big Mama walked in. Finally, the door was opened.

"Hey guys," Big Mama said with a big smile. "Michelle dear, fix your hair. You look like you've been up to something very naughty," Big Mama said as she winked at Mike. "Michelle, I have some news for you. I spoke with my club members, and we are going to take a bus trip to Biloxi this Saturday."

"Well, that sounds great," Michelle said as she continued to try, and rub her hair back into place.

"Alley's bed should be here no later then Friday, but of course she won't have a chance to sleep in it. You did tell James Alley was coming too, didn't you?" Big Mama asked.

"Yes mom. He said it would be okay if she came too."

Mike looked at Michelle very curiously.

"Good. I'm going to ask Ben if he wants to come with me. I know he will love it," Big Mama said. "Now, I can see that y'all might want to continue talking about what you were talking about before I walked in, so I will leave," Big Mama winked at Mike again.

Mike put his head down as his dimpled grin began to show.

"Good night y'all." Big Mama stood up, took her hat off, and then left the room.

Mike turned back to Michelle saying, "Why didn't you tell me the kid's father was picking them up this weekend?"

Michelle slowly looked up at Mike with a grin saying, "You didn't give me a chance."

"That is true," Mike said mischievously. "Michelle, I feel like I'm sixteen years old getting caught on your couch by your mother. We are too old for this. I want to finish what we started here."

"I do too Mike, but I feel it would be inappropriate to take you to my room with my kids here. And, you won't go to my room with my mother here either. So, what do you think we should do?"

"Come to my place this Saturday. I want to make dinner for you, a real Creole dinner. I promise you'll love it," Mike said.

"Okay. What time would you like for me to be there," Michelle asked.

"Come by around six on Saturday. That should give you enough time to do what ever you need to do."

"Okay," Michelle replied.

"Walk me to the door before I change my mind about going upstairs to your room."

Michelle walked Mike to the door, and he gave her one last passionate kiss before he said goodnight. Then he left.

*****

Thursday, school went by pretty quickly. It was a good day too. Toad and Stool saw Alley and me walking down the hall together, but this time they didn't say a word. They saw us, and walked off in the other direction. The whole school heard about what happened in the gym and now they are too ashamed to be seen around us. Alley and I giggled, and walked to our next class. It was nice seeing Alley smile again. Alley maybe a small fragile girl, but she is tougher than she looks. We had to go to aftercare today because Alley had to go to counseling again. When we got home, Alley grabbed my hand, and we ran upstairs to my room.

"Look!" She said.

Alley had a beautiful white iron daybed by the big picture window in my room. She had her own dresser in the corner of the room too.

Big Mama finally opened the door to our room, and said, "How do you like it."

"It's beautiful," Alley replied.

"Good, I'm glad you two like it. The bed wasn't supposed to get here until Friday, but the store delivered it early. Now Jasmine, you will have to share some of your closet space with Alley."

"Yes ma'am." I replied.

"All right," Big Mama said. Then she left the room.

That night, Alley and I talked for an hour sitting on her new bed until she kicked me out of it. She said she was tired, so I got into my bed, and we both fell asleep.

Friday after school, daddy came by to pick us up. Mama gave each of us a hug at the door. We all got into daddy's SUV, while he stayed on the porch talking to mama.

"James, make sure they finish their homework before you bring them back. I don't want them staying up late trying to finish it on Sunday night," mama said.

"Okay. How are you and Mike doing now?" He asked.

"We are just fine." Mama replied.

"Well, tell him he has a wonderful lady, but . . .," James paused with a little grin. "If he messes up, you can always come back to me."

"No, I can't James. Go on, the kids are waiting."

James walked away with that same grin. Mama walked back into the house, and put her purse down on the end table. She passed Big Mama in the kitchen, and patted Pee-Pee on the head. Then she got one of the kid's juice boxes out of the refrigerator.

"Michelle, I didn't cook anything because the kids were leaving today, but I can fix something for you," Big Mama said.

"No mom. That's okay. I'm going down to the center in a little while to see if the work is done. The inspector will be there on Monday."

"Did you hire any help, Michelle?"

"Yes. I hired two college students, and Sharon is going to help me until the business is up and running good."

"Michelle, I think Sharon is going to love her new job so much she won't leave."

"I don't know mom. Once she sees all the work she has to do, she might change her mind."

Big Mama looked up at Michelle with a smile. "You'll see," she replied.

"Mom, I've advertised my business in the paper, and yellow pages. I will start taking applications next week."

"Why didn't you advertise on the internet?" Big Mama asked.

"Because my business is small, and I don't want to be overwhelmed," she said. "Mom, I have to go. I'll get a salad while I am out. Do you want anything?"

"No thank you," Big Mama replied.

"Okay, I'll be back soon." She grabbed her purse off the coffee table, and left the room.

*****

Most of Saturday afternoon, Michelle lounged around the house. Big Mama and Mr. Davis had already left early this morning going to Biloxi. After lunch, Michelle got her hair, and nails done at her favorite salon. She knew that Devan, her stylist, would always make her hair look fabulous. Once she got home, it was almost time to meet Mike for dinner. Michelle went to her room to get dressed. She put on a short sleeve cotton white blouse, and a pair of black slacks. It took her a minute to dig through the mountain of shoes in her closet to find the pair of black strapped sandals she liked to wear for special occasions. Michelle took one more look in the mirror, and grabbed her purse. Then she left the house.

The sun was starting to set when she got to Mike's house. Michelle walked up to the big beautiful glass doors, and rang the doorbell. Mike opened the door looking up at Michelle, and said, *"Comment beau,"* which means how beautiful. Then he grabbed her by the hand, and kissed her on the cheek. "Come in."

Mike's house was as beautiful as it was the first time she saw it, but now it smelled good too. Mike was dressed in a nice shirt, and pair of jeans. Michelle felt a little over dressed when she saw that Mike didn't have any shoes on.

"Mike, what smells so good?" Michelle asked.

"Oh, that's a little gumbo, crawfish etouffee, and Creole vegetable kabobs."

"You're making me hungry," she said.

"Good, maybe I can tempt you with something else later."

Michelle laughed. Then Michelle took a small tour of the bottom half of the house. There were two more bedrooms, and a bathroom downstairs. Mike walked out of the kitchen, and said, "Finding everything okay?"

"Yeah," Michelle replied. "Your house is decorated beautifully."

"Thank you," he said. Once Mike got back into the kitchen, he turned the oven off.

"Let's eat," he said.

Michelle sat down at the table while Mike served her. Once Mike sat down to eat, Michelle said, "Why don't you come by the center next week. The guys are finished, and it looks beautiful."

"I'll bet it is," Mike said. "Are you excited?"

"I'm excited, and a little scared," Michelle said honestly.

"Why?"

"Well, today was my last day at work. I'm hoping I can make this business work."

"You will. Don't worry. You can always fall back on the money you still have left."

"I hope so, but I will never know what I'll need with a new business," Michelle said.

"Now, I think that's enough talk about business. Let's talk about you. You look absolutely stunning tonight," Mike said.

"Thank you. That's sweet," she said.

"No, I mean it. You were always beautiful, but today I just can't keep my eyes off of you."

"Well, I think you're beautiful too, but you need to eat before your gumbo gets cool. Anyway, sitting there staring at me will not satisfy you."

"Oh, but I think it will. But, I'll eat anyway." Mike said with a grin.

Michelle and Mike continued to eat dinner, and chat for a while until they were finished. Michelle offered to help Mike with the dishes, but Mike wouldn't hear of it. Michelle walked back into the den, and started looking through Mike's CD collection.

"Mike, you and I have the same taste in music. I love this one. I think she was the first woman to start the *Neo-Soul* movement."

"Take it out. We'll listen to it later."

Mike finished cleaning the kitchen, and putting the food away.

"Would you like some coffee?" He asked.

"No. If I drink it now, I will never go to sleep tonight. Are you sure you don't need any help?" She asked.

"No. I'm finished anyway. Would you like a piece of pie, or something?"

"No Mike," said Michelle. "I'm full. If you keep feeding me like this, I'll be as big as this house."

Mike laughed, and sat down on the couch by Michelle.

"Michelle, I've been wondering about something. After having three kids and two of them were twins, how did you manage to keep your figure?"

"Well, having three kids and two jobs leaves little time to eat. Also, going through a divorce will ruin your appetite too," replied Michelle. "At one time I was bigger, but the stress helped me loose weight. Also, I have scars. I am far from perfect."

"Well, you look perfect to me." Mike said sincerely.

"Thank you, Mike, but all women have their insecurities." Michelle replied.

"Well, you look great. Even your feet look great," Mike said looking at Michelle's shoes. "Michelle, your shoes are beautiful, but I know your feet can't be comfortable."

"Sore feet are the price women pay for beauty." Michelle said with a sigh.

"Put your feet up here," Mike said. Mike took off Michelle's shoes, and began rubbing her feet. Suddenly, Michelle jumped.

"Woo! That tickles," she said.

"Oh, does it?" Mike tickled her feet again until she finally pulled away. "Okay, I'm sorry. Put your feet back, please. What? You don't trust me?"

"You promise you won't tickle me anymore?"

"I promise."

Michelle put her feet back in Mike's lap, and be continued to rub her feet.

"Mike, if you keep rubbing my feet like this, you will put me to sleep."

"Well now, we can't have that. Come on. Let me show you the upstairs. Bring the CD."

Michelle stood up, and grabbed the CD. Then they both walked upstairs. There was a small hallway upstairs. On the right side of the hall, were small bedrooms, and bathrooms. Mike opened the door to his bedroom, and the view outside of the patio was amazing.

"Mike, this is beautiful. I can see downtown from here," she said.

"Yeah. Sometimes I like to stare up at the stars while I'm in bed."

Mike's large bed was in the middle of the room. There were two end tables beside the head board. He had a flat screen TV on one wall above a dresser. The room was decorated beautifully. Mike walked slowly over to Michelle, and wrapped his arms around her waist. He kissed her slowly down the side of her neck. Michelle could feel his hot breath in her ear as he nibbled on her earlobe. She began to tremble.

"Mike, I need to use the bathroom," she said.

Mike kissed her on the shoulder. Then he released her.

"The bathroom is over there," he said as he pointed the way.

Michelle walked into the bathroom, and Mike closed the patio curtains as he sat on the bed.

When Michelle came out of the bathroom, she said, "Mike, I love your bathroom. How many shower heads do you have in there?"

"A few. Why don't you put that CD in the player over there?"

Michelle walked over to the CD player, and put the CD in. The surround sound filled the atmosphere with sultry music. Mike dimmed the lights, and lit a few candles. Then he walked back to the bed, and sat down.

"Come here," he said.

Michelle's nervousness began to show. Being with another man was a little unnerving. She put her head down and slowly walked towards him. She sat down beside Mike on the bed gripping the mattress tightly.

"Michelle, are you nervous?"

"A little I guess," she replied shyly.

"Why?"

"I don't know."

"Michelle, nothing will happen that you don't want to happen."

Mike put his hand on Michelle's knee, and said, "It okay. Let's just lay here for a minute. I just want to hold you in my arms for a little while."

Michelle and Mike lay in the bed together like spoons in a drawer.

"How do you feel now?" He asked.

"Really good, and very comfortable too," she admitted.

"Good, because you feel good to me too."

Mike began kissing the back of Michelle's neck. Each erotic kiss sent shivers down her spine which caused her to curl up closer to him.

"I want to see you," Mike whispered in her ear.

He slowly unbuttoned Michelle's shirt, and unhooked her bra from the front. His eyes feasted upon her naked flesh. Mike placed his hand on Michelle's shoulder, and gently turned her towards him. His hand crept up Michelle's stomach, and cuffed her breast. He kissed her deeply. Michelle began to moan as Mike massaged her nipples between his fingers. Mike released Michelle's lips only to take her harden nipples into his mouth. Michelle's head went back into the pillow as her moans grew louder. She ran her finger through the soft curls of Mike's hair. Mike teased the hardened tip with his tongue sending shock waves of pleasure to her groin. He pleasured the other breast just as well as the first. He kissed and licked Michelle's chest, and stomach before his lips found her mouth again. When he released her from his kiss, he stared intensely into her eyes for a moment. Michelle was still slightly out of breath.

"I want to kiss you," Mike whispered.

Michelle puckered up to kiss him again. Mike gave her a gentle kiss, and said, "No, no. Not here."

He put his middle finger into his mouth, and slid his hand underneath her pants. Michelle inhaled deeply. "Here."

He watched her reaction. He knew it was only a matter of time before she found her release. Mike put one hand on her thighs to position her. Mike removed his hand from her pants, and slid down to kiss her stomach. He unzipped her pants, and slid them off. When Mike tried to take off Michelle's underwear, she panicked, and sat up.

"What's wrong?" He asked.

"I've never done this before, and I don't want you to see my scar," she said.

"You've never done this before?" Mike was shocked.

"No. My ex-husband wouldn't do it."

"Michelle, believe me, you will enjoy this. Just relax." Mike took off his shirt, and said, "Now, look at this." Mike turned around to show Michelle the scar on his back. It was a pretty big scar too.

"Mike, how did you get this?" She asked.

"I was stabbed in the back on a mission in the army. Now, you've seen my scar, can I see yours?"

Michelle hesitated for a brief moment then she pulled her underwear down to reveal the scar.

"Michelle, it's only four inches long. The scar is barely noticeable. You shouldn't be ashamed of this," he said.

Mike removed Michelle's hands from her underwear, and slid them down her legs. Once the panties were over her feet, Mike kissed her toes. Then he kissed the inside of her thighs. He paused for a moment to look deeply into Michelle eyes and then he pulled her towards him. Mike began kissing the little knob between her thighs. This sensation was something Michelle had never experienced before. The moment Mike's tongue touched her, she cried out. She arched her back grabbing a hand full of Mike's hair. Mike slowly removed her hand from his head, and brought her hand down to her side. The more Mike's insatiable tongue teased the little knob, the louder she became. Her head tossed about wildly as her hand gripped the comforter for stability. The sensations were becoming too much for her. She tried to pull back, but Mike held her steady. She felt vulnerable, and out of control. Mike inserted two fingers into the small canal. Michelle cried out again. With every stroke of Mike's fingers, and tongue Michelle could no longer resist him. She arched her back and screamed her released. The little spasms shook her to her core. Mike withdrew his fingers and released his kiss. Michelle's body lay on the bed as limp as a rag doll. She continued to pant loudly as Mike kissed her stomach, and positioned himself above her.

He kissed her jaw and whispered in her ear, "I could feel you cumming." He kissed her again. Then he looked deeply into her eyes, and whispered, "I want to be inside of you."

He cupped Michelle's breast with his hand, and took the harden nipple into his mouth again. Michelle grabbed a hand full of Mike's hair. Mike slowly pushed her hand away. Michelle's hand fell back hitting a picture on his side table. Mike gasped, and sat up on the side of the bed.

"What's wrong?" She asked.

"Nothing," Mike said without facing Michelle.

Michelle picked up the picture of Tracy, Mike's deceased wife. She sat on the side of the bed by Mike, and asked, "How did she die?"

Chapter 20
Katrina

Mike didn't look back at Michelle when she asked, but he did answer her.

"When my wife and I bought this house, we were planning on having a family. This house only had two bedrooms when we bought it. I built the room across the hall up here to be a nursery for our child. It's still decorated in blue for the boy we should have had. When Tracy told me she was pregnant, I was more excited than she was. The doctor told us it was going to be a boy. Before I even told Tracy, I wanted him to be named after me, but . . ." Mike paused.

Michelle put her arm around his waist. "What happen?" She asked.

"When I got home from work, Tracy told me she wasn't feeling well. She said she had a headache. She lay down for a while, but when I walked back into the bedroom to check on her, there was a trail of blood from the bed to the bathroom. I found her on the floor with blood pooling around her. The paramedics rushed her to the hospital."

Mike's voice grew shaky. Then he looked up at Michelle. "Tracy had a miscarriage after the fifth month of her pregnancy. My boy was small, but he was developed. Tracy never saw him, but I had too." Mike turned away from Michelle, and said, "The doctor couldn't stop the bleeding. Tracy bled to death." A tear rolled down Mike's cheek and Michelle suddenly started to cry too.

"She died that Tuesday evening. I loss my son and wife on the same day. Sometimes I think if I had checked in on her earlier maybe I could have saved her," Mike said with a tear running down his cheek.

"No Mike. You couldn't have saved her, and neither could the doctors. It was her time to go," Michelle said. "Remember you told me death is a part of life that we all must go through, but my mother told me long ago that we really don't die. She said our physical bodies may die, but our energy lives on forever. Tracy's body was suffering, but now she is at peace. Mike, you have to remember the happy times you had with her, and not linger over what you loss. Your marriage was a good one Mike, unlike mine, and you should remember that. You are lucky. Not everyone has what you have." Michelle wiped away Mike's tears, and kissed him on the cheek. "I'm going to go now," she said.

When she stood up, Mike grabbed her hand. "No, please don't go," he said. "Stay with me tonight."

"I thought you might want to be alone."

"I've been alone for two years Michelle. I don't want to be alone anymore. You are the first person I've ever brought up here in a long time, and I don't want you to go now. Please, stay until the morning."

"Okay, but just let me take off my shirt." Michelle took off her shirt, and put it on the back of a chair. Then she picked up her pants and folded them over the chair too. Mike looked a little disappointed when Michelle put her panties on that matched her bra, but he didn't complain. It was good to just have her here with him. Michelle blew out the candles, and got into bed with Mike. The warmth of her body was soothing to him, and it seemed to fill an empty void in his heart. Mike wrapped his arms around Michelle as they lay there for the rest of the night.

The next morning Michelle woke to the rays of sunlight coming through the shades that covered the patio doors. Michelle's eyes opened to see Mike staring down at her.

"Good morning," she said with a smile.

"I love you," Mike replied.

Michelle's mouth fell slightly opened. For a moment she was speechless. Then she said, "What?"

"I am in love with you Michelle. I've been in love with you for months. Your mother knew it, and I did too. I just didn't want to scare you away. I'm not trying to pressure you, but I want to be a part of your life. I don't want to share you with another man, and I don't want to be with anyone else."

Michelle started to speak, but Mike put his finger over her mouth.

"You don't have to say anything. I hope you feel the same way as I do, but if you don't, just let me have this one moment."

Michelle touched Mike's cheek, and lay back on the pillow staring at the ceiling.

"I feel the same way about you, but I can't say I'm not a little scared. I thought James loved me and you see how that ended. I will only get older, and there will always be someone new to come along. I can't go through that kind of pain again." Michelle kissed Mike's cheek, and said, "I better go."

"You haven't had breakfast yet." Mike put his hand around Michelle's waist, and pulled her closer to him. "Let's just take this one step at a time, okay."

Michelle shook her head in agreement. Then Mike kissed her brow. "Come on. Let's eat breakfast." Mike had taken off his pants at sometime during the night, and he was wearing nothing, but a pair of shorts when he went downstairs. Michelle got dressed, and walked downstairs. Mike prepared a mixture of fresh fruits, sausage links, beignets, and coffee for breakfast. Michelle sat down at the table while Mike poured the coffee. Mike finally sat down, and he put his hand on Michelle's shoulder. "I'm sorry about last night," he said.

"No Mike. You shouldn't apologize about something like that."

"Well, I had planned for last night to go a whole lot differently than it did. I was hoping you would take a bath with me this morning, and this breakfast would be a well deserved treat for our strenuous activities last night," Mike said with a big grin.

"Then you will have to invite me here again, but last night was wonderful."

"I'm glad you enjoyed it," he said with a smile. "But, there is so much more I need to show you than that."

Michelle grinned, and took a bite out of her beignet. Mike put his finger under Michelle's chin, and said, "I think you have some powder sugar on your lips. Here, let me get it off." He kissed Michelle gently until all the sugar was gone. Then he lifted her hand, and kissed her knuckles. "Mmm, that was sweet." Michelle grinned again.

"Mike, do you care if I turn the TV on?"

"No. Go ahead," he said. Michelle turned on the news channel, and the weather report was on. The meteorologist said the storm had rapidly intensified in the last twenty four hours after entering the gulf. The storm was now a category three. The forecaster stated that the president declared a state of emergency for Louisiana.

"Mike, I've been so consumed with Alley, and my business that I hadn't thought about the storm. My realtor told me that the last storm didn't affect my property, and that was the last time I even thought about the weather. Mike, have you talked to your family in New Orleans?"

"I talked to my aunt last week, but at that time the storm wasn't that close to New Orleans. My brother is on his way up here anyway to work on the case. He will be here tonight."

"Please call them Mike. Tell your aunt to get out of there. I've got a bad feeling about this."

"Okay, I'll call them. I know my brother, and sister-in-law will leave, but my aunt is stubborn."

"Mike, that city hasn't been hit with a hurricane like this in years. I know how devastating something like this can be. Do your best to get them out. Don't take this lightly," Michelle pleaded.

"Okay."

"I have to go. I need a bath," she said.

"You can take a bath here. I'll help you wash your back, and anything else that needs to be cleaned," he said with grin.

Michelle grinned. "Somehow, I don't think I'll stay clean if I stay here. You get on the phone, and call your folks. I'll see you later. Give me a call tonight."

"Okay, but I have to have one more kiss."

Mike kissed Michelle again, but Michelle pulled back from him, and said, "Are you trying to change my mind about leaving?"

"Now, would I do that?" Mike said looking as innocent as he could.

"I'll see you later. Call me." She stood up, and grabbed her purse. Mike walked Michelle to the door, and kissed her again. Then she left.

When Michelle got home, she thought she could get into her house before her mother got up. Michelle walked upon the porch. She turned the key slowly, and opened the door quietly as she could.

"Hey darling!" Big Mama said as Michelle entered the room. "Come on in here. Why are you trying to sneak into your own house anyway?"

Michelle shut the door, and walked into the den. She sat down on the couch beside Big Mama.

"Michelle, you, and Mike are sneaking around here like two teenagers. I know what's going on. You are grown now, and I am living with you remember? All I ask is that y'all be respectful around me and the kids because, I don't want to see any of it."

"Mom, nothing happened. I fell asleep over there and then I came home."

"Nothing happened?" Big Mama was shocked.

"Well," Michelle said with a pause. "Something happened. Mike said he loved me."

"I knew that," Big Mama said with a grin. "I'm just surprised he hadn't said it earlier. What did you say?"

"I said I felt the same way, but I didn't want to be in the same situation as I'm in now."

"Michelle, every man is not just like James."

"But, most are." She said flatly.

"Baby, you have to let go of the past, and think about your future. Mike is a good man. Don't push him away because you're scared."

"Mom, I'm not going to push him away. Even though he scares me, I can't seem to let him go."

"Mike is a better man than I thought," Big Mama said grinning again.

"Well, I'm going upstairs to take a bath."

"Are you going to church?"

"Yes, but we've got to get back here quickly to prepare for the storm," Michelle replied.

"I know baby." Big Mama's mood suddenly changed. "I'm going to pray for them, but I know things will be bad for a long time. You go on now and get dressed."

Michelle gave Big Mama a concerned smile, and walked upstairs.

*****

That afternoon Mike came by Michelle's house after church. Mike told Michelle and Big Mama that his sister in-law would be heading up here tonight too."

"Mike, have you spoken to your aunt?" Michelle asked.

"Yes, and she told me that her neighbor is going to take her to a shelter downtown."

"That's good," Michelle said. "She can come back sooner if nothing really bad happens."

Big Mama put her head down, and said "She won't come back. There will be too much water."

"It does flood a lot down there," Mike replied.

"Mike, this won't be just another storm. There will be deaths, and destruction like you've never seen before." Big Mama replied in a melancholy tone.

"Mom, you're starting to scare him." Michelle replied.

"I'm sorry Michelle. I just wanted Mike to be prepared," Big Mama stood up, and walked into the kitchen. "Mike, would you like something to eat?"

"Yes ma'am," Mike replied.

Michelle and Mike walked into the kitchen with Big Mama. Big Mama took the food out of the refrigerator she prepared earlier for Sunday's brunch. Michelle and Big Mama were preparing their plates when the doorbell rang.

"I'll get it," Mike said. Mike walked to the door, and opened it.

"Hello, hello!" It was Mr. Davis.

"Come on in," Mike said.

"Ben, would you like something to eat?" Big Mama asked.

"Sure." He replied.

"You know the president has declared a state of emergency for Mississippi, and Alabama too. It looks like we are going to have a long day tomorrow."

"I think so too Ben," Big Mama agreed.

Everyone was seated at the table and after Big Mama said grace. They began to eat.

"The inspector was supposed to come by on Monday. I guess I could call him, and see if he could come by earlier," Michelle said.

"That would be a good idea. I know I won't have to go to work tomorrow, so I can go with you," Mike replied.

"Okay. Mom, Mr. Davis, would you two like to come too?" Michelle asked.

They both said yes.

"Mike, when will your brother get here?"

"He is already here, but he's working. Lisa won't get her until eight o'clock tonight."

"Good, at least they will be out of harms way."

The doorbell rang again. Michelle and Pee-Pee answered the door. All the kids walked into the house, and greeted everyone inside. James walked inside the front doors carrying a few of the kid's bags.

"Michelle, does that dog always come to the door with you?" James asked.

"Yes. He protects me from strangers," Michelle said with a smirk.

"You're not funny, Michelle." James greeted everyone, and said, "I better go. I've got to put some things away before the storm comes. Bye y'all."

James waved goodbye, and left rather quickly. The kids ate brunch with everyone at the table. Later on that evening, Mike got a phone call. He said he had to go meet his sister in-law. He kissed Michelle goodbye, and left. Jasmine watched Mike through the window as he walked to his truck, and drove away. She was scared. The old feelings she had during the last storm were coming back to her as she saw him walking away. Jasmine knew that tomorrow would bring great sorrow and devastation to so many. Mike would feel this sorrow too. There was nothing she could do. She turned to see Big Mama staring at her. She sensed the same thing Jasmine was feeling.

"Jasmine, come over here, and play with Alley, "said Big Mama. "There's nothing we can do now, but trust in God."

Big Mama's speech was slow, and cryptic. But, Jasmine did what she said, and left the window.

*****

On Monday morning everyone was up early. The TV was turned on to the news channel. Big Mama and mama were all ready sitting in the den drinking coffee, and watching TV when I came downstairs. My brothers and Alley were sitting on the floor watching TV too. The meteorologist called the storm "Katrina." He said the hurricane turned a little in the night around 6:10am making its initial landfall near Buras, Louisiana. He said there was severe damage, and flooding in that area, but it was too soon to report injuries, or deaths. The meteorologist said the storm will cross Mississippi by this afternoon leaving tremendous amounts of destruction in its path. He recommended that anyone on Alabama's western boarder seek shelter. He said the storm wouldn't reach our area until late this afternoon, or sometime into the night. The reporter stated that many tornados may spin off from this storm, so no one should take this situation lightly.

"Kids, y'all go upstairs, and get ready for school. I don't know if your school will let y'all out early, but most likely they probably will. Mom, I'm going to get dressed, and take them to school. I'll call the inspector to see if he is still coming today, but I'm quite sure he won't," said mama.

"Michelle, you need to call Mike too, and let him know," Big Mama said.

"I will. Come on guys."

I walked away from the den, and wondered to myself how such a pretty name could be given to something this destructive. My thoughts of the anticipated storm terrorized me, and saddened me too. I knew this day would not end well. After breakfast, we all headed out of the front door leaving Big Mama behind. On our way out of the house, Mr. Davis came by. Big Mama invited him in, and told him mama would be back shortly. The sky was clear and beautiful this morning. I was amazed how quickly that would change. Mr. Davis and Big Mama waved to us as we left for school.

****

When Michelle got home, she called the inspector's office. The inspector said he wouldn't come by the center today because of the storm, but he would come by on Friday. Michelle looked a little disappointed.

"Michelle, it's okay. We can still see your place without the inspector," Big Mama said.

"Okay," Michelle replied. "I need to get over there anyway to make sure everything is put away, and y'all can help."

Big Mama and Mr. Davis agreed to help. They continued to chat about the weather when the doorbell rang. Pee-Pee gave a loud bark, and walked to the door with Michelle. Michelle opened the door. It was Mike.

"Good morning beautiful," Mike said. Then he kissed Michelle on the cheek.

"Mike, I meant to call you. The inspector won't be coming by until Friday. Mom and Mr. Davis said they still wanted to see the center. So, we are just going down there to visit. Do you still want to come?"

"Yeah, I would love to," Mike replied.

Mike and Michelle walked back into the den. They sat down on the adjacent couch from Big Mama and Mr. Davis.

"Mike, is your sister in-law here now," Big Mama asked.

"Yes ma'am. She got here last night. I gave my brother a key, so they could come and go without me being there."

"Mike, have you talked to your aunt?" Michelle asked.

"No, she has a cell phone, but I haven't been able to get through to her phone all morning. I have to admit, I'm getting a little worried about her," Mike said.

"Don't worry Mike. She went to a shelter. She will be all right," Michelle replied. "Come on guys. Let's go to the center. Maybe it will take our minds off the storm."

Everyone got up, and left the house. The center was only fifteen minutes from Michelle's house. The building looks like it once was a small retirement home. There was a circular driveway out front. Michelle parked in front of the covered walkway, and everyone got out. There was a sign out front in large print that read: *Jenkins's Senior Care Center*. Michelle unlocked the front glass doors, and hit the handicapped button which automatically opened the doors. Then she did the same thing to the next set of doors. Once they were in the lobby, Big Mama said it was decorated like a beautiful home. There was a large desk in the middle of the lobby. It was completely stocked with files, and two computers. There was a small sitting area passed the desk by the back window. To the right side of the office were ten small bedrooms on either side of a long hallway. Everyone followed Michelle down the hall. Each room had a single bed, TV, dresser, and bathroom. There was a picture that hung over each bed and each room had its own window. Michelle walked with everyone across the hall to a large open recreational area. This area had two couches, four cushioned chairs, and a huge sixty five inch flat screen TV mounted on the wall. There was a pool table, and chairs on the other side of the room. In the center of the recreation area was a large wooden table with ten chairs around it. Michelle continued the tour to the kitchen. There were five round tables in the dinning area. In front of the kitchen stood a buffet counter completely stocked with trays, and silverware. Michelle walked everyone back to the small restaurant style kitchen. The floor was covered with terracotta tiles and rubber floor mats. The appliances and sinks were made of stainless steel. After Michelle's tour of the kitchen, everyone followed her outside to a small courtyard. There was a small table on the patio with six chairs, and a few benches spread around the courtyard. A beautiful flower bed was planted by a big shed. Inside the flower bed was a stone birdbath that looked like an angel holding a big bowl.

"Michelle, this is beautiful," Big Mama said. "When did you buy all this stuff?"

"I didn't. Mr. Taylor included it in the asking price for the building. All I had to do was repair the kitchen, and buy some more dishes. I paid to have the sign changed out front and I had to clean up a little too. I asked a man named Joe who did a lot of the maintenance here to work a few hours a day cleaning, and maintaining the yard for me. The staff will be doing the cleaning, and caring for the patients," Michelle said.

"Michelle, later on you may want to add some shade trees out here. It's cloudy now, but it will get really hot out here during the summer," Mike said.

"I like the trees Mike, but you see how they fall around my house. This is such a small yard. I don't want to risk anything falling on the building. I think I might put umbrellas over the tables out here, or something. Anyway, no one is going to sit out here too long. Now, I need your help." Everyone turned to Michelle as she continued. "I need y'all to help me put the patio chairs, and table into the shed. I don't know how bad the wind is going to get, and I don't want one of these chairs crashing into the side of the building."

Everyone picked up a chair, and walked to the shed. Michelle opened the shed so everyone could stack the chairs against the wall. Michelle and Mike walked back to get the tables.

Once everything was put away, Michelle said, "It's starting to get darker out here. I think we need to go back home."

They all walked back through the building, and Michelle turned everything off. She locked the doors and everyone got back into the van. Then Michelle drove home. Before Michelle could open the front door, her cell phone rang. Big Mama unlocked the door to let everyone in while Michelle answered the phone.

Michelle entered the room behind them saying, "That was the school calling. The school will close early today by noon due to the weather. Mom, what time is it now?"

"It's about ten forty five a.m. I'll make lunch Michelle. You take care of the kids."

"Okay," Michelle replied.

"Michelle, I need to use your phone," Mike said.

"It's over there," she said as she pointed in the direction of the phone.

"Well Bertha, I better make sure everything is locked down at my house," Mr. Davis said. "I'll see y'all later."

Then he left the house. Michelle and Big Mama sat on the couch, and turned the TV on. The weather report was on every channel. Mike hung up the phone and sat on the couch too.

"Are you okay Mike?" Michelle asked.

Mike hesitated for a moment, and said, "Yeah. My brother told me there was a breach in the canal levees this morning. He said the Ninth Ward was flooded."

"Thank God your aunt was out of there," Michelle replied.

Michelle began unconsciously stroking Mike's back. She could tell that he was worried. The news reporter didn't help sooth Mike's nerves either. The broadcast showed pictures of the superdome's roof being ripped off by the mighty winds. Michelle sat there with Mike for twenty minutes before she said she had to go. Once Michelle was gone, Big Mama walked into the kitchen. Big Mama pulled several things out of the refrigerator, and put them on the table. She sat at the table mixing some ingredients in a bowl to make chicken salad. Mike walked to the table, and sat down with Big Mama.

"I know that you can see things that no one else can see," he said. "Tell me, is my aunt alive?"

Big Mama stopped stirring the chicken salad. She knew what he was going to ask before he sat down. She slowly looked up at Mike, and said, "Mike, I don't like to give people bad news."

"Bertha, you told me earlier that you wanted to prepare me. Prepare me for what?"

"Mike, Michelle doesn't want me to talk about this. If I upset you, she will never forgive me," Big Mama said as she continued stirring the salad.

"Bertha, I won't say anything to her, but I have to know. Please, tell me."

Big Mama stopped stirring the salad, and sat back in the chair.

"Mike, where you grew up will no longer exist in the way you remember it. Before this nightfall, the Ninth Ward will be underwater. Many will die. Some of their bodies may never be found. When the water is finally gone, what is left of your neighborhood will be bulldozed to the ground. Your life is here now. None of your family will ever go home again. Mike, you will find happiness here. Your sadness will not last forever."

"What about my aunt?" He asked.

"Mike, please don't ask me anymore."

Big Mama started to get up, but Mike grabbed her arm.

"Please don't go. I have to know," Mike pleaded.

Big Mama sat back down, and sighed deeply. "Mike, she is alive for now, but she's in a place that is filled with despair. Many will cry out for help, but no one will come for days. And for some, it will be too late. The few lawless criminals will wreak havoc upon the survivors. Mike, this will not be an easy time for you, but you must find your aunt. She doesn't have much time left. Take Michelle with you. Believe me, you will need her strength."

Mike sat there in a bit of shock. Suddenly, Mike's cell phone rang. He got up, and walked back to the den to answer it. Mike talked on the phone for about fifteen minutes before the front door opened. Michelle walked inside the house, and was followed by the children. Mike hung up the phone, and met Michelle at the front door.

"Michelle, I need to talk to you," Mike said.

"Okay. Kids y'all go into the kitchen, and eat lunch."

"Michelle, let me stay here tonight. I can't go home right now."

"Okay, but you can't stay down here on the couch either. Stay in my room, and I'll sleep down here," she said.

"I can't do that."

"Yes, you can, and I insist. Let me do something for you."

"Okay." Mike kissed Michelle, and they walked back into the den.

*****

By nightfall the power went out. I sat there with Alley, and cried. We heard more trees falling in the distances. The loud crashing sound and the whistling winds caused Pee-Pee to bark hysterically. He ran to mama's side. Suddenly, the dog started to howl. I looked out of the window, and I saw the angel. The angel took my mind to a far away place by the big river. I saw the souls of the dead rising, and going with the angels. Then there was a beautiful song they sang that I had never heard before. Through this terrifying night, I saw a great peace, and ever lasting joy that no man living will ever know.

"Where are you taking them?" I asked the angel.

The angel answered me, but her voice could only be heard in my head. "They will be taken to a place to wait in peace until their final judgment. Then they will forever live in peace. Do not mourn for the dead, for their sorrows are over. It is the living that will have to suffer this world's evil. But, know He is with us until the end. Do not fear little one, for He watches over us all. Find her mother sweet *Ayin,* and bring her mother home."

The angel smiled at me, and disappeared.

"Jasmine, what are you talking about?" Alley asked.

"Oh honey, she's just talking to the angel," Big Mama replied with a smile.

Pee-Pee stopped howling after the angel disappeared, and the storm suddenly stopped. All I could hear now was the faint sound of rain falling.

"Kids, take the flash light upstairs, and go to bed. I think the worst is over now," mama said.

Big Mama stood up, and said in a slow cryptic voice, "I wish that was true. How, I wish that was true."

Big Mama touched Mikes shoulder, and left the room.

"Mike, come on honey. Go upstairs," Michelle said.

"No. Michelle, stay with me for a little while longer."

"Okay."

Mike held Michelle in his arms for another hour before she demanded that he go to bed.

Chapter 21
The News

Michelle woke up early this morning. Her night on the couch wasn't a very comfortable one, but at least this time she was better prepared than she was during the last storm. Michelle took Mike's advice, and bought a portable generator. Her only regret was that she wished she would have thought to bring it out of the shed yesterday. Michelle also bought a battery-operated TV. The house was still quiet when Michelle walked outside. The storm left debris all over the house, and yard. There was a large branch that had fallen into Big Mama's garden that Michelle had to cross to get to the shed. Looking out over the yard, she could tell that the water from the small creek behind her house had flooded her yard. Debris from the water marked the trees, and shed about five inches above the ground. Michelle opened the door to the shed easily, but she struggled to pull the generator outside. She turned around suddenly to find Mike standing behind her.

"Do you need some help?" He asked.

"Yeah, thanks. I didn't mean to wake you though," Michelle said.

"Don't worry, I was up anyway. Your bed is really comfortable, but I couldn't sleep. Hold on a minute. Let me move this branch." Mike dragged the large branch from the garden, and rolled the generator out of the shed.

"Mike, let's put it here on the patio," said Michelle. "We don't want the fumes to get into the house."

Mike rolled the generator under the kitchen window.

"Mike, the man at the store told me this generator should power my refrigerator, or stove, but I could only use one of them at a time. I think we should plug the stove up first. I'm hungry," Michelle said.

Mike read the instructions that came with the generator, and ran a heavy duty cord through the window to plug up the stove.

"You know something, Michelle," Mike said. "When I talked about a generator, I meant for the whole house."

"I know, but I had to use that money for the business. Don't worry. I'll get one later."

Michelle and Mike began cooking breakfast when Big Mama walked into the kitchen.

"Good morning. It smells good in here," said Big Mama.

"Mom, I'm boiling some water for the instant coffee. It will be ready in a minute."

"Honey, take your time. Do y'all need some help?" Big Mama asked.

"No mom. We got it," mama replied.

Mike and Michelle continue cooking while Big Mama chatted on about her trip to Biloxi. Alley walked downstairs, and sat at the kitchen table.

"Good morning, dear," Big Mama said. "How did you sleep?"

"I couldn't sleep at all last night," Alley said. "Jasmine talked all night in her sleep. I woke her up twice. She looked like she was terrified."

"I'll go talk to her," Big Mama said.

Big Mama stood up to walk out of the kitchen when Jordan and Jonathan ran to the table. Jonathan sat down first.

"I won! I won!" Jonathan said.

"Boys, stop running in here. Jordan, you almost knocked me down," Big Mama shouted.

Then she left the kitchen, and walked upstairs to Jasmine's room.

"Jasmine," Big Mama said as she opened the door.

Jasmine jumped when she heard her name. She was breathing very hard. Her eyes were opened wide, and filled with panic. Big Mama walked over to her bed, and sat down.

"Honey, are you okay?" Big Mama asked.

"Big Mama, the people! They're in the water! Some of them have stayed on their roofs all night."

Even though Jasmine was awake, she was still terrified by my dreams. She felt like she was really there. Jasmine got out of bed, and hugged Big Mama. "Big Mama, tell me it's not true! Please, tell me it's not true."

As the nightmares replayed themselves in her head, she found herself crying unconsciously on Big Mama's shoulder.

Big Mama held her for a moment. Then she said, "Jasmine, sometimes the gifts God has given us comes with a price. He allows us to see both the good, and the bad. But He only allows us to see what He wants us to see. I know this is sad, but he wants you to help someone. Who did you see?"

"The little girl. I saw a little girl holding onto her mother's hand. The water was pulling the little girl so hard that she could barely hold on. Something fell. I think it was a board, or tree limb, but it hit the little girl in the head. She let go. Her mother screamed for her, but she couldn't see where she went in the darkness. Her mother is still there, Big Mama."

"I know, but we have to find out what this means. Jasmine, don't be upset. Her mother will find peace again, and her daughter is with God now. We can't stop the bad things from happening in this world, but as long as He is in control, it we will be okay. Have faith that God will take care of them. Now, you go wash your face. Then come downstairs, and eat breakfast, okay."

Big Mama smiled at her, and left the room. Jasmine took Big Mama's advice, and decided to have faith. She finally got out of bed. Jasmine did what she told her to do. Everybody was sitting at the table talking when Jasmine came downstairs.

"Morning sweetie. Are you okay?" Michelle asked.

Jasmine shook my head, and said, "Yes ma'am," as she sat down at the table.

Michelle prepared her breakfast, and put the plate in front of her. Jasmine said a little prayer for the people along the gulf and then she began to eat.

When Michelle sat down, she said, "Kids, I don't think y'all will have school today. The storm hit our area harder than I thought it would. I'll have to check the weather report later to make sure."

"Good," Jordan said. "Now I don't have to take that test."

"But, you'll still have to study for it," Michelle replied.

"I think I'll go check on Mrs. Madison and Ben later on today to see how they're doing," Big Mama said. "They aren't as lucky to have a generator like us. Mike, have you talked to your brother?"

"Yes. I called him this morning. He's a little worried about his house, but they are okay. Trey said my power is out at my house too."

"Hey guys, I forgot something in the shed. I'll be right back." Michelle got up from the table, and walked outside the back door. When she came back, she had a small portable TV with her. Michelle put the small four inch screen TV on the counter, and turned it on. "Now, we can see what going on," she said.

Big Mama put her fork down, and lowered her head. The tiny black and white screen was clear. The news was on. The news report showed pictures of the storm's devastation. The pictures were worse than my dreams. Men, women, and children made signs pleading for help. Some areas were hit so hard by the storm that the broadcast could only be shown by helicopter. Entire families were treading through the water looking for higher ground. I was shocked to see buildings on fire in all that water. Then the camera man interviewed people in Mississippi who watched their entire families drown in front of them. There were families swept away by the menacing flood waters from the hands of their own love one's. In our state of Alabama, the city of Mobile looked like it was a part of the sea. A big oil barge crashed into the bridge on US highway 98 over the Mobile River. There were pictures of shrimp boats tossed about on the land like kid's toys. The homes of the rich, and poor were equally destroyed. The reporter said thousands in our area were left without power. Tornados spread out as far as Arkansas, and Georgia. This one storm has left more devastation than any storm in our history. The news report showed pictures of Louisiana again. The faces of the people in the shelter were filled with shock, and despair. Children that were younger than me were left wandering in the water crying out for parents that weren't there, or no longer alive. Over night our country changed from hope to despair. Then Mike leaned towards the TV. There was a man with a child on his shoulders treading through the waters with his wife at his side. Mike stood up, and left the room. We all turned to see Mike walk outside the front door.

"Michelle, go see if he's all right," Big Mama said.

Michelle got up, and walked outside. Mike was sitting on the steps with his face in his hands.

"Mike, I know this won't be easy, but we will get through this together," mama said.

Mike wiped his eyes, and turned his head. "I knew the man that was in the water. We grew up together. I even went to his wedding."

"Well, let's be thankful that he is still alive," Michelle said.

"But for how long?" Mike turned to face Michelle abruptly. "No wonder I couldn't get through to my aunt's cell phone. There are no cell towers. There is nothing left. I saw the camera pass by dead bodies on the street. This is like a nightmare that I can't wake up from."

"Mike, what can I do to help?" Michelle asked.

"I don't know, but I have to talk to my brother. We have to find my aunt."

"I know Mike. If you need me, just ask. No matter what time it is, I'll be there." Michelle kissed Mike on the side of his face as she rubbed the soft curls on the back of his head.

"I've got to go. I'll call you tonight. Please tell everyone goodbye for me."

He stood up, and helped Michelle up. Then he kissed her gently, and left. Michelle felt helpless as she watched him drive off. This problem was so massive that she felt helpless to do anything. She walked back into the house, and shut the door. The power did finally come back on sometime in the early morning the next day, and the children had to go to school. Michelle took them to school this morning.

"Guys, I have left my new number in the office, and everybody knows my cell phone number, don't you?" She asked.

 They all said, "Yes ma'am."

"Alley, do you have my number?"

"Yes ma'am." She replied.

"Okay," mama said. "Love yah guys. I'm going to the center. I'll see you this afternoon."

Then Michelle drove to the center. When she pulled up to the circular drive, Joe was outside blowing away debris from the grounds with a leaf blower. He waved at Michelle, and walked over to her van.

"Mrs. Patterson the building looks fine. You had a lot of trash on the ground out here, but I cleaned it up. Your mail came today. I put it on your desk."

"Thanks Joe. Joe, the inspector couldn't come by on Monday, but he will be here on Friday. I'm not going to open the center until the week after next, but I want you to come in on Thursday to take care of the grounds, okay."

"Yes ma'am," Joe replied. "Michelle, how is your family?"

"Okay, but my friend's family needs help. They are from Louisiana."

Mr. Joe gasped, and said, "Oh no."

"That's why I'm going to wait a week to open, but no matter what Joe, we will open that Monday. Thanks for coming in. I'm going inside to open all that mail."

Michelle got out of the van, and went inside of the center. When she walked to the desk, there were three boxes of applications for Michelle to go through. She couldn't believe that she would have this many applications before the center even opened, but her sitting service was the only one of its kind in the city. Michelle was overwhelmed. She made a decision that she wouldn't take any more application after today. She called the newspaper to stop them from running the advertisement for her business. Then Michelle called Sharon on the phone. They talked to each other on the phone for about thirty minutes. Michelle asked Sharon to come down to the center, and thirty minutes later Sharon arrived there. Michelle gave her a small tour before they started going through the box of applications. She and Sharon completely sorted through one box of applications before lunch.

"Sharon, I'm not going to open the center for at least another week. The inspector won't come by until Friday and . . ." Suddenly Michelle hesitated.

"What's wrong Michelle?" Sharon asked. "Is it Mike?"

Michelle shook her head.

"I saw how bad it was on the news. Those people are still down there in that mess. The government won't let anybody into New Orleans without a two-day approval from FEMA. Who knows how many could be injured, or dying by then," Sharon said.

"Mike saw his friend walking through the water with his wife, and child. He hasn't heard from his aunt yet either. I haven't talked to Mike since yesterday, but he said he would call me. Sharon, I don't know how I can help him."

"Michelle, he may need a little time to sort this out. This is a lot to deal with. Give him a little time and then call him. Just be there for him when he needs you. That's all you can do."

"Sharon, what would I do without you?" Michelle asked with a smile.

"Find another old lady to take my place."

Sharon and Michelle laughed.

"Believe me Sharon. No one can take your place."

"Michelle, don't worry about the center. I'll fill in here if you need more time."

Michelle hugged Sharon, and said, "Thank you. Now, let's go eat. I know a beautiful restaurant down the street that you will just love. That is if they are open today."

"Well, come on. Let's go. I am starving, and since you're the boss, I know you are paying," Sharon said with a grin.

"I'll buy today, but you are now my manager, so you will be making a decent salary too. And, the next lunch will be on you."

"Okay Michelle." Sharon agreed.

The two friends filed the rest of the papers they wanted to keep, and left the other applications in the boxes. Then they went to lunch.

Michelle and Sharon had a long lunch together. When they got back to the center, Michelle decided to end the day early. They both went home. Big Mama had cleaned the debris from the yard, and she hung the swing back up too. Michelle walked into the house. She saw Big Mama sitting on the couch watching TV, and drinking tea. The news channel was running continuous reports of the after effects of Hurricane Katrina. Michelle walked into the den, and sat down on the couch by Big Mama.

"Mom, what's going on now?"

"There are so many people on roof tops, and highways that it seems impossible to rescue them all. People are begging for help. The saddest part of this tragedy is that the children are being separated from their parents. There is total chaos out there," replied Big Mama.

"Mom, look at that. A few of them are stealing."

"Michelle, most of them are stealing to survive. Within a week, any food down there in that heat, and water will be ruined anyway. I say let them have it. I know that there are always a few criminals that terrorize people in every society, but the majority of these people are good. Just look at them. They just want help," Big Mama said.

"Mom, I can't look at it anymore. It's too painful for me to watch this. I can't imagine walking passed dead bodies on the street. I'm going upstairs to take a nap."

"Okay baby. I'll pick up the kids today," Big Mama said.

"Mom, let's go out to dinner today. I don't feel like cooking tonight."

"All right," replied Big Mama.

Michelle walked upstairs, and got into bed. Her bed became a welcoming refuge from such a chaotic world. She fell fast asleep.

*****

Today Big Mama picked us up from school. On our way home Big Mama said, "Kids, we are going out to eat tonight, so y'all have to start your homework when we get home."

"Oh man!" Jordan said.

"And, I want y'all to be quiet while your mother is sleeping. Do you understand Jordan?" Big Mama said looking in her rearview mirror.

"Yes ma'am."

"Okay." Big Mama said with a stern look.

As Big Mama continued to drive through the city, I noticed there were a lot of cars on the street with Louisiana, and Mississippi tags. Once we got to our house, we all walked inside very quietly. We put our books on the table, and sat down at the kitchen table to do our homework. Big Mama walked into the kitchen to make some snacks for us. Big Mama put a bowl of cookies on the table. Then she brought out four cups of juice and sat them on the table.

"Now, that should give y'all a little energy to finish your homework," she said.

Then she walked into the laundry room, and began sorting the clothes. Forty minutes later we finished doing our homework, and Big Mama let us go outside. We saw Plump standing at Mrs. Madison's gate. Mrs. Madison gave Plump a hand full of candy, and told her to share it with the rest of us. Plump ran across the street to our yard. She gave each of us a piece of candy.

We all yelled, "Thanks Mrs. Madison," and began eating.

Mrs. Madison waved back to us, and walked back onto her porch. Plump, Alley, my brothers, and I played a game of *"Red Light/ Green Light"* in the front yard most of the afternoon until Plump's mother drove into their driveway. There was another car that pulled up behind her mother's car.

"Plump who's that?" I asked.

"That's my uncle. He's going to stay with us for a while. His house was destroyed in the storm. I got to go. I'll see y'all tomorrow." Plump waved as she left the yard.

Mama walked outside onto the front porch, and said, "Kids, come in the house, and wash your hands. It's time to go."

Mama and Big Mama decided to go to a Chinese restaurant. Mama drove the van to the south side of town. When we pulled into the restaurant's parking lot, I noticed that our van was the only vehicle from Alabama. All the other vehicles were from either Mississippi, or Louisiana. We got out of the van, and walked over a small bridge. Under the bridge was a pond that was filled with a large yellow, orange, and white Koi. My brothers, Alley, and I stopped to ogle the fish. We ran from one side of the bridge to the other chasing, and pointing at the fish that were trying to get away from us.

"Come on guys. I'm hungry," mama said.

We walked inside the restaurant, and a little Asian lady wearing a red apron asked, "How many?"

Big Mama said, "Six."

"Follow me please," the waitress said. She seated us at a beautiful carved dark wooden table. She took our drink orders and we all got up, and went to the buffet tables. Jordan's plate was piled so high with food it looked like a small volcano. Once we sat down, I looked around the room. The people in the restaurant were unusually quiet. They were chatting amongst themselves. Some of them even smiled, but the majority looked like they were still in shock.

I turned to Big Mama, and said, "Big Mama, I saw a pastor on TV saying that the people in Louisiana were sinners, and that's why God has done this to them. Is that true?"

Big Mama and mama looked at each other for a moment.

Then Big Mama said, "Baby, the people in Louisiana are no worse than the man that said that. We all have sin. That storm didn't just hit Louisiana. It hit Alabama and Mississippi too. I'm always amazed at people who think they can speak for God. I don't know how God feels, but I wouldn't want these people to speak for me. Baby, that man thinks he is better than other people, or that his sins are some how less than theirs. We have all sinned, and no sin is better than another. The God of this universe is so much bigger than this."

"Big Mama, why do you think a storm like this has happened?" I asked.

Big Mama looked up at me sadly, and said, "I'm not sure. It could be because of greedy men who kill our environment. They are criminals. They poison the air, land, and water killing the earth's creatures in the process. It was only a matter of time before what they have done starts to kill people too. The earth has gotten hotter than it was when I was a child. But, remember what I told you."

"Mom, let's change the subject. People are starting to stare," mama said.

We all looked around, and everyone was looking at us.

"Guys, I think y'all are watching too much TV. Y'all should be playing games, and having fun. Believe me. You will have plenty of time to worry about the world when you grow up. Come on let's eat."

We continued to eat, and chat about everything else except the storm. When we left the restaurant, mama stopped by a drive thru ice cream shop, and bought all of us a cup of ice cream. That night Alley asked me if I thought all the people in the Superdome were going to die. I said no, but I told her this storm would be something they will never forget.

*****

Thursday, Big Mama took the kids to school. Michelle arrived at the center early today. She wanted to finish going through the applications. Because her business was so small, she could only accept twenty patients from the three hundred applications that were sent to her. This task was so enormous that she decided to wait for Sharon to arrive. Michelle made a pot of coffee, and turned on the big screen TV in the recreation area. She poured a cup of coffee, and sat down to watch the news. The reporter showed pictures of explosions, and lawless criminals shooting at the police. She shook her head, and took another sip of her coffee. Then she heard the buzzer at the front door. Michelle got up to open the door. It was Sharon.

"Hey honey," Sharon said. "Whatcha doing?"

"I'm watching that madness on TV," Michelle said.

"I saw it myself this morning. If they don't get those people out of there by tomorrow, I'm afraid a lot of people will die," Sharon replied.

"I told Mike I was glad his aunt left the Ninth Ward, but I am afraid she may not survive in that shelter either."

"Well, at least in the shelter she has a chance. Come on Michelle, I want to show you something."

Sharon gave Michelle activity schedule for the first month. Michelle and Sharon continued discussing business, and menu plans for most of the morning. Michelle gave Sharon a key. She asked Sharon to meet her on Friday when the inspector comes by. After Lunch, they finished sorting the last two boxes of applications. Tomorrow they would have to decide on the final list of people they would accept. Michelle and Sharon ended the day early so that Michelle could pick the kids up from school. When Michelle and the kids got home, Mike was sitting on the front porch with Big Mama. They all got out of the van, and greeted Mike and Big Mama on the porch.

"Kids, y'all go on into the house, and let your mama and Big Mike talk for a moment," said Big Mama

Everyone walked inside leaving Michelle, Mike, and Big Mama on the porch.

"Michelle, some of the roads have been cleared in Mississippi, and my brother, Lisa, and I are going down to see what we can save. Trey is going to drive my truck, but I would like you to come with me in your van. Michelle, there will be a lot of devastation down there, and there is no telling what we will see," Mike said. "We need your help, but if you decide not to go, I will understand."

"Mike, what time are you leaving tomorrow?" Michelle asked.

"We are going to leave tomorrow morning at six a.m. Is that okay?"

"Yes, but . . ." Michelle hesitated.

"What?" Mike asked.

"I told Sharon we would make our final decision on the applications tomorrow. Also, the inspector is coming. I guess I'll call Sharon, and have her meet the inspector. We can go through the list next week," Michelle said.

"Will you go Michelle?" Big Mama asked.

"Of course, but that is if you don't mind looking after the children for me," Michelle asked Big Mama.

"Of course not," Big Mama said with a smile. "I'm going to check on them now. Y'all go on, and talk."

Big Mama stood up, and walked back into the house. Michelle sat down on the swing by Mike.

"How are you doing?" She asked.

"I don't know Michelle. I guess I'm still in a state of shock. I can't believe what's going on down there. I'm so angry, but I don't know who to blame. I feel that the mayor should have done more to get the people out of the city. I feel that the governor should have done more to restore the order, and most of all I blame FEMA. People were dying, and they wouldn't let anyone come into the city to help without a two-day background check. FEMA still has supplies that aren't being given to the people that need them the most. This is insane. I've been making calls for two days now, and they still won't let me into New Orleans. I don't know if my aunt is alive, or dead. They won't even let my brother in there right now."

Mike turned from Michelle, but she could see the rage in his face. He was so angry his hands began to shake.

"These people made it through the storm Michelle. They didn't have to die."

"I know Mike. We will find her. Don't worry." Michelle put her arms around Mike while they sat in silence. Then Michelle stood up, and told Mike to come inside. She asked him to have dinner with them. Mike walked inside the house with Michelle. During dinner that night, Mike's seemed to be feeling a little better. He even laughed at Jordan's stupid *knock-knock* jokes. After dinner, Michelle put a movie in the DVD player. She didn't want the children to see any more news tonight. Around nine o'clock Mike left. Jasmine heard Michelle talking on the phone, and packing before she fell asleep.

*****

Friday morning Big Mama was up early. I came downstairs, and walked into the kitchen.

"Big Mama, whatcha doing?" I asked.

"I'm packing some food, and water for your mother's trip. Where she is going there probably won't be many places to stop, and eat." Big Mama said.

Pee-Pee was crunching very loudly on the kibble in his bowl in the corner when I sat down at the table.

"Big Mama, I had that dream again about the little girl, but this time mama was talking to her mother. Do you think it has something to do with mama's trip?" I asked.

Big Mama stopped packing. "What happened in your dream? What did you see?"

"She's a little girl with blond hair. She is about five years old I think, and she has this old nasty looking doll. She told me to tell her mother to come, and get her."

"Where is she Jasmine?" Big Mama asked.

"She's under the old shed door." I said.

"Who's under a shed door?" Mama asked as she suddenly walked up behind us.

Big Mama and I turned back to see mama standing there. Mama was fully dressed, and ready to go when she walked into the kitchen.

"Jasmine, you go upstairs, and get dressed. Let me talk to your mother," Big Mama said.

After Jasmine left the kitchen, Big Mama told her about Jasmine's dream. Mama was in shock.

"Mom, you want me to find somebody?"

"Yes."

"Mom, this trip is going to be hard enough for me as it is. I'm not looking for anyone."

"Michelle, if you see the lady just tell her, okay."

"All right Mom."

"Here," Big Mama said. "I've packed a few things for you to take on your trip."

"Thanks mom. I'll put this in the van." Michelle loaded her bags in the van, and before long everybody was downstairs eating breakfast. The doorbell rang. Mama answered it. Big Mike and Mr. Davis walked inside to greet us.

"Michelle, are you ready?" Mike asked.

"No, but I'm ready as I'm going to be," she replied.

"Okay, let's go." Mike said.

Mama hugged everyone, and said goodbye as Mike and mama got into the van. Trey and Lisa were behind them in Mike's truck. We waved at them as they drove away. I was a little sad to see her go, but I knew she had to.

Chapter 22
Getting up again

The ride to Mississippi was a long one. Michelle and Trey made one stop inside of the Mississippi boarder for gas, and a bathroom break. Then they headed down south of Interstate 59 to Bay St. Louis. The closer they got to Bay St. Louis the more damage and destruction they saw. The pictures on TV couldn't compare to the massive devastation they witnessed. There was heavy machinery everywhere clearing the roads. Some of the roads were closed with detour signs guiding Trey and Michelle into an unknown direction. Every bridge they came to was damaged, or completely destroyed. This trip would normally take only a few hours, but due to the massive destruction it took two hours longer than normal. When they finally got near Trey's and Lisa's neighborhood, there was a road block. Two State Troopers were checking everyone's driver's identification. The trooper on the right side of the road waved to Michelle to stop the van. Michelle pulled up beside him, and rolled her window down.

"Ma'am, I need to see your license, and proof of insurance," the trooper said.

Michelle reached into her purse, and gave the officer what he needed.

"Ma'am this road is closed to everyone, but the residents of this area."

"Officer, we are with the truck in front of us. He is a resident here. This is his brother Mike," Michelle said.

"Officer, my brother asked us to come down to help him salvage some of his belongings," Mike said.

The trooper looked at the truck, and said, "Y'all wait here."

He walked to Mike's truck, and spoke to Trey. When the trooper wrote the tag numbers from the truck and van down on his note pad. Once he finished, he walked back to the van.

"Okay ma'am. You can go, but you will only have two hours in there. It's getting late, and there won't be any security down here after dark."

"Okay," Michelle said.

The first trooper removed the barriers, and Trey drove through first. Michelle followed behind him. The only things left from some of the houses were the foundations. Trey drove slowly down his street. Everything looked different to him now. He was trying to find anything that was familiar to him. Finally, Trey pulled the truck over into the grass. Michelle parked behind them, and they all got out of their vehicles. Michelle and Mike met Trey and Lisa on the sidewalk. Most of their house was still standing, but the back side of their house was demolished. The whole house seemed to slope down at an angle in the back. Lisa put her head down. The reality of having lost everything she ever owned was real now.

"The only thing I recognized from the house is the mail box on the ground. "With all the bills we had, that was the one thing we could afford to lose," Trey said.

Mike and Trey laughed, but Lisa started to cry.

"Lisa, are you okay?" Michelle asked.

"No. I thought that some how we could come back, but it's all gone. And, my dog's gone too."

"Your dog was here?" Michelle replied in shock.

"Yes!" Lisa cried. "I left Peanut here because I didn't think the storm would come here. I am so sorry."

Lisa continued to cry. Then Trey walked over to her, and held her as she cried on his shoulder. Michelle saw something moving under a piece of siding.

"Peanut?" Michelle asked curiously.

The dog walked out onto the grass towards them. Lisa suddenly turned from Trey to see what Michelle was referring to. The little brown dog looked like "*Toto*" from the "*Wizard of Oz.*" The dog yelped, and wagged his tail. Lisa and the dog both ran to each other crying, and yelping. The dog jumped into Lisa's arms as she fell to her knees. They both cried tears of joy.

"Well, at least something good came out of this madness," Trey replied. "Come on guys. We've got a lot of work ahead of us."

Lisa took the dog back to the truck, and gave Peanut some water. She didn't have any dog food, but the dog enjoyed her sandwich just as well. Lisa walked back to the rubble, and started picking up pictures and cherished memorabilia. Lisa even found her wedding photo album. Some of the pictures had a little water damage, but most of them were intact.

Everyone salvaged as much furniture, clothing, and mementos as they could find. They worked for an hour until Michelle saw a lady walking down the street. Even though the lady had on sunglasses, Michelle could tell she was crying. Michelle saw the lady sit down on the curve next door to Trey's property. She was a petite white lady with short dark curly hair. She was too neatly dressed in her white shirt, and khaki shorts to be sitting on the ground, but Michelle could tell that she didn't care. While everyone continued to work, Michelle walked over to the lady, and sat down on the curve beside her. Michelle didn't say anything for a moment. The lady didn't even acknowledge that Michelle was there. The lady just continued staring at all the debris crying. Michelle sat there looking over the debris too.

Michelle never looked at the lady, but she said, "You know, I was afraid to come down here because I was afraid of what I might see. Then I remembered a song my mother liked to play on my CD player. You see, my mother is a big fan of "*Mahalia Jackson*." I've listened to "*Mahalia's*" music most of my life, but for some reason the song titled "*Precious Lord*" by Thomas Dorsey stuck in my head all the way down here." Then Michelle started to sing. The lady stopped crying, and turned to listen to Michelle. Michelle stopped singing and said, "Let's go get some of your things."

Michelle extended her hand to help the lady up. She and the lady searched through the debris on the lady's property. Michelle got a bag from Mike's truck to put the lady's belongings into. They continued to search until Michelle came across a picture of a beautiful blond little girl with blue eyes. The picture was a little damaged from the water, and the frame was broken.

Michelle walked back to the lady, and said, "Who is this?"

"That's my daughter. The night it stormed the water rose so high I had to climb out of the window. I pulled myself onto the roof. I reached down to pull my daughter up, but the water was pulling us so hard she could barely hold on. Then a limb from that tree hit my daughter on the head, and she let go."

The lady didn't cry, but her voice was getting shaky. The lady continued.

"The same tree that killed my daughter saved my life. The roof started to collapse. I jumped into the tree. I stayed there all night until a reservist rescued me. I don't believe my daughter is still alive, but I'd give anything to find her. I just want to give her a proper burial."

The lady paused, and took the picture from Michelle. "Thank you for finding it for me."

The lady traced her daughter's image on the photo with her finger. Michelle turned from the lady because she understood now what Big Mama wanted her to do. Michelle walked slowly to the shed that was turned over, and leaning against a pole. She was shaking. She lifted the door, and saw a small child. The little girl's body looked more like a broken rag doll than a child's body.

"Mike!" Michelle yelled.

Everyone turned around. The lady screamed, and ran stumbling over the debris towards the child. Mike ran to Michelle. Michelle grabbed Mike, and began to cry on his shoulder. Lisa couldn't move. The lady fell to her knees, and cradled the child in her arms. The lady screamed continuously, and cried hysterically. Trey tried to free the lady's hands from the child, but she wouldn't let go.

Trey walked back to Mike, and said, "I'm going to get the state troopers, stay with her."

Trey ran to the truck, and sped away. Twenty minutes later Trey came back with two state trooper's cars, and a coroner's hearse. The lady wasn't screaming anymore, but she sat there cradling the child. Tears were falling from her eyes as she rocked back and forth. She talked to the child as if the little girl was just sleeping. But, the ladies eyes were as dazed as a mad man's.

Trey walked to the lady saying, "Come on. Let's take her home."

Trey helped the lady up with the child still cradled in her arms as they walked to the hearse. Michelle, Lisa, and Mike followed them. The lady laid the child's body down in the back of the hearse. Then she got into the hearse with the coroner. The troopers got back into their cars too and they both drove away. Mike and Trey decided it was time to go too. Lisa and Trey walked back to the truck where the happy faced dog was waiting for them. Mike held Michelle around the waist, and walked her back to the van. Mike helped Michelle get into the passenger side of the van. Then he got into the driver's side, and started the van. Mike followed his truck out of the neighborhood. Michelle put her head on the side of her seat, and cried for an hour until Mike drove out of the city. It was dark now when Mike drove passed the Louisiana boarder. Trey and Mike stopped at a small bed and breakfast inn outside of Baton Rouge. This was the only place that still had any rooms left. It was an expensive price to pay for the room, but everyone needed some sleep. Mike and Trey each rented a room for the night. Mike and Michelle walked to their room without saying a word. Michelle sat down on the window seat, and stared at the night sky. Mike put their bags down and walked over to her.

"Darling, are you okay?" He asked.

Michelle didn't say anything, but she did shake her head in agreement.

"Okay," Mike said. "I'm going to take a shower."

Mike got some personal things out of his suitcase, and walked into the bathroom to take a shower. Soon Mike walked out of the bathroom with a pair of shorts on. Michelle was still sitting in the window seat when he came out. She hadn't said a word since they left Mississippi.

"Honey, why don't you take a shower, and come to bed," he said.

Michelle never spoke. She picked up her overnight bag, and walked into the bathroom. After Michelle got out of the shower, she put on a satin pajama short set. When she walked out of the bathroom, Mike was sitting at the table quietly staring at the walls. Tears were cascading down his cheeks. His once beautiful big brown eyes were red, and swollen. Michelle sat down in the other chair, and didn't say anything for a moment.

"Mike, you told me this wouldn't be easy. The first time I was confronted by this devastation, and death I fell apart," Michelle said. "I'm sorry."

"No Michelle. I'm sorry for bringing you here. My world has been destroyed overnight. The wind and water have taken every bit of happiness I've ever known. There will be nothing, but death where we are going."

"That's not true. These people are not victims of this storm. They are survivors, and so are you. When we get to New Orleans, we will not find death. These people are alive, and they will have a chance to start over again. I don't know what we will see once we get to New Orleans, but I will be with you every step of the way. I prayed in the bathroom, and I asked God to give us the strength to get through this journey. Mike, you've just got to have faith that everything will get better. Don't look back. Just keep looking forward."

"How do I do that Michelle? I feel that I am walking through Hell."

"Because Mike, even though we may walk through the valley of shadows of death, He is with us. I know I am sounding like my mother, but she is right," Michelle said. "Now Mike, sometimes you just have to do what needs to be done."

"How do I do that?"

"Just take my hand," Michelle said.

Mike took Michelle's hand and stood up. Michelle led Mike to the bed and they both got in.

Michelle said, "When you can't go on anymore, I'll be there for you, okay. We are in this together. I know this is your family, but we will get through this together."

Michelle fell asleep with her arms wrapped around Mike's waist most of the night.

When Michelle woke up this morning, she could see how beautiful the room was. The whole room was filled with antique furniture, and art. Michelle decided to get dressed early. Because Mike had such a long day yesterday, she decided to let him sleep a little longer. She knew she would be going on a long drive today, so she put on her grey Capri sweat pants, and matching t-shirt. She finally had to wake Mike. He got dressed in a pair of jeans, and t-shirt. He called his brother to meet him downstairs for breakfast. Mike and Michelle were sitting at a small wooden table eating a gourmet breakfast when Trey and Lisa walked in. They sat down at the table when the young waitress came over, and took their orders.

"Mike, we might have to take a few back roads to get out of here, but the interstates are still looking good," Trey said. "How are you two doing?"

Mike and Michelle looked at each other, and Michelle said, "We were going to ask you the same thing."

"I'm not upset about that house. I hated to lose my things, but at least I have my family. We can get another house," Trey said.

"Yeah, and now we have Peanut back, our family is almost complete," Lisa replied.

"I heard on the radio that the Superdome in New Orleans was emptied yesterday," Trey said. "Our best chance of finding Aunt Frances will be at the Superdome in Houston.

"Guys, I want to do something for the survivors on our way back," Michelle stated. "There are so many people living out here in trailers in this heat, and without running water, or power. I would like to stop somewhere, and buy some water and ice to give them. We can't take very much with us, but maybe we can do something to help. Guys, do y'all mind?"

Mike grabbed Michelle's hand, and kissed her cheek. "That's a wonderful idea," he said.

Then Michelle thought about Peanut being in the truck all night.

"Lisa, is Peanut still in the truck?" Michelle asked.

"No. Trey told the manager about our situation, and he allowed us to bring the dog in since we would only be here for one night. He even brought the dog a dog bowl and dog food this morning. Trey walked him this morning, and no one has complained about the dog yet."

"I am glad he understands. Thank God there are still a few good people left in the world, "Michelle said with a smile.

The group continued to eat, and chat for the next twenty minutes. Then it was time to go. Everyone loaded up the vehicles, and pulled out of the parking lot. Trey and Mike stopped their vehicles once for gas. Then they were back on the road again. They drove out of the state without stopping. They did, however, stop inside of the Texas boarder for gas, and a bathroom break. The price of gas was getting more expensive with every stop they made. After pumping the gas, Trey walked the dog while Michelle and Lisa went to the bathroom. Michelle used the restroom first. When she walked out of the stall to wash her hands, she turned around suddenly when she heard someone vomiting.

"Lisa, are you okay?" Michelle asked.

"Yeah, I'm okay," Lisa said.

She flushed the toilet, and walked out of the bathroom. Both Lisa and Michelle washed their hands. Then Lisa started to rinse her mouth from the facet's water.

"Lisa, how long have you been feeling this way?" Michelle asked.

"I've been feeling this way for about a month. I think I must have acid reflux, or something. I'm always hungry, but some foods that I eat just make me sick." Lisa replied.

"Do you think you are pregnant?" Michelle asked.

"Are you kidding? Trey hasn't been home long enough to get me pregnant."

"Well, it doesn't take any longer than two minutes," Michelle said with a grin. "Even less for some."

They both laughed.

"Don't take any medicines before you see a doctor. I think you've been sick for too long, and you need to get checked out. I have some crackers in my van that my mother packed for me. I believe that it will help. I have some mint tea that would sooth your stomach, but I have a lemon lime soda in the front seat of the van too. Come on. I'll get them for you."

"Do you really think it will help?" Lisa asked.

"Oh yes. It has work for me many times. Trust me. It will work for you too. Come on."

Michelle and Lisa walked out of the bathroom to Michelle's van. Michelle gave Lisa the crackers, and soda. Then they both got back into their vehicles. Mike and Trey started the vehicles up again, and soon they were driving down the interstate. Trey and Mike drove straight to the Superdome. They parked their vehicles in the large parking lot. It was still early in the morning, and Trey rolled down the window so that the dog could get some air. Everyone walked up to some security guards standing in front of the entrance. People were coming, and going as more buses drove up. Mike told the officers they were looking for his aunt Frances Mitchell. The guard instructed them to go inside to the information desk.

The massive circular building was lit up like a football game was about to start. People were walking back and forth through the circular hallway chatting, and wandering about. There was a big message board near the entrance filled with messages for the people who were still missing their love ones. Trey, Mike, Lisa, and Michelle walked into the arena. People filled the stands as well as the ground floor. The young and the old camped down under the Superdome's lights with mattresses, sleeping bags, and old lawn chairs. It was hard to believe that anyone could sleep under these bright lights, and loud noises, but the body can do amazing things when it is exhausted.

Trey, Lisa, Mike, and Michelle maneuvered down through the crowd when a man yelled, "Mike! Trey!"

It was Mike's friend Michelle saw on TV. Mike's friend was alive, and well. He ran down the stadium steps towards him. Mike's face was filled with utter happiness to see that his friend had survived the flood. The two men embraced, and shook hands. Then the man embraced Trey just as hard, and shook his hand too.

"Man, it is good to see y'all! Did y'all just get here? Man, I thought y'all left town long ago," said the man.

"We just got here, but we didn't come from Louisiana," Mike said. "Man, I've been living in Alabama for years now, and Trey lives in Mississippi."

"Oh man. You're in the same situation as we are Trey. I wouldn't wish this on anybody," the man said. "Did everybody in your family get out?"

"Yeah," Trey replied.

"Well, it is good to see somebody I know, except I don't think I know these two lovely ladies," the man said smiling from ear to ear.

"Oh, I'm sorry," Trey said. "This is my wife Lisa, and this is Mike's friend Michelle. Lisa, Michelle this is David Goodwater. We all grew up together."

The two ladies gave David a polite greeting.

"Now Mike, she must be more than a friend to come down here to this madness," David replied.

"She is," Mike agreed. "How is your family?"

"Oh man! Come, and meet them. They're sitting up there."

David pointed to his family, and they waved back. Everyone walked up the stadium steps to greet David's family. David said to his wife, "Sandra, you remember Mike and Trey."

Sandra stood up, and hugged them both.

"Sandra, this is Mike's friend Michelle, and Trey's wife Lisa. The women exchanged greetings. Then a shy little girl looked around Sandra's leg peering up at Michelle.

"And, who might you be?" Michelle asked.

"Oh, this is my little girl Dee-Dee. Say hello Dee-Dee," Sandra said. The beautiful little girl just waved, and darted back behind her mother's leg. "She's a little shy."

Mike turned to David, and said, "Man, I saw you on the news. Are you okay?"

"I am now, but we've got to get out of this place," he replied.

"David, where are you going to go now?" Mike asked.

"Well, I am a truck driver, and this man came by the center earlier today. He offered me a job in Atlanta. We are going to be bused to Atlanta, Georgia tomorrow. He told me to come by, and fill out an application when we got settled, but we'll still have to stay in a shelter for a couple of days until we find an apartment. At least that shelter is a smaller place than here. We will have our own rooms too."

"That's good," Mike said.

"Yeah, I'm lucky. I had my wallet with me when I left. Some of these people don't have a dime. All they came here with is the shirts on their backs."

"Mike, were you in a shelter?" Sandra asked.

"No, no. I came from Alabama to look for my aunt," Mike replied.

"Mike, you let me go on without telling me that?" David asked. "I saw your aunt yesterday, but she's not here now. I think they took her to the hospital. I don't think she was feeling well."

"What?" Trey and Mike said in union.

"Yeah. She said she wasn't feeling well, so they took her to the hospital, but I'm not sure of which one." David replied.

"How can we find out where they've taken her?" Trey asked.

"Go down there to that help desk. They can help you." David replied.

"Good seeing you David, but we have to go," Trey said.

Mike and Trey ran down the stadium steps with Lisa and Michelle behind them.

David yelled, "It was good to see y'all! I hope she's all right!"

When Mike and Trey reached the desk, they were slightly out of breath. The little blond middle age lady jumped back a little in her seat when she saw everyone running towards her desk at once. The middle aged lady fixed her glasses, and said, "May I help you?"

"Yes. We are looking for Mrs. Frances Mitchell. We were told she was here, and she was sent to a hospital," Trey said.

"Yes sir, and who might you be?" She asked.

"I'm her nephew Trey Raimond."

Trey opened his wallet to show the lady his FBI identification card.

"Well, we have the real FBI here," the lady said with a raised brow.

"Please ma'am. We are in a bit of a hurry. Can you tell us where to find my aunt?" Trey insisted.

"Yes, yes. Hold on a minute." Then she began typing information into the computer. "She is at the county hospital about a mile from here. Here, let me write down the address." The lady wrote the address down on a piece of paper, and handed it to Trey.

"Thanks," he said.

They all ran back up the stadium stairs, through the arena, and outside to the parking lot. Everyone got back into their vehicles. Mike followed Trey to the hospital. Luckily the hospital had a covered parking deck. Lisa left some water in a bowl for the dog on the floor of the truck. Trey let the window down in the truck about half way so the inside of the truck wouldn't get too hot. They left the vehicles, and walked across a covered bridge to the hospital. Mike walked up to the information desk, and asked the lady behind the counter for information about his aunt.

The lady said, "She is on the second floor in room 212." They took a short ride up the elevator to the second floor. The TV was on when they entered the room. Mike's aunt was a small woman with silvery grey hair. She had an IV inserted into her arm, and an EKG monitoring her heart.

"Hey boys. Oh my, I am so glad to see y'all," she said.

Mike and Trey walked to either side of the bed, and each one of them kissed their aunt on the brow. There was a tear that rolled down Aunt Frances's cheek. Lisa walked to the side of the bed by Trey, and kissed Aunt Frances too.

"Lisa baby, it has been too long since I've seen you. Honey, you are practically glowing," Aunt Frances said. "Honey, who might you be?"

"Oh, Aunt Frances this is Michelle," Mike said.

"Is she your wife Mike?" Aunt Frances asked.

"No ma'am. Not yet," Mike said with a grin.

Michelle stood there staring at Mike with her mouth slightly opened. She couldn't believe what she just heard.

"Well baby, don't just stand over there with your mouth opened. Come over here."

Michelle walked closer to the bed.

"Mike, she's a beautiful girl. She must be special. Mike, you hold on to this one. Any women that would follow you down here into this mess, is a good woman. Mike, Trey, I'm glad I could see y'all for the last time," Aunt Frances said sadly.

"Oh, Aunt Frances, you're going to out live us all," Trey replied.

"Honey, I wish that was true, but my heart can't take anymore." Aunt Frances breathing had become labored.

"In one night, my world turned into a living Hell. I went to a place that I thought I would be safe, but instead we were forgotten. We were left to die. One man did just that. I saw a man fall to his death. I don't think I'll ever forget that. I heard rumors of all sorts of crimes being committed. There were no police to call, or security to protect us. I haven't had a glass of water since yesterday when I came here, but I survived. God let me survive long enough to see y'all again. Don't worry about me. I'm old. I . . . I just want . . ."

Aunt Frances could barely catch her breath. The monitor behind her bed started beeping sporadically.

"I . . . want y'all to know I love . . . you."

Then there was a solid buzzing from the machine.

"Aunt Frances!" Mike screamed.

Two nurses and a doctor ran into the room. One of the nurses said, "I am sorry, but I'm going to have to ask y'all to step outside of the room."

The nurse opened the door.

Mike yelled, "What's going on?"

"Please sir. Let us help your aunt," the nurse said.

"Come on Mike," Trey said as he grabbed Mike's shoulder.

Everyone rushed out of the room. They waited in the waiting room for an hour before the nurse asked everyone to follow her.

She took them to another small room, and said, "Please have a seat. The doctor will be here in a moment."

A few minutes later the doctor entered the room.

"I'm sorry you've waited so long, but I did all I could do to save your aunt's life. She was pronounced dead twenty minutes ago. I'm sorry."

Mike sat there in a state of shock. He could not speak. Lisa started to cry.

"How did she die?" Trey asked.

"Your aunt has been through a lot in the last four days. She was severely dehydrated when she came here. She hasn't eaten since that Monday night when she first arrived at the shelter. When she came to the Houston shelter, someone gave her some potato chips. She said she ate them because she was so hungry. The salt didn't help her high blood pressure. Her heart was weak. Her body couldn't take the stress. I am sorry," the doctor said.

"What's going to happen to her now?" Trey asked.

"That's up to you," the doctor replied. "You can make arrangements with the nurse."

"We will take her to Alabama," Mike said.

Everyone turned suddenly to Mike. He hadn't said a word the whole time Trey talked to the doctor.

"What?" Trey asked. "She was born, and raised in Louisiana. We should burry her there."

"Trey, our home is gone, and there is no telling if we'll ever be able to come back. Let's keep her close to us Trey. None of us can go back right now. Even if we did, it would never be the same. Doctor, give me the information, and I'll handle the arrangements," Mike said.

Mike stood up, and shook the doctor's hand.

"Thank you for taking care of her."

Mike then turned, and left the room. Everyone followed him to the nurse's station. Mike gave the nurse his information, and said he would have the funeral home call them for a time to send her remains to them. Michelle and Lisa were both in tears. Michelle could tell that Mike and Trey were visibly shaken by their aunt's sudden death, but neither man shed a tear.

Chapter 23
Riverside

The drive back to Baton Rouge was a long one. Mike didn't say very much on his way back. Michelle and Trey stopped the vehicles at a familiar gas station in Texas for gas, and a bathroom break. Trey pumped the gas into the truck while Lisa walked the dog. Michelle pulled up to the pump, and turned to Mike.

"Are you okay?" She asked.

"I don't know," Mike said. "Let me pay for the gas. That's the least I could do since I brought you down here."

"It's okay Mike. I can pump the gas." Michelle said.

"No Michelle. I need to get out anyway."

"Can I get you anything?" She asked.

"No thanks," he said with a smile.

Michelle walked inside of the convenience store to use the restroom.

When she came out of the restroom, Lisa ran passed her saying, "I got to go," and then she slammed the bathroom door.

Michelle bought two sodas for herself, and Mike. Once Lisa left the restroom, she bought chips, hot dogs, pickles, popcorn, a candy bar, and sodas. Michelle was astounded at the sight of all the food Lisa was carrying.

"Lisa, are you hungry?" Michelle asked.

"Yes. I don't know why I am so hungry. I eat a lot, but it seems that I can never get full."

"Lisa, don't eat all that junk. Why don't we stop for lunch?"

"Okay. Let's tell the guys," Lisa said.

When Mike and Trey came back to the front of the store, Lisa and Michelle told them they wanted to stop for lunch. Everyone got back into their vehicles, and drove to a drive-in restaurant. They ate outside under a covered picnic area. Lisa let Peanut out of the truck too. Since they were eating outside anyway, Lisa didn't think anyone would mind. She feed the dog while everyone ate. After lunch, everyone got back into their vehicles, and got on the road again. They didn't stop until they reached Baton

Rouge. They stayed in the same bed and breakfast inn that they stayed in before. Lisa and Trey even got the same room. Michelle and Mike stayed in a smaller room this time. Mike still wasn't very talkative that evening, but Michelle didn't pressure him to talk either. Later on, that evening, the group met in the dinning room. Both brothers chatted with each other, but neither one spoke of their aunt. That night Mike wrapped his arms around Michelle, and held her all night as they slept.

Michelle got up early the next morning. She got dressed as quietly as she could. Then she wrote a note, and left it on the table for Mike. She quietly left the room. When Mike woke up, he was a little surprised to find Michelle gone. He sat up, and called her name, but there was no answer. Once Mike got out of bed, he found the letter Michelle had written to him. The letter read:

> *"Mike,*
> *I'll be back soon. Go on, and have breakfast with your brother. I'll meet you in the dining room.*
> *Michelle"*

Mike got dressed, and called his brother to meet him downstairs. Mike, Trey, and Lisa were seated at a small round wooden table in the dinning room when Michelle walked in.

"Hey guys," Michelle said.

"Darling, you should have waked me," Mike said.

"No, no Mike. You were sleeping so peacefully I didn't have the heart to wake you. Besides, I bought a lot of stuff to help the people here and packed it into the van. Getting it out will be the trick. I'm hungry. What are you having?" Michelle asked.

"I'm having Eggs Benedict," Mike said.

"Hmm? That sounds good."

Michelle sat down with everyone, and ordered Eggs Benedict too.

After breakfast, they left the bed and breakfast, and drove to the interstate. Mike and Trey drove until they came to a sign in Mississippi that read: *Picayune* one mile.

"Mike, let's stop here," Michelle said.

Mike and Trey turned their vehicles into the gas station's parking lot. There were several trailers parked on the gas station's side lot. Michelle got out of her van, and went inside to talk to the merchant.

She walked up to the man behind the counter, and said, "Sir, why are there so many RVs in your parking lot?"

"Ma'am, those belong to people who escaped the storm. The boss lets them use the lot because there was no place else for them to go."

"Do you think they might need some ice, or water?" Michelle asked.

"Sure. They would probably take anything, but they don't need it. Those people had enough money to buy those RVs. Also, they have enough money to buy ice, and everything else they need from me. Ma'am, if you really want to give something to someone, I think you should give it to someone who can really use it. It's a church about a mile down the street from here. There are a lot of people staying there who have lost everything, and they have no money. The church doesn't have any power either. The church is asking for any donations people are willing to give. You should take that ice, and water down there. Those people will appreciate what you have."

"Sir, who told you about this church," Michelle asked.

"No one ma'am. I've been living there myself since the storm, but I'm lucky. I still have a job. Believe me, they will appreciate it."

Michelle couldn't believe the man was still smiling after what he told her. She asked, "Sir, what's the name of the church?"

"*Saving Grace Temple* ma'am. You can't miss it."

Michelle thanked the man, and left the building. She walked to the truck, and told Trey to follow her.

Then she got back in the van, and said, "Mike, move over. I'm driving. We've got a stop to make."

Michelle got into the van, and drove away. She drove one mile down the road when she saw the small church from the interstate. She stopped the van in the church parking lot. Michelle was the only one to get out of the van. She walked up a few steps, and knocked on the church door. A middle aged black man with graying side burns answered the door. The man was neatly dressed when he walked outside to speak to Michelle. No one in the vehicle could hear what Michelle was saying, but the man hugged her, and picked her up off the ground. The man walked back into the church. A group of people both black and white came back outside with him. There was a black family living there that came outside with a small baby. The young white couple ran to Michelle, and gave her a hug. Mike, Trey, and Lisa got out of their vehicles, and walked to the group.

Michelle walked up to Mike, and said, "This is Reverend Porter. There are a few people living here until they can find another place to go."

The minister shook Mike's and Trey's hand. He thanked all of them, and told them what a blessing they were. Mike and Trey helped Michelle unload the water, and ice out of the van. Since Michelle was going straight home from here, she decided to give the box of food to the people that Big Mama packed for her trip. When Michelle grabbed the box, she noticed there were two baby bottles, and a jar of baby formula in the box. Michelle thought to herself, no *wonder Mom packed so much*. Michelle gave the food to the minister. Everyone said their goodbyes and then they left.

Mike drove the van back to the interstate as Trey followed closely behind him in the truck. They drove until they got inside of Alabama state boarder. They stopped once for gas, and then they drove straight to Mike's house. Mike and Trey unloaded Michelle's van, and put most of the furniture in the shed. They did the same thing with the items in the truck. Lisa and Michelle took the clothing into the house. They also grabbed some mementos from the van, and brought them into the house too. Peanut jumped out of the truck, and ran behind Lisa everywhere she went. Once they had finished unloading the vehicles, Michelle hugged Trey and Lisa, and said goodbye. Michelle's friendship with Trey and Lisa had grown over the course of time it took them to drive from Alabama to Texas, and back. She would miss Mike's family, but she was excited to see her own. Mike walked Michelle back to her van.

"Michelle, I don't want you to go," he said.

"Mike, your family needs you here. Y'all have a lot to discuss. Don't worry, I am not going anywhere. You can come by anytime, okay."

"Thank you for being there with me. I don't think I could have done this without you."

"Yes, you could Mike. You are a very strong man."

"I love you, Michelle."

Then he kissed Michelle gently on the lips. Once he released her, Michelle got into the van, and drove away.

When she got home, Michelle struggled to open the front door while holding onto her luggage. The kids screamed, and ran to her. She stumbled back a little when the kids wrapped their arms around her waist, and hips. Big Mama walked over to Michelle, and hugged her too. Michelle sat her luggage down in the hallway, and walked to the kitchen. Big Mama prepared dinner, and they all sat down to eat. It was nice hearing the children's laughter again. Michelle was glad to be home, but she wanted to take a bath.

Michelle got up from the table, and said, "I'm going to take a bath. Mom, I will take the kids to school tomorrow. Kids, why don't y'all help Big Mama clean the kitchen, and get ready for school tomorrow."

All the kids moaned, and said, "Yes ma'am."

Michelle got up from the table, and the kids cleared the table. Then she stopped in mid stride, and turned back slowly to Big Mama.

"Oh yeah Mom, the lady in the church wanted to say thanks for the baby formula, and I think Lisa is pregnant too. Just don't tell Mike. Let him be surprised, okay," Michelle said.

"Okay darling, but do you want to know if it's a girl or a boy?" Big Mama asked.

"Let's keep that a surprise too," she replied.

Michelle picked up her luggage, and walked upstairs. She took a long hot bath, and went to bed.

*****

Today I woke up without any bad dreams this Tuesday morning. I knew it was going to be a good day. Alley was still sleeping when I woke up. I lay in the bed for a little while longer enjoying the silence. Then I got up to get ready for school. Once I got dressed, I went downstairs. Mama was up early this morning too. She was humming to herself, and cooking breakfast. I walked into the kitchen, and sat down sat the kitchen table.

"Good morning sweetie," mama said. "How was school yesterday?"

"Fine," I replied.

"Just fine, Jasmine? Come on. You can tell me more then that."

"Well, yesterday Teach fell asleep in the classroom, and passed gas. My English teacher wanted us to write a paper about what we want to be when we grew up, and Toad and Stool have started bothering Alley again."

"Jasmine, do I need to go to the school, and talk to the principal?" Mama asked.

"No ma'am."

"Well, let me know if something else happens. I don't want those two boys bothering you two, okay."

"Okay," I said. "Mama, what happened to the little girl? I don't see her in my dreams anymore."

Michelle stopped stirring the grits. She hesitated to answer Jasmine.

"Jasmine, I know you and mom share this gift. I am sorry you had to see that, even though it was just a dream. The little girl was found, and she will be laid to rest."

"Yes Jasmine. Her soul is at peace with God," Big Mama said.

Mama and I turned to see Big Mama walking into the kitchen.

"Michelle, you got a letter yesterday. I put it on the coffee table with the mail. What's cooking? Something smells good," Big Mama said.

"Well, I made some grits, eggs, and sausage. And for you, I chopped up some fruit," mama replied.

Big Mama has lost so much weight that her face even looks smaller. Big Mama told me that she has lost forty pounds.

"That sounds good Michelle," Big Mama said. Then she poured herself a cup of coffee, and sat down at the table. Soon Alley and my brothers ran downstairs. They sat down at the table, and chatted on about school. Mama and Big Mama prepared plates of food for all of us. Mama said a prayer then we began to eat. Once we finished, we all got up, and cleared the table. After putting the dishes in the dish washer, mama picked up the mail, and took us to school.

She pulled up to the front door of the school, and said, "Love yah, guys. Have a good day." Then she left.

****

Michelle drove to the center to check on the building, and to get the mail. She parked at the front entrance, and walked in. She walked up to the front counter, and picked up a piece of paper off the desk that read in big letters, APROVED. She walked into the recreational area and then she called Sharon on the phone. Michelle and Sharon talked for an hour. Sharon told Michelle that the inspector checked everything. She said that the building didn't suffer any damage during the storm, so the inspector gave his approval. Michelle began telling Sharon about her trip to Mississippi, and Texas. She told Sharon in graphic details about the destruction she saw. Michelle cried when she told Sharon the story about the little girl she found, and about Mike's aunt. The two friends continued to talk until Michelle stopped crying. She asked Sharon to be with her on the opening day. Then she hung up the phone. She turned the TV on, and started going through the mail. Most of the mail was junk. Then Michelle separated the bills from the junk mail when she came across a letter. The letter's return address was from Mississippi. Michelle opened the letter that read:

> *"Dear Michelle,*
>
> *My name is Cathy McCullon. I have been trying to reach you ever since that day you found my daughter. I've finally convinced the troopers to give me your name, and to tell me where you were from. I have searched very long, and hard to find you, so I'm hoping you will understand why I had to write to you. I just wanted to say thank you for finding my daughter. I don't know if you have children, but you can't imagine what a parent goes through when that child is missing. Each day I wake up is a struggle for me to get through the day knowing that she is gone. But, I thank you for giving me a piece of my heart back, so at least I can give my daughter a proper burial. I will be eternally grateful to you for what you have done for my family.*
>
> *Thank you,*
> *Cathy"*

A tear fell from Michelle's eye. Before Michelle put the letter down, she noticed there was something else in the envelope. Michelle turned the envelope upside down and a small photo of the little girl fell out. She picked up the photo from her lap. It was the same photo that she had found in the rubble, but the image of the picture looked perfect. It was smaller than the original, and there were no water spots. Michelle marveled over the technology that was used to restore the picture. Seeing the little girl's face made Michelle smile and then she turned suddenly when she heard the buzzer at the front door. She put the mail aside, and got up to answer the door. Mike was standing on the other side of the glass doors. Michelle opened the doors to let him in.

"Hey honey. I didn't think I'd see you today," she said.

"I just wanted to see you. What were you doing?" Mike asked.

"Oh, I was just going through some mail in the rec-room. Come on. Let's sit down."

Mike followed Michelle into the recreation area. He moved the letters to sit down on the couch. Then he noticed the picture of the little girl on the couch.

"I'm sorry Mike. Here, let me move that stuff out of your way." Michelle tried to gather up all of the mail when Mike picked up the picture.

"Is this the little girl you found in Mississippi?" He asked.

"Yes."

Mike gave Michelle the picture. Then he began to cry silently. Michelle sat down beside him, and put her arm around his waist. Mike cried for a few more minutes on her shoulder before he turned away from her.

"It is undignified for a man to cry this way," he said.

"No, it isn't, Mike. I rather you cry than to stand in a clock tower shooting a gun," Michelle replied.

Mike smiled a little, but he continued to cry. "I can't do this Michelle."

"You can't do what?"

"My aunt's body will be at the funeral home tomorrow, and I don't know what to do. My brother said since I wanted her to come here, I should take care of the arrangements. I don't know what to do. This is too hard. I've seen death before, but this is my aunt. This woman practically raised my brother, and me. Now, I have to burry her. I'm so angry. I just want to hit something. What do I do now?"

Mike sat there quietly staring in the distance. His rage left him depressed, and exhausted. Michelle leaned back on the couch, and thought for a moment.

"Mike, if you and your brother don't mind, I could handle all the arrangements for you," Michelle said.

"What?"

"Mike, I know it is too difficult to think about funeral arrangements when you have loss someone so close to you. Let me do this for you, and your brother. Y'all have enough to deal with."

"I can't ask you to do this. I've put you through enough."

"And, you aren't asking me Mike. You haven't put me through anything either. I'm an adult, and I knew what I was getting into. Let me do this for you. We can have the funeral at my church."

"Okay," Mike said. "Let me call my brother."

After Mike got off the phone, he told Michelle his brother thought that would be a good idea. Michelle called the church, and spoke to the church secretary. The secretary took down Michelle's information, and told her the minister would get in touch with her. After Michelle ended her phone call to the church secretary, she and Mike left the center. They spent the rest of the day together.

The next day Michelle and Mike met with the funeral director, and the minister at the funeral home to plan the service. Michelle was surprised to see that Mike had a life insurance policy for his aunt. Mike told Michelle that his aunt gave him the policy in case something happened to her. He said she would have given it to Trey, but he moved around too much. The funeral was planned for Saturday at one o'clock in the afternoon.

The night before the funeral Mike stayed at Michelle's house. Everyone got up early that morning to get dressed. Mike helped the boys tie their neck ties. Michelle combed Jasmine's hair into two pony tails. Then she brushed Alley's hair, and put a blue head band on her head that matched her dress. Once everyone was dressed and ready, they all went downstairs. Big Mama and Mr. Davis were sitting on the couch waiting for everyone. Michelle and Mike got into Mike's car. Everyone else got into the van. They drove to the church.

When everyone arrived at the church, Mike was surprised to see so many people there. Mike didn't know that the minister told everyone at the church services Wednesday night about Mike's aunt's story. People that Mike had never met before showed up to pay their respects to his aunt. Mike, Michelle, Trey and Lisa lined up at the church door to view the body. Big Mama, Mr. Davis, and the kids were behind them. They all walked in to view the body. Mike's aunt looked more like a large doll than a real person. Jonathan and Jordan didn't want to walk near the casket. Alley didn't want to walk near it either. Once everyone was seated, the choir began to sing. The service wasn't very long, but the preacher spoke highly of Mike's aunt. He preached of hope, and faith during troubled times. They all walked outside, and got into the limo. Two policemen on motorcycles drove beside the limo with their lights, and sirens on. When the limo stopped, they got out, and walked into a large cemetery. The graveyard held an eerie silence that was noticeable to everyone. There were no sounds of birds, or even traffic passing by. It was strange to Jasmine that she didn't see any souls in the grave yard. Normally, she would see souls everywhere, but not here. There were a few rows of chairs in front of the casket for the family to sit. Michelle, Mike, Trey, and Lisa sat in the front seats. Everyone else sat in the back. The church members gathered around them. As the preacher continued to preach his last sermon, Jasmine looked down the row to see Mike. And, there beside Mike stood the soul of his deceased aunt. Her spirit had a beautiful iridescent white light surrounding it. She smiled at Jasmine. Then she put her finger to her lips signaling Jasmine not to say anything.

The angel appeared behind the aunt's soul, and said, "It's time to go."

Mike's aunt waved at Jasmine then touched Mike on the shoulder. Then she was gone. Jasmine knew Mike must have felt her presence too because he looked down at his shoulder as if someone touched him. Then he looked in the direction that his aunt was standing in. The minister gave everyone on the front row a rose, and the funeral was finally over. Jasmine hadn't noticed the small band behind them until now. Soon as the funeral ended, they started to play *Down by the Riverside*," in a jazzy Creole style. They played until everyone left the graveyard. The family got back into the limo, and went back to the church. The church's cooks prepared a big Creole feast for everyone, but Michelle and Mike didn't stay to eat. Big Mama hugged Lisa and Trey as she gave her condolences. Then Big Mama, Mr. Davis and the kids left. Big Mama talked to Mr. Davis all the way home, but no one else said a thing. Jonathan, Jordan, Alley, and Jasmine were just glad to be going home.

Chapter 24
Trick or Treat

A month has passed since Mike's aunt's funeral, and summer was turning into fall again. Mama's center is becoming a great place to play. Big Mama takes us to school in the morning, and mama picks us up in the afternoons. Then mama brings us back to the center. I love the center. The old people are so funny, and friendly. After we've finished our homework, Alley and I would show a few of the ladies how to jump rope, or play *Jacks*. Mrs. Hattie Mae Robertson reminds me of Big Mama. She is a petite little black lady that is really good at playing cards. Mrs. Mary Johnson has beautiful cotton white hair, and sparking blue eyes. She tried to teach us how to knit, but my string would always turn into a knot. Mrs. Gray and Mrs. Peters were two twin ladies with pale wrinkled skin, and gray hair. They love to read stories to us. Some of their stories were as fascinating as Big Mama's. Mr. Mack is an elderly black man that walks with a slight limp. He has a favorite cap he wears all the time, and he always has a tooth pick in his mouth. It's amazing to me that he can play pool as well as he does because Mama told me he could barely see. Mr. Dixon has a sharp mind. Like most of the people here, Mr. Dixon gets around in a wheel chair. He has thinning gray hair, and the arthritis in his hands is so bad that his fingers turn to the side. His green eyes sparkle through his thick glasses. When he smiles, his pale wrinkled skin turns upward to reveal years of happiness, and laughter from his youth. Sharon really likes Mr. Dixon. She said he is a retired accountant, but his mind is still sharp. It's a shame that his body won't allow his mind to do what it wants to do, but he never complains.

Terri and LaShundra are the college students that help mama and Sharon run the center. LaShundra is a slightly overweight black girl who is a student at a culinary school. She helps mama prepare breakfast in the morning, and lunch in the afternoon. Mama and LaShundra would feed some of the patients there by hand. Terri is a young black nursing student that works at the center in the afternoon. Sharon and Terri clean the patients, and their rooms. They would even have to change the patient's diapers. I didn't even know grown people wore diapers until Alley and I saw Mr. Dixon's diaper when Mrs. Sharon was helping him into his wheel chair.

At the end of the day, mama would wait for the patient's family members to come by, and pick them up. So far no one has been late. Mama said they won't be late because they don't want to pay an extra fee. Mama would lock up the building, and then we would go home.

Fall seemed to come to Alabama over night. The evening sun seemed to go down sooner, and the nights were getting cooler. After dinner, I decided to put my favorite pajamas on early. The soft pajamas pants were covered with images of sleeping bears. The long sleeved shirt had a big print of a sleeping bear on the front. When I put the pants on, the hem was an inch and half too short. Then I put on the shirt. It was too little too. I walked downstairs to show mama.

"Mama, look at my pajamas!" I said.

Everyone in the den turned around to look at me. My brothers laughed.

"Jasmine, you've grown. I guess it is time to go shopping again," mama replied.

"Alley needs some more clothes too," Big Mama said.

"Well, why don't I take y'all shopping this weekend," mama replied. "Jasmine, just put on your gown?"

"Okay," I replied.

Before I walked upstairs to change, there was a knock on the door. Mama and Pee-Pee got up to answer the door.

"Hi Mike," mama said.

"*Belle dame*, you're looking lovely this evening," Mike said. Then he kissed her on the cheek.

"Come in," she said.

Mike and mama walked into the den. Mike exchanged greetings with everyone in the room. He sat on the sofa by mama, and said, "I have some good news to tell y'all."

"What's that Mike?" Michelle asked.

"Lisa is pregnant!" Mike said with a huge dimpled smile.

Mama and Big Mama looked at each other then turned back to Mike, and said, "Congratulations." My brothers, Alley and I cheered. Mike looked at mama and Big Mama strangely.

"Wait a minute. You two already knew, didn't you?" Mike said suspiciously.

"Well Mike," mama said with a slight grin, "I thought she might be pregnant when I saw her getting sick in the bathroom. I told her to go see a doctor then."

"I'll bet your mother knew all the time. Isn't that right Bertha?" Mike asked.

"Yes, I knew. I'm a Seer. What can I say," Big Mama replied with a grin.

"But Mike, mom promises not to tell us what the sex of the child will be, right mom?" Mama said turning to Big Mama.

"Yes, yes. I want them to be surprised too," Big Mama replied.

Big Mike stared at Big Mama curiously with a grin on his face. "So, tell me Bertha. What do you see in my future? Will Michelle and I have any children in our future?"

Big Mama took one look at mama. Then she looked back at Mike and said, "Come on children. Y'all go upstairs and play in your rooms. Let's leave these two love birds alone."

My brothers, Alley, and I left the room. Big Mama stood up, and giggled a little bit before she left the room too.

Mama looked back at Mike like she couldn't believe he just asked that question. Mike had a mischievous grin on his face. Then he put his head down, and laughed.

"Mike, you're bad," mama said with a grin.

"Well, not as bad as I want to be."

"I would love for you to be too, but now we have a bigger problem. I think it's great that your family is here. At least now you won't be alone, but it is going to be hard to finish what we started," mama said.

"I know," Mike replied.

"It's good to see you smile again," mama said with a smile.

Mama laid her head on Mike's chest as they talked, and watched TV. Mike decided it was time to go when mama fell asleep on his chest. He kissed her gently then said goodbye.

*****

On Saturday, mama agreed with Big Mama that she would take us to the mall while Big Mama went to the grocery store. Mama took us to a sport store first. Alley and I tried on our tennis shoes first. Jordan and Jonathan played a game of miniature basket ball in the corner of the store. Neither one of my brothers wanted to end the game, but mama demanded that they come over, and try the shoes on. Jordan and Jonathan had so much fun in the sport store that they didn't want to leave. While mama paid for the shoes, Jordan and Jonathan tried on goalie masks, and football helmets. They played with the baseballs and bats too. Mama had to yell at them telling them it was time to go. The next store we went to was a children's clothing store. Mama picked outfits out for my brothers, but she told Alley and me we could pick out something for ourselves. Of course, mama would make the final decision on whether she would buy the outfits. This store wasn't my brother's favorite store to shop in. They were bored, but Alley and I pretended that we were runway models. We tried on just about everything we could fit into. Even mama got tired of us changing so many times. She made us stop. Once mama paid for the clothing, we all went back to the van. Mama took us to lunch then we shopped for another two hours. Mama bought all of us new pajamas, and jackets.

On the way back home, Jordan said, "Mama, we haven't gotten our Halloween costumes yet."

"That's right," Jonathan said. "I want to be '*Dracula.*'"

"I want to be '*Spiderman,*'" Jordan replied.

"Then you don't need a costume, Jordan. You look like a spider anyway," I said grinning. Alley and Jonathan laughed.

"Well, you look like a--."

"That's enough Jordan," mama interrupted. "I'll take y'all to the costume store."

We all cheered, but Jordan stuck his tongue out at me. Mama turned the van around, and drove us to the costume store. She parked the van by the store's entrance. There was a big scary sign with a picture of a hooded skeleton hanging over the door that read: *Enter at your own risk.* My brothers ran inside the door. Alley and I huddled together as we walked inside. Mama followed behind us. Once we were inside, there was silly Halloween music playing throughout the store. It was brightly lit inside the store. The cashier and other store workers were dressed as their favorite characters. Some of the workers looked like witches, and mummies. There was a guy dressed like *"Frankenstein's Monster"* standing in a corner. He looked like he was part of the decorations.

When Jonathan walked over to touch his hand, the monster came to life and said, "NO!"

Then the monster walked away. Jonathan jumped back so fast I thought he was going to have a heart attack. Jordan, Alley, and I laughed as the stiff walking monster continued to walk away. There were so many interesting things in the store like fake skeletons, and talking witch statues. Mama called us over to try on our costumes. Of course, Jordan got a "*Spiderman*" costume. Jonathan got a "*Dracula*" costume, but Alley got a princess costume. Her gown was pink and blue with long sleeves. She wore a pointy hat with a long train in the back of it. I tried on an angel costume with large white wings, and a golden halo. I put on white tights under the gown. Mama tied a golden sash around my waist.

"Now Jasmine, you look like a real angel," mama said.

"An angel? Mama, are sure there aren't any horns that go with that costume?" Jordan asked.

"Shut up Jordan! You're the only little devil in this family," I said with a bit of a pout and I tried to push him.

"You're a devil!" He shouted back.

"Quit it guys! Go change Jasmine," mama said.

After mama paid for the costumes and some candy, we walked to the door where a witch was giving out candy. The bowl she held had a face in the middle of it. Each time one of us grabbed a piece of candy, the eyes on the face in the bowl would move, and the scary voice from the bowl said, "*Trick or Treat*." We all left the store, and got into the van.

I was a little tired from this long day of shopping. I think my brothers were tired too. They didn't say a word while mama drove us back home. Soon mama turned onto the corner of our neighborhood street. The sun was going down, and beautiful brilliant colors filled the evening sky. Alley watched the sun coming down as the van came near her old house. When she looked down from the sky to the window of her old house, she thought she saw something move. Then she gasped loudly. There he was in the window. His bright blond hair and pale blue eyes showed vividly through the window. There was an evil grin on his face. Then he stepped back, and disappeared in the darkness of the room. Suddenly Alley screamed.

"Ah!" He's here! He's here!" She cried.

Mama stopped the van.

"Alley, stop screaming! Who's here?" Mama asked.

"Daddy! Daddy's here!" She screamed, and pointed to her house.

Tears ran freely down her face wetting the collar of her shirt. She was visibly shaken.

"What?" Mama yelled. Then she reversed the van, and backed up to look into the house.

"No! No! Don't let him take me back! I won't go back!" Alley cried. Then she grabbed me, and held me tight. "Jasmine, you said he wasn't going to take me away. Please, don't let him take me away."

Alley continued crying on my shoulder.

"No one is going to take you anywhere Alley," mama said. "I just want to see for myself, and I don't see him."

"He's there! He's there!" Alley cried.

"Okay, okay. Let's go." Mama said. "I'm going to call the police. They can check out the house."

Mama put the van into gear, and then drove home. Once mama opened the door to the house, Alley ran upstairs to my room.

"Jasmine, you go upstairs with her. Maybe you can calm her down," mama said.

I said, "Yes ma'am," and went upstairs.

"What's going on?" Big Mama asked as she walked into the den from the kitchen.

"Boys, y'all go upstairs too. Let me talk to mom," mama said.

Jordan and Jonathan mumbled something under their breath. They didn't want to go upstairs. Mama walked into the den, and grabbed the cordless phone off the coffee table.

"Come here mom, and please sit down."

Once Big Mama was seated, mama said, "Mom, Alley said she saw her father in the window when we passed by her house."

Big Mama gasped slightly.

"I knew he'd come back," she said.

"Mom, are all the doors, and windows locked?"

"Yes." Big Mama replied.

"Good. I'm calling the police."

Mama called the police. Then she called Mike and told him to tell his brother. Within twenty minutes the police, Mike, and Trey arrived at the door. Trey left with the police to search Billy's house while Mike stayed with mama. Thirty minutes had passed before Trey came back. Trey walked into the den, and sat down on the couch.

"We didn't find him," Trey said, "but we could tell that someone had been in the house. The back door lock was broken, and a lot of his personal stuff was missing. The police will put a patrol car in front of your house tonight."

"Just for tonight?" Mama asked.

"They will make more patrols in your neighborhood too. Don't worry Michelle. We will do all that we can to catch him. Well, I got to get back to collect some finger prints samples. I'll see y'all later on," Trey said.

"Trey, would you like to eat dinner with us?" Big Mama asked.

"I would love to, but I don't have the time, maybe next time," he replied.

"Okay," Big Mama said.

Trey said goodbye, and left the house.

"Well, the kids still have to eat," Big Mama said. "Let me go get them." Big Mama got up, and went upstairs.

Mama hugged Mike then she kissed him. "Thank you for coming by Mike."

"Wow, will you do that every time I come by?" Mike asked.

"Only if you want me to," mama said with a grin. Mike leaned over to kiss her when the kids ran down the steps.

"Mike! Mike!" Alley yelled. Then she ran to him, and gave him a hug. Will you stay with us tonight, please?" Alley pleaded.

"I don't mind, but it's not up to me," Mike said.

"Can he stay Mrs. Michelle, please?" Alley pleaded.

Mama looked down into Alley's big blue eyes as she pleaded. Mama knew Alley would be too afraid to sleep tonight if Mike wasn't here. Then mama looked into Mike big beautiful brown eyes, and saw something more erotic.

"Okay," mama said.

Big Mike leaned over to mama, and kissed her on the brow. Mike and mama ate dinner together with the family. Later on, that night, Mike slept in mama's room, and she slept on the couch. The next morning Mike woke up with her lying beside him in the bed.

"Good morning," she said.

Mike was surprised to see her there. "Good morning to you. Didn't I leave you downstairs last night?" He asked.

"Yeah, but I couldn't sleep on that couch, so I came back up here. I hope you don't mind."

"Oh no, I don't mind," Mike said. Then he kissed her. His hand slid underneath the loosely fitted t-shirt. She moaned softly while Mike massaged her nipples, and kissed her deeply. He stopped abruptly when he heard a knock at the door.

"Who is it?" Mama asked.

"Mama, what am I wearing to church today?" Jordan asked, but he didn't open the door.

"I'll get you something out in a minute. Go on, and wash up. I'll be out in a minute," mama said. "I'm sorry Mike. I bet you are ready to leave me."

"Are you kidding?" He asked. "I'm ready to do something, but I'm not going to leave you. I love you Michelle and I can wait." Mike kissed mama gently and then she got out of the bed.

"Your tooth brush is still in the bathroom. You can take a shower if you want. Come downstairs later, and have breakfast with us," she said.

"All right," Mike replied.

Mama started to walk out of the room when she stopped at the door, and said, "Hey Mike, Halloween is this Saturday, and I'm taking the kids to '*DC's Hunted Mansion.*' Would you like to come?"

"Of course," he said with a dimpled grin.

"Good. We'll leave here by six o'clock."

Mama left the room, and went downstairs to help Big Mama prepare breakfast.

*****

Every kid at school couldn't wait for Halloween this Saturday. Plump, Teach, and Carlos said they were going to the *DC's Haunted Mansion* too. Mama had a big party at the center for the patients on Friday. Everyone dressed in costumes at the center. Mama prepared a table full of snacks for the patients to eat, but Alley and my brothers ate most of it. They played music and games at the center too. All the seniors left the center with a bag full of treats. The party was fun, but it was no *DC's Haunted Mansion*.

Today was finally Saturday, and Halloween was here. Big Mama helped us get into our costumes, but she decided not to go with us. She said she would stay at home in case any trick-or-treaters came by for some candy. Mama came downstairs in a long black fitted fringed dress, and a pointed witch's hat. Alley came downstairs dressed like a princess. Jonathan was already downstairs with me. He was dressed like *"Dracula"* with fake teeth in his mouth. Big Mama was helping me put on my wings and halo. Jordan jumped down the steps looking like *"Spiderman."*

"Stop Jordan before you hurt yourself," mama said.

Soon the door bell rang, and mama answered the door with Pee-Pee by her side. Mike was standing outside of the door dressed like a cowboy.

"Wow! Getty up Cowboy. You look great!" Mama said looking him up and down.

"So do you. I hope you're a good little witch," he replied.

"Oh no, I'm bad," she said with a wink.

"Well, little lady, that sounds even better." Mike tried to kiss mama, but their hats got in the way. Big Mama cleared her throat.

"Hmm, hmm? We have children present. Come on in Mike, and let me see your outfit," Big Mama said.

Mike wore some leather steel toe boots, blue jeans that fitted nicely over his muscular legs, and a white t-shirt. He had on a beige suede fringe jacket which matched his hat.

"Man, you look good Mike," Big Mama said. "Let me get my camera. I want to take a picture of y'all." Big Mama grabbed her camera off the kitchen table, and said, "Now y'all, stand together, and say cheese." Then she took the picture.

Alley, my brothers, and I grabbed our plastic pumpkins candy holders, and left the house with mama and Big Mike. We waved goodbye to Big Mama as we left.

It took us only fifteen minutes to drive to the haunted mansion. Mama parked the van, and we all got out. People both young and young at heart were dressed in costumes filled both sides of the street, and sidewalks. After we went through the gate, we met Plump, Teach, and Carlos by the entrance. We all took a hay ride up to the Mansion. The lady on the ride told us a ghost story as we rode up the hill. When we came to the mansion, I was scared. I clung to Alley, and Plump clung onto me. My brothers were too stupid to be scared. They ran to get in line ahead of Teach and Carlos.

As we walked through the Mansion, there were skeletons hanging from the ceiling, people screaming, and witches giving out candy. There was one room with flashing lights. When we walked through there, there was a big scary face at the end of it. Once we got outside, the costume parade was about to start. Any kid that wanted to be in it would have to line up at the entrance. Alley, my brothers, Teach, Plump, and I all got in line while mama and Mike watched. Alley walked across the stage, and curtseyed to the crowd. Jonathan showed his fangs, and Jordan jumped like "*Spiderman.*" When I saw all those people, I was so afraid that I ran across the stage. None of us won, but mama bought us a toy at the gift shop anyway. The last exhibit was a walking path through the hunted forest. It was supposed to be a scary walk, but mama and Mike were holding hands.

"Our children look beautiful," Mike said.

"Our children?" Michelle replied lifting a brow.

"Well, if you can adopt, why can't I? I love your family, Michelle."

"And, we love you too, Mike."

In the darkness Alley and I turned to see mama and Mike kissing.

"Yuck!" We said in unison.

We continued to walk through the forest until we got to the end. A skeleton was standing at the gate with a sign that read: *We hope we'll see you again soon. Nothing stays buried here for too long.* Our trip through the *DC's Haunted Mansion* was over. We said goodbye to Plump, Teach, and Carlos. Then we got into the van, and mama drove away.

*****

Big Mama sat at the kitchen table sipping ice tea, and reading the paper. She wanted to enjoy this night without the kids. Only a few trick-or-treaters came by, so Big Mama felt that she could have a peaceful relaxing evening for a short while, but Pee-Pee kept interrupting this moment. The dog kept barking, and growling.

"What in the world is wrong with that dog?" Big Mama said to herself. "Come on Pee-Pee. Maybe you need to go outside."

Big Mama opened the back door, and let the dog outside. Then she went to the refrigerator to refill her glass of ice tea. When Big Mama sat back down, she realized something. "Oh, I didn't shut the side gate. The dog will get out," she said out loud to herself.

Big Mama put the newspaper down, and opened the back door. She started to walk outside when she stopped in mid stride. Big Mama's heart was pounding in her chest. She slowly raised her hands up in the air, and backed up.

A low sinister Southern accented voice said, "Trick or treat."

It was Billy. He had a pistol pointed at Big Mama's head. Once he was inside the laundry room, Billy shut the door.

"Turn around, and walk into the kitchen," he said.

Big Mama turned around slowly, and did as she was told.

"You know Billy. You don't have to point that gun at me. I can walk without it," Big Mama said.

"Shut up! Sit down over there."

Big Mama sat down at the end of the table.

"Where is she?" He asked.

"Who?" Big Mama asked.

"Don't play dumb with me old woman. I don't want to hurt you, but I will."

"Just like your dad hurt your mom?"

"Old woman, you don't know anything about me," Billy said in anger.

"I know he beat your mother so badly that she almost died. She left your father, didn't she? I see you as that scared little boy when she left you with that monster. He turned is anger towards you when she left, and you blamed her for it, didn't you. You beat Alley's mother like your father beat you," said Big Mama.

Billy turned away from Big Mama. When he turned back to her, he slapped her as hard as he could across the face. The blow sent Big Mama's head sailing towards the table. She steadied herself against the table's edge with her hands. The blow sent shock waves of pain through her jaw, the side of her face, and her eye. She couldn't see for a moment.

Billy yelled in a fit of rage, "Shut up, Nigger! Who told you this stuff about me? I'll kill them!"

"Like you did Alley's mother?" Big Mama said without turning to face him.

She was still leaning over the table, and slightly out of breath. Billy walked towards her, and pointed the gun towards her face.

"What did you say?" He said in a low slow voice.

Big Mama gasped a little when he put the gun to the side of her head.

Then he yelled, "Tell me where my daughter is now old woman, or I'll blow your God damn head off!"

"Why would I? So, you can hurt her again like your uncle did to you?" Big Mama turned abruptly to face him. Billy gasped, and stepped back.

"Yes, I know what your uncle made you do in his room. I can even hear your screams. You know how bad this was for you, how could you do this to your own child?"

Billy was amazed. "Woman, how could you know that? No one knew what he did except for my . . ." Billy hesitated.

"Except your father," Big Mama continued. "Your father wasn't going to put his own brother in jail for you, so he let it go on. Now, you are listening to those demons, and you have become the monster you had nightmares about. I would die before I give her back to you!"

"Then old woman, you are about to die." Billy was so furious that his hands were shaking. He lifted the gun up to her head, and cocked the hammer back.

Chapter 25
The Hero

When mama pulled up into the driveway, we saw Pee-Pee barking, and scratching at the front door. We all got out of the van, and walked onto the porch.

"What's wrong boy?" Mike asked. The dog kept scratching at the door, and growling.

"Here Mike," mama said. "Take my keys, and open the door. Maybe he just wants to get in."

As soon as Mike put the key in the door, Pee-Pee stopped barking, and put his nose to the bottom of the door. I knew the moment Mike opened the door he would take off, and he did. The dog ran through the opened door like a greyhound at the track. He was quiet too. Billy didn't see, or hear the dog running. Pee-Pee jumped up, and bit Billy's wrist causing the gun to drop out of his hands. The dog shook, and ripped flesh from Billy's wrist. Billy wailed in pain. Then he kicked the dog sending Pee-Pee sliding across the kitchen floor yelping. Before Mike could get the key out of the door, he ran into the kitchen. Mama screamed when she saw Billy in her house.

"Daddy!" Alley cried.

Billy stumbled backwards against the sink griping his wrist. Mike ran toward Billy, and punched him in the face. Mike punched Billy continuously until Billy's face started to bleed. Mama ran to the phone, and dialed 911. Billy grabbed Mike around the chest, and slammed him down into the table. Big Mama jumped up, and scrambled for the gun. Then Billy grabbed a pitcher of ice tea that was sitting on the table, and slammed it down towards Mike's face. Glass and Tea went everywhere. Luckily, Mike turned his face before the pitcher came down, but the glass cut the side of Mike's head. Mike grabbed Billy by the collar, and punched him straight in the face causing Billy to stagger backward. Mike jumped off the table. He punched Billy in the side sending him wailing, and crashing to the floor. He kicked Billy with his steel toe leather boots over, and over again. Then he punched Billy in the face until his fist was as bloody as Billy's face. Big Mama found the gun, and picked it up.

"That enough Mike," Big Mama said.

Mama ran into the kitchen, and grabbed Big Mike's arm before he could hit Billy again.

"Stop Mike! You'll kill him!" Mama yelled.

Mike stood up. Then he kicked Billy in the stomach again. Billy rolled over retching, and screaming in pain. Jonathan heard the police sirens, so he ran to the window. Alley and I were crying, and too afraid to move. Jordan was standing there frozen, and in shock. Jonathan saw the police walking onto the porch. He ran to the door, and let them in. The sirens and lights lit up the night sky. People started to gather outside. Billy was handcuffed, and taken out of the house. Trey ran inside the house, and walked into the kitchen where Mike was sitting at the kitchen table. The kitchen was still in a mess, but the paramedics were doing their best to repair the wound on Mike's head. Alley, my brothers, and I were all sitting on the couch while mama talked to the police officers in the kitchen. Big Mama was sitting in the kitchen too. A paramedic gave her an ice pack to put on her eye.

"Well Mike, it looks like you got him," Trey said.

"Well, the dog got him first," Mike replied.

"Yeah. I would be dead if that dog hadn't jump up, and bit him when he did," Big Mama said. Big Mama continued telling Trey what happened before Mike got there. Mama started to cry when she heard what happened. Then she looked down to see Pee-Pee panting very loudly, and wagging his tail. Mama was still wearing her costume when she tried to pet the dog. It was hard for her to get on the floor, but some how she managed.

"Come here my dog. You're my hero," mama said.

"Now he's your dog?" Big Mama said looking surprised.

Mama tried to hug the dog, but Pee-Pee yelped when she grabbed him. She quickly let him go.

"Mom, Mike, we've got to get you two to the hospital, and the dog needs to see a vet. How long do you think it will take for the police to finish up here Trey?" Mama asked.

"Michelle, the evidence tech has to collect a little more evidence before we leave," he said. "I'll stay here until you come back."

"Okay, but let us change out of these costumes." Mama walked back to the den where we were sitting and said, "Guys let's change out of these clothes. You can put on some sweats if you like, because we have to take Big Mama and Mike to the hospital. I will probably come back, and get Pee-Pee too. He needs to see a vet. Go on guys, and Jonathan, wash that makeup off your face."

We all stood up, and walked upstairs. A few minutes later we all came downstairs in sweats suits. Even mama had on a sweat suit. Big Mama's eye was swollen shut, so mama had to help her get into the van. Mike could barely see too, but he wouldn't accept any help. Once everyone was in the van, the police cleared the driveway, so that mama could back out. Mama drove up to the emergency room's door, and parked the van. She got out and then went inside the hospital. She came back with a nurse, and a wheel chair. She helped Big Mama get out of the van, and into the wheel chair. Mike was pressing a towel against the side of his head when he staggered out of the van, and slowly walked towards the hospital door. Once he was inside the hospital, the nurse convinced him that he needed to get into a wheel chair too. Mama got back into the van, and parked the van in the parking lot. We all got out, and walked into the hospital's waiting room. Then mama walked up to the front desk, and asked about Big Mama and Mike. The lady told mama to have a seat and that someone would be with her in a minute. She sat down and waited with us. After twenty minutes, Big Mama came out to the waiting room.

The doctor said, "Mrs. Thomas is a tough lady. We took an x-ray, and she has no fractures, or loose teeth. I checked her eye, and there is a lot of swelling, so if she has any problems with it, I want her to see an ophthalmologist. Mrs. Thomas, your eye will be red for a few days. Also, keep some ice packs on that side of your face until the swelling goes down." Then he gave Big Mama a prescription for pain medicine. "Mrs. Patterson, may I speak to you for a moment," the doctor continued. Mama stood up, and walked to the front desk with the doctor. "Mr. Raimond is asking for you. Follow me."

Mama and the doctor walked through a large set of double doors and down the hall to a small room on the right. The nurse was putting a bandage on his head when mama and the doctor walked in. Mike's fist that he used to punch Billy was bandaged, but both of his hands had bruises, and cuts on them.

"I hear that Mike is a hero," the doctor said.

"Yes, he is," mama replied. "And, my dog too. They both saved my mother's life."

"Mike, take these two prescriptions. One is for pain, and the other is for infections. You might want to take some of the pain medicine tonight, but eat first. It might make you sleepy. Mike, you need some rest tonight. You've lost a lot of blood, so put your boxing gloves down tonight, and get some rest," said the doctor with a grin.

Michelle grinned.

"Well, I'll let y'all talk," the doctor said. "Mike, you're ready to go anytime."

"Okay doc," Mike said and then the doctor and nurse left the room.

"Mike, how you are feeling?" Mama asked.

"Mad, and a little sore, but I'll be all right."

"Mike, I want you to stay with me for a couple of days. And, I'm not going to sleep on the couch either. We are going to stay in my room together. I will talk to my mother, so don't worry about offending her. I'll take you home if you want me to, but I really can't blame you if you don't want to stay. But, . . ."

Mike put his bruised finger up to mama's lips to stop her from speaking.

"Michelle, I want to stay. I was going to ask you the same thing. That's why I wanted you to come in here."

"I think everyone will sleep better if you're there, Mike. Come on. Let's go home."

Mike and Michelle walked back out to the waiting room. Big Mama was still sitting in the wheel chair when they walked out. Mama left us in the waiting room to go get the van. She drove the van around the circular driveway, and parked in front of the hospital doors. Mike pushed Big Mama to the van in the wheel chair then helped her in, and then the rest of us got into the van. Mama stopped at the pharmacy first to fill the prescriptions. Then she stopped at a drive thru restaurant to get some food for all of us to eat. Finally, we went home. Trey opened the door when we got there. We walked inside, and sat down in the den.

"Well, how is everybody?" Trey asked.

"Sore," Big Mama said. "But, we'll live."

"How about your convict?" Mike asked.

"Oh Billy?" Trey replied. "He's still at the hospital. I think you might have cracked a couple of his ribs. He has a concussion too. You worked him over pretty hard, but I'm glad you caught him. With all the evidences we have on him, I think he'll be put away for a long time."

"That's good. I know everyone in this neighborhood will sleep easier tonight," Mike said,

"Well, I'm going to go now," Trey replied. "I guess you'll be staying here for a few days. Lisa called, and said she would come by tomorrow. I'll have her to bring some clothes for you to change into. I'm going to go now, and check in on Lisa. I'll see y'all later."

Trey let himself out while the rest of us began to eat. After dinner mama told us to go upstairs, and go to bed. Alley, my brothers, and I got up, and left the room.

"Mom, I want to talk to you," mama said. "Mom, Mike is going to stay here tonight. He will sleep in my bed. Since there are no more beds in this house for me to sleep in, I will be sleeping in my bed as well. We don't want to offend you, but since I have to take care of everyone, I'm going to need some rest, and I'm not staying on that couch."

"Michelle, Mike saved my life. I really don't care were he sleeps. You two are grown. Y'all figure it out. I'm going to bed."

Then she got up, and left the room. Mama was a little shocked by her mother's reaction. Then she started to giggle. Mike grinned too.

"Mike, I have to take the dog to the vet. There is an emergency vet about fifteen minutes from here. I won't be gone long, but I'm going to stop by a store, and get you something to change into. I'll be back," she said.

"Okay and I'll wait up for you."

Mama kissed Mike, and called Pee-Pee. The dog followed her outside, and they both got into the van.

                                    ****

The next morning Mike awoke with mama asleep at his side. He lay there watching her sleeping. She was just as beautiful sleeping as she was awake. Mama awoke to Mike gazing down at her.

"Morning," he said.

"Good morning. How are you feeling today?" Mama asked.

"A little sore, but I'll live. How is the dog?"

"The vet said he has a bruise on his chest were Billy kicked him. The vet gave me some pain medicine for him that will help the swelling too. She told me to put a pill in a piece of cheese before I give it to him."

"Why cheese?" Mike asked curiously.

"So he won't taste the pill, and spit it out."

"Dogs are just like children," he said with a giggle.

"Yeah, but they don't talk as much."

"Speaking of the children, do you think they are up yet?"

"I don't hear them," she said.

"Good. It is getting harder for me to sleep next to you without . . ."

"Shh! Not so loud Mike. You might wake the children."

"Well, I promise not to get loud if you promise not to," he said with a slight grin.

With one hand holding the back of her head he kissed her softly. His tongue teased her own as his hand slid down to her breast. When he tried to position himself on top of her, he cried out in pain.

"What's wrong?" She asked.

"Oh, my back is a little sore because of that little fool that slammed me against the table."

"Mike, let me see."

Mike sat up on the side of the bed. Then Michelle lifted his shirt to view his back.

"Oh Mike! You have a huge bruise on your back. Do you want me to get some ice?"

"No. I'll take one of those pills in a minute, but later on I let you give me a back rub. Hey, where are you going?"

"To feed y'all. Someone has to cook, and I want to get that glass up before the kids get into it. Besides, you're too sore to handle me right now anyway." Mama giggled and walked to the door. "I bought you a sweat suit, and some clean underwear. It's over there." She pointed to the vanity chair. "You can take a bath if you like. You know where everything is. I'm going downstairs, and to cleaning the kitchen."

Mama walked downstairs to a huge mess that was left in her kitchen. Glass, dried tea, and blood were everywhere. The sink cabinet was scratched were Mike and Billy had been fighting. She swept up the glass, and mopped up the tea, and blood stains off the floor. She cleaned off the table, and straightened up the kitchen. Except for the scratch on the cabinet, the kitchen looked, and smelled like nothing ever happened. Mama opened the refrigerator to search for a piece of cheese. The only cheese she could find was shredded cheese. Mama tried to give the dog the pill without hiding it in food, but Pee-Pee sniffed it, and turned his head.

"Oh, don't be that way Pee-Pee. Take it," she said. Mama tried to give it to him again, but he turned his nose away again.

"Fine! Don't take it," she said.

Then she realized that she had some leftover lunch meat. "Let's see if you will like this," she said out loud.

She took the meat out of the refrigerator. Wrapped the pill up in a slice of it and handed it to Pee-Pee. He wolfed it down without even chewing it. "Now that I know what you like, this want be so hard the next time."

Mama patted the dog on the head then she let him outside the back door. When she walked back into the kitchen, Jasmine and Alley were sitting down at the table.

"Hey guys. How did you sleep?" Mama asked.

"Not well," I said.

"Yeah, Jasmine talked in her sleep all night again," Alley said. "Can I sleep in your room?"

"Oh no. I have enough people sleeping in my room. Jasmine, what were you dreaming about?" Mama asked.

"The lady. I kept dreaming about the lady. I told you about her before Big Mama moved in here with us."

"How often have you had this dream?" Mama asked.

"I had this dream again on the Friday before Halloween."

Alley put her head down, and started to cry.

"Alley, what's the matter?" Mama asked.

"It's my fault he came back. I didn't want Big Mama, or Big Mike to get hurt. I didn't want anybody to get hurt. I know how he can be. I'm so sorry."

Mama knelt down beside Alley's chair, and said, "Alley it's not your fault. He is a grown man, and you're not responsible for what he does. Big Mama knew the risk. We all should have been better prepared, but no matter what, he is the only person responsible for what he has done here. Not you, okay."

Alley shook her head in agreement.

"Come on give me a hug," mama said.

Their hug was abruptly interrupted by a knock at the door. Mama answered the door. It was Mike's sister in-law, Lisa.

"Hey Lisa, Mike told us the good news. Congratulations!" Mama hugged Lisa at the door.

"Thank you, but I know that you already knew about it."

Mama tried to look shocked. "What do you mean?"

"Come on Michelle. You offered me crackers. You told me to go see a doctor. You asked me if I was pregnant."

"Okay, I knew," mama finally admitted. "After all, I do have three kids. Come on in, and give me that bag."

Mama took the bag Lisa was holding. They both walked into the den, and sat down on the couch.

"Lisa, that bag was heavy. What did you bring him?" Mama asked.

"Mike stays here more than he stays at home. I didn't know how long he would be here, so I brought him some extra clothing just in case he runs out."

"Believe me, he will be back before then," mama replied. "I was just about to start breakfast would you like to help?"

"Oh yeah. I love to be around food lately. Let's go," Lisa said as they walked into the kitchen.

Alley and I greeted Lisa as mama and Lisa continued to talk. Big Mama walked into the kitchen, and hugged Lisa. She congratulated her, and sat down at the table with us. The swelling around Big Mama's eye had gone down a little, but Big Mama's eye was still red, and bruised. Lisa asked Big Mama what happened last night. Big Mama hesitated then told Alley and me to go into the den until breakfast was ready. We left the kitchen, but I could still hear Big Mama explaining to Lisa what happened that night. Lisa put her hand over her mouth in shock. Then I saw her hug Big Mama. Soon Mike came downstairs. He greeted us, and then walked into the kitchen. I knew he must have had a shower because he smelled good. Lisa ran over to give him a hug.

"Easy Lisa. My back is a little sore," Mike said.

"Are you okay?" She asked.

"Yeah, you should have seen the other guy," Mike replied with a laughed.

"It's not funny Mike, and where did you get those clothes? That's a nice sweat suit you're wearing."

"Michelle bought it for me last night." He replied.

Lisa folded her arms, and looked at mama. Then she turned back to Mike. "Will we be hearing a proposal from you soon, Mike?" Lisa asked with a raised brow.

"You never know," Mike said with a grin.

Mama's mouth was slightly opened as she looked at the two of them. Then mama caught Big Mama staring at her. Mama turned from Big Mama. She knew that Big Mama could see the fear all over her face. Big Mama decided to change the subject. Lisa ate breakfast, and lunch with us today. She stayed at our house until Trey came by that evening. Lisa and Trey left, but Mike stayed until the next day with Big Mama. Big Mama put some kind of ointment on Mike's back that Monday, and he said that his back was much better. He ate dinner with us, and left that night.

*****

We had mid-term exams this week. Mama took us home in the evenings instead of bringing us to the center. Mama said we needed more time to study. Every evening Big Mama would make us a snack while we went over our study guides. Jonathan would always finish first. Then he would quiz Alley and me on history, or literature. Jonathan is smart enough to be in my grade, but I think he likes goofing off with the other boys in his class. Jordan was always the last person to finish his homework. Sometimes we would be outside playing while he was still finishing up. Big Mama tried to help him, but most of the time his mind was just not into doing his homework. By Friday, all our exams were over. No one was happier than Jordan.

He ran outside of the school's front doors jumping, and screaming, "I'm finished! I'm finished!" Everyone outside was staring at him.

"Well Jordan, now that you've finished, let's just hope you've passed," Teach said in a fit of laughter.

Jordan ran after Teach chasing him around the school grounds. Mama drove up, and got out of the van.

"Jordan! Stop chasing him, and come on!" She yelled.

We all turned around suddenly to see mama standing there. Then we walked to the van.

"I'm going to get you back Teach," Jordan said.

"Yeah, right," Teach said as his mother drove up.

Jordan got into the van and mama drove us to the center. When we got to the center, Mrs. Johnson had started a knitting class with some of the ladies there. Mrs. Robertson didn't know how to knit, but she knew how to make quilts.

"Mama, what are they doing?" I asked.

"A lot of the ladies here need extra money around the holidays, so Sharon went to the mall, and opened a booth for them to sell their crafts," she said.

The ladies made sweaters, children's clothing, and beautiful quilts. I was amazed to see what these ladies have done in such a short time. Sharon was sitting at the table with Mr. Dixon when I walked over to her.

"Mrs. Sharon, whatcha doing?" I asked.

"Oh, Mr. Dixon and I are helping some of my friends do their taxes for a small fee. The end of the year is approaching fast, and Mr. Dixon can use the extra money."

"Yeah. I can't type anymore, so she is doing it for me," Mr. Dixon said.

"Kids, y'all go on outside, and let us finish here," mama replied.

Alley and I ran outside to the courtyard while Jordan and Jonathan played pool with Mr. Mack. When the last patient went home, mama locked the center's doors, and took us home. After a long week of studying, I went to bed early.

Saturday afternoon Mike came by our house. He ran onto the porch where mama and Big Mama were sitting.

"Hey, guess what?" He asked.

Mama and Big Mama looked at each other.

"What Mike?" Mama asked.

"I've found a building for my business. Come on. I want to show it to you."

"Now?" Mama asked.

"Yes. Get the kids. We can all go."

Mama called out to us in the front yard, and said, "Kids, let's go."

We said goodbye to Teach and Plump and got into the van. Mike drove us to an empty gas station, and repair shop with a for sale sign in front of it. Mike jumped out of the van with a huge smile on his face.

Once we all got out of the van, he said, "Come on. Let's look around."

The realtor gave Mike a key, and he let us inside. There was a small waiting room area with a couch on the left side. On the right side there was a counter, and a cash register. Next to the waiting room area was a small hall that led to an office on the right side. There were two bathrooms on the left side. A large garage with two large garage doors on the front was right outside of the waiting area door. A few tools were lying about, and the whole place was dirty.

"Well, what do you think?" Mike asked.

Mama looked around, and said, "It's great!"

My mouth fell open. I couldn't believe what she just said.

"But, you'll have to take a bath before you come near me," she replied with a smile.

"What, you don't like your man a little dirty?" Mike said grabbing mama around the waist, and giggling.

"Um, Hmm!" Big Mama cleared her throat. "We have children present. With a little paint this place could be great Mike."

I was dumfounded. I looked at Alley in utter amazement. She just shrugged her shoulder, and turned back to Mike. My brothers weren't listening. They were too busy playing with the tools. Mike went on telling mama and Big Mama his plans for the garage, and how he was going to finance it. They both agreed that his ideas would be a great one. We all walked back to the van, and got in.

"Oh Jasmine, Alley, y'all left your new pajamas in the back of the van," Mama said. "With all of the excitement this past weekend, I forgot about it. Take the bags into the house when we get home."

Mike chatted all the way home about his new business. We all could see how excited he was. Mama didn't interrupt him while he talked. Once we were home, Alley and I grabbed the bags, and took them to our rooms. Alley started putting her things away, but I wanted to play dress up. I grabbed an old hat from my closet, and danced around the room. Alley giggled a little when she saw the silly hat on my head. Then I saw her necklace. I grabbed it to put it on, but Alley tried to snatch it away from me.

"Don't play with that!" She shouted, but when she tried to grab the locket from me, it hit the floor, and opened up. It was the lady. The picture in the locket was the lady in my nightmares. This time she was holding a baby.

"Alley, who is that?" I asked.

Alley picked the locket up, and said as she pointed towards the picture, "That's me when I was a baby, and that's my mom," she replied.

"I've seen her before. Alley, we have to show this to Big Mama."

"Why?"

"Because I think I know where your mother is. Come on. Bring the locket."

Alley and I ran down the steps, and outside the front door.

"Big Mama, I know where her mother is!" Then I looked around. "Where are Jordan and Jonathan?"

"They went to the store with Carlos," Big Mama said. "What are you talking about Jasmine?"

"Alley, show Big Mama the locket."

Alley opened the shiny carved silver locket to reveal the only picture she had of her mother.

"Big Mama, this is the lady in my dreams. I've seen her at the hunting club when we went to Pine Mountain this summer. She is in the forest, Big Mama."

"Alley, here. You take this back to your room. Mike, why don't we call your brother," Big Mama said.

"And, say what?" Mama asked. "That Jasmine had a dream?"

"Yes," Mike said. "He will check it out no matter what. I'll call him."

Mike got up, and called his brother. About fifteen minutes later, Trey showed up at their door. Trey greeted everyone when he walked onto the porch.

When Jordan and Jonathan walked into the yard with Carlos, Jordan said, "What's going on?"

"Boys, why don't y'all go around to the backyard, and play," mama said. "Alley, Jasmine, why don't y'all go too. I'll call you if I need you."

Alley and I said yes ma'am in unison. Then we left. Mike told his brother about Big Mama's and my gifts. He told Trey that I knew where to find Alley's mother.

Then Big Mama interrupted him saying, "Mike, Jasmine saw Alley's mother's soul. I don't believe that her mother is still alive, but Jasmine has to find her," Big Mama said. "What?" Mama was shocked. "Mom, I can't put those girls through anymore."

"Michelle, her dreams won't stop until she fulfills her destiny. She is the only one that can find her mother. She has to go, and I'll go with her. I promise I won't let anything happen to her."

"Neither will I," Trey said. "If she can lead us to her mother, this will definitely help our investigation."

"I'll go too," Mike said.

"Wait a minute," mama said sternly. "She's my daughter, and I think I should go."

"Okay," Big Mama agreed.

"Wait mom, we can't all go," replied mama.

"Yes, we can. I'll call Lisa over here to watch the children, if that's all right with you," Trey said to mama. "But, we are going to need some help. Let me make a few phone calls. Oh yeah, where did you say her body was?"

"Hold on. Let me go get Jasmine," mama said.

Mama walked around to the side yard and told me to come here. I was a little scared when I saw everyone sitting on the front porch.

"Come on Jasmine. You're not in any trouble," Big Mama assured me. "We just wanted to know where you saw Alley's mother."

"She's in the forest where the *"Spotted Buck Hunt Club"* sign is."

"Jasmine, do you think you can take us to her mother?" Big Mama asked.

"I think so."

"Okay honey," Big Mama said, "and don't worry. We will all be with you."

Somehow, that didn't ease my nerves, but I hoped I could find Alley's mother. Maybe if I found her, she would have one person in her family that loves her.

I turned to Big Mama, and said, "Okay."

Chapter 26
Going Home

Mama told me to go, and put my heavy jacket on while we waited for Lisa to get here. She said the sun would be going down soon, and it was getting cooler in the evening. Mama got up to get her jacket and Big Mama's too. About twenty minutes later Lisa drove up. When she got out of the car, she was still wearing her regular clothes, but her growing belly was undeniable.

"Hey everyone. Where are the rest of the kids?" Lisa asked.

"They are around back," Trey replied. "I'm not sure when we will get back, so if you need me, just call or text me."

"Okay," Lisa replied. "Y'all please be careful."

Trey kissed Lisa, and got into his car. Mama, Mike, Big Mama, and I got into the van while Mike drove us to the hunter's club. I was nervous the whole time he drove. Mama put her arm around me trying to sooth my nerves, but it didn't help. Mike drove us out of the city, and across the long bridge. The sun was starting to set casting beautiful hues of color over the lake. Because of the changing seasons only a few boats were on the lake today. Mike continued to drive until we passed the lake and then we were surrounded by a thick forest on either side of the road. He drove passed the sign that read: *"Spotted Buck Hunt Club"* one mile. Mike followed the sign, and turned the van onto the road that led to the hunter's club.

As we drove down the road, I saw the angel smiling at me from the side of the road. I could hear her speaking to me in my mind.

"Jasmine, do not be afraid for He is with us. She will meet you on the path. Follow her sweet *Ayin,* and don't get off the path. Bring her mother home."

I closed my eyes for a second. When I looked up, she was gone. Mike parked the van next to Trey's car. There were several FBI agents standing outside the main office of the hunt club. I saw one of the agents hand the owner a piece of paper, and said that this was a search warrant to search the land. The man was reluctant, but he took the warrant.

"Is Billy Hope a member of this club?" Trey asked the man.

"Yes," the owner replied.

Trey asked another investigator to question him then he walked towards me. "Jasmine, which direction should we go into first?" Trey asked.

I looked around for a moment, and then I saw the lady. She looked like she was glowing in the dim evening light.

"That way," I said as I pointed to her then I ran towards her.

"Jasmine, wait!" Mama shouted.

Everybody followed me into the forest, but when I turned around, I didn't see anyone. The angel said to follow her, and stay on the path so I did.

"Where in the Hell did she go?" Trey said out of frustration.

Then another agent walked up to Trey. "Trey, what's going on?" He asked.

"The girl knows where the body is," he said. "We have to find her."

"How does she know?" He asked.

"She saw her when she came out here on a field trip this summer with her summer camp group. Look, I'll explain later. Come on," Trey said.

"Wait a minute. I know where she went," Big Mama said.

"What?" Trey asked.

Then everyone turned to Big Mama.

"The angel said, 'Upon His rock through the shifting sand.' Look at the ground." The red sandy soil held foot prints in the direction that Jasmine was running.

"Come on," Trey shouted.

They followed the path through the woods flashing their flash lights. Jasmine continued to follow the lady. The lady ran through the forest as if someone was still chasing her.

"Where are you going?" I yelled.

But, she didn't answer me. I turned to see the lights from the flashlights searching the forest, and following me in the distant. I could hear them calling my name, but I didn't stop. I had to find Alley's mother. The lady ran behind three huge boulders, and sat down.

I sat down beside her. "Let's go!" I said. She still didn't respond. Her bruised face was terrified. She was still trying to move something with her deformed hand, but suddenly she put her hands up.

"Please, who is going to take care of our child if I die?" She asked.

Then her head and body fell forward. I jumped back, and landed on my bottom. Then the lady's soul stood up, and so did I.

"Follow me," she said.

Out of no where Big Mama, Mike, mama, Trey, and the FBI agents walked out of the woods onto the clearing.

"His rock!" Big Mama shouted.

"Jasmine!" Mama cried.

I pointed to the lady saying, "She's there!"

The lady walked away, and I followed behind her. She walked through the forest passing more huge boulders, and trees until we came near a cliff. When I looked out over the cliff, I noticed Pine Mountain's cliff was on the other side. It was dark now, and I was afraid. I could hear owls hooting, and wolves howling.

The lady turned to me, and said, "Sweet *Ayin*, do not be afraid for He is with us. Follow me."

We continued down the path until we came to another clearing that looked over the mountain side. As I continued to follow her, the souls of children, four little girls, arose from the ground, and followed me. Then the lady stopped in front of me.

"I am here, below you. Your heavenly '*Eye*' has allowed you to find me. Since the day that I was murdered, I've wandered these woods for years in hope that one day my soul could rest. Now that day is here. Thank you sweet *Ayin* for bring my soul, and the children's souls to the light. Please tell my daughter that I love her, and that she will never be alone."

I was startled by the presence of the angel that was behind me.

"Don't be afraid sweet *Ayin* for it is time for us to go home. Take my hand," the angel said.

Then Alley's mother grabbed my other hand, and a bright glowing light shined down on us from the heavens. It was beautiful. I felt a peace unlike anything I've ever felt before. There was no sadness, or fear in the light. I only felt joy, and eternal happiness. When I looked down, my feet hovered over the ground. The girls started to run towards the light too. Then the angel took a step forward, and my soul left my body. When I stepped forward with the angel and Alley's mother, the four girls ran passed me giggling, and laughing into the abyss. I put my feet down onto a beautiful pearl floor, and walked down the aisle. The angel and the elders clapped as I approached the throne. When I turned to see where the angel went, she was standing with the other angels clapping. I turned to see

Alley's mother standing beside the little girls smiling, and clapping too. A man with his hands stretched out to me walked towards me. At first, I couldn't see his face because the bright light surrounding him, but I did notice the holes in his hands. He grabbed my hands and kneeled down in front of me. Then I could see his face.

"Hello little one," He said. "You have completed a great task, and your name shall be written in the *Book of Life*."

"Where am I? Is this heaven?" I asked.

He just smiled at me and then said, "This is my Father's house, and all around you is heaven."

"Are you God?"

"No," He said. "I'm the one who will return one day to call my people home."

"You're Jesus! But, you don't look anything like your picture."

He laughed, and stood up.

"You must go back now. You still have another task to perform. You will not remember this place, but you will remember me." He dropped my hands, and stepped back from me. I ran to him, and hugged him.

"I don't want to go back. Please, let me stay with you."

He lifted my chin with his finger, and said, "No Jasmine. It is not your time. You will live a very long and fulfilled life. Tell the people about me on your journey through this life."

"Well, what about Alley's mother? I was told by the angel I had to bring her home."

"Jasmine, this is her home now, and one day it will be yours too. Now give me a hug. It's time for you to go, but remember, I'll be with you always."

I hugged him, and that was the last thing I remember. Mama, Big Mama, Mike, Trey, and the agents found me, but they stood there in utter amazement. They saw the light of God shinning down on me, and I was floating above the ground. Mama put her hand over her mouth, and gasped.

Big Mama said, "She's okay. She is with God now."

My body slowly came back down to the earth.

"Mike, go get her. It's okay," Big Mama assured him.

Before I came back to the ground Mike caught me. The next thing I remembered was seeing Mike's face.

"Hi Mike," I said.

He smiled at me. "She's okay," he said. Nobody moved. They were stunned by what they just saw.

"She's down there," I said as I pointed towards the ground.

"Come on guys. Let's mark the spot. Come on!" Trey said. The men looked at each other curiously.

One man said to Trey, "What was that?"

Trey didn't look at the man when he hesitated to say, "I don't know. Come on."

"The girls are out here too," I said.

"What?" Trey said. He was shocked, and so was everybody else.

"There is a little girl here, here, here, and over here," I said as I ran over, and pointed to the places that they were buried. "Billy killed them all."

Trey took a bright orange spray can of paint, and marked the shallow graves.

"Okay guys, I'm going to call in more agents. Y'all have to go now. We'll get in touch with you if we need to," Trey replied.

Then he called one of the agents over to escort us out of the forest. Mama, Big Mike, Big Mama, and I walked back to the van. The agent gave mama a card then he went back into the woods. Mike drove us back home. On the way home there was an odd silence in the van. No one wanted to be the first to speak. Big Mama sat in the back with me on the way home.

Big Mama finally broke the silence by saying, "You know something Jasmine, when I was your age, the same thing happened to me. I remember him well. To be the Son of the most High, He is very humble." Big Mama giggled. "I don't remember much about heaven, but I do remember his face. It's nice when people can believe without seeing Him. Even when those that do believe in Him actually see his awesome power, well they are still amazed. You and I know how great He is, so we don't have to be scared. We just have to have respect, that's all."

"Are we different from other people, Big Mama?" I asked curiously.

"Oh no child. We are just a little more sensitive than most. Why if people really wanted to hear God's voice, all they have to do is listen. I mean really listen, and close their minds to everything else. He will answer. It may not be how they want to hear it, but he will answer."

"So, you don't think I'm weird?" I said looking up biting my lip.

"No honey, but you are funny. You and your brothers make me laugh so much that sometimes I'm brought to tears," Big Mama laughed again. "Now, your friend Plump, she's a little weird. I've never seen a child talk so much. It's like she had diarrhea of the mouth."

I giggled.

"I'm glad to see you smile," Big Mama said.

"Big Mama, what about Alley? Should I tell her about her mother?"

Big Mama suddenly stopped smiling, and became very serious. "No Jasmine. I'll tell her. Just let her sleep tonight, okay."

"Yes ma'am," I replied.

"Jasmine, you are a good friend. Alley is lucky to have a friend like you," said Big Mama.

"Thank you, Big Mama."

"Give me a hug baby." I hugged Big Mama, and we continued to talk all the way home.

The next morning Alley didn't go to church with us, and neither did Big Mama. Mama told us that Big Mama was going to tell Alley about her mother today. Once we were at church, I really wasn't concentrating on anything that was happening around me. The choir was singing. People were clapping, and shouting, "Praise the Lord!" I wasn't involved in any of it. My body was there, but my mind was somewhere else. I was worried about Alley. It has taken all summer long to bring some happiness to her life. Within one night, I've taken that all away. I know how happy her mother is because I saw her in heaven, but I also know how Alley longed to find her mother. The news of her mother's death will be devastating. After church, mama didn't hang around like she normally did. We all got into the van and drove away. On the way home mama warned us. "Now, I want y'all to be nice to Alley for the next few days. She will be upset for a while. Jordan, Jonathan, I don't want y'all teasing her, or hurting her feelings. No jokes, especially you Jordan. If I hear of anybody teasing her, you will have to answer to me."

We all said yes ma'am as mama continued to drive. When we got home, Alley was in our room. She wasn't crying, but the melancholy look that was on her face months ago was back. She lay across her bed staring out into the distant.

"Alley, are you okay?" I asked as I sat on the end of her bed.

"No," she replied.

"Are you mad at me?"

"Why would I be mad at you, Jasmine?"

"Because I found her. I thought she would be alive because the angels wanted me to bring her home, but I didn't know her home was heaven. I talked to her Alley."

"You did?" Alley's big blue eyes looked up at me, and her melancholy face seemed to brighten up when I said this.

"Yes, I talked to her. You know you look just like your mother."

"What did she say?" Alley insisted. Then she sat beside me on the edge of her bed.

"She thanked me for freeing her soul, and the souls of the children."

"There were other children there too?" Alley said with shock.

"Yes."

The news of the children was like another stab to Alley's already broken heart. She held her head down, and began crying again. I put my arms around her, and gave her a hug.

"Alley, it's all right. They're happy now too. I saw them in heaven, and you will never believe how wonderful it can be."

Alley's huge blue eyes looked up at me. Then she asked, "Are they happy?"

"Oh yeah," I replied. "I didn't even want to go home myself. I don't remember much about the way heaven looked, but I felt a great sense of peace. The girls ran passed me giggling, and cheering. Then they welcomed your mother home too. Now her soul will never have to wander around in that forest again. She's home Alley, and she is happy. I know she wishes she could be here with you, but she wanted me to tell you something."

"What?" Alley asked looking at me curiously.

"She wanted me to tell you that she loves you, and that you will never be alone."

"But, I am alone Jasmine!"

"No, you're not. You are apart of our family now, and we will never leave you alone again. Also, your mother is watching over you too, so you have a big family now."

"Jay-Jay, do you think I'll ever meet any of my other relatives?" Alley asked.

"I don't know, but we'll always be here for you no matter what. Come on. Let's go outside."

"Okay," Alley said, "but you better take off that dress first, or your mother will kill you if you get it dirty."

I giggled. "Okay," I said.

After I changed, we went outside to play. Alley didn't go to school on Monday, but she did go see her counselor. I could tell she had been crying when we got home. By Tuesday Alley decided to go back to school. The week seemed to go by quickly, but on Friday mama had to go to Mr. McBeavie's office. She didn't get back until it was dark. Saturday at two o'clock we all went to the funeral home for Alley's mother's funeral. Mike and his family were there too. The organist played soft music while the preacher preached a short sermon. At the cemetery, mama ordered a beautiful head stone for Alley's mother. Alley cried as she laid flowers by her mother's head stone. Then the funeral was over.

A week had passed, and Alley was becoming her old self again. My brothers even started teasing her again. I was surprised to see that they went this long, but soon they started teasing both of us.

*****

The Saturday before Thanksgiving, Mama and Big Mama went shopping together. As usual my brothers were sneaking things into the basket. Mama bought a huge ham, and two turkeys. Mama said she had to buy food for the center's party too. Before we left the store Big Mama and mama had two buggies piled high with food. Even the areas under the buggies were full. Mama let the third row of seats down in back of the van to put the food in. My brothers, Alley, and I had to sit together on one row of seats. There were bags of food on the floor of the van by our feet too. Mama managed to back out of the parking lot with all those bags of food covering the back window. She and Big Mama cooked most of the day on Saturday, and part of the day on Sunday. Some of the food had to be stored in the deep freezer.

The Wednesday before Thanksgiving, Mama and Sharon had a big Thanksgiving dinner at the center for the patients. Some of the patient's family members came too. Mr. Dixon's son, Christopher, was there. Mrs. Gray's daughter and twin grandsons were there to see her, and Mrs. Peters. I think Mrs. Robertson's whole family came to the dinner. There were so many of them I didn't think we would have enough food. Mama and the college students brought out some long folding tables, and chairs from the shed. They set them up in the recreational area. The whole center was decorated in fall colors with autumn leaves on the counters, and tables. There was a horn of plenty on each table, and a scare crow at the entrance. Everyone sipped punch, and mingled while Jonathan and Jordan ate up most of the "After Dinner" mints. Once mama announced that dinner was ready, everyone sat down at the tables to eat. Even Mr. Joe sat down with us. Mama, the students, and Sharon served everyone at the tables. Alley, my brothers, and I ate so much that we couldn't move. Mama and LaShundra fed the patients that couldn't feed themselves while Sharon and Terrie ate. Once they were finished eating Sharon and Terri cleaned off the tables while Mama and LaShundra ate. By the time everyone was finished, Mama and her co-workers worked as a team cleaning up the center, and cleaning the patients. Mr. Joe helped mama take down the tables. Then he took out the trash. Many patients left after dinner with their families, but a few of them stayed until it was time to close. Mama said that the center would be closed for the next two days just like our school. When we got home that night, no one wanted anything to eat. Big Mama and Pee-Pee decided to share some of the ham in the refrigerator, and Big Mama ate some of the vegetable casserole too. Mama and Big Mama played games with us that night until it was time to go to bed.

****

Today was Thanksgiving Day. Even though we had taken a bath this morning, mama made us wash up again. Mama laid our clothes out for us on our beds, and told us not to get dirty. My brothers, Alley, and I played a game of cards on the coffee table until everyone arrived for dinner. The first person to ring the doorbell was Mr. Davis. Mama answered the door with Pee-Pee.

"Hey Mr. Davis, come on in," mama said. "Would you like me to take your jacket?"

"Sure," Mr. Davis replied.

"Come on in Ben. Now, what do you have there?" Big Mama asked.

Mr. Davis handed Big Mama a large covered glass bowl.

"This here is my famous corn bread," he replied.

Big Mama lifted the cover off the dish to sniff the delicious smelling bread.

"Ben, it smells great, and it's warm too. I'll take it to the kitchen."

Mr. Davis walked into the den, and sat down on the couch.

"Now, who's winning?" Jonathan raised his hand. "Boy, you're getting pretty good with those cards. You know I'm getting better myself. Hey, don't say anything to your grandmother, but I believe I can beat her at a game now." Then Mr. Davis winked at Jonathan.

"No, you can't, Ben! I'll always beat you. Just stick with what you know, Bingo."

"Bertha, you heard me all the way from there?" Mr. Davis asked. My brothers, Alley, and I giggled.

"Yeah Ben," Big Mama replied. "My hearing is still good."

Mr. Davis laughed when the door bell rang again. Mama and Pee-Pee answered the door.

"*Mon amour*," mama said which means my love.

"You've learned a few French words. I'm impressed," Mike said. Then he kissed mama's cheek.

"Well, my love, are you going to say some beautiful words to us?" Trey asked.

"You're special Trey, but not enough for me to speak in French," mama replied with a slight grin. Lisa laughed.

"Y'all come on in, and give me a hug," mama said.

Mama hugged Lisa, but when she tried to hug Trey, he was holding a chocolate cake.

"Oh Trey, I'm sorry," she said. "You can take the cake to the kitchen. Trey walked to the den, and handed the cake to Big Mama. Mike, Lisa, and Trey walked into the den and greeted everyone giving Big Mama a hug as they passed by her.

"Oh Ben, I forgot to tell you that Trey here is going to be a father," Big Mama said.

"Well, congratulations!" Mr. Davis replied. "Well Trey, are you hoping for a girl, or a boy?"

"I am just hoping it will be healthy," he said.

Soon they sat down, and started to chat. Mike turned the football game on. For a moment, the three men made the den sound like they were at a live game. The door bell rang again, but this time Pee-Pee didn't bark. He just followed mama to the door.

"Hello guys," mama said.

It was Mr. Greg and Mrs. Sharon at the door. Mama gave them a hug, and invited them in. I couldn't hear what they were saying because of all the cheering over the game, but Sharon was carrying a pecan pie. She took the pie to the kitchen, and hugged Big Mama. Before mama could shut the door Uncle Pete walked in.

"What's up?!" Uncle Pete was loud enough to hear over the cheering.

"Hey Pete," mama said.

Uncle Pete gave mama a bear hug. Mama hated this. Then he put his arm around her shoulders, and shut the door.

As she walked into the den, Uncle Pete said, "Little sis, you, and mom got it smelling real good in here. Hey, who are these folks? What's up?"

Uncle Pete kind of stunned everyone when they turned abruptly to face him.

"Uncle Pete!" I yelled. Alley, my brothers, and I ran to give him a hug.

Not to risk anymore embarrassment, mama jumped in front of Pete, and said, "This is my brother Peter Thomas. Pete this is Trey, Mike's brother, and Lisa is Mike's sister in-law. I think you know everyone else."

Everyone greeted Uncle Pete politely, but Uncle Pete said very loudly, "What's up?!"

"Y'all have to forgive my loud son. He's always like this," Big Mama said.

"Mama!" Uncle Pete walked into the kitchen, and gave Big Mama a hug.

"Hey Pete," she said. Then the door bell rang again. "I wonder who that could be?"

Uncle Pete and Big Mama walked into the den to see who it was. Mama answered the door.

"Hey James, I'm surprised to see you here," mama said.

Everyone in the den had an uncomfortable and shocked look on their faces when daddy walked in.

"Well, look who's coming to dinner!" Uncle Pete said. Big Mama elbowed him in the arm. "Ouch Mama! That hurts!"

"Be quiet Pete. James, come on in," Big Mama said.

James greeted everyone. My brothers, Alley, and I gave daddy a hug. Mike greeted daddy, but he gave him a very suspicious look.

Mama walked beside daddy, and said very quietly, "What are you doing here?"

"Come on Michelle, after all these years can't we have dinner together? Anyway, I came by to see the kids. I'm not here to start any trouble."

Mama gave him a suspicious look too. "Okay James," mama said. Then mama walked over, and sat down by Mike.

"Now that everyone is here, I would like to say a prayer thanking God for this food, but before I do, it has been a tradition in our family to say what we are thankful for. Ben, would you like to start?" Big Mama asked.

"Okay, I'm thankful that I met a wonderful woman like you."

Trey said, "I'm thankful that my family is safe." Lisa agreed with him.

Mike said, "I'm thankful that I met Michelle."

Mama said she was thankful for having her mother, and Mike here. Mrs. Sharon and Mr. Greg were thankful for Mama, and the center. Daddy said he was thankful they allowed him to be here with his children today. Alley said she was thankful for having a family. Jordan said he was thankful that he didn't have to go to school. Jonathan was thankful for desserts. I said I was thankful that Alley was here.

Finally, Uncle Pete said, "I will be thankful when we hurry up, and get something to eat." Everyone laughed, but Big Mama.

"Okay Pete," Big Mama said sternly. "Let's pray. Dear Lord, we are all thankful that you brought us through the storms, and trials of life. We pray that you forgive us, and bless this food. We also pray for the many that are in need of you right now. We asked that you will be with them, and supply their needs, Amen. Let's eat."

The one room that kids were never allowed to go into was the dining room. The dining room was on the right side of the hall in front of Big Mama's room. The food was severed buffet style. Mama set up another table in the dining room for extra seating, but my brothers, Alley, and I had to eat at the kitchen table. We could hear everybody laughing, and talking in the dinning room while we had to sit in the kitchen with Pee-Pee. Once we finished, my brothers, Alley, and I went back in the den to play a game. Soon, everyone else came back into the den to eat dessert, and drink coffee. The women helped Big Mama and mama clean up. When they were finished, they sat down too. They chatted about the game, church, and the weather for about an hour.

Then mama said, "Hey guys. Mike is opening his own business, and before y'all go home, I want to show you the place."

Everyone congratulated Mike and mama got up to get everyone's jackets out of the hall closet.

"Mom, do you mind driving?" Michelle asked.

"No baby," Big Mama replied.

"Good," mama said. "Let's go."

Once we got our jackets on, we all left the house. Mama locked the doors. All of us kids got into the van with mama and Big Mike. Trey and Lisa drove their own car, and so did Mr. Greg and Mrs. Sharon. Mr. Davis, Uncle Pete, and Daddy rode with Big Mama to the gas station. Once we got there, the realtor's sign out front read: *Sold*.

"What?!" Mike shouted.

Mama parked the van, and Mike jumped out. Mama opened the door for us. Mike was mad.

He paced around for a moment and said, "I can't believe they sold it from under me!"

Soon everyone parked their cars, and got out. We all gathered around mama.

Mike started to speak when mama said, "Wait Mike, I have something to tell you all. The one thing I'm most thankful for is that Mike saved my mother's life. So, to show my gratitude, I bought this business for him." Everyone gasped. Mike was speechless. He stumbled back a little in shock.

"What?" He asked.

"Mike, I sold some of my stock a few weeks ago. The stock tripled in value and it was enough to buy this place. Mr. McBeavie handled the paper work for me. Then I signed it over to you. Mom." Mama called Big Mama.

Big Mama walked up to Mike, and handed him the deed. Mama gave Mike the keys to the station. Mike hugged Big Mama then he picked mama up, and spun her around in the air. Mike leaned mama down, and kissed her fervently in front of everyone. Everyone yelled, cheered, and clapped as they kissed, except for daddy silently looked on.

Chapter 27
Nicky

The Monday after Thanksgiving, Trey came by our house. He told Big Mama he had some information about the case. He said he needed to speak to her and mama privately. We all knew that meant that Alley, my brothers, and I would have to leave the room. We all went upstairs to my brother's room to play video games. Jordan and Alley played together first while Jonathan and I waited. Soon, I got up to leave the room Jonathan asked, "Where are you going?"

"To the bathroom," I replied, but I was really going to the edge of the staircase to listen in on the conversation going on downstairs. I left the room, and walked to the edge of the staircase.

I heard Trey saying, "We matched the bullets found in the bones to an old hunting riffle we found in Billy's rented car. Some of the girls Jasmine found had been missing for over six years. There were reports of Billy's car being seen in the area where the girls were missing, but no one saw him with any of them. We do know he sold drugs in the areas where the girls were missing."

"If no one saw Billy taking the girls, how did he get them?" Big Mama asked.

"We think he might have gotten the meth addicts to trick the girls into meeting Billy somewhere that he wouldn't be seen taking them," Trey said.

"That's horrible. I can't imagine what those parents are going through. The world is getting so bad that it's unsafe to let your kids go outside," Big Mama said.

"Trey, what I don't understand is why did he kill Alley's mother?" Mama asked. "She had to know what he was doing."

"Well, not necessarily. Shortly after the girls had gone missing, there was a 911 phone call made from Billy's house. The dispatcher called back, but Billy said it was an accident. He said the baby was playing on the phone, so the dispatcher didn't send the police. We aren't sure about the actual events, but we believe he killed her that night because--"

"--because Alley's mother found out about the girls, and she wanted the police to stop him before he hurt his own daughter," Big Mama said interrupting him.

"Yes," Trey continued, "but there could be more children out there we haven't found. Billy confessed to harming his daughter because we had a DNA sample on him already, but he won't confess to any of the other murders. All though he did agree to testify against the officers for a reduce sentence if he gave us information on the police officer scam. Don't worry about the police officers either. They are in custody too."

"He doesn't have to because the jury will find him guilty anyway," Big Mama said. "He will get the death penalty."

"And, he deserves it too," Trey replied. "Well, I better go. I've got to pick up dinner tonight. I'll see y'all later."

"Okay," Big Mama said. "Jasmine, come down here!"

I froze for a moment. Then I walked downstairs. Big Mama, Trey, and mama met me at the bottom of the steps.

"Jasmine, how long have you been up there?" Mama asked.

"Not long."

"Jasmine, I don't want you to tell Alley about anything you've heard down here, okay. She is dealing with enough right now, and this would only hurt her more."

"Yes mama."

"Now, you go back upstairs. We'll call you when dinner is ready." Mama replied.

I slowly walked back upstairs, but I never thought about what would happen to Billy after I found Alley's mother. The whole ordeal just made me sad. I walked back into my brother's room, and I didn't say anything to Alley. She was having such a good time playing the game with my brother, and I didn't want to give her any more grief.

After school Wednesday, Big Mama came to pick us up. When I got into her car, I asked, "Big Mama, where is mama?"

"She's at the center. I'm going to drive y'all to the center today, but Alley, I want to talk to you after I drop them off."

"About what, Big Mama?" She asked.

"Oh, just a few things. I'll tell you about it when I drop them off."

Big Mama drove us through the city, and ten minutes later we were at the center. My brothers and I got out of the car, but Alley stayed in the car with Big Mama. Then Big Mama drove Alley to the park by the lake. It was a beautiful day to be outside. The weather was a little warmer than it normally was. The sky had a few cottony white clouds floating by, and the lake was as blue as the sky. It was quiet in the park today. Only a few joggers were in the park, and a lady with a small child who was feeding the ducks. Big Mama saw a bench by the water, and asked Alley to sit down with her here there.

"Alley, I've asked you to come out here because I got a phone call from your father this morning. He wants to see you."

"What?" Alley said in shock. Knowing he called their house was shocking enough, but did he actually think that she would want to see him again?

"Alley, listen to me," Big Mama said. "Your father's trial will probably start in a few months after Christmas, and I believe he will get the death penalty. Alley, I think you should talk to him."

"No!" Alley said staring at Big Mama in shock.

"Alley."

"No Big Mama! He tried to kill you! He killed my mother, and four little girls that were almost the same age as I am."

"Who told you that?"

"Jasmine did, but I also saw it in the newspaper at school too. Everyone knows about Jasmine, and how she found the bodies. Our school's picture is in the paper, and everything."

Big Mama closed her eyes, and sighed. She didn't think about the publicity, or how it would affect any of the kids at school. Big Mama opened her eyes, and turned to Alley. "Alley, I'm sorry. I didn't want you to be hurt anymore, but you still need to see him."

"After what he has done to me, you still want me to see him?"

"Yes Alley, just this once, and I'll be there with you," said Big Mama assuring her.

"Why?" Alley asked looking confused.

"Because Alley, you have to face him, and you have to forgive him."

Alley's bright blue eyes grew large with shock when she looked back at Big Mama. "You want me to forgive him?"

"Yes. Alley, I can't force you to forgive him, but I hope you will. This maybe the last time you will ever see him alive. If you don't see him now, you may regret this for the rest of your life."

"Big Mama, what do you think I will regret it?"

"Not knowing why, or not saying what you need to say to him. Maybe seeing the only relative you know, but Alley you need to forgive him for yourself. I don't know how he will react to this, but it doesn't matter. You can't expect him to change even if you forgive him. You must do this for yourself. The pain and anger you're holding onto will not hurt him. It will only hurt you. You have a long life ahead of you Alley. Don't let your future be clouded with anger, and resentment from your past. I know a few kids like you that have turned to drugs, alcohol, sex, or even suicide because they can't let go of their past. I don't want this to happen to you. What is done is done Alley. Your father can't change the past, and neither can you. I don't want you to grow up, and become just like him. You've got to end this cycle of violence in your family, or your children's fate will be the same as yours. Your father is not a role model for the men you will want to date, or marry. Billy's life should stand as a warning sign for you, so that you don't get evolved with a man like him. Your mother has paid a terrible price for that lesson, but now you have a choice. You can choose to forgive him and learn from the past, or you can hang on to your animosity, and become just like the very one you hate the most. The choice is up to you Alley. Will you go with me to see him? I'll be with you the whole time."

Alley looked out over the water meditating over the words Big Mama spoke. Big Mama could see the despair in her eyes as she struggled to do the right thing. Big Mama thought for a moment that Alley might cry, but her emotions were drained and she had no tears left to shed.

"Okay Big Mama. I'll go." Alley said sadly.

Big Mama hugged Alley then they got up to leave the park. Big Mama drove Alley to the county jail that was at least an hour away. She parked the car, and said, "Are you okay?"

"I guess." Alley replied.

"Sweetie, have courage and face your fears. Be free of this man," replied Big Mama.

Big Mama and Alley walked through a special entrance designed for visitors. The guards checked Big Mama's purse as they walked through a metal detector. They took Alley and Big Mama to a little room to wait, but Big Mama had to leave her purse with the guards until she was ready to go. The guards opened the door to the room, and told Big Mama he will see them now. Big Mama told the guard she wanted to see him first. The guard escorted Big Mama from the room while Alley waited in the small waiting room by herself. Big Mama walked down the small hallway passed several booths. Each booth had a metal chair in front of it, and a telephone on the right side of the divider. There was a thick piece of

Plexiglas that went all the way to the roof. The visitor's side of the booth was completely sealed off from the prisoner's side. When Billy saw Big Mama, she couldn't hear what Billy just said because they weren't on the phone yet, but she knew he had just cursed. Big Mama sat down, and picked up the phone. Soon as Billy calmed down, he picked up the phone too.

"Where is she?" Billy asked.

"She is here," Big Mama said, "but I wanted to talk to you first."

"About what?"

"Billy, it has taken a lot of courage for her to come here, so don't say anything that will upset her."

"Lady, don't tell me what to say. That's my daughter."

"She's not yours anymore Billy and you will listen to me, or we will leave!" Big Mama said in a very stern tone. "She knows everything, so don't lie to her. I will be here beside her the whole time. Don't upset her Billy."

"I won't, Hell! Let me speak to her."

"Okay," Big Mama said. She walked back to the waiting room. When she came back, Alley was with her.

"Have a seat Alley, and pick up the phone," said Big Mama.

Alley looked up at her father behind the Plexiglas wearing a prison uniform. His spiked blond hair and his huge grin made him look even more sinister than before.

"Hey darling," Billy greeted.

"Hi daddy," she said softly. "Why did you call me here?"

"Well, I just wanted to see how you were doing and . . ." Billy hesitated, and fidgeted around in his chair.

"And, what daddy?" She asked.

"And, I wanted to say how sorry I'm about all of this."

"Why Daddy?"

For a moment Billy was speechless. Then he put his head down. When he looked up again, he said, "I . . . I have a problem darling, and I need help."

"Were you going to do the same thing to me as you did to the other girls?" Alley asked curiously.

"No! I would never hurt you."

"But, you did daddy," Alley replied quickly. "You did hurt me."

Billy stared at her for a moment then he said, "I was drunk, and stupid. I . . . I wish I could have stopped myself."

"What about mama?" Alley said staring directly into his eyes.

Billy didn't say anything for a moment. He began fidgeting around in the chair again looking for something to keep his hands busy. When he finally stopped, he said, "Alley, I'm sorry. I was drinking that night too. Things got out of hand. I know I shouldn't ask you for anything, but can you ever forgive me?"

Alley stared at him for a moment and then she said, "I've hated you for years, and I been afraid of you longer than I can remember. For months you have been the monster in my nightmares, but I'm not afraid of you anymore. You can't hurt me or anyone else anymore. As much as I wanted to hate you, I don't now. Now, I just pity you."

Big Mama could see the fury in Billy's eyes. Billy started to grit his teeth the more Alley talked.

"I forgive you daddy," Alley said, "but I don't want to ever see you again."

Alley hung up the phone, and quietly walked away.

Billy went ballistic. He yelled into the phone receiver shouting, "You can't talk to me like that!" Then he punched the Plexiglas. He continued yelling, and screaming as Big Mama and Alley walked away. The guards had to run in, and stop him from punching the Plexiglas.

Once Big Mama and Alley were back to the car, Big Mama turned towards Alley, and said, "Alley, are you okay?"

"I am now," she said with a smile.

Big Mama smiled too. "Alley, I'm proud of you. You faced your fears, and you stood up to him. Come on Alley. Let's go home."

When Alley and Big Mama got home that night, Alley was eating an ice cream cone before dinner. I don't know where Big Mama and Alley went after school, but she came back happier than she has been in the last two weeks.

The next few days at school Alley seemed to be getting tougher. Alley finally stood up to Toad and Stool. She had grown tired of Toad tripping her in the hallway, so she decided to get him back. On Wednesday, it was raining about an hour before school was about to end, and there was a huge puddle of water outside of the school's front door. Alley saw Toad coming outside of the school doors, so she decided to hide behind the shrubberies that lined the front side of the school. Stool walked around the puddle, but before Toad could walk around it, Alley pushed him down. When Stool turned around the muddy water splashed all over the front of his clothes. Toad's books, clothing, shoes, and body were covered in mud. Alley ran before either one of them could get close enough to grab her. Luckily, mama drove up just in time, so she could escape Toad's wrath. Alley opened the van door, and jumped inside quickly. Alley was giggling hysterically when I and my brothers got into the van.

"Alley, what is so funny?" Mama asked.

Alley quickly stopped giggling. We all got really quiet too. Everyone looked at Alley.

"Okay," mama said. "I know that look. Y'all are up to something. All right, don't tell me. I better not hear anything bad from your principal, or someone is going to get it."

Mama started the van, and drove away. Alley put her hand over her mouth, and giggled again. Some how I knew that this would be the last time Alley would ever be a victim again.

*****

Saturday morning was a quiet one for Michelle. The kids were gone with James for the weekend to some kind of holiday theme park. Big Mama and Pee-Pee were outside in the yard. Michelle saw Big Mama and Mr. Davis talking to each other over the fence from her bedroom window. The sight of the two friends talking made Michelle smile, but she turned around abruptly when the phone rang. Michelle picked up the cordless phone from her nightstand, and walked back to the window.

"Hello," she said.

"Hi beautiful," Mike said. "Are you busy this afternoon?"

"No," she replied.

"Well, I want to take you out to this new restaurant, and night club that just opened up called *Scandals*. Do you want to go?"

"Yeah."

"Good. I'll pick you up by seven."

"Okay," Michelle replied.

"See you tonight," Mike said.

When Michelle hung up the phone, she looked down at herself. She was wearing a pair of sweat pants, and a t-shirt.

"I'll need something to wear tonight," she said to herself.

Michelle looked through her closet, and dresser for something to wear, but everything she had was from last year. She had been so busy with work that she hadn't really found time to shop for herself. The changing seasons made Michelle want to change her wardrobe too. She grabbed her jacket, and decided to go shopping. When Michelle walked down the steps, Big Mama and Pee-Pee were walking inside from the back door.

"Mom, I'm going shopping," Michelle said. "I'll be back in a little while."

"You must have a date tonight," Big Mama replied with a raised brow.

"Yeah. Mike wants to take me to this new club. What are you going to do today?" Michelle asked.

Big Mama thought for a moment and then she said, "Nothing."

"Nothing?" Michelle asked in a bit of shock.

"Yeah. These passed few weeks have just worn me out. I'm going to watch TV, and eat some left-overs. Ben said he was coming over later, so we are going to sit here, and do nothing together."

"Okay mom." Michelle started to walk out of the door when suddenly she stopped. "Oh yeah, mom what has happened to Alley?"

"What do you mean?" Big Mama asked.

"Well, she is a lot bolder than she was before. Something must have changed her at that jail because she is not the same," Michelle replied.

"Oh darling, it's just a little confidence. That's all," Big Mama said. "I'll talk to her if she gets out of hand."

"Okay mom," Michelle replied.

Then Michelle left. Michelle shopped for four hours. She bought a black suit and shoes for her date with Mike tonight. She also bought a purse, two pairs of pants, two more suits, jeans, shirts, and lingerie. Michelle had just as many bags as she did when she went shopping for the kids. She had to rush to get everything in the house because she was running a little behind on the time. Michelle dropped the bags on the floor in her room then she went into the bathroom to take a shower. When she came out of the shower, she pulled the tags off the garments, and laid the suit on the bed. Michelle put on the matching bra and panties when suddenly the door bell rang.

"Oh no!" She said.

Michelle walked out into the hallway in her underwear.

"Mom, please get the door for me, and tell Mike I'll be down in a moment."

"Okay," Big Mama yelled back to her.

Michelle went back into her room to finish dressing. She didn't have time to do anything fancy with her hair, so she just brushed it, and put her make up on. She took one more look in the mirror before she left. Then she grabbed her purse, and went downstairs.

"I'm sorry Mike. I went shopping today, and I'm running late."

"It's okay," he replied. "You're worth the wait."

"Come on. I don't want you to wait any longer. Bye mom." Michelle said.

Mike and Michelle left the house. When they got to *Scandals*, Michelle and Mike had to wait for a table. The club was packed full with people. Finally, the hostess found a booth in the corner for them. Michelle looked around the room. The atmosphere wasn't as laid back as *Jamaica Man*. The waiters and waitress all wore white shirts, black pants, and black ties. The night club was separated from the dinning room, but the music could still be heard. Michelle thought to herself, the food had better be good because she didn't like this place already. Michelle turned to Mike, and said, "Mike, go on an order my drink. I'm going to the restroom."

"Okay. What would you like for me to order?" He asked.

"I'll just have some water," Michelle said.

Then she left. Mike tried to get the waitress attention, but the club was so busy she didn't see him. He did manage to get someone's attention though. A beautiful slender young lady with long brown hair waved to him. She was wearing a white fur jacket, tight black leather pants, and four inched high heeled boots. Mike really couldn't see who she was through the crowd, but she jumped down from the barstool, and walked towards him.

"Nicky?" Mike said. It was his old girl friend. He hadn't seen her in over a year.

"Hey Mike!" Nicky ran over to Mike's booth, and gave him a big hug. "How have you been?" She asked.

"Fine Nicky. Where is the old man?" Mike asked

"Oh, we broke up. So, what have you been doing all this time?"

"I've started my own business, and I've met someone too." Mike replied.

"So, you finally became a business owner. Mike, I'm proud of you."

"And," Mike said again, "I've met someone."

"You have?" Nicky said raising a brow. "Well, is she as good as I was?" Nicky rubbed the curls on the back of Mike's head.

"Stop it, Nicky," Mike said sternly, but Nicky just giggled. "You have to leave before she comes back."

"Can I meet her?"

"No!" Mike said firmly. "Now go."

Nicky put her head down, and pretended to pout like a small child. "Okay. I'll go, but you got to give me one thing."

"What?" Mike asked curiously.

"Come here," Nicky said mischievously. "I don't want to say it out loud. Come here. I'm not going to bite you."

Mike leaned over towards her. Nicky grabbed Mike by the collar, and pulled him to her. She kissed him deeply. Mike had to grab the table to keep from falling on her. When Nicky let go of him, she started to giggle again. Mike and Nicky slowly looked up at the same time. Michelle was standing there with her mouth slightly opened. Michelle stood there unable to move for a moment.

"Michelle!" Mike shouted, but it was too late.

Michelle grabbed her purse, and ran outside. Mike tried to run after her, but Nicky blocked his path. When Mike and Nicky finally got out of the booth, Michelle was no where to be found.

"Nicky, how could you do this?" Mike shouted.

"I'm sorry Mike," Nicky said with a little guilt. "I was just playing."

"What the Hell would make you think I'd want to kiss you anyway? Why don't you go find that old man you left me for, and kiss him?!" Mike shouted.

"Mike, I'm sorry. I'll make it up to you."

"Just get away from me." He demanded.

"But Mike . . ."

"Now!"

Nicky jumped back, and gasped for a moment. She thought Mike might hit her, but she knew he was never that type of man. Everyone in the dinning room was quietly staring at Mike and Nicky. Mike was still enraged when he stormed out of the club leaving Nicky with a little bit of embarrassment. Nicky brushed her hair back over her shoulder, and went back to the bar. Mike looked around the club, but he didn't see Michelle. He thought she might be waiting at his car, but she wasn't there either.

Mike leaned against his car, and sighed. Then he decided to call Michelle's house. The phone rang for a moment then someone picked up.

"Hello! Hello!" Mike said.

"Mike, is that you?" Big Mama asked.

"Yes. Have you seen Michelle?"

"What? No. I thought she was with you," confused Big Mama replied.

"Bertha, something has happened tonight, and she left. Please call me if she comes home."

"Okay Mike," Big Mama said curiously.

Mike hung up the phone. Then he started to walk down the street. A cab pulled up in front of a small diner. He saw a woman that looked like Michelle walking out of the diner.

He called out to her. "Michelle!" Mike shouted.

She looked at him, and ran to the cab. She got in the cab, and the driver sped off before Mike could get close to her. Mike ran back to his car. He got into it as fast as he could then he sped away. Mike got to Michelle's house a little bit before the cab pulled up. When Michelle got home, she paid the cab driver, and walked to her front door as fast as she possibly could. Mike met her at the door. He stopped her from putting the key in the lock.

"Michelle, wait," he said. "I know how this looks, but it's not what you think."

"Oh, you know what I think?" Michelle said gritting her teeth.

"No Michelle. I just--."

"Mike look, you don't need to explain anything to me. We aren't married. You can see as many women as you want. Besides, nothing happened between us anyway."

"Michelle, listen to me," Mike pleaded.

"Why Mike? I don't need to hear anymore lies from any more men. Go back to her. I'm sure she will be waiting for you at the bar. Maybe you'll get lucky this time."

That last statement from Michelle infuriated Mike. "Yeah, what about your ex-husband? He's been coming around here trying to get you back for months. I guess you will be going back to him now?"

"I don't go back, Mike, unlike you!" Michelle shouted.

"You don't have to go back to him. He is here all the time!" Mike shouted back.

Michelle gritted her teeth, and her eyes narrowed. Then she walked up to him. "Yes, he does come by here to see his children, but unlike you, I didn't kiss him! Now, get off my porch before I call the police!"

Michelle's last words seem like a low blow that hit Mike the hardest. Michelle opened the door, and slammed it shut, locking it behind her. Mike walked towards the door as it slammed. He touched the door as if he was touching her and then he walked away. Michelle walked upstairs. Her tears seemed to burn her eyes as she shut her bedroom door. She leaned against the door covering her face with her hands, and cried. Michelle stayed there for a few minutes until she could move again. Once she got off the door, she changed her clothes, and got in bed. This day that started out so wonderful has changed back into the old familiar pain she once knew. How could she ever trust another man again?

Chapter 28
Trusting Again

When Michelle woke up this morning, her eyes were so swollen, and puffy that she could barely see. She got up to shut the blinds because the glare from the sunlight was blocking what little vision she had left. Michelle went to the bathroom, and rinsed her face with cold water. Then she walked downstairs. Big Mama was already up and making breakfast when Michelle walked into the kitchen. Pee-Pee seemed to smile, and wagged his tail when she walked in.

"Good morning darling. Would you like some coffee?" Big Mama asked.

"Yes ma'am. Thank you," she replied.

Pee-Pee walked over to Michelle, and licked her knee. Michelle felt that in some way the dog was trying to console her. She patted the dog on the head and walked to the cabinet to get a coffee cup.

"What happened, Michelle? What was the big argument about?" Big Mama asked.

"Oh, you heard," she replied.

"Baby, half the town heard you two."

"I'm sorry mom."

"That's okay. Are you all right?"

"I guess I will be. After all, I've been through this before."

"What have you been through before Michelle?"

"Mom, last night in the club, I saw Mike kissing another woman. He almost fell on her. I took a cab home, and that's when the shouting started. I told him to go back to the bar where his friend was waiting for him. He told me to go back to James. What a jerk. I guess men are all the same. At least I found out now. There's no telling how long he has been seeing that girl."

"Michelle, I can't believe Mike would do that to you."

"I didn't think he would either, but this is my own fault. I told myself not to get involved with him, but I did it anyway. Now, I am back in the same place I started in."

"Don't say that Michelle," said Big Mama. "Maybe this is just a misunderstanding."

"I guess I misunderstood the part where he was kissing another woman," Michelle said sarcastically. "Mom, I don't want to talk about it anymore. It just makes me upset all over again."

"Are you going to church today?" Big Mama asked.

"No. I'm going to stay here, and cook today. I just need some time alone."

"Okay baby," Big Mama said. "I'll call Ben. He might want to go."

Big Mama and Michelle continued to chat about everything, but Mike. Then they ate breakfast together. After breakfast, Big Mama went to her room to get dressed for church. The doorbell rang, and Michelle answered the door.

"Good morning," Mr. Davis said.

"Good morning Mr. Davis," Michelle replied. "You look mighty handsome today."

"Oh, I can look pretty cute when I get cleaned up." Mr. Davis said with a grin.

Michelle laughed.

"Well, don't you look handsome," Big Mama said as she walked out of her room.

"Thank you," Mr. Davis replied.

"Now, I think y'all look like the perfect couple. Your outfits even match."

Both Big Mama and Mr. Davis wore gray pinstriped suits, and Big Mama had on a hat to match.

"Michelle, are you going to be okay here?" Big Mama asked.

"Oh yeah, don't worry about me. Y'all go on. Church is about to start."

Big Mama hugged Michelle, and they left. Michelle cleaned up the kitchen, and sat on the couch looking outside the window. The cool fall gray cloudy day did nothing to improve Michelle's mood. The more she sat there and thought about Mike the lonelier, and depressed she became. Michelle got up, and went upstairs to take a shower. Once she was dressed, she started cleaning the house. The boy's room took the most time to clean.

Since this was the first weekend after Thanksgiving, Michelle took out the Christmas decorations, and started decorating the house. She put a beautiful reef on the front door, and electric holiday candles in the windows. The candles gave the house a warm majestic glow. She hung the kid's stockings by the fire place. Then she realized she had to get Alley a stocking later. She put a reef above the fireplace mantel and two statues of angels blowing their horns on one corner of the mantel. She put a small twelve-inch artificial Christmas tree on the dinning room table, and two nutcrackers on the buffet. Michelle went outside to the shed to bring the Christmas tree inside the house. Pee-Pee followed her outside the back door. It was a hard job dragging the tree into the house, but some how she managed. Michelle decided to wait until the children came home to decorate the tree. She knew how excited they would be, so she got the decorations out for the tree, and put the boxes on the floor by the window. Michelle got a glass of ice tea from the refrigerator, and took a small break. But, soon those old feeling started to come back, so she decided it was time to cook. Michelle kept the portable TV in the kitchen, and watched the news while she cooked. The smell of the roasted chicken, and casserole in the oven was driving Pee-Pee mad. The dog yelped, and begged for the cooked food.

"Oh no Pee-Pee, this is ours," Michelle said. "Let me feed you."

Michelle put a scoop kibble in Pee-Pee's food bowl, and fresh water in his other bowl. She also gave him two dog treats while he waited. When Big Mama walked through the front door, she was amazed. Big Mama took off her hat, and walked into the kitchen.

"Michelle, the house is beautiful. You must have been working since I left."

"Do you like it?" She asked.

"I love it!" Big Mama replied. "Do you need some help in the kitchen?"

"No mom. The food is almost done."

"I asked Ben to come by later, and eat with us. Is that all right?"

"Of course," Michelle replied.

"Good. I'm going to change out of these clothes."

Once Big Mama left the room the doorbell rang. Michelle answered the door with Pee-Pee.

"Hey mama," Jordan said. It was James, and the kids.

"Hey baby," she replied.

The kids gave Michelle a hug as they entered the house. They were astounded by the beautiful Christmas decorations that were displayed around the house.

"Kids, after dinner we will decorate the tree," Michelle said.

James brought the kid's bags inside the house as the kids hung up their jackets.

"Michelle, the house looks great," James replied. "Do you want to do mine?"

"No," she said. Michelle looked outside the front door, and saw a lady sitting in the front seat of James's truck. "Who is that, James?"

"Oh, she's a friend of mine. I got tired of waiting for you to come back to me," he said with a grin.

"Well, at least she looks mature. You go on. Don't keep her waiting." Michelle replied.

James said goodbye and left. Mr. Davis came by later, and ate dinner. Michelle didn't eat very much, but after dinner she seemed to smile more as we all decorated the tree. Mr. Davis helped too. Then Michelle put the star on the top of the tree. It was beautiful.

*****

This week was the week of our final exams. Mama took us to school this morning, and she warned Jordan that he had better pass everything with at least a C+, or greater.

Jordan said in a very monotone voice, "Yes ma'am."

Big Mama picked us up from school, and took us straight home. She told us that mama had been really busy this week at the center, and we needed to study so we had to go straight home. Big Mama said she went to the center this morning with mama, and the girls had decorated the place beautifully. She also said that mama was having a party the Friday before Christmas Eve.

I know mama had a lot to do, but I can't help feeling that she was doing all of this to keep her mind from thinking about Big Mike. I am starting to miss Big Mike too. I know my brothers and Alley miss him. They don't have anybody to wrestle with now. He calls our house sometimes, but mama won't talk to him. I just wondered if we will see him on Christmas Day.

Once Big Mama parked the car, we all got out, and put our books on the kitchen table. Big Mama made us a snack. We ate our snacks, but soon we had to start on our study guides. We studied for about an hour. Jonathan quizzed Alley and me as usual, but this time Jordan asked for help too. We all finished our homework earlier than usual, but we couldn't go outside. Big Mama said it was too cold, and wet outside. She told us to go upstairs, and play today. On the way upstairs, I heard the phone ring, so I stopped to listen.

I heard Big Mama say, "Hi Mike. She's not home yet. Can I take a message? I'm sorry Mike. I don't know why she hasn't called you back. Michelle only told me a little about what happened. I'm not trying to pry, but what happened between you too?"

Then all I heard Big Mama say was, "Um hmm, um hmm? And oh, and oh no!" Next, Big Mama said, "I think y'all need to talk. Mike the kids are in a Christmas play at school. Why don't you come? Stop by here tomorrow, so I can give you a ticket. Okay, that's a great idea. I'll see you then. Bye, bye."

Big Mama hung up the phone. I knew Big Mama was up to something. I believe Friday would be an interesting night for all of us.

*****

Mama left work early Friday, so that she could take us to the play. "*A Christmas Carol*" was the name of the play we were performing tonight. Alley played the "*Ghost of Christmas Present.*" My brothers and I played as the party guests. We came downstairs dressed in our costumes. Alley had a ring of flowers on her head. Our costumes looked like they were centuries old. Big Mama and Mr. Davis were dressed, and ready to go.

Mama yelled downstairs, "I'll be there in a minute."

Soon she came running down the steps in a black dress, and jacket trying to put on her earrings at the same time.

"Y'all ready?" Mama asked.

Everyone said, "Yes."

"Let's go," she replied.

Mama drove all of us in the van, and parked near the school's entrance. We all got out, and walked in. She took us backstage to the dressing room while Big Mama and Mr. Davis waited in the foyer.

"Guys, do y'all have everything?" Mama asked.

We all said, "Yes ma'am."

"Good. Now, have a good time, and smile."

Mama walked back to the lobby's foyer and met Big Mama and Ben.

"Michelle, you go on inside the auditorium. I think I saw someone I want to talk to," Big Mama said.

"Okay mom, but don't be too long. The play is about to start."

Mama gave the lady at the entrance her ticket, and found her seat. The lights in the auditorium started to dim. Mama looked back at the entrance to see if Big Mama and Mr. Davis were walking in. When she looked back, she saw Mike. Mama gasped, and turned around quickly.

"What is he doing here?" She whispered aloud to herself.

Mike was dressed very nicely in navy jacket, white striped shirt, and matching slacks. He was good looking. Damn good. Michelle was happy to see him even though she wasn't going to admit it, but she was still mad at him. He was carrying some beautiful flowers with him when he sat down beside her.

"Michelle, look who I found," Big Mama said with a sweet smile. Mama glared at Big Mama.

"Hello Michelle. These are for you." Mike tried to hand Michelle the flowers, but she just sat there looking at him.

"Oh, go on, and take the flowers Michelle. Don't make a scene," Big Mama said.

Mama took the flowers from Mike and then she whispered to him, "What are you doing here?"

"Shh! The play is about to start," Big Mama said.

When the play began, mama had her hand on the armrest of the seat. Mike saw her hand, and grabbed it. Michelle tried to pull her hand away, but Mike held on to it. She glared at him, but he gave her a slight dimpled smile. Then he picked her hand up, and kissed her palm. Mama finally snatched her hand free from Mike's grip. She tried to rub the kiss off on the side of the chair. Mike giggled a little, but mama decided to just ignore him.

The play started off with a musical number, and Plump had a solo in the chorus. Mama was impressed by her vocal abilities. She thought to herself, how can she sing so beautifully when her voice is so irritating? Mama laughed when Teach entered the scene to play the "*Ghost of Christmas Past.*" Big Mama pulled the camera out of her purse, and took pictures of every scene. When the play was over, everyone came back onto the stage, and took a bow. The crowd gave them a standing ovation. Big Mama and Mr. Davis walked ahead of Mike and mama. When mama and Mike reached the lobby, they met Big Mama and Mr. Davis.

"Wasn't that a good play? Who knew Bernadette could sing like that?" Big Mama said.

"Yes, she can really sing?" Mama said staring at Mike.

"Are you okay Michelle?" Mike asked.

"Yes. I'm fine. How is your girlfriend?" Mama asked with one eye brow raised.

Mike glared back at her, and said very slowly, "Well, you just said you were fine."

"I meant your new girl friend, or shall I say your old flame," mama said slowly.

"I don't have another girlfriend, Michelle."

"Why sure you do Mike. I saw you two kissing remember."

Big Mama interrupted them. "Mike, Michelle, this is not the time, or the place to discuss this. There are children here. You can talk about this later." Mama was still glaring at Mike while Big Mama continued to talk. "Hey Mike. Why don't you come by the house? I made your favorite, chocolate cake."

Mama quickly turned to Big Mama and gasped.

"Certainly. You know I love your chocolate cake," Mike said before mama could respond.

"Good. Oh look, here come the children. Dear, close your mouth. You're liable to catch a fly," Big Mama said to mama.

The kids ran over to Mike, and hugged him.

"Mike! Mike!" They yelled.

"Man, we haven't seen you all week," Jordan said.

"Well, I guess I have to come around more often," Mike replied with a grin.

Mama rolled her eyes.

"Mike, did you see me? I was playing the violin at the Christmas party," Jonathan said.

"Did you see me?" Alley said excitedly. "I was the '*Ghost of Christmas Present.*'"

"Jordan and I were in the chorus." I said sadly.

"Jasmine, you all were great. Everyone did a great job. Don't you think so Michelle?" Mike asked.

"Yes. Y'all were wonderful," mama said as she tried to force a smile on her face. "Come on guys. Let's go."

"Mike, you'll meet us at the house, won't you?" Big Mama asked.

"Sure," he replied.

"Good. Well, we'll see you there."

"Mama, where did you get the flowers?" Jasmine asked.

"Mike gave them to me."

"Cool!" I said.

Everyone walked outside of the school's lobby, and into the parking lot. Mr. Davis and the kids got into the back seat. Big Mama got into the front passenger seat. Mama got into the van, and slammed the door. She quickly turned to Big Mama, and stared for a moment. Mama whispered to Big Mama, "Why did you invite him over?"

"Michelle, don't whisper. It's rude. Besides, we can all hear you anyway. Mike is not just your friend. He is all of ours, right kids?" Big Mama said as she turned to look over the seat at us.

Everyone in the back seat said, yah! Mama was out numbered. She didn't say anything else. She just drove home in silence. Once they were home, mama opened the front door for everyone without saying a word.

"Are you all right Michelle?" Big Mama asked.

Mama gave Big Mama a malevolent look. She locked the door behind everyone, and started to go upstairs. Everybody else walked into the den when suddenly Big Mama stopped.

"Michelle, where are you going? We have guests," Big Mama said.

"No mom, you have guests. I'm going to bed."

"Young lady, you get down here now," Big Mama demanded.

"Mom, I am not a young lady, and this is my house. I will go wherever I please."

"Michelle, please stop," Big Mama pleaded.

"Mom, I have never meddled in yours, and daddy's business, so why do you think you can get into mine?"

"Dear, I wasn't trying to pry, but I think that you should talk to him. Just hear him out, okay? If you still want him to go, I won't say another word."

"Mom . . .!"

"Bertha, I think I'll have that piece of cake tomorrow. I'll see you later," Mr. Davis said.

"Ah Ben, you can't stay?" Big Mama pleaded.

"No, no. I'll come back when things are a little less heated. See y'all tomorrow."

Ben opened the front door, and left the house.

"I guess I'll be going too. I didn't come here to start any trouble between you two," Mike said.

"No Mike, no." Big Mama replied. "Michelle, this was my idea, so if you're going to be mad at somebody, be mad at me. Just talk to him. I promise you I'll never get in your business again. Baby, don't let your pride get in the way of doing what is right."

Mama looked at Big Mama, and then she looked at Mike. The anger in mama's face couldn't be hidden.

"Okay Mike. What do you have to say to me?" Mama asked.

"Wait a minute Mike, Michelle. Let's not do this here." Big Mama said. "Kids, let's go into the kitchen. I'll cut y'all a piece of cake, but you'll have to take it to your rooms."

They all shook their heads as they stared over the back of the couch watching the scene.

"Come on kids. Mike, Michelle, why don't y'all go into the den." Big Mama pointed them in that direction.

Big Mama walked into the kitchen as Mike and mama sat on the couch. Big Mama cut a piece of cake for the kids, and told them to take it upstairs.

"Guys, when you finish eating that cake, take a bath," mama said. They all moaned and complained.

"She gets mad at Big Mama, and takes it out on us," Jordan mumbled.

"What Jordan?" Mama shouted. All the kids ran upstairs, and shut the door.

"Mike, I wrapped a piece of cake up for you, so if you don't want it now, you can take it with you," Big Mama said.

Big Mama put the cake on the coffee table, and patted Mike on the shoulder. Then she left the room.

He turned to Michelle, and said, "Michelle, you shouldn't talk to your mother that way."

"Mike, what did you have to say to me?" She asked quickly to change the subject.

Mike sighed deeply, and tried to control his temper. "Michelle, Nicky is my ex-girl friend that I told you about. She's the one that was fooling around with another man while we were together."

"Well, it seems like you got over it," mama said.

"Let me finish. I haven't seen her in over a year. When you left me to go to the bathroom, I tried to get the waitress attention, but Nicky saw me first. She came running to my table, and hugged me. She told me that she broke up with the old man. I tried to get her to leave, but she said she wanted to tell me something. When I leaned over to hear it, that's when she grabbed me by the collar, and kissed me. Now, you didn't see me touching her, did you? She kissed me," Mike said.

"Is that all?"

"No," he replied. "She came by my house."

Mama closed her eyes, and put her head down. "Did you sleep with her?"

"No Michelle. She wanted me back. She tried to apologize for what she did. She told me she saw us when we walked in. She waited for you to leave so she could make her move. She said she saw you coming back. That's why she kissed me. She was hoping she could get rid of you, and later she would apologize then try to come back to me."

Mama shook her head, and said, "What a bitch. Did she try to have sex with you?"

"Yes."

"What did you do?"

"I put her out of my house," Mike replied. "Michelle, I haven't had sex with anyone else since I met you, and I don't want too either. I told you that I love you. You are the only person I want to have sex with."

"She's a pretty girl Mike, and a lot more glamorous looking than I am," mama admitted.

"She is silly too, and I told you. I don't like to share. Michelle, you are beautiful too. You've just been listening to your ex-husband for so long that now you don't believe it, but I see how other men look at you."

"But you kissed her Mike!"

Mike grabbed Michelle's hand, and this time she didn't pull away. "I washed my face, and brushed my teeth. I'm not sick either. Don't you trust me?" Mike got closer to Michelle. "Don't you trust me, Michelle?"

"Mike," mama replied cautiously.

"Don't you?" He said leaning over to kiss her.

"Yes," she said finally.

"Then kiss me," he said.

Michelle became nervous as a school girl. Mike tried to kiss her, but she put her head down. "Mike, I don't want to be hurt again."

"I won't hurt you. Now, kiss me." Mike leaned forward again, but this time he grabbed the back of her head.

"Mike, I can't."

"Yes you can."

He leaned her back until they were finally lying on the couch. His amorous kiss made her moan softly. He wouldn't let her pull away until she gave up her resistance. She ran her fingers through the soft curls on the back of his head. Mike kissed her neck, and chest. Then he massaged her perky breast through the silky black dress. He laid his head on her chest, and continued to massage her breast. Michelle continued to moan softly, and uncontrollably. Having him in her arms again just felt right. She missed him too. Holding Michelle like this was soothing to him. He was so happy that this misunderstanding was finally over.

"Michelle, I am sorry about what I said about you and your ex-husband."

"I'm sorry about what I said too," she replied.

Then Mike sat up to look into Michelle's eyes. "I love you Michelle, and I wish I could stay with you forever." He traced Michelle's lower lip with his finger. Then he kissed her again, but this time the kiss was more erotic. His hot tongue entered her mouth, and she could feel his harden erection against her thighs.

"Oh, I'm sorry. I thought y'all where gone. Never mind me I was just going in the kitchen to get something to drink for the kids," Big Mama said.

"Mom!" Michelle shouted.

Mike and Michelle sat up, and tried to adjust their clothing.

"Well, I would have knocked dear, but there is no door."

Big Mama walked into the kitchen, and got four juice boxes. Before she left, she said, "I'm glad to see that the arguing has ended. Y'all carry on where you left off. I'm going to bed. Good night y'all."

"Good night mom."

"Good night, Bertha." Mike said.

Then Big Mama walked out of the room.

"We've got to think of a place that we can go for a little privacy," Michelle said.

"How about your bedroom? I dying to have you up there," Mike said with an erotic grin.

"Mike, we wouldn't be alone for long. My kids would be in there with us all night."

"I'll tell you what. Let me think of something, and I'll surprise you, okay. I had better go. Come on and walk me to the door," Mike said.

"Mike, will you be available next Friday?" Michelle asked.

"Yes."

"Good. I'm having a party at the center. Why don't you stop by?" Michelle asked.

"Sure. Now, walk me to the door."

Michelle walked Mike to the front door. He gave her another passionate kiss. His hands slowly massaged her back. Then his hands firmly gripped her hips as he pulled her closer to him. He released her from his kiss, but not her hips.

"Good night, beautiful lady," he said.

He kissed her brow and he released her. Then he left.

*****

This was the last week of school before fall break, and everyone was ready to get out of school for the holidays. All of our exams were over last week, and we all passed. I think mama's words really helped Jordan because he made three B's, and two C's. This is the best he has ever done in school all year. When we got out of school on Friday, we ran outside to find Mike's car. Mike waved to us to come over to him.

We walked over to him, and he said, "I'm taking y'all to the center today. Come on. Put your bags in the trunk."

We all got into Mike's red sports car. It was beautiful. I was so happy I got to sit in the front. My brothers loved his car. Once we got to the center, Mike parked the car, and we all got out. We all walked through the entrance, and the two students at the desk saw Mike walking in, and gasped.

I heard Terri say, "Girl, he is fine."

I think Mike heard them too because his dimples started to show.

"Sir, may we help you?" Terri asked sweetly with a big smile.

"Yes. I'm looking for Michelle," Mike replied.

"Oh, she's in the recreational area. Just go on in," Terri replied.

Terri and LaShundra giggled, and ogled Mike as they followed behind us. A few of the church choir members were dressed in their church robes singing Christmas carols by the television set. Mama prepared a table full of appetizers today because she said the patients were still full from Thanksgiving dinner. She said they didn't want all that food today. Mama walked over to Mike, and gave him a kiss. Mike walked back over to the buffet table with the kids, and prepared a plate for himself. Big Mama was talking to Mr. Mack when mama sat down beside her. Terri and LaShundra were both flirting with Mike. LaShundra was trying to fix another plate of food for him.

"Michelle, those two girls are flirting their heads off, but that what happens when you get involved with such a pretty man," Big Mama said.

"I know mom, and I'm sorry about last week too."

"Oh, don't worry about that. I was playing match maker, but I'm glad to see y'all back together again."

Mike walked over, and sat down by mama, Big Mama, and Sharon. Most of the patient's family members came by too. By the time the party ended, mama gave all the patients a goody bag as they left the center. Big Mama rode home with mama, but Mike took my brothers, Alley, and me home. He said he had to go shopping so he couldn't stay, but he would come by tomorrow. I was glad too. Christmas would be great this year. Not just because of Santa, but this year Alley and Mike would be here too. Our whole family would be together on Christmas day. I can't wait.

Chapter 29
Christmas

The next day, mama and Big Mama were in the kitchen preparing the big meal for Christmas day. After they finished, mama said she had to go to the store for some more wrapping paper. She came back about two hours later. She said she had to go to three different stores before she could find one store that was still open on Christmas Eve. Mama started wrapping Mrs. Sharon's gift when the doorbell rang. She got up to answer the door with Pee-Pee at her side.

"Hey beautiful. Come outside with me," Mike said.

"Okay. Just let me get my jacket. Jasmine, Alley, do y'all want to finish wrapping that gift for me?" Mama asked.

"Yeah!" We both said in unison.

Mama got her jacket from the hall closet, and walked back to the front door.

"Oh yeah Michelle, get your keys," Mike said.

Mama got her keys out of her purse and walked outside the front door.

"What's up Mike?" She asked.

"Come here." Mike walked to his truck, and took the tarp off the back truck bed to reveal four brand new beautiful shiny bikes. Mama gasped putting her hand over her mouth.

"Mike, they are beautiful. They will love them." Mama gave Mike a big hug.

"Shh, Michelle! They'll hear you. Come on. Help me put them into the shed."

Mama helped Mike take the bikes off his truck and then they took them around the side of the house to the shed. She came back to Mike's truck to help him get the rest of the gifts. They walked into the house, and put the gifts under the tree. Mike sat down on the couch, and started playing with my brothers.

"Kids, if Santa Clause is going to come tonight, y'all have to go to bed. Come on. It's almost nine o'clock," Big Mama said. "Y'all tell Mike good night."

We all said good night and went upstairs to bed.

"Well, I better go to bed too if I want to see Santa myself. Good night y'all," said Big Mama.

Then she went to bed. Mama and Big Mike were left sitting on the couch in front of the fire place sipping on hot chocolate when we all went to bed.

*****

Alley, my brothers, and I woke up early on Christmas morning. When we ran downstairs, we were amazed. All the stocking were filled. There was even a full stocking for Pee-Pee too. Jordan got a race track, skateboard, and a *Walkie-Talkie*. Jonathan got a robot, skateboard, and a microscope. Alley and I had two dolls, skateboards, and a hand-held computer games. Santa also brought us some movies, and video games we had to share. Big Mama was in the kitchen feeding Pee-Pee, and cooking breakfast when we ran downstairs. Mama came downstairs in her robe, and grabbed the camera.

"Hey guys. Everybody say, cheese." Then she took a picture of us all dressed in Christmas pajamas. "Mom, it's your turn. Come on. I want to get a picture of you too. And, you too Pee-Pee," Mama said.

Big Mama stood behind us. Pee-Pee sat down in front of me.

"Say cheese," she said.

"Cheese!" We all said in unison. Then mama took the picture.

"Come on everybody. Breakfast is ready," Big Mama replied. We all went into the kitchen to eat.

Because this year Christmas fell on a Sunday, Big Mama demanded that we go to church. After breakfast we went upstairs to get dressed. Church service was short today, and the youth group put on a short play that honored the birth of Jesus. The preacher wanted to give the people more time to be with their families. He knew that a lot of people would be here from out of town, so he decided not to have evening services today. When we got home, we changed out of our dress clothes, and went outside to skateboard. We saw Plump outside riding her new bike with Teach and Carlos. Mike drove up, and parked in the driveway.

He walked up to us, and said, "Hey guys. Where are your bikes?"

We all looked at each other, and said in unison, "What Bikes?"

"Hold on," Mike said. Then he walked up to the front door, and knocked. Soon mama came to the door. "Michelle, where are their bikes?" He asked.

"Well, I wanted to wait until you got here, so you could give them their bikes."

"Come on Michelle. Let's go get their bikes. Kids, go into the house, and put your jackets on. Then come back out here," Mike said.

Mike and mama walked around to the backyard. When we walked back outside, mama and Mike had four shinny new bikes with them. We screamed, and ran down the steps to give Mike a big hug. I got the purple bike, and Alley got a pink bike. Jordan got the black bike. Mike gave Jonathan the sparkly blue bike. We got on the bikes, and rode until we caught up with Plump, Teach, and Carlos. Mike and mama sat on the porch swing huddled together watching us ride. Mr. Davis came over to our house carrying a few presents with him.

"Hey Mr. Davis," mama said. "Go on in, and take those things into the house. The door is open."

Mr. Davis walked into the house, and put the presents under the tree. Then he came back outside, and sat in the rocker.

"I see Santa was good to the kids. How has he been treating you good folks?" Mr. Davis asked.

"Oh, he has been treating us just fine," mama replied.

"That's good, that's good." Mr. Davis said, "And, it's good to see y'all together again too."

"I think so too Mr. Davis," Mike replied. Then he kissed mama's hand.

"You know, I would drive my wife crazy. Oh yeah, I loved to argue with her because making up with her was so much fun, ha, ha, ha." Mr. Davis laughed.

Mama and Mike laughed too. Soon Big Mama came outside holding a plate of Christmas cookies.

"Well, hey y'all. It's kind of cool out here. Don't y'all want to come inside?" Big Mama asked.

"We'll go inside in a minute. The kids wanted to ride their bikes," mama said.

"Okay. I'll be back in a minute. I'm going to take Mrs. Madison some cookies."

Big Mama left the porch, and walked across the street to Mrs. Madison's house. They couldn't hear what Big Mama and Mrs. Madison were saying, but mama, Mike, and Mr. Davis waved to her from the porch. When Big Mama came back to the porch, Uncle Pete walked towards the porch with two large bags.

"What's up?" Uncle Pete shouted.

Everyone greeted Uncle Pete as he walked onto the porch.

"Hey sis, grab one of these bags because Santa Clause has come to town."

"Here Pete, let me take them," mama replied. Mama got up, and took Uncle Pete's presents into the house.

"Hey mom! Merry Christmas!" Pete Shouted.

Uncle Pete gave Big Mama a big hug. Then he shook hands with Mike and Mr. Davis. Uncle Pete sat down in the other rocker. Mama came back outside, and sat down on the swing beside Mike.

"Well, I'm getting cool, so I'm going back into the house," Big Mama said.

"Mike, is that your brother?" Uncle Pete asked.

Everybody turned to see Lisa and Trey approaching the porch.

"Well, there's my long-lost brother," Trey remarked. "How's everybody doing this Christmas?"

Everybody on the porch greeted Trey and Lisa.

"Trey, I see that you have been busy." Pete said.

"I guess so, but this time it worked." Trey said with a grin.

All the men laughed, but Lisa rolled her eyes.

"Come on everyone. Let's go into the house," mama replied. "Kids, put the bikes up, and come inside."

Everybody left the front porch, and went inside the house. They hung up their jackets and coats and walked into the den gathering around the fire place. Mama put on a soulful Christmas CD. The soft rhythmic music set the tone for the evening. Big Mama gave everyone a cup of eggnog.

"Mama, did you put a shot of rum or *Bourbon* in this?" Uncle Pete asked.

"No Pete!" She said sternly. "The kids and Lisa are going to drink it too."

"What kind of eggnog doesn't have rum or *Bourbon* in it?"

"Mine Pete! Just drink your eggnog," Big Mama said.

Pee-Pee barked when Alley, my brothers, and I walked inside the house from the back door.

"Kids, go wash your hands," Big Mama said.

We all went to the bathroom down the hall to wash our hands. Then we sat down on the floor around the fire place. The doorbell rang again. Mama and faithful Pee-Pee answered it.

"Hey, hey, hey! Merry Christmas!" Mr. Greg said.

Mama hugged Sharon and Greg. Then she took their jackets, and hung them up in the hall closet.

"Come on in here!" Uncle Pete said.

Greg walked into the den, and shook hands with the men in the den. Then he hugged Big Mama and Lisa. Mrs. Sharon greeted everyone too, and put the present under the tree. Everyone talked for thirty minutes while mama and Big Mama set the food out on the buffet. Before we all started to eat, Big Mama came back into the den, and asked everyone to bow their heads in prayer. Once everyone said amen, we entered the dinning room. The food was set up on the buffet like it was for Thanksgiving. The adults ate in the dinning room and of course, the kids ate in the kitchen. All of us kids finished eating before the adults did. We walked back out into the den to play with our toys while the adults continued to talk and laugh. Once they were finished, the women helped mama and Big Mama clean up, and put the food away. Then mama poured coffee for all the adults except for Lisa, and everybody got a dessert.

After everyone finished eating, it was time to open the presents. The adults decided to draw names this year. Mama called out the names on the presents from under the tree. Mr. Davis got a quilt from mama, and all of us. Mr. Davis gave Big Mama a nice pair of earrings. Big Mama gave Mike a new leather jacket to replace the one that was destroyed in the fight. Trey gave Mr. Greg a watch. Sharon gave Lisa a picture frame. Uncle Pete gave Sharon a coffee maker and Mr. Greg gave Trey a CD player. Lisa gave Uncle Pete a radio. Everyone gave Lisa and Trey baby stuff. All the kids got more toys from the guests. Mama gave Sharon a pin set for her desk as a special gift for working with her at the center. Then I realized that mama hadn't gotten a gift.

"Michelle, you haven't opened your gift," Mike said.

"Well, there aren't any more present under the tree," she replied.

"Oh, that's right. Let me go get it out of my truck." Mike walked outside to his truck, and came back with a big box. He sat the box on the floor in front of everyone. Everyone stared, and mumbled to each other. "Go on. Open it," he said.

The box was huge. Mama unwrapped the paper very gently so not to tear the wrapping paper.

"Oh Michelle, we will be here all night if you do it that way. Just rip it. We aren't going to save the paper anyway," Big Mama said.

"Okay, okay." Mama tore the box open. There was a lot of packing stuff in the box and then she found another box. Mama ripped that box opened too to find a third box. Inside of the third box was a cereal box.

"Mike, I hope you didn't go through all that trouble just to give me a box of cereal," mama said.

"Keep looking."

Mama opened the box of cereal to find a small popcorn box.

"Ha, ha. How funny," mama said sarcastically.

"Keep looking," he demanded.

Mama pulled the paper out of the popcorn box and found a little black box. She gasped. Then she put her hand over her mouth. Everyone else gasped too.

"Open it," Mike said.

Mama's shaky hands opened the box to find a three diamond princes cut platinum ban ring in the small black velvet box. She staggered back for a moment.

"Mike, is this real?" Shocked, mama asked.

"Well, it better be. I paid a lot of money for it. Why don't you try it on?" Then Mike took the ring out of the box, and got down on one knee. Everyone gasped.

"Michelle, I know we've been through a lot this year, but you've always been by my side. You followed me to the biggest devastation this country has ever witnessed, and you were there for me when my aunt died. Michelle, I love you, and I love your family too. I want to be a part of your life forever."

Then Mike put the ring on mama's shaky finger. She started to cry, and so did Big Mama.

"Michelle, you'll make me the happiest man in the world if you would agree to marry me."

Everyone clapped, and cheered. Mike kissed mama before she could say anything.

"Well Michelle, are you going to answer the man?" Uncle Pete asked.

Mama looked around the room. She began to panic, and slowly backed away from Mike. Then she turned away from him, and walked into the kitchen. Mike looked devastated. He followed her into the kitchen.

"Michelle, what's wrong?" He asked.

Tears poured from mama's eyes. She wouldn't face him. "Mike, I can't get married again."

"Can you face me?" Mike asked with a little bit of irritation in the sound his voice. Michelle slowly turned around.

"Mike, I am so sorry, but . . ."

"--but what? Don't you love me?"

"I do, but it just too soon."

"Too soon for what? Do I have to keep paying for what your ex-husband has done?"

"No Mike," mama said shaking her head. "That's not it."

"Yes, it is. I guess you're going to be another one of those lonely bitter black women," Mike said with anger.

That last statement left mama shocked, and angry. She quickly took the ring off her finger.

"Here Mike! I wouldn't want you to be with a lonely bitter black woman. Take your ring, and go."

Mike stared at the ring and then he looked into her eyes. God, he loved this woman. He had hoped this night would be the beginning of a wonderful life together. Instead, this night has become a night of pain, and humiliation. He was tired of going home leaving what has become his family to go home to a lonely bed. He wanted to stay with her and make love to her all through the night. Then rise in the morning with her at his side to do it again. He knew this day will never be. His heart ached, but he knew he had to accept whatever she had to offer. Having her as his girlfriend was better than not having her at all.

"No Michelle. I bought it for you. I don't want it back. I love you Michelle, and I am not trying to pressure you. I think I had better go now. Good night."

He put the ring back on her finger, and kissed it. Then he kissed her brow, and left. Trey ran outside the front door to catch up with Mike. Mama was still in the kitchen when Sharon and Greg decided to go too.

"Well, we better go Bertha. I've got a busy day tomorrow," Sharon said.

Mr. Davis said he had to go too. Lisa stood up, and walked to the front door.

"Big Mama, do you think she will be okay?" Lisa asked.

"Yes. It may take some time, but she will," Big Mama replied.

"He loves her, Big Mama," Lisa said sincerely.

"I know."

"Tell her if she needs to talk, she can call me."

"Okay," Big Mama replied.

Uncle Pete stood up, and walked to the door. Big Mama got the guests their coats and jackets from the hall closet, and handed them to their rightful owner. Then everyone hugged Big Mama as they left the house.

Before Uncle Pete left, he said, "Well Mama, everything was wonderful, but my little sister can really clear out a house."

"Shut up, Pete," Big Mama said sternly. "You be careful going home."

"Yes ma'am," Uncle Pete said. Then he left too.

Big Mama walked back into the den.

"Kids, take some of your toys upstairs, and get ready for bed," Big Mama said.

We all walked upstairs while Big Mama and mama stayed downstairs. Big Mama started picking up the Christmas wrapping paper, and small boxes when mama slowly walked back into the room and sat down on the couch.

"Mom, do you think he will ever see me again?" She asked

"Right now, I don't think he can leave you if he wanted to, but you are frustrating him," Big Mama replied.

"I know, but I'm not trying to. Mom, how will I know if it will work out this time? Who is to say that Mike won't find a young girl, and leave me for like James did? You know, I thought I couldn't survive without James when he left me. I was devastated."

"Michelle, Mike is not James."

"I know mom. Tell me something since you can see into the future, if I marry Mike, will he leave me for someone else?"

Big Mama stopped picking up the paper, and sat on the other couch. "Michelle, God's gift for me doesn't work like that. I'm not a fortune teller. I can only see what he wants me to see. Michelle, I told you that only time will tell what's truly in a man's heart, but one thing I do know is this. God does not want us to fear to live!"

Mama was speechless for a moment. She just stared at Big Mama dumfounded by the truth. She turned from Big Mama, and put her head down.

When she could speak again, she said, "What would you have me to do? Should I marry him?"

"Michelle, I'm not going to tell you who to marry. I didn't do that with your first husband, and I'm not going to do it now. But, you are afraid to live."

In shock, Michelle turned back to face Big Mama.

"We've all made mistakes, and bad things happen to everyone. You can't dwell on the past because you can't change it. What has happened is over now, but it is up to you to determine your future. This man has been in love with you after the first month he started dating you. He sees your kids as his own, Michelle. God has let me see that much, but the choice is yours now. You can live each day in the moment, accepting this man's love to the fullest, or you can live in fear, and lose the only true love you might every have again. The choice is yours," said Big Mama.

Mama put her head down, and started to cry. Big Mama got up, and sat down on the couch beside her.

"Mom, what have I done?" Michelle asked.

Big Mama put her arms around her shoulders, and said, "Its okay baby. Give him a few days. Then go, and talk to him, okay."

Michelle cried on Big Mama's shoulder a few minutes longer. Then Big Mama told mama to go to bed. She said she would clean everything up in the morning.

*****

The next few days after Christmas, Michelle focused on her work. Sharon wanted to ask her how she was doing and about Mike, but she decided it was best not to. Mike was hard at work preparing his new business for opening day too. He and a few of his friends were doing most of the repair work themselves. Wednesday afternoon, Michelle told Sharon she was going out for lunch, and she might be a little late getting back. Sharon said okay, and Michelle left. She drove to a flower shop where she found a beautiful bouquet of sunflowers on a side table.

"Now, these should brighten anyone's day," Michelle said.

She paid for the flowers, and left the store. She drove to Mike's repair shop. She found several people outside cleaning, and painting the building. Michelle parked the van, and walked inside of the building. The inside waiting area had been cleaned, and painted. There was a new cash register, and seating area. Michelle looked around the office, and admired the men's handiwork. A man walked into the waiting area covered in speckles of paint.

"Excuse me Sir. Have you seen Mike Raimond?" Michelle asked.

"Ma'am he's in the office."

"Thank you." She replied.

Michelle was nervous when she walked back to Mike's office. She took a deep breath, and knocked on the door.

"Come in."

Michelle slowly opened the door. "Hey," she said softly.

Mike looked up, but he didn't smile.

"What are you doing here?" He asked.

"I just wanted to come by, and see how you are doing. That's all," Michelle replied.

"I'm fine," he said flatly. "Now, you can go."

"Can't we talk for a little while?"

"I'm busy," Mike said without looking up.

"I bought you some flowers."

"You can leave them over there." Mike said pointing to the corner of his desk.

"Mike, you don't have to be so rude to me. I just wanted to talk to you. Why can't we be friends?"

Mike looked up slowly. "Is that all I am to you now, just a friend?" He asked.

Michelle's eyes narrowed. "Fine! Here are your flowers!" She shouted and slammed them down on his desk. "And, here is your ring! I'm glad I didn't make a mistake of marrying a man that can't talk to me!"

Michelle took the ring off her finger, and slammed it down on the desk too. Then she turned to leave the office.

"Wait! Wait!" Mike jumped up, and ran towards her putting his hand on the door. "Don't go. I'm sorry. Please come back."

Michelle silently walked back, and sat in one of the office's chairs. Mike grabbed the ring off of his desk, and put it back on her finger.

"Mike, I came by here to say that I'm sorry," Michelle said.

"For what? You don't want to marry me. What's to be sorry for," he said as he walked back to his chair.

"Mike, I know I said I didn't want to get married, but the truth is that I can't marry you now. I have only been divorced for seven months and I just have to make sure that I'm not going to make another mistake again. I love you Mike, and I didn't mean to hurt you."

"What can I do to prove to you that I'm not going to hurt you?" He asked.

"Just give me a little time."

Mike reached across the desk, and held Michelle's hands. "Okay, I'll wait to have you as my wife, but I can't wait anymore to have you. Come here, and kiss me."

He pulled Michelle's hand towards him, and kissed her gently standing over his desk. Then there was a knock at the door. The door opened.

"Hey boss, do you want me . . . Woo! Oops!"

Michelle and Mike turned around abruptly to see one of the painters enter the office.

"Sorry boss," he said.

"That's okay Tom. Give me a minute in here. I'll be out in a second," Mike replied.

"Okay." Tom said. Then he closed the door, and left.

"Well, we can't do this here. Not that I would want to anyway," Michelle said. Mike sat back in his desk chair, and grinned.

"You're right. The first time should be special. I'll tell you what, let me surprise you," Mike said with a grin.

"Surprise me? Should I be scared?" Michelle said with a raised brow.

"No. You should be excited," he said impishly.

Michelle laughed. "Mike, I came here to ask you to go to lunch with me too."

"I'm sorry. I've really had too much to do here right now, and I'm waiting on a guy to get here," Mike replied.

"Okay," Michelle said, "but why don't you come by the house this Saturday? Jasmine's birthday is on New Year's Day, and we always stay up to celebrate. Would you like to come?"

"I'll be there."

"Good. Now, walk me to the door, and kiss me again before anyone else comes in here," replied Michelle.

Mike did as he was told, and they both agreed not to argue anymore.

*****

My party didn't start until nine o'clock on Saturday night. Plump's parents were going out tonight, so Plump spent the night with us. The house was decorated with screamers, and signs that read: *Happy Birthday*, and *Happy New Year*. Mama covered the kitchen table with a table cloth, and put the big beautiful pink sheet cake in the middle of the table. Everybody went outside in the middle of the night to light the fireworks. Mama let Pee-Pee outside, and Big Mama followed behind him.

"Hold on guys. Let me get my lighter," mama said from the back door.

She walked back into the house, and searched through the kitchen drawers for a lighter when the doorbell rang. She grabbed the lighter out of the drawer, and left the kitchen to answer the door.

"*Laissez les bon temps roulez* and *Happy New Year*," Mike said which is a French Creole way of saying, let the good times roll.

"Not yet, Mike. Come on. We're in the backyard."

When Mike and mama entered the backyard, Mr. Davis was giggling with Big Mama.

"Hey folks! Are y'all ready for the fireworks," Mike asked everyone.

"We are ready. Let them rip!" Mr. Davis said.

"Well, just one more minute. I have something for the birthday girl." Mike reached into a bag that mama hadn't noticed him carrying before now. Then he pulled out a beautifully wrapped box, and handed it to me.

"That's not all I have," Mike said.

He reached in the bag, and pulled out a bottle of champagne. All the adults cheered.

"I'll take that Mike," mama said. "Here, you light the fireworks while I go get us some glasses."

Mama handed Mike the lighter, and took the champagne bottle. She took the presents into the house too.

"Okay kids! Stand back!" Mike said.

Plump put her fingers in her ears, and closed her eyes.

"Plump, how are you going to see the fireworks with your eyes closed?" Jordan asked.

"I'll open them later," Plump replied. "Fireworks scare me."

Mike put a big bottle rocket in the ground, and lit it. Before he could run from it, the rocket zoomed in the air leaving yellow sparks, and a smoky trail following behind it. Within a few seconds the bottle rocket burst into flames of red, blue, and yellow sparkles. My brothers, Alley, and I said, oh and ah, over the magnificent burst of colors. I don't think Plump saw any of it. Plump still had her eyes closed, and her fingers in her ears. Jordan tried to pull her hands away from her ears and she hit him. Pee-Pee didn't like the bottle rockets at all. The dog took off running towards the back door. Once he got there, he whined, and barked until mama let him inside. Mama walked back outside with four champagne glasses, and the opened champagne bottle. She also put on her coat.

Mike set off three bottle rockets at one time. He looked like a big kid with a new toy. We all cheered when some of the rockets began to spiral into shades of green and purple. Soon other people in the neighborhood started to shoot off their fireworks too. It was getting closer to midnight now. We could hear the melody of "*Auld Lang Syne*" being sung by the neighbors in the street. The sound of fireworks grew louder as the crowds in the street grew larger. It was almost midnight when mama poured the adults a glass of champagne. Mike setup ten bottle rockets in the ground, and tied the fuses together.

Then mama looked at her watch, and started counting down. "Ten, nine, eight, seven, six . . ."

Mike ran to ignite the bottle rockets fuses.

"--five, four, three . . .," Mama continued to count along with everyone else. Mike ran back to mama slightly out of breath, and wet from perspiration in the chilled night air. He grabbed his glass, and counted along with everyone else.

"-two, one. Happy New Year!" We all said in unison.

Every rocket shot off at once. Not just in our yard, but the whole neighborhood sounded like a war zone. Multiple fireworks were blasting in the air. The night sky was lit with beautiful colors, and filled with large sonic booms. The rockets and cherry bombs going off sent Pee-Pee into a frenzy. Pee-Pee made a few maddening dashes to the back door, and barked hysterically. Big Mama and Mr. Davis toasted, and sipped their champagne. Mr. Davis even kissed Big Mama on the cheek which caused her to giggle shyly, and turn away. When Big Mama looked up, she and Mr. Davis gasped. They saw mama and Big Mike passionately kissing. Big Mama tried to clear her throat, but neither Mike, nor mama could hear her amongst the multiple explosions. When they finally stopped kissing, they stared into each others eyes. We could see that they were both a little dazed by the kiss. Then Big Mike kissed mama's brow lovingly. Mama smiled slightly and turned to see all of us staring. She gasped. Everyone was staring and astounded. Mama quickly looked down so that no one could see the embarrassment on her face. Mike looked down too, but he was grinning.

When mama looked up, she yelled, "Its cold! Let's go inside the house!"

Once we got into the house, and took off our jackets, Pee-Pee seemed to calm down. The explosions continued outside while we gathered around the table. Mama lit the candles on the cake while everyone sang *Happy Birthday* as loud as they could. We all ate cake, and ice cream and everyone chatted until one o'clock in the morning. Finally, Mama made us go to bed. Big Mama went to bed when we did. Mr. Davis left right after Big Mama went to bed. Even though the noise had finally died down outside, Mama didn't want Mike to go home. He said he would come by for dinner tomorrow, and have another piece of cake with her. He kissed mama, and said goodnight. Then he left. Mama put the dishes in the dishwasher, and went to bed too.

The next day no one got up before twelve o'clock in the afternoon. Plump's mother didn't come by to get her until two o'clock that day. Needlessly to say, no one went to church today. Today was a very relaxing day. We played most of the day until it was time to eat dinner. Big Mama had already cooked a traditional meal for New Year's Day. Each dish she prepared was made according to an old wives' tale. The black-eyed peas were cooked for luck, collard greens were eaten to bring money into the New Year, and fish was eaten for wisdom. The corn bread was made just to go with the meal. But, one thing that Big Mama made that I had no clue of its meaning was chitterlings. Yuck! These things stunk up the whole house, but Big Mama said Uncle Pete liked them.

Twenty minutes before dinner started, mama started a fire in the fire place. My brothers were playing with their race cars and Big Mama put on a gospel CD in the CD player. Alley and I decided to dress Pee-Pee in our doll clothes. Big Mama laughed at us as she hummed to the rhythm of the gospel music. The table was set, and the food was warming on top of the stove. I was getting hungry. Then there was a knock at the door. Pee-Pee barked.

"I'll get it," Big Mama said. Big Mama walked to the door still humming the same tune. "Hey Ben! Happy New Year!"

"My year is going to be great now that I see you. They say if the first person a man sees is a woman, then his year will be full of good luck," Mr. Davis said.

"Well, I guess I am your good luck charm." Big Mama replied. "Come on in."

Mr. Davis laughed, and handed Big Mama his jacket. Mr. Davis walked into the room, and greeted everyone in the den. Then he sat down on the couch.

"Now, this fire is cozy," he said. "I bricked my fire place up years ago."

"Now Ben, why would you do a thing like that?" Big Mama asked.

"Oh, I don't know. My wife was gone, and it seemed like the best thing to do at the time."

"Maybe one day, you should have that fire place opened up again. It could save you a little money on your heating bill," Big Mama suggested.

Pee-Pee barked again, and walked over to the front door. The happy face dog sat down in front of the door, and wagged his tail. Mama looked at Pee-Pee strangely. Then she walked over to him.

"What wrong boy?" Mama asked.

"Michelle, he might want to go outside," Big Mama replied.

Mama opened the door to find Mike holding on to Uncle Pete.

"Hey beautiful. I was just about to ring the doorbell when I had to grab Pete here. I think he has been celebrating just a little too much," Mike said.

Uncle Pete turned to Mike, and said with a slur, "I have not."

"Ugh!" Mike said as he turned away from Uncle Pete's breath.

"Bring him in, Mike," mama replied with an irritated look. Uncle Pete staggered inside the house with Mike holding him up.

"What's up?" Uncle Pete shouted.

"Sit down Pete," Big Mama said very sternly.

Uncle Pete sat down on the couch, and Mr. Davis got up.

"Lookie here at what I got!" Uncle Pete held up a bottle of champagne in the air.

"I'll take that Pete," mama replied. "You've had enough."

Big Mama turned to Pete looking a little irritated, and said, "Pete, can you come to the table?"

"Oh yeah! I can come to the table all right."

Uncle Pete staggered into the kitchen, and flopped down into the chair. Everyone else followed Pete to the table, and sat down too. Big Mama said a prayer then they started piling food on their plates. Mama put everything Big Mama made on my brother's, Alley's, and my plates. She even included the chitterlings. The adults continued laughing and talking while the kids wondered about this stuff on our plates. Well, that is, everyone except for Jordan. He ate those chitterlings like he had just eaten his last meal. Jonathon started to eat everything except the chitterlings. Alley picked one up with her fork, and looked at it curiously. I looked down, and shook my head.

Big Mama was sitting beside me when I looked up, and said, "Big Mama, do I have to eat those chitterlings?"

Looking down into Jasmine's big green eyes, Big Mama laughed. "No baby, but it is a tradition."

"Why Big Mama?"

"Well, they say chitterlings will bring you good luck."

"How can something this stinky, bring anyone good luck?" Jonathan asked. "You have bad luck when you walk into the house, and smell it."

All the adults laughed.

"I'll take yours if you don't want them," Jordan said.

"Okay!" We all said in union.

Jonathan, Alley, and I scraped the chitterlings onto Jordan's plate. He ate until he was full. Everyone continued talking when Uncle Pete stood up, and staggered with his plate to the stove.

"Pete, what are you doing?" Big Mama asked.

"I'm . . . I'm just getting a little sumpton, sumpton. You know I love chittlins."

"Pete, get away from that stove," Big Mama said firmly. "Let me get it for you."

"I is grown folk now, mama! I can get my own chittlins," Pete demanded with a slur.

Pete grabbed a kitchen fork, and dumped a pile of chitterlings on his plate. Then he staggered towards the stove. Next, he took two steps back, and crashed to the floor.

"Pete!" Mama yelled.

Big Mama and Mike jumped up. The rest of us sat there in shock. Mike helped Uncle Pete stand up. Big Mama got up, and walked over to Pete.

"Pete, you are going to help me clean this mess up. Michelle, don't worry about it. I'll handle it. Y'all have some more birthday cake in the den. Go on." Big Mama demanded.

Everyone left the table, and mama stayed behind to cut the cake. Then she passed the cake out to everyone in the den. Big Mama and Uncle Pete stayed in the kitchen to clean. Uncle Pete was on his hands and knees picking up chitterlings, and putting them into the trash. Big Mama cleared the table, and made sure he got every chitterling off the floor. Big Mama even made Uncle Pete mop the kitchen floor. Mama, Mike and Mr. Davis just laughed at them while they sat in the den enjoying their cake. As I looked around the den and kitchen, I knew this year was already off to an unusual start.

Chapter 30
The Deans

School was still out, so none of us felt the need to get up early except for mama and Big Mama. Big Mama was in the kitchen cooking breakfast, and cleaning whatever was still left in a mess after Uncle Pete's fiasco last night. Mama was getting dressed to go to work when the phone rang. She answered the phone from her room. Big Mama went upstairs, and knocked on our doors.

"Breakfast is ready," she said.

All of us kids followed Big Mama downstairs. We all sat at the table while Big Mama prepared our plates. As I looked around the room, I noticed that Alley and my brothers could barely keep their eyes opened. The weekend of partying had left us all tired, and a bit worn out. I felt sorry for mama. She stayed up later than we did. Mama was dressed for work when she walked into the kitchen. She looked like she was about to cry.

"Mom, come into the den with me for a moment. I need to talk to you," mama said.

"Hold on a minute," Big Mama replied curiously. She turned the pot of grits off, and put a top on the pot. Then Big Mama walked into the den, and sat beside mama.

"Baby, what's the matter? You look like you're about to cry."

"Mom, that was Mrs. Green on the phone, and she said she has found Alley's grandparents."

"What?" Big Mama said. Then she sat back on the couch in a bit of shock. "When?"

"Mrs. Green told me that Alley's grandparents called her sometime before Christmas. She saw Alley's picture in the paper, and read the news article. Alley's grandparents took her mother's birth certificate to the mortuary to claim her daughter's body, but the director told her that we had already buried her. She talked to the police, and told them that Alley was her granddaughter. The police called Mrs. Green, and she did a little background check of the lady's story, and she found out her story was true. She wants to come by, and see Alley."

"Are these good people, Michelle? We don't want to give her back to the same kinds of people that would hurt her again."

"Mom, Mrs. Green said she checked their backgrounds, and they have no prior criminal records. They live on the rich side of town too. Alley's grandparents have nothing to do with Billy. Mrs. Green told me they didn't want anything to do with him. He got Alley's mother hooked on drugs, and she ran away with Billy. Mrs. Green said they hadn't seen, or heard from their daughter in over eleven years. Her daughter was eighteen when she left home with Billy, so there was nothing they could do to make her come back home. They will be here today around five o'clock. I will take off from work early today to be with you when they get here. Do you want me to tell the children?" Mama asked.

"No Michelle. They are tired, and they haven't finished eating yet. Let them get some rest today, and I'll tell them Alley's grandparents will be coming by this afternoon. We don't need to upset them now. Just let them relax, and have fun today before we have to tell them because Jasmine will really be upset by this news."

Mama shook her head in agreement, but Big Mama knew mama was still upset.

"Michelle, we will all miss her, but at least she'll get to know her family. Cheer up, and come on. Let's eat breakfast," said Big Mama.

Mama and Big Mama walked back into the kitchen. Mama was smiling this time, but I knew she was still upset. We finished breakfast, and put our dishes in the dishwasher. Mama gave all of us a hug. Then she kissed Alley on the head, and went to work. After breakfast, Big Mama told us if we wanted to go back to bed, we could. Alley, my brothers, and I ran upstairs and got back in our beds again. Once I got into bed, I drifted off to sleep fast. I started dreaming about a fairy I was chasing through a thick dark enchanted forest with many pixies flying like fireflies. A toad spoke to me, and said, "If you want to catch the fairy, she is hiding behind that toadstool over there, but I wouldn't want to touch those dirty creatures. They get gold dust all over you."

Then the toad jumped into a mud puddle, and caught a fly with his tongue. I saw the fairy's head peeking at me from behind the toadstool. Then she quickly ducked back behind it. I slowly walked up to her, and cupped my hands around her, and the stool.

When I opened my hands, the little fairy looked at me saying, "Why do you chase me?"

"Little Miss Fairy, you are so beautiful I just had to see you up close," I said.

The fairy blushed. "Since you are such a sweet little girl, I want to show you something, but be prepared. These people you will see will bring you shocking news," she said.

The fairy told me to look at the sky. A cloud turned into a vision of a lady, and man entering into our house. Mrs. Green was with them. The lady and man looked like Mr. and Mrs. Clause. The man had a snow white beard, and thinning white hair on top of his head. His dimpled smile gave way to a jolly laugh. The stocky lady had beautiful cotton white hair, and sparkling blue eyes. The lady's eyes looked very familiar. Maybe in the lady's youth, she might have looked like Alley. Oh no! Could these people be Alley's relatives? I woke up abruptly, and sat up in my bed. Alley was still sleeping when I walked downstairs. I found Big Mama sitting on the couch sipping coffee. Pee-Pee was sitting at her side enjoying a few passing scratches behind his ear from Big Mama's hand.

As I approached the back of the couch, Big Mama never turned around, but she said, "Come in, and sit down Jasmine. I know you know Alley's grandparents have come to take her home."

I was speechless for a moment, but then I sat down on the other couch. Before I could look up into Big Mama's eyes, tears started falling from my eyes like droplets of rain. I was devastated.

"Jasmine, I don't want her to go either, but it would be selfish of us to keep her here. She has a right to know her family, and we are going to help her to do just that."

"But Big Mama, I don't want her to leave. She has become my sister. I will really miss her if she goes away."

"I know Jasmine, but just because she leaves this house don't mean you won't see her again. I will have a talk with Mrs. Green. I heard Alley's grandparents are descent people. I think they will agree to let the two of you visit sometimes, but for now, I want you, and Alley to play together. Y'all have as much fun as you can. Then we'll all sit down together, and tell her before her grandparents arrive."

"Okay," I said.

"Have a talk about what?" Alley asked.

Big Mama and I turned suddenly to see Alley standing at the bottom of the staircase. Big Mama told Alley to come, and sit down on the couch. When she did, my brothers ran down the steps too. Big Mama asked them to sit down with us. She told everyone that Alley's grandparents were coming by to see her today. The news was as shocking to Alley as it was to me. Alley didn't cry, but she was curious. After Big Mama told Alley everything, she told us to go upstairs, and get dressed. Once we all got dressed, we put on our jackets, and went outside to ride our bikes.

Big Mama yelled at us from the front door, "Watch out for the cars, and don't go too far."

We all said, "Yes ma'am."

Then we rode our bikes to the community center. When we got there, a few of the neighborhood boys were playing basketball. My brothers and a few guys started playing basketball from a hoop on the other side of the court. Alley and I went to the game room to play *ping pong*. We couldn't play as well as some of the big kids. Alley and I chased the ball more than we returned it. We played for a little while until we saw a few girls playing *Double Dutch* in the gym. Alley and I immediately stopped play *ping pong*, and ran over to them. The girls let us play, and we jumped rope until we had to go home for lunch. After lunch, we stayed inside, and played inside the house. It started to rain outside, and it was too cool to go back out again. Mama came home early today. She started a fire in the fire place then she went upstairs. Once the fire started burning Pee-Pee walked over, and lay down in front of it closing his eyes. Big Mama was about to tell us a story when the door bell rang. Big Mama got up to answer the door.

"Hey Mike. We didn't expect to see you today," Big Mama said.

"Michelle called me, and asked me to come by. She told me about Alley's grandparents, and I just wanted to be here for her."

Mike walked inside. Big Mama took his jacket, and shut the door behind him. Mama walked down the steps, and stood on her tip toes to kiss Mike on the cheek.

"I'm glad you made it. I know you're busy, but I really appreciate you coming over like this," mama said.

"Anytime, beautiful lady," he replied.

Everyone walked into the den, and sat down on the couch. My brothers, Alley, and I played a game of cards on the floor. Mama, Big Mama, and Mike chatted quietly, but everyone was nervously awaiting Alley's grandparent's arrival. Jordan heard a car pulling into the driveway, so he ran to the window.

"They're here," he said.

Soon there was a knock at the door. Pee-Pee barked.

"I'll get it," mama replied.

Mama walked to the door with Pee-Pee at her side. "Hello Mrs. Green and it's nice to meet you all. Come on in."

Michelle took everyone's jackets, and told them to have a seat in the den. Mama hung their jackets in the hall closet. Then she walked back into the den, and sat beside Mike. Alley's grandparents looked the exact same way as they did in my dream. Mrs. Green spoke first.

"Everyone, I want to introduce you all to Alleys' grandparents. This is Mrs. Betty Dean, and her husband Paul Dean."

Everyone exchanged greetings. Mama introduced everyone else in the room to Alley's grandparents. Pee-Pee walked over to Betty Dean, and licked her hand that hung over the side of the couch.

"Oh, what a pretty dog," Mrs. Dean said. "This dog looks like a show dog. The breeder that you bought him from must have been very selective."

"I didn't buy him," mama replied. "He showed up at my front door one day, and he's been here ever since."

"Really?" Mrs. Dean said with surprise. "Well, you're very lucky to have found him. What is his name?"

"Pee-Pee," mama replied.

Mrs. Dean looked at Mr. Dean who was grinning, and they both laughed.

"Pee-Pee, you are a beautiful dog to have such a funny name," Mrs. Dean said.

She patted Pee-Pee on the head. Then Pee-Pee left Mrs. Dean, and lay on the floor by mama's feet.

"Alexandria honey, come over here and give us a hug. We have been searching for you for so long. I thought we would never find you, but Thank God we did," Mrs. Dean said.

Alley cautiously walked over to them. She knew they were her grandparents, but they also were strangers to her. Alley hugged them both, and then she sat back down on floor.

"How long have been looking for Alley?" Mama asked.

"After our daughter left, we heard from one of her friends at school that she was pregnant. She never told us, but thinking back now, I remember her symptoms. I believe that's why she left with Billy. She knew how we felt about Billy, and I guess she was too scared to tell us the truth," Mrs. Dean said.

"How did you know that Alley was your granddaughter?" Big Mama asked.

"Because of this." Mrs. Dean reached into her purse, and pulled out a picture. She gave the picture to Alley. It was a picture of Alley's mother when she was ten years old.

"You see? I instantly knew you were my granddaughter when I saw your picture in the newspaper."

Alley showed the picture to me. Alley looks a lot like her mother except for her hair. Alley's mother's hair was darker, and she had a few more freckles on her face.

"Alley, let me see," Big Mama said.

Alley gave the picture to Big Mama who showed it to all of us.

"I see why you thought Alley was your granddaughter. She looks exactly like her mother," Big Mama said.

Mama looked at the picture, and handed it back to Mrs. Dean.

"After a few years had passed, we finally gave up hope of ever finding her, but now we've found you. And, it's taken a lot to prove to everyone that we are who we said we are. I had to show your mother's birth certificate to the police before they would call Mrs. Green. Honey, we have done all of this because we have loved you before we ever knew you. I know it might take some time for you to get to know us, and this must be a bit of a shock for you. Also, we wanted to thank y'all for taking care of her. Mrs. Green has told us about all that you have done for her. I will be eternally grateful to you for stepping in, and protecting her from that monster," Mrs. Dean said with tears in her bright blue eyes as her voice began to shake.

"Now Alley, we know you have lived here for a few months now, and it is wonderful that they have accepted you into their family, but we would like to ask you to come, and live with us," Mr. Dean said.

Alley's blue eyes grew large.

"What?" Alley surprisingly said.

"We want you to come, and live with us," Mr. Dean said again. "Alley, you have a cousin that's almost your age, and relatives that want to meet you honey. Now that your mother is gone, you are all that we have left of her. So, what do you say?"

"I don't know what to say," she replied.

"Alley, everyone should know where they've come from," Big Mama replied.

"Will I ever see y'all again?" Alley asked.

"Yes honey. You are going to stay in the same school for now, and you can visit with everyone on the weekends if that's okay?" Mrs. Dean asked.

"Of course," Big Mama agreed. "Alley is apart of this family now. Anytime she wants to come over, just let us know, and I'll even come over to get her."

"Do I have to leave now?" Alley asked.

"No, no honey. That's another thing we wanted to talk to y'all about," Mrs. Dean said. "Alexandria's room won't be ready for at least another two weeks. We are renovating your mother's old room. Honey, you will love it, but I wanted to ask y'all if it would be okay for me and my husband to come by, and visit with y'all during that time. I think this will give Alley a chance to get to know me and Paul a little better. Also, when it is finished, we want everyone to come over, and see it."

"We would love too, and you can come by here anytime," Big Mama replied.

"We would like to get to know y'all too. The kids will be out of school for the rest of this week, but they have to go back to school on Monday. Why don't you come by tomorrow. Would that be okay with y'all?"

"That sounds great. I would love too. Well, we should be going now," Mrs. Dean said.

Everyone stood up and walked to the front door.

"Mrs. Thomas and Mrs. Patterson, I think we'll be seeing a lot of each other now that Alexandria has two families," said Mr. Dean.

"Well, I hope so," Big Mama said.

"Alexandria, can we have a hug before we go?" Mrs. Dean asked.

Alley hugged Mrs. Dean and Mr. Dean around the waist and then they left.

The next day Mrs. Dean came by to see us. Big Mama and Mrs. Dean talked, and laughed over a cup of coffee. Mrs. Dean read a book to Alley and me. Then she played a game of cards with us. After Mrs. Dean ate lunch with us, she said she had to go home, but she would be back every day this week. She was true to word too. Mrs. Dean came by every day except for Sunday.

On Saturday, Mrs. Dean took us ice skating. Mr. Dean came too, but he didn't skate. Mrs. Dean skates very well. Alley caught on pretty quickly too. I had to hold onto the side of the wall, but my brothers just fell. Every time they got up they fell down. Jordan tried to help Jonathan up, and they fell on top of each other. Finally, Mr. Dean made them sit down on the bench before they hurt themselves. I finally figured out how to balance myself on the skates, and I let go of the wall. Alley grabbed my hand, and we skated off together. I really had a good time with Mrs. Dean. She is so funny too. It was fun skating with Mrs. Dean and Alley, but I don't want to ice skate anymore. Once we got off the ice, my feet ached.

The first week back at school was a very long one. Mrs. Dean came by for dinner once this week, but that was the only time we saw them this week. By Thursday Big Mama had packed most of Alley's things. The reality of her leaving had suddenly become real to me. The thought of her leaving made me sad.

Even though the week was slow, Saturday got here fast. Mama and Big Mama packed all of Alley's belonging into the van except for her bike. Big Mama said she would be back next weekend, and she needed something to ride on when she is here with us. Once we all got into the van, mama drove away.

We drove over the mountain to a beautiful woodland neighborhood. The houses in this neighborhood were huge. Some of the houses looked like castles from a fairy tale. The trees cast shadows over the street, and neighbors were jogging along the nice cool shady sidewalks. Mama turned onto a long driveway that proceeded to a grand old brick house with two large circular staircases that lead up to the upstairs balcony. The front entrance was under the balcony that was held up by two large off white pillars. Mama parked on the circular driveway, and we all got out. We walked down the entrance way that was lined with beautiful flowers. The circular front steps led us up to the wooden and cut stained glass double doors. Large windows covered the front of the beautiful house. Mama rung the doorbell, and a young maid answered the door.

"Afternoon," the maid said. "We were expecting you. Come in, and follow me."

Mama and Big Mama ogled, and pointed at the beautiful foyer. There was a large water fountain and a huge marbled table in the middle of the foyer. The maid led everyone to the den where Mr. and Mrs. Dean were sitting. The den was huge, and brightly lit. There were a few bookcases, and family mementos on the walls. A warm glowing fire in the fire place kept the room nice, and cozy. A beautiful Persian rug was on the floor in front of the fire place surrounded by two large rich leather sofas, and two over stuffed chairs where Mr. and Mrs. Dean were sitting. The den was filled with beautiful glass, and wooden furniture. The Deans stood up when we walked in.

"Well, hey y'all. You made it. Kids y'all come over here, and give me a hug." Mrs. Dean said.

We all ran over to Mrs. Dean and hugged her.

"Y'all have a seat," she said.

Everyone sat down on the beautiful leather sofa, and chairs.

"Was it hard to find this place?" She asked.

"Oh no. We came right to it," mama said. "Betty, your house is beautiful."

"Well, Paul here found this old house. When we first moved in here, it was a mess. Ceiling tiles were falling off, and plaster was all over the place. It took us ten years to fully restore this house."

"Who is that in the picture?" Alley asked.

"Oh, that's your aunt Amanda. She is your mother's sister. The picture over there of the girl, and boy are her kids, Tracy and Chad," Mrs. Dean said. "The picture on the bookcase is a picture of your uncle Kenny, and his family. Kenny's wife and your aunt's name is Barbara. The two boys in the picture are your cousins Jason and Chris. They live in Illinois, but your aunt Amanda will be here later this afternoon. Say, would y'all like to see the rest of the house?"

"Sure," we all said.

"Well, come on," replied Mrs. Dean.

Mr. Dean laid back in the leather recliner, and watched football on the large flat screen TV while we toured the house. Mrs. Dean took us up a curved staircase with a mahogany railing. The walls along the hall had beautiful raised panel wooden frames, and pictures of Alley's ancestors. Mrs. Dean took us to several different rooms upstairs, and told us all about the repair work that was done on each of them. The last room upstairs we came to was Alley's room. Mrs. Dean opened the door, and Alley walked into it first. Her blue eyes grew to the size of large marbles when she saw it.

"Wow! Alley, your room is as big as my brothers, and my room combined," I said.

Alley's room was huge. There was a big canopy bed between two large windows. The color of her bedding was cream with a toile print of pale pink scenes from the old English story of "*Alice and Wonderland.*" The walls were painted in the same pale pink color with a cream colored chair rails, and raised wooded panels. There was a second daybed by the window on the other side of the room in the same fabric with stuffed bunnies on it. Her dresser and night stands were painted cream, and trimmed in a pale pink. Two bookcases lined either side of the desk were Alley had her own laptop computer. On the other side of the room, were two cream colored upholstered arm chairs with a pale pink rope trimmed by the TV cabinet. Everyone entered the room in amazement.

"This is just beautiful," Big Mama said. "Betty, you have done a wonderful job."

Alley walked to the dresser, and picked up a picture. "Grandma, is this a picture of my mother?" She asked.

"Yes. I thought you might like to have it here. This was your mother's old room, and I just wanted to keep a piece of her in here for you."

Alley hugged her grandmother, and said, "Thank you."

As everyone walked downstairs to the sun room in the back of the house, Jordan and Jonathan said, wow, when they saw the large pool, and fountain.

"Boys, y'all are going to have to see me this summer so we can take a dip in that pool. Now, I hope y'all don't have to go too soon. I wanted my daughter to meet y'all. I thought we could have lunch together out here."

"Thank you," mama said.

"Great!" Mrs. Dean pushed the intercom button on the wall, and called the maid.

"Maria, we will have lunch in the sun room," she said.

"Yes ma'am," the maid replied.

Amongst the flowers and plants in the sun room, there stood a large cage with two large white cockatoos inside.

I walked over to the large bird cage, and said, "What a pretty bird."

"Pretty bird! Pretty bird! Quack!" The bird squawked. I jumped back.

"Oh honey, that's just Birdy. He won't hurt a fly. I've had him for years now," Mrs. Dean said.

"Does the other one talk too?" I asked.

"Oh yeah. Sometimes they talk for hours to each other. We have to put a blanket over their cage just to keep them quiet. Oh good. The food is here."

We all sat down around a large round table to eat. Maria put the food in the middle of the table with a pitcher of ice tea. Once we were finished eating, we went back into the den where Mr. Dean had fallen asleep. He woke up quickly when we entered the room. When we all sat down, Alley's aunt and cousins entered the room. Amanda gave her mother and father a hug then greeted everyone else. Mrs. Dean introduced us to everyone. Tracy, Alley's cousin, was a shy little girl with blond hair. She was the same age as Alley and me. Her brother Chad was younger, and shorter than Tracy. He had brown hair and freckles. He was also missing a tooth, but that didn't stop him from talking. He saw my brothers, and said, "Wow, y'all look just alike."

"That's because we are twins," Jordan said.

"Hey guys, do you want to play cards with me?" Chad asked.

"Yeah! Jordan and Jonathan said in unison.

Chad continued to talk the whole time they played cards. Tracy took Alley and me to Alley's new room where we played with the stuffed bunnies on her bed.

"Grandma bought you a video game. Do you want to play?" Tracy asked.

"Sure!" We said.

Tracy opened the small cabinet, and plugged the game into the TV. We played the game for about an hour before the maid told us it was time to go. Alley and Tracy walked downstairs with me.

"It's going to be strange not seeing you at home anymore," I said to Alley.

"I know," she replied.

"Well, I'll still see you at school," Jasmine said sadly.

"Yah. Are you still coming over to my house this weekend?" I asked.

Alley looked up at Mr. and Mrs. Dean. "Will I get to see them this weekend?" She asked.

"Oh yes, sugar. You can see them anytime you want," replied Mrs. Dean.

"Mama, what about Alley's things," I asked.

"The maids got them out of the van already."

"Oh, okay," I replied.

Alley and I hugged. Then Alley hugged everyone else in my family including my two brothers. Finally, mama said we have to go. Alley waved to us from the door as we drove away. It was quiet when I got back in the van.

My brothers named all the cars on the street saying, "That's mine! That's mine!"

Suddenly, I felt all alone again with two annoying brothers. I looked at them playing, and pointing, I wondered about Alley.

I turned to Big Mama, and said, "Big Mama, do you think they'll be nice to her?" I asked.

"Oh yeah, honey. At first, they are going to spoil her rotten. Once Alley gets settled in, she will just be another part of their family, but remember this, Jasmine. We can't be selfish."

"Yes ma'am," I said.

The rest of the journey home I remained quiet. That afternoon Plump came over to play with me. I told her about Alley's grandparent's big house, and about her cousins. Plump just sat there, and listened to me. This was the first time Plump has ever just sat there, and listened to what I had to say without completely taking over my conversation. I could really talk to her now. Suddenly, I didn't feel so alone anymore. Plump and I played until she had to go home.

On Monday, we had to get up early for school, and none of us wanted to go. Big Mama took us to school as mama went off to work. School was pretty normal except when I saw Alley stomping on Toads foot. He had stuck his foot out again to trip Alley, but this time she stomped his foot as hard as she could. While he wailed in pain, I ran over to Alley, and gave her a hug. We left before Toad got up. Seeing her again made the rest of my day much brighter. She was happier too. She wore a new locket around her neck today. When I asked her about it, she opened it, and showed me the picture of her grandparents on the right side of the locket, and a picture of her mother on the left. She told me her grandmother gave it to her yesterday. I understood now that Alley's family was complete. She had finally found people who were related to her that loved her.

It was odd seeing Alley leaving with her grandparents, but at least now I knew she was happy. Alley and her grandmother came by our house on Saturday. We played like she had never left. Alley's grandmother drank tea with Big Mama, and talked to her most of the afternoon before she left Alley with us. Big Mama and Mrs. Dean were becoming fast friends. When Mrs. Dean came by to pick up Alley the next day, she decided to stay for dinner. I thought to myself that not only had Big Mama found a new friend, but now Alley has two families that love her. What can be better than that?

Chapter 31
Valentine

This year Valentine's Day was on a Tuesday, and love was in the air. All around the city the shops were decorated in red hearts, and roses. The week before Valentine's Day was a busy one for Michelle. She was preparing for another party at the center. The students decorated the lobby and recreational area with paper hearts, and cherubs. They put a bouquet of roses on the lobby's desk. Paper red and white garland was draped over the top of the front doorway, and over the edge of the front desk. Michelle put out little bowls of chocolate candy on the counters, and tables for the patients. There was even sugar free candy for the patients that couldn't eat regular candy. Michelle was tired when she left the center today. When she got home, she noticed Trey's car in the driveway. She was a little curious to know why his car was here, but she was too tired to care. She walked into the den to see Lisa sitting at the kitchen table talking to Big Mama. As Michelle turned the corner to walk into the kitchen, she saw Lisa giving something to Big Mama, but she couldn't tell what it actually was. When Lisa saw Michelle entering the kitchen, she turned towards her immediately.

"Hey Michelle!" How was work today?" Lisa asked.

"Okay," Michelle replied. "What are y'all up to?"

Big Mama just smiled.

"Hey Michelle, why don't we go into the den," Lisa said. "We haven't talked in a long while."

"Okay." Michelle replied.

Lisa struggled as she tried to get out of the chair. Her swollen belly made it difficult for her to maneuver around the table. She finally got out of the chair, and waddled over to the couch.

"Lisa, how have you been?" Michelle asked.

"I've been getting bigger," she replied.

"I can see that. The baby is growing. Can you feel it kicking you now?"

"Can I," Lisa replied. "This baby kicks so hard you can see my shirt move."

Michelle laughed. "I remember when I was carrying my two boys. I thought they were fighting in there. Hey, where are my kids anyway?" Michelle asked.

Big Mama shouted from the kitchen, "They're upstairs playing a video game."

"Oh, okay. Well Lisa, I'm glad you came to see us. I was about to ask Mike about you and Trey. How is Trey doing anyway?"

"Oh, he's off on some kind of mission. He will be back in two weeks he says. I told him that he better be home for his child's birth, or I was going to give him some labor pains, if you know what I mean."

Michelle laughed.

"So, have you changed your mind about becoming my sister in-law?" Lisa asked with a raised brow.

Michelle didn't say anything at first. Then she said, "I just need a little time."

"Take as much time as you need, but you are apart of our family now, and we won't have another."

Michelle really didn't want to talk about her relationship with Mike, so she tried to change the subject.

"Lisa, do you and Trey know what sex the baby is going to be, or do you want to be surprised?"

"Oh Michelle, we don't need anymore surprises. It's a girl. Mike is letting us fix up the nursery for our baby."

"That's sweet of him," Michelle said.

"Well, for a while the baby will stay downstairs with us. I can't imagine myself going up, and down those steps for those four a.m. feedings. So, tell me something," Lisa said with a pause. "What do you and Mike have planned for this weekend?"

"I'm really not sure," Michelle replied.

"If I know Mike, he's going to surprise you because that's the kind of man he is. Whatever y'all decide to do, just have a good time, and give me the details," Lisa said with a laugh.

Michelle grinned.

"Look, I better go." Lisa said.

"Oh Lisa. You're not going to stay for dinner?" Michelle asked.

"No. no. Big Mama has feed me enough already. Why else would I be in your kitchen. Come on. Walk me to the door."

Lisa and Michelle stood up to walk to the door. Lisa turned to say goodbye to Big Mama. Then she left. Michelle thought about Valentine's

Day, and the surprise Mike was planning for her. Then she realized that she hadn't gotten Mike anything.

Michelle walked back into the kitchen, and said, "Mom, what do you think I should give Mike for Valentine's Day?"

Big Mama thought for a moment and then she said, "A watch."

"Why a watch, mom?"

"Michelle, have you seen Mike's watch? He has one of those old digital watches that he wears everywhere. You can barely see the face on that watch with all of the scratches on it. I think he works in it too. He needs a watch that is classy, and durable."

"Mom, that's not a bad idea. I'll go look for one tomorrow. Do you need any help with dinner?"

"No baby," Big Mama replied. "It's almost ready."

"Okay," Michelle replied. "I'm going upstairs to say hey to the kids, and change. I'll be back in a moment."

"Oh Michelle, remember that the kid's are staying with Mrs. Dean this weekend. Alley's birthday is this weekend," Big Mama said.

"Oh, that's right. I'll make sure to buy her something too."

Then Michelle went upstairs to greet the kids. They were playing a video game when Michelle entered the boy's room. She greeted the kids, and they returned her greeting with a very monotone hello. None of them wanted to stop playing the game long enough to give her a proper greeting. Michelle left the room, and decided to go to her room to take a shower. When she got out of the shower, she got dressed, and walked downstairs to eat dinner. The kids were friendlier at the table than they were upstairs. After dinner, Michelle played a game with the children until they all went to bed.

The next day after work, Michelle went to the mall. She bought Alley the one thing she knew Alley would love to have, a gumball machine. It was a beautiful old fashion metal, and glass machine. Michelle thought that she would enjoy the gum as well as learn to save money too. Michelle also bought Alley a beautiful dress. Now, buying for Alley was easy because she knew what Alley liked, but buying a gift for Mike was a little more complicated. Michelle took Big Mama's advice to buy Mike a watch, but she didn't say what kind to buy. She looked at the different styles. Some of them were very casual while others were very elegant. She didn't want to give him something that would just stay in the bottom of his drawer. Michelle continued to look until she found a watch that was just right. She spotted a beautiful silver watch with a black shinny face.

"Ma'am, are you looking for something for that special someone?" The salesman at the counter asked.

"Yes," Michelle replied. "Tell me about the features of this watch."

The clerk pointed out, and demonstrated the many features of the watch. He told Michelle the watch was water proof too.

"Wow! I'll take it," Michelle said.

"What would you like to have engraved on the back?" The salesman asked.

"I can have it engraved too?" Happily, surprised she asked.

"Sure. What would you like for it to say?" Michelle thought for a moment and then she said, "Do you have a piece of paper?"

"Yes."

The salesman handed her a piece of paper and Michelle wrote: *Toujours et pour toujours mon amour* on the paper, and handed it to the salesman.

The clerk looked at the note, then he looked at Michelle, and said, "Ma'am, what kind of language is that?"

"It's French, and believe me, he will understand."

"Okay," replied the salesman. The man gave Michelle a strange look, and took the watch to the back with the paper. While Michelle waited for the watch, her phone rang.

"Hello."

"Hi beautiful. Whatcha up to?" Mike asked.

"Just shopping."

"Well, this Saturday is the last weekend before Valentine's Day. So, do you want to go out with me?"

"Of course, but Valentine's Day is on Tuesday," She replied.

"I know, but you are going to have a party at the center so you will probably be too tired to go out. Besides, I have this weekend off, so we can be together all day, or all night if necessary."

"Really, will it take all night?" Michelle asked curiously.

"It might."

"Now, you've peeked my curiosity, Mike."

"Good," Mike said. "Why don't I pick you up at five o'clock Saturday afternoon?"

"I'll be waiting," replied Michelle

"See you then pretty lady."

"Okay, bye." Then she hung up the phone. Michelle thought about Mike's words, 'all night if necessary.' She wondered what he meant by this.

Her thoughts were abruptly interrupted when the clerk said, "Ma'am, your watch is ready. He showed Michelle the engraving, and she loved it. She paid for the watch, and took the gifts upstairs to be gift wrapped.

*****

Friday when Michelle got to work, she put her purse in the office locker, and walked back to the recreational area to help LaShundra prepare breakfast. When she walked into the recreational area, she was met by Sharon.

"Sharon, what are you doing here this early?" Michelle asked.

"Michelle, Mike asked me to come in this morning for you. He wanted me to give you this." Sharon gave Michelle an envelope.

"Well, open it," she said.

Michelle opened the envelope that had a coupon inside for a day at *Valley Spa.*

"Read it Michelle," Sharon demanded.

"Okay."

"To my beautiful lady,

I know how hard you work, so this day is for you. My gift for you is a day of relaxation. You deserve it honey.

Happy Valentine's Day,
Mike."

"Oh, how sweet. Michelle, this man is as romantic as he is beautiful. Girl, how did you get so lucky?" Sharon asked.

"Well, I'm not that lucky. I can't go," Michelle replied.

"What do you mean you can't go?"

"Sharon, I can't leave you all with all this work."

"You're not. LaShundra!"

Sharon called her from the kitchen. LaShundra walked out of the kitchen with a very shy and petite black girl.

"You see Michelle, I asked LaShundra if she knew anybody who wanted to make some extra money today, and Brittany agreed to help us."

Michelle greeted Brittany, and thanked her for coming in on such a short notice and she offered her a job if she wanted it.

"So, you see Michelle, you have no excuses, and you better go now," Sharon said.

"Now?" Michelle asked.

"Yes now, or Mike will have my hide if you don't, so have a good time."

"Thank you, Sharon."

The two friends hugged. Then Michelle left the center and drove to the Southside of town to a huge beautiful spa. When she walked towards the spa, there were two waterfalls on either side of glass door entrance way. Michelle walked up the sandy stone steps passed the Roman columns to the lobby's foyer. There were lots of tall ferns, and plantings in the lobby. Soft rhythmic music played as Michelle walked up to the front counter.

Michelle handed the coupon to the lady at the counter, and the lady said, "Well, it looks like someone has ordered a very special package for you today. Come with me."

Michelle followed the lady to a locker room where she changed out of her clothes, and she put on a long white robe. Once Michelle locked up her belongings, she followed the lady to a mineral bath. After the bath, Michelle received several treatments such as a full body massage with hot stones, pedicure, manicure, and her hair styled. When Michelle got home, she felt like a new woman. She walked inside the house, and everyone cheered and gasped.

"Michelle, you look wonderful! Your hair is beautiful." Big Mama said.

"Mike surprised me with a day at that beautiful spa."

"Well, you look great," Big Mama said.

"Thank you," she replied.

"Mama, are you going somewhere," Jasmine asked.

"Yes. I'm going to take mom out to dinner after Mrs. Dean comes to pick y'all up."

All the kids moaned, and complained.

"You guys will have so much food at Mrs. Dean's house that you won't need, or want to go to dinner with us. Y'all have a good time at the party, and let mom and I have a good time tonight."

Michelle turned and walked upstairs.

"Michelle, where are you going?" Big Mama asked.

"I'm going upstairs to call Mike, and thank him."

Michelle ran upstairs to her room, and shut the door. She grabbed the cordless phone, and called Mike.

"Hey you," Michelle said to Mike on the phone

"Well, hello beautiful. How was the spa?" Mike asked.

"It was great. I was so relaxed when I drove home, I almost fell asleep."

"Well, we can't have that," Mike said. "Tomorrow will be a little more exciting for you."

"Really? Mike, what kind of twisted surprise are you planning for me tomorrow?"

"You will see," he said impishly, "so, don't be late."

"Okay. Would you like to eat dinner with us tonight?" Michelle asked. "It's my treat."

"I can't," Mike replied. "My brother came back earlier, and I promised him that I would go out with him tonight. I've neglected him too much Michelle. I can't say no now."

"Okay. Mike, you go with Trey, and I'll see you tomorrow. Oh damn!"

"What's wrong?" Mike asked.

"The doorbell rang. The Dean's are here for the children."

"That's okay," Mike replied. "I'll see you tomorrow."

"All right, Goodnight darling," she said. Michelle smiled as she hung up the phone. She walked downstairs to see Alley, Mrs. Dean, and Mr. Dean at the bottom of the steps.

"Hey, you look like a movie star," Mrs. Dean said.

Michelle walked down the steps, and hugged the Deans and Alley.

"Thank you," she said. "Mike gave me a day at the spa for Valentine's Day."

"Well, honey you hold on to that one. He's a keeper," replied Mrs. Dean. "Kids, do y'all have everything?"

"Yes," Jasmine and her brothers said in unison.

"Good."

"Now Mrs. Dean, the boys can be a little rambunctious, but we told them to be on their best behavior," Big Mama said.

"Oh, I'm sure they will be perfect little angels," Mrs. Dean said with a smile. "Well, now y'all come on. Let's get this party started. Y'all tell your mama and Big Mama goodbye."

All the kids waved goodbye as they started to walk outside of the front door when Michelle stopped them.

"Oh, Alley don't forget your gifts," mama said as she handed her the big birthday bag.

They all waved goodbye to mama and Big Mama at the front door, and then they left.

"Mom, I believe Mrs. Dean will have her hands full this weekend," Michelle said.

"I know," Big Mama replied with a smile. "Let's just hope they'll be on their best behavior this weekend like they promised me."

"Come on mom. Let's get our purses, and go eat," replied Michelle.

Michelle and Big Mama walked back inside the house, and shut the door.

*****

Saturday evening Michelle was excited about her date with Mike. She bought a nice black dress with a long jacket for tonight. The dress was comfortable, but it was sexy too. The plunging neckline and fitted dress hugged her curves in all the right places. She didn't want her hair in a style that was too fussy tonight, so she fixed it in the same smooth style it was in when she left the spa. Michelle checked herself out in the mirror again, and knew she was looking pretty good. She grabbed her purse and Mike's gift then she walked downstairs to the kitchen to find Big Mama and Mr. Davis sitting at the table.

"Wow! Look at you. Sexy! Sexy!" Big Mama said.

"Michelle, you look great," said Mr. Davis.

"Thanks. I thought Mike would be here already. He told me not to be late. Now he's late. It's five minutes after five, and he's not here," Michelle said.

"Oh, be patient Michelle. He'll be here in a moment," Big Mama said. "So, what are y'all going to do tonight?"

"I really don't know," Michelle said honestly. "Mike was very secretive."

Big Mama and Mr. Davis looked at each other with a raised eye brow, and slight grin on their faces.

"Kind of mysterious if you ask me," Mr. Davis said.

"Me too Ben," Big Mama replied.

"Oh wait, I think I hear a car outside." Michelle walked to the window in the den, and looked outside. Then she stepped back, and put her hand over her mouth. When she could speak again, she said, "There is a limo outside!"

She turned around to see Pee-Pee carrying an envelope in his mouth. Michelle took the envelope from the dog and opened it.

"Read it Michelle. What does it say," Big Mama asked. "Well, if it's not too personal that is."

"It's not," she replied. "The letter says:"

> *"Man's best friend is a dog indeed, but outside awaits a limo with much more speed. You will arrive by limo to the lake where we walked hand and hand on our very first date. Another clue awaits you under the gazebo on the bench where we kissed. It's under the box of chocolates, you just can't miss."*

The poem brought a gentle smile to Michelle's face then she realized something. "Mom, I think it a scavenger hunt." The thought of a hunt intrigued Michelle.

"That's the surprise?" Big Mama asked.

Michelle laughed. "Yep, but what's at the end of this hunt?" Michelle said curiously.

"I don't know, but knowing Mike it will be something special," Big Mama replied.

Mr. Davis looked at Michelle, and said, "Back in my day, we were more up front about our dating. We walked to the young lady's front door, and gave her a box of candy, or flowers. We didn't make her hunt for it."

"Oh, pipe down Ben. This is romantic. Go on Michelle. He's waiting for you."

"Mom, you wouldn't have had anything to do with this would you?" Michelle asked suspiciously.

"What do you mean?"

"Come on mom. I know Mike didn't give this letter to Pee-Pee."

"Okay Michelle," Big Mama admitted. "The day Lisa came by she told me about the limo, and gave me the note. She wanted me to tape it to

Pee-Pee's collar, but that dog follows you everywhere so I knew he would bring it to you."

"Well, you're a good dog Pee-Pee," Michelle said patting the dog's head.

"Michelle, he's waiting." Big Mama insisted.

"Oh yeah. Bye y'all," replied Michelle.

"Have a good time darling," Big Mama said.

"Don't do what I can't do either," Mr. Davis replied.

Michelle grinned as she left the house.

"Oh Ben, you're a bad boy," Big Mama said with a grin.

When Michelle got to the limousine, she thought she would find Mike there, but he wasn't.

The chauffer opened the door for Michelle, and said, "Sorry for the delay ma'am. There was traffic."

"That's okay," she replied. "We'd better go."

The chauffer shut the door after Michelle got into the limo, and then he drove away. There was a bottle of champagne, and some champagne in a crystal glass waiting for her inside the limo. She took a sip, and it was really good too. Michelle relaxed, and sipped on more champagne until the driver stopped at the park's entrance. The chauffer got out of the limousine, and opened the passenger door for her.

"Is he here?" She asked.

"Who ma'am?" The chauffer asked curiously.

"Mike Raimond," she replied.

"No ma'am, but he asked me to bring you here."

"Okay," Michelle replied, "but don't leave me."

"Yes ma'am. I'll wait here until you come back."

The chauffer held out his hand to help Michelle out of the limousine. She left her purse and Mike's gift inside the limo while she walked into the park. Michelle walked down the pathway to the runner's trail were runners passed her as she walked by. The sky was clear, but hues of yellow and orange lined the sky as the sun began to set. The air outside was getting cooler and Michelle was glad she wore her high hill black boots as she wrapped her dress coat around her waist. She looked around the park to see if Mike was there, but he was no where to be found.

"Well, he said in the letter to go to the bench under the gazebo, so I guess that's were I'll go," Michelle said to herself.

Michelle passed a few more joggers, and ducks that were begging for bread crumbs from passing strangers. When she approached the bench where she sat on her first date with Mike, she saw a beautiful wrapped box of assorted chocolate truffles. Michele picked up the pretty red box with the large white bow on top of it to find another envelope. She sat down on the bench, and put the box beside her. Then she opened the envelope. Even though she was alone on the bench, she read the letter out loud.

> *"Sweets for the sweetie, just for you my dear, but beware of clowns that might appear. Don't be frightened by this clowning around, another surprise awaits you by that rock that I found. Upon this rock by the bridge, you will see a red rose that was placed there for you, from me."*

Michelle stood up. She grabbed the box, and the letter. She walked to the bridge, and she smiled when she saw the single red rose on top of the large boulder. When she got close enough to grab it, a clown jumped from behind the rock. Michelle screamed, and jumped back.

The clown giggled, and said, "Sorry to scare you dear lady, but I fell asleep back there waiting for you."

"You were waiting for me?" Michelle asked.

"Why yes! I'm Red Nose the Clown, and I can really get on down. Let me show you a little something."

The clown pushed a button on his radio, and started to break dance. The joggers in the park slowed down, or just stopped to watch the clown. When the clown stopped break dancing, he stopped the music, and bowed to the crowd. The joggers clapped, and Michelle burst out into laughter. The clown picked up the rose, and handed it to her.

"Dear lady, you forgot your rose," the clown said.

Michelle took the rose, and pressed the petals to her nose. Then the clown burst into a loud silly laughter.

"Dancing is not all the Red Nose Clown can do in the *Red Nose Clown show*. I can do magic tricks too."

The clown made a coin disappear from his hand, and reappear behind Michelle's ear. He asked her if she needed a tissue, and before she answered him, he pulled multicolored scarves from his sleeve. Then the clown handed Michelle another envelope from his pocket.

"Here, this is for you," the Red Nose Clown said with a silly laugh. Michelle opened the letter, and read it out loud.

"A single red rose will never do. There must be eleven more this clown has for you. So, close your eyes, and count to three. Another surprise awaits you, from me."

"Well, my lady, close your eyes," the clown said.

Michelle grinned, and said, "Okay. One, two, three."

When she opened her eyes, the clown had a long clear plastic box of red roses for her. Michelle gasped and held her hands out for the flowers.

She grabbed the flower from the clown, and the clown said, "Open the box. There is a note inside."

"Okay. Will you hold this?" She asked.

She gave the clown the box of truffles, the single flower, and the other poems to him. Then she put the box of flowers on the large bolder, and opened it. She took the letter out, and read it aloud.

"Clowns! Clowns! Stop clowning around! A French dinner is waiting for you downtown. So, get in the limo, and away from this clown. Dinner is waiting and a night on the town. I can't wait to see you. I can't wait anymore, so come to dinner my darling.
Mon amour."

"How sweet," Michelle said.

"How sappy. Well, you better go now. Yes go!" The clown said.

Michelle gathered up her flowers, chocolates, and poems. Then she ran back to the limo. The chauffer opened the door for Michelle and closed it behind her. Once she was inside the limousine, the chauffer drove away. Michelle put the poems and single rose in the box with the other roses. Then she took another sip of the champagne. She put her head back, and let the driver drive her to her next unknown surprise. Twenty minutes later the limo stopped in front of a grand old hotel downtown. The valet opened the passenger door, and extended his hand to her. Michelle got out of the limo grabbing her purse, and Mike's gift.

"Wait! Wait!" Michelle said. "My flowers are in there."

"I'll get them for you," the valet said.

"The candy too," Michelle replied.

"Yes ma'am." The valet reached into the back seat of the limo. He grabbed Michelle's gifts, and walked through the lobby's rotating glass and brass front door behind her. The floor of the grand hotel lobby was made of white marble. Large ferns and plants surrounded the lobby's seating area. Passed the elevators Michelle saw Mike sitting by the front desk wearing a nicely fitted black tuxedo. He stood up when Michelle walked in. His dimpled smile just seemed to melt her heart when she saw him. Michelle ran over to him and gave him a hug. Not only did he look good, but he smelled good too.

"Hello handsome. I feel slightly under dressed. Look at you. You're gorgeous," Michelle said.

"Thank you, beautiful lady. I'm starving too. Let's go eat," Mike replied.

"Oh Mike," Michelle said. "What about my flowers, and candy?"

"It's okay. I'll ask the valet to take them to my room."

Mike walked over to the valet and gave him the room number. He asked him to take them upstairs. Then Mike gave him a tip.

"Come on lovely lady. Dinner waits."

Mike extended his arm, and Michelle quickly latched onto it. They walked across a beautiful bridge surrounded by tropical plants, and a Koi lagoon that ran underneath the bridge. Soft string music was playing behind Michelle and Mike by a small string quartet as they sat at an intimate table in the corner.

"Mike, I have to say you've surprised me. Mom told me how you got my dog involved, and who knew you were such a poet. But, a break-dancing clown. I thought I was going to have to take a pill," Michelle said with a laugh. "I don't think I've ever laughed so hard."

Mike laughed, and said, "I didn't know he was going to break dance."

"Mike, you've done so much for me I just want to give you something. I know it's not much compared to the spa, and the scavenger hunt, but I wanted to give you something from my heart."

Michelle handed Mike a little golden gift bag. Mike took the little wrapped box out of the bag, and opened it up.

"This is nice Michelle."

"Take it out."

Mike took the watch out of the box, and he started to put it on when Michelle stopped him.

"No, no Mike. Read it," replied Michelle.

Mike turned the watch over, and read the engraving silently. Soon Michelle could see his dimpled smile emerging.

"Mike, read it out loud."

He looked up at Michelle, and said, "Always and forever my love."

"Do you like it?" She asked.

"I love it."

Mike took the watch he had on his wrist off, and put the new one on.

"Mike, you have done so much for me. I really can't thank you enough."

"You deserve it Michelle, and the day is not over."

"There's more?" She said with curiosity.

"Much more, but for now let me order us some wine." Mike waved to the waiter to come over to their table. The waiter started passing out the menus as he boasted about the house specialties. When the waiter opened the wine list, he spoke in French. Mike spoke back to him in French. The two men carried on speaking in French to one another as if they were long lost foreign friends. The only words Michelle could understand from their conversation were Louisiana, and Canada. Mike abruptly stopped speaking in French and turned to Michelle. Then he started to speak in English again.

"Michelle, would you like dry, or a sweet wine?" He asked.

"Sweet," she replied.

Mike turned back to the waiter, and continued to speck in French. Then he stopped again to ask Michelle if she wanted to order now. She said yes. Mike gave the waiter their orders and the menus back.

"Mike, what did you say to him?"

"Oh, I just asked him where he was from because he speaks French very well. He said he was from Canada, but his parents are originally from France. He heard my accent, and said I must be from Louisiana. Now, what would make him say something like that?" Mike asked with a grin.

"Well, you can't hide your accent, Mike."

"I guess not. Later on, after dinner, I want to show you something."

"All right," Michelle replied.

They chatted for a short while until their dinners arrived. Michelle and Mike both had steak dinners. Michelle refused the dessert tray because she was just too full. After dinner, they walked over the bridge hand in hand to get a better view of the Koi. Mike caught Michelle by surprise when he lifted her chin with his finger to kiss her. A couple giggled as they walked passed them. Michelle stopped kissing Mike abruptly when she caught a glimpse of the woman smiling at her. Michelle shyly smiled back at the lady as she walked by.

"Michelle, I want to show you something now, so follow me."

"Okay" she replied.

Michelle and Mike walked hand in hand to the elevator. They rode the elevator to the top floor. Once they exit the elevator, they walked a short distant to a suite. Michelle stopped outside the door, and looked up at Mike.

"Is this the end of this scavenger hunt you've sent me on?" She asked.

"Yes, but I want you to see the view," Mike said with a smile. "Come on."

Chapter 32
New Beginnings

Mike opened the door to a huge suite. There was a seating area near the balcony, and a large king size bed across from a big flat screen TV. The bathroom had a separate shower stall, and whirlpool tub. There was a large dinning room table with the flowers, candy, champagne, and large basket on it next to a fully stocked bar and refrigerator. Mike passed by the table to open the patio curtains to reveal the spectacular view of the city.

"Do you like it?" He asked.

When Michelle walked into the room she was amazed by the view. Then she walked to the patio doors.

"It's beautiful," she replied.

Mike walked behind Michelle, and put his arms around her waist. Michelle became a little nervous, and excited about the thought of being with Mike for the first time.

"Are you nervous?" He asked.

"I guess I am a little," she admitted.

Mike kissed the back of Michelle's neck sending familiar tiny shivers down her spine.

"Michelle, when I said that I love you, that's what I meant. I don't want to just have sex with you. I want to make love to you over, and over again. There is no need to be nervous around me. I want you to feel comfortable enough around me to do anything you want to do, and I'll stop at anytime you want me to."

Michelle turned around, and looked up into Mike's big beautiful eyes with a mischievous smile.

"Anything?" She asked.

"Yes, but I want you to see this first." Mike grabbed Michelle's hand, and walked her over to the table.

"Mike, what is this?"

"Take a look," he replied.

Michelle picked up the basket, and looked at it a little closer.

"Mike, there are flavored condoms, lubricants, and massage oils in there. What's this? Bath salt for sore muscles?" Michelle laughed.

"I also have this," Mike said and he handed Michelle a piece of paper. Michelle read it.

"Mike, is this a STD test?"

"Yes," Mike said with a grin.

Michelle laughed even louder. "Man, you are too much."

"Well, I know how you felt about this kind of stuff, and I don't want you to worry. I am very healthy," he said with a big grin.

Then he took his jacket, and tie off as Michelle opened the basket to explore what was inside. Mike unbuttoned his shirt, and walked back to the table. Then he took off his cuff links, and set them on the table next to the flowers. He walked up behind Michelle and slowly removed her dress coat. He unzipped her dress, and rubbed his hand up her spine pushing the dress off her shoulders. Michelle started to turn around, but he stopped her.

"No, no Michelle. Let me undress you," he said softly.

He took off Michelle's slip off then he turned her around. She was wearing nothing more than her boots, and matching bra and panties. Mike slowly looked up into her eyes. He picked her up, and placed her gently on the bed. He unzipped the boots one at a time, and took them off slowly. Then he removed the matching bra and panties. Mike climbed on top of her, and began kissing her. His tongue teased, and tangled with hers. He kissed her neck as his cupped her full breast. Michelle moaned softly when Mike lowered his mouth to her tight perky nipples. He eagerly paid loving attention to the other breast as well. Michelle ran her finger through the soft curls on the back of his head as he continued to tease, and lick her perky nipples. Each flick of his tongue sent waves of heat, and passion to her groin. Michelle continues to caress the back of Mike's head as he kissed down her stomach. Mike stopped kissing her only for moment to look into her eyes. Then he slid down between her thighs, and positioned her legs. He didn't hesitate. He spread the small lips between her thighs, and devoured the little knob. Michelle cried out. Each flick of his tongue was like a burst of passion in her groin that was about to explode. Michelle tried to hold onto the bed, but each flick of his tongue, and gentle suck brought her closer to her own release. Michelle's breathing grew very rapid and shallow. Her moans grew louder. Finally, she arched her back, and screamed her release. Her legs trembled as Mike gave her one last fiery lick. Mike kissed her stomach, chest, and then her neck. Finally, he whispered into her ear, "You taste so sweet."

He sat up to look into her dazed eyes then he kissed her lips, and sat on the side of the bed. Mike kicked his shoes off, and stood up. He pulled off his pants. Then he walked over to the table. He leaned against the table watching her in the dim light wearing nothing, but his shirt. Michelle's eye lingered over his muscular chest, and flat rock hard abdomen. Her eyes stopped at the beautiful, but large package that was erect and waiting between his muscular thighs. She thought to herself that this must be the reason why they call him Big Mike.

Michelle sat up on her elbows. "Mike, what you are doing?" She asked.

"I just want to see you," he said.

Michelle got out of the bed, and seductively walked up to him. She grabbed a bottle of favored lubricant, and gave him a mischievous smile. She poured a little in her hand and got down on her knees to massage, and stroke his pulsating erection. Then Michelle took the harden tip into her mouth. Mike gripped the table tightly as his legs began to tremble. With one hand Michelle stroked his lean thighs, and buttocks. Mike's moans grew louder. Finally, he gently pushed her away.

"What? Did I do something wrong?" She asked.

"No, but if you keep doing that, all this will come to an end very quickly."

Michelle grinned. Mike picked Michelle up, and carried her to the bed. He gently laid her down. Then he took off his shirt, and positioned himself between her thighs. He gave her a soft gentle kiss before he entered the small tight canal. Michelle cried out a little with each passionate thrust. The sensations were becoming too much for her. Michelle started to pull away from him.

"Wait, wait," she cried out.

Mike looked down into her eyes. He wanted her to enjoy their first time together, not pull away from him. He knew his size might be a bit too much for her in this position the first time. He kissed her gently then rolled her over positioning her on top of him.

"Ah! Mike what are you doing?" She asked.

"I'm just making you a little more comfortable," he replied.

And, he did too. Michelle enjoyed being in this position. Mike didn't move at first, but Michelle did. Michelle's inhibitions were fading as she accepted more of him. For a moment Michelle put her head back, and enjoyed every inch of him. Mike began touching her, and kissing her breast as her thrusting increased. Mike knew it was only a matter of time before she came again. He held onto her hips as she climaxed. The little spasms shook her as she slowly lay down on Mike's chest like a fallen leaf. Mike held her in his arms while she slowly recovered.

"I could feel you cumming," he said as he kissed the top of her head, "and now it's my turn."

Mike rolled Michelle over onto her back, and they made love again until they both screamed their release. Mike withdrew himself, and laid beside Michelle staring into her dazed eyes.

They both were slightly out of breath when Michelle turned to Mike, and said, "I love you."

"I know," Mike said with a mischievous smile, "but I love you too. How are you feeling right now?"

"Satisfied," Michelle said with a smile.

"Satisfied?" Mike said with a raised brow.

"Yes. Aren't you?" She asked with concern.

"Not yet," he said with a dimpled grin, "but I am thirsty. Would you like something to drink? I think there is some bottled water in the refrigerator by the table."

"Sure, and I'm going to have one of those chocolates too," Michelle replied.

They both got out of bed wear nothing more then their birthday suits. Michelle did have some of the water Mike offered her, but she decided to open the champagne too. When they got back into the bed, Michelle feed Mike some of the chocolate truffles she was eating, and they both sipped on the champagne.

As the evening progressed, the couple grew tired, and fell asleep. It was almost midnight when Mike awoke. The lights were still on, but the room was dim. Mike watched Michelle sleeping peacefully beside him. She was lying on her side. Although her hair wasn't still as neat as it was before, she was very beautiful. Her beautiful copper colored skin tone was smooth, and glistening in the soft dim light. Her round apple shaped bottom aroused him, and he wanted her once more. He began touching the smooth silky skin on her back then his hands firmly gripped her back side. Michelle stirred a little, and moaned softly with the sensation of Mike's touch.

Mike kissed the back of her neck, and whispered into her ear, "I'm still not satisfied. I'm going to get something out of the basket that will make this a little more comfortable for you. Don't move."

Michelle's sleepy eyes barely opened when Mike came back to the bed. He lay down beside her, and cupped his hand around her breast. Michelle woke up suddenly when Mike slipped his fingers into the small tight canal between her thighs. Michelle gasped, and grabbed his wrist.

"Mike! Ah!" She cried out when Mike turned her over onto her stomach.

He grabbed a pillow and slid it underneath her hips. Then he grabbed the lubricant from the side table, and poured a small amount into his hand. He rubbed the lubricant between the small lips that lie between her thighs. Michelle gasped softly as he inserted two fingers into her womb stroking her gently.

Then he lay on top of her kissing the back of her neck, and whispering into her ear, "I love you."

Next, he grabbed her hips, and replaced his finger with his strong pulsating erection. With each thrust Michelle cried out. Soon Mike found a rhythm that brought both of them pleasure with each stroke. Michelle moaned softly until Mike pulled her up to his chest. He cupped her breast with one hand, and with the other he massaged the little knob between her thighs. The sensations overwhelmed her. She came quickly. Then Mike lowered her down gently until her chest lay on the bed. Michelle gripped the sheets as Mike's thrusting increased. Soon Mike own cries grew to match hers. The erotic sensations overtook them, and the spasms shook them both. Mike lay on top of her for a moment. Then he kissed the side of her head, and lay by her side. Michelle turned over and looked into his dazed eyes. Slightly out of breath, she was unable to speak. He pulled her closer to him. After a long night of love making, they were completely exhausted. Naked and satisfied they lay together in the bed like spoons in a drawer until the next morning.

The light through the patio door shined brightly the next morning when Michelle woke up beside Mike still in the same position she was in when they fell asleep. She smiled when she thought of the erotic scenes of her last rendezvous with Mike last night. She turned to see him still sleeping peacefully beside her. She stroked his beautiful face with the back of her hand. Then she got up to go to the bathroom. On her way out of the bedroom, she looked into the mirror. Michelle tried to brush her hair back into place with her hands, but she needed a comb. Once she was in the bathroom, she was happy to see that the hotel had two new tooth brushes, and tooth paste for their guests that might have forgotten their own. Michelle brushed her teeth, and washed her face. She walked out of the bathroom to find Mike sitting up in the bed.

"Come here, *belle dame*," he said.

Michelle crawled over to him, and they begin to kiss. Mike pulled Michelle towards him until she straddled his lap. The thoughts of how this woman made him feel last night was driving him mad. He had to have her again. Last night was a night he catered to her needs, but this morning he wanted a piece of her for himself. His kisses grow stronger, and more erotic. He had to have her now. He inserted himself into her with one stroke. Michelle cried out, but Mike held her hips steady. With a few good thrust, he was completely inside her. With every thrust, the hardened head of his erection tingled, and set his senses on fire. She felt good in everyway to him. He rubbed his hands down her back then he gripped her hips. Mike shifted to the side of the bed, and stood up lifting her.

"Hold me," his husky voice cried.

Michelle couldn't answer him. She screamed and moaned as Mike's thrusting sent her bobbing up, and down in his arms. She had no way of resisting him. She held onto him as he put one hand out against the wall to steady himself. Mike stopped his thrusting long enough to carry Michelle back to the bed. He laid her down gently. Then he lifted her hips up with his hands. Each stroke he made was harder than the last. Michelle cried out each time. Soon he found that old familiar rhythm that pleased them both. A very powerful orgasm shook both of them as they cried out together. Mike withdrew himself, and lay breathlessly beside her. Michelle moaned as she rolled over.

"Are you all right?" Mike asked.

"I . . . I'm a little sore," she admitted.

"I think it is time we take a hot bath," he replied.

Mike got up and went into the bathroom. He ran a bath for them in the whirlpool tub. He turned the massage jets on, and added the body salts to the water. Michelle got into the tub first. The soothing water and massaging jets seemed to soothe every sore muscle in her body. Mike bushed his teeth while Michelle began to bathe. Then he got into the tub, and sat down behind her.

"I wished I had brought my razor. I think I need to shave," he said.

"I think the shadow looks good on you," replied Michelle. "Besides, nothing could hurt that beautiful face."

"Are you okay now?" He asked.

"Yes," Michelle said with a shy smile.

"You came a lot last night. Is that normal for you?"

"It has happened before, but not in a very long time. Maybe, it was you Mike," she replied.

"Am I that good?" He said with a large grin.

"Mike, I don't know if it is you, or the fact that I haven't done this in years, but it was wonderful."

"It was, wasn't it," Mike said as he wrapped his arms around her.

"You know Mike, I think we had better get married now, or my mother is going to kill me."

"What?" Mike asked with a surprised look.

"Mike, I love you, and I was scared to take a chance again, but if you say no I will--."

Mike leaned Michelle back, and kissed her fervently before she could say anything else. Then he hugged her. "Of course, I want to marry you," Mike said.

"Mike, what about your brother?"

"What about him?" He asked.

"He seemed pretty upset when I turned you down the first time. How do you think he will feel about me now?" Michelle said with concern.

"Michelle, Trey knows about your divorce, so he understands. Both Lisa and Trey love you too."

"Okay. Well, there is one thing we have left to do," Michelle said.

"What's that?" He asked.

"Tell mom."

Mike laughed. "Of course, it was her idea to bring you here."

"Y'all planned this?" Michelle looked surprised.

"No, no. She told me to bring you here for dinner. I decided to get the room," Mike admitted.

"And, I'm glad you did," Michelle admitted. "You know, I don't know how wonderful our honeymoon will be compared to this, but tonight was the best night of my life."

Mike kissed the side of Michelle's head, and said, "The best is yet to come."

*****

It was the first week of June, and we were out of school. Today was a beautiful hot Saturday, and A.M. E. Zion Baptist Church was decorated in blue flowers with huge white ribbon bows that cascaded down the church's stair railings. The same color flowers and bows were on either side of the church doors. A big bouquet of flowers was displayed on a table in the church foyer. People were gathering in the foyer as the usher seated them in different sections of the church. There was one section for both families to sit in that was marked by beautiful white ribbon bows. We had so many family members there that they took up the whole center aisle of the church. I had cousins there that lived as far away as California. The Dean's were there too. Mike's uncle from Florida was there, and his friend that had to relocate to Atlanta, Georgia was there with his family. All of our neighbors, and friends came to the wedding too. Uncle Pete sat on the front row with Big Mama and Mr. Davis. Big Mama was holding my soon to be cousin, Aunt Lisa's baby girl she named Jessica Michelle Raimond. The baby girl had beautiful dark curly hair like Lisa's, and dimples like Trey's and Mike's. Big Mama would talk in baby talk to her, and the baby would coo, and giggle every time. The church's altar was beautiful. There was a brass arbor covered with white, green, and blue flowers. Flower stands were placed on either side of the brass arbor. The minister had on a white robe with a golden trim.

"It's almost time Jasmine. Get downstairs, and get in line with the rest of the wedding party," the pushy wedding coordinator said. "And, where are your brothers?"

We both peeked back inside of the church doors to see my brothers playing a game of tag with my cousins.

"Oh no! I'll go get them. You get downstairs."

I ran downstairs to find the wedding party chatting amongst themselves. I scurried around them, and entered the bathroom. Mama was sitting in front of the huge sink, and mirror adjusting her veil. She looked like a princess. Her dress was strapless, and beaded across the chest. The dress tied like a corset in the back. The dress had a beautiful long train in the back that made mama look like royalty.

"Mama, you look beautiful," I said.

"Thank you, sweetie," she replied. "Come here."

When I walked over to mama, she gave me a big hug. "How's my girl doing?" She asked.

"Fine," I replied. "Mama, will we have to move once you marry Mike?"

"No baby. Mike is coming to live with us," she said.

"What is he going to do with his house?"

"Nothing. Lisa and Trey just had a baby, and they'll stay in the house for now until their house is rebuilt."

"Okay, but is Mike going to be our daddy now?" I asked curiously.

"No, Jasmine. Mike isn't going to be your daddy. You already have a daddy, but you will have to respect what he says, and we will decide on any punishment y'all receive together, okay. He will be your stepfather. Now, that's enough questions. Let me make sure I have what I need," mama replied.

"Do you have something old?" I asked

"Yes. I am wearing mom's pearl earrings, and I have something new too. Mike gave me this pearl bracelet as a wedding present."

"Mama, what about the borrowed, and blue part?"

"Well, Big Mama's earrings are borrowed too, and as for the blue part." Mama lifted her dress to reveal a blue garter belt around her thigh.

"Mama!" I said in surprise.

Michelle laughed. "It's supposed to be there, Jasmine."

Then the pushy wedding coordinator came into the bathroom. "It's time. Jasmine what are you doing here. Come on. Get in line."

I ran outside of the bathroom, and walked upstairs. Soft music was playing as I got in line, and stood by Alley. Then the pushy wedding coordinator gave us a basket of rose petals. The photographer took pictures of Mike, Trey, and Mr. Greg coming down the aisle first. They all wore off white tuxedos with mixed green and light blue printed vest and ties. Sharon walked out next and then Lisa followed behind her. They both were wearing light blue spaghetti strapped dresses with a green sashes tied on the side. Alley and I came down the aisle side by side dropping rose petals as we walked. Our long white dresses had small pearl buttons that lined the back. Both of our dresses had huge ribbons that tied around our waist, and large blue and green colored ribbon bows that trailed down the back of the dresses. My brothers walked out together wearing the same tuxedos as the men. Today, they actually looked pretty good. Jordan was the ring bearer, and Jonathan had a bell to ring to announce the coming of the bride.

Once the wedding party was standing by the altar, the minister raised his hands for everyone to stand. Jonathan rang the bell and to announce the coming of the bride. Everyone turned to see mama standing in the entrance with the veil covering her face. She was beautiful. Mama seemed to glide down the aisle as the organist played, *"Here Comes the Bride."* Once mama got to the altar, she put her beautiful bouquet of lilies in her left hand, and with her right hand she held onto Mike's hand. He kissed her hand as they approached the minister. The minister recited the *Lord's Prayer*. The soloist began to sing as mama and Mike lit the unity candles. Then Sharon walked to the office's door by the side of the altar, and came back with a bouquet of red roses. She handed them to Mike. Michelle and Mike walked to Big Mama to give her the flowers. They couldn't give the flowers directly to Big Mama because she was holding the baby, so Mike gave the flower to Mr. Davis to hold. Then mama and Mike kissed Big Mama on the cheeks, and walked back to the altar. Big Mama was so touched by their gesture tears began to roll down her cheeks. Next, the minister announced that mama and Mike would recite their own vows.

Mama didn't remove the veil from her face, but she turned toward Mike holding his hand, and said, "I wasn't expecting to find love so soon, but then you came along. I was afraid that a love this great could not be real, so I didn't trust it, but you've stood by me through the good times, and bad. And, you didn't give up on me. My family has grown to love you just as much as I have. I vow to you to be there for you through sickness and health, for richer or for poorer, through good times and bad, forsaking all others, and to love you till death do we part."

Mike looked down into Michelle's eyes saying, "My beautiful lady, I think I fell in love with you after the first month I met you. I didn't think I would find love so quickly either, but then I met you. After being alone for the last two years, I never thought I could have a family, or a chance to have children again. I want to thank you for giving a lonely man his hearts desires, and for being with my family during the worst natural disaster this country has ever known. I vow to you Michelle to be with you through the good times and bad, for richer or poorer, through sickness and health, forsaking all others," Mike said as he stepped closer to Michelle, and lifted her chin with his finger. "And, that's includes kissing another too. I vow to love you until death do we part."

Mike stepped closer to Michelle as if he was going to kiss her, but the minister stopped him.

"Hold on son, we haven't gotten to that part yet," replied the minister.

The audience laughed. Mike and mama exchanged the rings, and the minister said, "Now I present to you Mr. and Mrs. Raimond. I pronounce you husband and wife. Mike, now you may kiss your bride."

Michelle struggled a little when she tried to lift the layers of the veil over her face, but Mike lifted it for her. Once he saw her beautiful face looking up at him, he leaned her back, and kissed her passionately right there in church. They kissed each other as if no one else was around. The audience laughed, and cheered. When Mike released Michelle, she was a little embarrassed, but she was excited too. They walked down the aisle and the wedding party followed behind them. A limousine was waiting outside of the church to take them to a big reception hall downtown. The crowd followed them outside, and waved to them as they left.

Uncle Pete walked outside with Big Mama and Mr. Davis, and said, "Now, Let's get this party started right."

The crowd soon left the church, and met back at the reception hall. When we entered the hall, a band was playing soft music in front of a small wooden dance floor. The tables were covered in white linen table cloths with flowers, and glowing candle lit lanterns in the center of each table. There was a large table for the wedding party, and another table for the food. In the center of the food table, was a huge three layer wedding cake. The groom's cake was beside the bride's. His wasn't quit as high, but it was wider than the bride's cake. It had three layers of chocolate cake with chocolate covered strawberries cascading down the sides of it. There was so much food on the table I couldn't name it all. The photographer took pictures with mama and Mike. Then he took pictures of the wedding party, and families. There was a bar, and of course, Uncle Pete was there. Big Mama had to make him come to the table to eat. After dinner, the pushy wedding coordinator pulled mama and Mike out onto the dance floor for their first dance as husband and wife. They danced for a short while, and were soon joined by others on the dance floor. After mama and Mike left the dance floor, Uncle Pete asked the band to play something more up beat. Suddenly, Uncle Pete took over the dance floor. He did a split. Then he jumped up, and he got down again. My brothers walked over to him, and started to break dance. Uncle Pete watched them for a little while and then he started to break dance too.

The crowd laughed, and chanted, "Go Pete! Go Pete!"

Mama laughed, but Big Mama was embarrassed. Later on, I was embarrassed when Big Mike took off mama's garter belt, and threw it.

Then mama threw her bouquet, but none of the women caught it. The bouquet sailed over the women's heads, and when Uncle Pete turned around it landed in his hands. Everyone laughed.

Uncle Pete looked at the flowers with a bit of shock, and he said, "I'm still a player, ain't that right Jordan!"

Then he gave Jordan a high five, and he gave me the flowers. Finally, it was time for mama and Mike to go on their honeymoon. As they walked out of the reception hall, people threw bird seed at them. Mama shouted to my brothers and me from the limo telling us to be good while she was gone. Then they left. I was a little sad to watch her go, but Big Mama told me they would be back in a week.

I walked back towards the reception hall with Big Mama, and said, "Big Mama, where are they going?"

"Jamaica," she replied.

"Jamaica? Is that a fun place?" I asked.

"Oh yes," Big Mama said.

"Why can't we go?"

"Baby, kids don't go on honeymoons with their parents."

"Oh," I said in a sad tone. "Big Mama, will they be happy together?"

"Oh yeah. I can see that, and you might even have that little sister you've always wanted."

I was suddenly excited. "Really Big Mama!"

"Yes."

Then I thought about something. "Big Mama, how do you know this?" I asked.

"The angel told me. She is over there." Big Mama pointed in her direction. I turned to see the angel standing by the curve as the people unknowingly passed her by. She waved to me, and I waved back.

"See, the angel likes a good wedding too. Come on inside, and I'll tell you a story about how I met your grandfather."

Big Mama continued to talk as we walked inside. I looked back at the angel, and wondered about my destiny as an *Ayin*. Would this be the end, or could this just be the beginning. But, like Big Mama always says, only time will tell.

www.ingramcontent.com/pod-product-compliance
Lightning Source LLC
Chambersburg PA
CBHW061509020726
47502CB00006B/1995